DESOLATION
CREEK

WILLIAM W. JOHNSTONE
AND J.A. JOHNSTONE

DESOLATION CREEK

PINNACLE BOOKS
Kensington Publishing Corp.
www.kensingtonbooks.com

PINNACLE BOOKS are published by

Kensington Publishing Corp.
119 West 40th Street
New York, NY 10018

PUBLISHER'S NOTE: Following the death of William W. Johnstone, the Johnstone family is working with a carefully selected writer to organize and complete Mr. Johnstone's outlines and many unfinished manuscripts to create additional novels in all of his series like The Last Gunfighter, Mountain Man, and Eagles, among others. This novel was inspired by Mr. Johnstone's superb storytelling.

All Kensington titles, imprints, and distributed lines are available at special quantity discounts for bulk purchases for sales promotion, premiums, fundraising, and educational or institutional use.

Special book excerpts or customized printings can also be created to fit specific needs. For details, write or phone the office of the Kensington Sales Manager: Kensington Publishing Corp., 119 West 40th Street, New York, NY 10018. Attn. Sales Department. Phone: 1-800-221-2647.

Pinnacle Books, the Pinnacle logo, and the WWJ steer head logo Reg. U.S. Pat. & TM Off.

First Kensington hardcover printing: April 2023
First Pinnacle mass market printing: June 2023
ISBN-13: 978-0-7860-4985-1
ISBN-13: 978-0-7860-4992-9 (eBook)

10 9 8 7 6 5 4 3 2 1

Printed in the United States of America

CHAPTER 1

When a bullet zipped past Smoke Jensen's ear, leaving a hot, crimson streak in its wake, he had a realization.

Trouble sure had a way of following him.

He hadn't come to Big Rock with anything on his mind other than taking care of his business, maybe saying hello to a few friends, chief among them Sheriff Monte Carson and Louis Longmont, and then getting on back to the Sugarloaf.

Of course, his wife, Sally, had it in mind to do some shopping, but that was harmless enough, except for the damage it did to his pocketbook. So, no reasonable explanation existed as to why he found himself smack-dab in the middle of a shooting scrape.

Or rather, *another* shooting scrape.

The last thing he wanted was trouble. He wasn't the type to just stand idly by when bullets were flying, though. He might catch one of them. Or worse, innocent folks might get shot. So, he drew his Colt with lightning speed and took aim at the man who had just emerged from the general store.

A wisp of powder smoke still curled up from the muzzle of the gun in the man's fist. He had already shifted his focus elsewhere after firing that first round. Evidently, he caught Smoke's movement in his peripheral vision and turned his attention back in that direction. He leveled his weapon and sneered.

"I wouldn't," Smoke said.

The warning fell on deaf ears and the man's finger twitched, ready to squeeze off another shot. Smoke's keen eyes saw that, and his gun roared first.

The bullet hammered into the fella's chest, sending him backward as his feet flew from beneath him. He landed flat on his back. His fingers went slack and he released the revolver. Smoke ran to the gun and kicked it away. One quick glance told him the gesture hadn't been necessary, although erring on the side of caution was always better.

A scarlet ring was spreading on the man's dirty, tattered shirt. Dull, glassy eyes, with the life fading from them, stared up at Smoke.

"Who in the—" Smoke began, wanting to know who he had just shot, and why.

He didn't have time to finish the question as another shot rang out from inside the general store.

"Sally," he said, working to rein in the worry he felt rising in his chest. He swung his gun up, while quickly stepping away from the dead hombre, who lay sprawled out in the middle of the street. Eager to check on his wife, who'd gone inside the store a few minutes earlier, Smoke was about to close the gap between himself and the structure, when the door flew open again.

Another gunman burst onto the store's porch, spinning wildly as if trying to assess his surroundings, but not moving cautiously enough to gain a true lay of the land. This gave Smoke all the time he needed to dive behind a water trough. He reached the cover just in time as the panic-stricken gunman sent two wild shots into the air. As far as Smoke could tell, no one was hit. Most of the folks who had been on the boardwalks or in the street had scrambled for cover when the shooting started.

Just who was this fella and what was he all fired up about? Maybe, Smoke thought, he could end this without any more bloodshed. He didn't care for the fact that a fresh corpse was only a few feet away. Smoke didn't hesitate to kill when necessary, but he didn't take any pleasure in it. If he had his way, he'd never be mixed up in gunplay again.

Smoke rested his arm on the trough and drew a bead, his hand steady, his aim sure.

"Put that gun down!" he called. "No one else has to get hurt. Or worse."

A few townspeople were hustling around, trying to get out of the line of fire. Two old men who'd been sitting on a bench, enjoying the shade the boardwalk's overhanging roof offered, dove off the side and onto the ground. Smoke had to chuckle, realizing the impact had probably jarred the old-timers. They were in one piece, though, and didn't have any bullets in them as they crawled beneath the porch. Thankfully, it seemed as if everyone was out of harm's way.

Until the little girl dashed past.

Smoke hadn't even noticed her before now. She couldn't be any older than six, but might have been as young as four. She was a little thing, and scared, as she screamed for her ma. She tried to make it off the porch, but the gun-wielding hombre extended his free arm and scooped up the child, jerking her back onto the porch before Smoke could react.

The man held on to the girl tightly, using her as a shield as he swept his gun from side to side. She squirmed and kicked her legs as she continued screaming, but she had no chance of escaping the man's brutal grip.

Smoke regretted not having put a bullet into the wild-eyed varmint as soon as he laid eyes on the man. That would have ended this before he had a chance to grab that poor child.

"I'm gonna get out of here!" he yelled. "You all hear me?"

Smoke caught a glimpse of movement up the street and swiveled his head to see Sheriff Monte Carson hurrying toward the scene, with two deputies following him. Unfortunately, the crazed gunman on the porch noticed them, too, and sent a shot in their direction. Monte and the deputies instinctively split up as the bullet whistled between them. Monte took cover in one of the alcoves along the boardwalk, while the two deputies crouched behind a parked wagon.

The little girl screamed even louder after the shot, but her captor only tightened the arm he had looped around her body under her arms.

"Shut up!" he snarled at the girl. He turned his attention back to the sheriff and yelled, "Stay back! I swear I'll put a bullet in this here child's brain!"

Smoke's blood was boiling. He'd encountered some low-down prairie scum in his day, but anyone who would hurt a child was the worst of the worst. He had to smile, though, when the girl started writhing even harder beneath the man's arm. She tried throwing her elbows back and even sent a few more kicks toward him, but his strength put an end to the struggle quickly. Still, Smoke admired her fighting spirit. He aimed to tell her as much, too. He'd get a chance, since he would never let that little girl die.

"What is it you want?" Smoke called.

He wasn't the law in Big Rock, but with the sheriff and his deputies pinned down and unable to get closer, he was in the best position to act.

"I want out of here," the gunman said. "I want to make it to my horse down yonder, climb in the saddle, and get out of town without any trouble!"

"Sure, friend," Smoke replied in an affable tone. "Just let the young'un go and you can mosey on out of here. No one will stop you."

The man's lips curled back, revealing jagged yellow teeth. "That ain't how this works. She comes with me. I'll leave her down the trail when I'm free and clear."

Smoke's back stiffened. He couldn't let the hard case ride out of town with that little girl. If she was carried off by him, she was probably as good as dead.

"My daughter!" a loud, terror-stricken voice screamed. "He has my daughter!"

The hard case swung his gun hand around to cover the panicking woman who ran out of the store next door, holding her dress up as she sprinted. Her feet kicked up gravel and dust, but she didn't slow down any, until the man jabbed his gun toward her.

"Don't come any closer! I'll shoot her!" He jammed the hard barrel back against the child's skull, causing her to cry out. She tried reaching for her mother, the gesture causing the woman to cry even louder and stretch her arms out, too, as she skidded to a stop in the road.

Smoke had seen more than enough. He couldn't get a shot off, though. He was good—probably one of the best there was—but even he couldn't guarantee a clean shot under these circumstances. It was just too risky. And he'd be damned if any harm came to a child because of him.

But he couldn't *not act*, either.

The street was eerily silent. Smoke could see the two old-timers crawling quietly beneath the porch, headed toward the gunman, obviously intent on intervening. There was an opening where they could get out, not far behind the man. Smoke hoped it wouldn't spook the varmint, causing him to shoot the child.

Smoke cast his eyes toward the sheriff. Monte Carson peered around the corner of the alcove where he had taken cover, but he made no move toward the gunman. His deputies stood motionless behind the wagon, following his example.

The tension was thick. Normally, Smoke was as calm as could be in situations like this, but now his heart felt as if it might beat right out of his chest. Perhaps the child's presence did it. Or maybe his not knowing what had happened to Sally. Had that shot he'd heard earlier hit her? Was she okay? Heaven help that crazed outlaw if she wasn't. Whatever the reason, his nerves were a bit more frayed than usual.

He fought hard to control his emotions. He needed to proceed with a clear head. He didn't give a darn about his own life.

Right now, that little girl was all that mattered.

And Sally.

Smoke drew a deep breath, exhaled slowly, and fought down his anger. Now wasn't the time to be blinded by rage. A wry smile tugged at his lips as a plan began to take shape inside his mind. What he needed was a distraction. Maybe those two old-timers would give it to him. They were edging closer, shifting beneath the porch and looking as if they were ready to scramble out and spring up at any moment.

Just like that, though, in the blink of an eye, the old men and Smoke's plan became irrelevant.

The outlaw had taken a few steps back on the porch, toward the store's door. He never bothered to check behind him.

That had been a mistake.

A bottle broke into a dozen pieces as it crashed against his head. One jagged shard tore into his scalp, slicing away the flesh and leaving a hot, wet, bloody streak.

Out of instinct, he dropped the child. She leaped off the porch as quickly as possible and into her mother's arms. For a moment, Smoke feared the outlaw would trigger his gun, but the man just pawed at his flowing wound. Confusion registered in his eyes as he swayed unsteadily on his feet. His gun slid from his fingers.

"What the—"

He tried spinning around, but didn't have a chance before a second bottle smashed into him, sending him to the ground, out cold.

Smoke was already at the porch now, his gun still drawn, when he realized who had saved the day.

There in the doorway, with the neck of a broken bottle in her hand, stood Sally.

CHAPTER 2

"What on earth is going on here?" Monte Carson asked. Smoke finished thumbing a fresh cartridge into his walnut-butted Colt and then pouched the iron. "I was wondering that myself." He looked to Sally and arched an eyebrow. "Here I was worried about *you*, and I should have been worried about *him*." He jerked his head toward the unconscious gunman who lay on the porch's puncheon floor.

One of the sheriff's deputies was standing over the downed man, relieving him of his weapons. A small derringer was up his right sleeve, along with a knife in one of his boots. The deputy then rummaged through the man's pockets and pulled out a wad of greenbacks and waved them toward the sheriff.

"Those are mine!" Don Baker said.

He was a large, easygoing man who ran the mercantile, along with help from his clerk, Ike Hairston. Ike was out on the porch now, too, and hurried to the downed brigand. He reared his foot back, but Sheriff Carson stopped him.

"You can't kick him now. He's laid out cold!"

"Well, I oughta," Ike said, and then his voice trailed off

into a consortium of jumbled curse words. "They tried to hold up the store."

"They didn't *try*," his boss corrected him. "They did rob us. Would have gotten away with it, too, if it hadn't been for Jensen."

"Which one?" Smoke said with a smile. His eyes darted to Sally, who was now off the porch and checking on the terrified mother and child.

"Thank God she's okay," Sally said, rubbing the girl's back.

The two old-timers had rolled out from under the porch and, after considerable effort, were finally stumbling to their feet.

"Sheriff, I think Walt done broke his backside," one of them said.

The other groaned as he rubbed his rear end. It took considerable effort for Smoke to control his laughter, and one look at Sally told him she was having the same struggle.

Monte seemed somewhat annoyed when he said, "Will someone just tell me exactly what happened?"

"I'll tell you," Ike said, still red-faced with anger. "Those two no-accounts came in the store, acted like they were shopping, but then drew their pistols and demanded the money from the register. They were also trying to take off with a few supplies, jerky and coffee, mostly." He jabbed a bony finger toward the dead man in the street and said, "He got spooked and told his partner they had to get out of there. That's when he came out shooting!"

"That explains your ear," Monte said, looking at Smoke.

Smoke remembered the close call and touched his ear. It stung a little, but the blood had dried now. He'd had a lot worse done to him over the years.

"Guess I was in the wrong place at the wrong time," Smoke said with a chuckle.

"Or the right place," Monte said. "He may have hit someone with those wild shots, had you not taken him down. Reckon the town is obliged to you for that. Once again."

Smoke nodded.

It seemed as if Monte took every opportunity he could to state how much the town of Big Rock owed Smoke. In fact, Smoke was mostly responsible for the settlement's founding, having led an exodus here of folks escaping from the outlaw town of Fontana, several miles away. They had fled to escape the reign of terror carried out by brutal mine owner Tilden Franklin and his hired guns.

Now, a couple of years later, Franklin was dead, and Fontana was an abandoned town, nothing left but moldering ruins, while Big Rock was growing and thriving. Monte Carson wasn't the only one who gave Smoke a lot of the credit for that happening.

Smoke, however, wasn't interested in accolades. He was thankful when the storekeeper started talking again.

"Anyway," Ike Hairston continued, "that spooked his partner inside the store and he started shooting, too."

"Anyone hit?" the sheriff asked.

"No, but he plugged the dang cracker barrel!" Ike said. He looked as if he wanted to kick the man again. His anger subsiding, he shrugged and said, "That's when he came out onto the porch, and, well, you saw the rest."

Sally was at Smoke's side now. They joined Sheriff Carson in examining the two outlaws. Both wore dirty, torn homespun and it seemed as if neither had bathed in a long while.

Smoke thumbed his curled-brim hat back, revealing more of his ash-blond hair, and scratched his forehead. "Looks like these two had fallen on hard times."

"Explains why they were so desperate," Monte said with a frown. "Still doesn't give them call to carry on like this."

"Sure doesn't," Smoke agreed. "Reckon they could have gotten a meal just about anywhere here in town."

Smoke wasn't exaggerating. Big Rock was a friendly community, where folks could find plenty of help if they needed it. Smoke might have even given the two work at the Sugarloaf, had they dropped by. Of course, the fact that one had held a little girl hostage showed he was *not* simply a good man who'd fallen on desperate times, so Smoke doubted if they'd had any intent on working for an honest day's wages.

The one Sally had laid out was now starting to groan as he came to.

"Let's get him on down to the jail," Monte told his deputies. "I'll send for Doc Spaulding to patch him up."

"He needs to take a look at my rear, too!" Walt said, still rubbing his derriere.

"Maybe he can get you one of those sittin' pillows," the other old-timer said. "Feels better than resting your cheeks on a hard chair, that's for sure!"

Monte rolled his eyes and mumbled, "Lord help me." He turned his focus to the corpse, which lay in the street, and winced as he saw that flies had already started to gather. "I'll get the undertaker down here, too. I'll look through the wanted dodgers I have back at the office. Could be that you have some reward money coming, Smoke."

Smoke snorted. "A bounty-hunting Jensen? Now that's a thought."

"Don't you go getting any ideas. We don't need any more trouble," Sally said. "Besides, you're a rancher. Remember?"

Smoke held up his hands in mock surrender. "Believe me, I've had my fill of trouble. I'm not looking for more." His smile disappeared as he turned his gaze toward the sheriff. He scratched his strong, angular chin and asked, "Do I need to stick around and appear before Judge Proctor?"

"Nah," Monte said. "This is pretty cut-and-dried. The way I figure it, you did the town a favor. You too," he said, smiling at Sally. "Smoke, you sure married one with a bit of sass in her."

Smoke laughed, nodding in agreement.

He certainly couldn't argue that point.

The ride back to the Sugarloaf was seven miles and Smoke didn't mind the journey one bit. The country was mighty pretty, and he had an even prettier woman by his side. As he guided his black stallion, Drifter, beside the buckboard Sally drove, he took a moment to soak it all in.

She had an infectious smile, which he never tired of. Her brown hair hung in bouncing curls. With Sally set against the backdrop of the rugged Rocky Mountains, Smoke wondered if he'd indeed been shot back in Big Rock and was now in heaven.

"What are you looking at?" Sally said, though her smile hinted that she already knew the answer.

"The woman of my dreams," he said without hesitation.

She smiled even wider. "And what are you thinking about?"

Smoke laughed. He made a show of looking around and said, "Well, I suppose I could tell you, since there's no one else around."

Now Sally laughed loudly. "Easy. We've got a few miles to go before we're back home."

"Like I said, there's no one else around."

Sally cast him one last devilish grin before turning her attention back to the trail before her. Smoke did the same.

They rode in silence for a few minutes before he said, "That was some stunt you pulled back there, walloping that owlhoot like that. You could've been hurt."

"And that little girl could've been killed."

"True," Smoke admitted. "Reckon I can't be too upset."

"Upset? You knew I was a handful when you put the ring on my finger."

Smoke chuckled. "That I did. And I wouldn't have you any other way. I just want you to be careful, is all. I intend to grow old with you."

"Of course," she said. "I'll be sitting by your side on the porch in our rockers. We can look out over the Sugarloaf. It will be massive by then."

"You have big plans," he said.

"*We* have big plans," she said.

"Yep. And they don't include gunfighting, that's for sure."

She gave him a pointed stare. "It really bothered you, what happened back in town?"

He nodded. Drifter continued to pick his way over the trail, staying beside the buckboard, moving at a measured pace. It seemed as if the horses were just as content to enjoy the pleasant evening as night fell around them as Smoke and Sally were.

The falling sun painted the picturesque landscape in pink and yellow hues. A cloud of gnats hovered just off the road. A few grasshoppers leaped in the brushy grass to Smoke's left. Smoke sucked in a lungful of air and held it a moment, enjoying the smell of the upcoming summer. Something about this time of year called to him. Something peaceful. Thinking about peace, he said, "I just hope this valley is tamed one day, and sooner rather than later. I've had more than enough gunplay to last me a lifetime."

"There will be peace around these parts soon enough," she said. "Men like you and Preacher have worked hard to make this land safe for decent folks. One day, our children will thank you for it."

Smoke smiled once again. He sure liked the sound of that.

Children.

Of course, if they turned out anything like their pa—or ma, for that matter—they'd keep him and Sally on their toes.

They finished their trip in silence, content to simply be in each other's presence. The relaxing ride did wonders in washing away the unpleasantness that had occurred back in town, and by the time they arrived home, it was already nothing but a memory.

That peacefulness didn't last long, though. Upon riding up to the house, Smoke realized they had company. Two saddle mounts he didn't recognize, along with a couple of pack animals, were tied in front of the log ranch house.

Something stirred deep inside his stomach, telling him that all was not well. He remembered that realization he'd had back in town when the shooting had started.

Trouble just had a way of finding him.

CHAPTER 3

Smoke relaxed when he saw the visitors sitting on the porch and realized who they were. His good-natured laugh cut the night silence as he swung down from his horse and started for the steps.

"Audie? Nighthawk? What are you two doing here?"

Some of his excitement faded when his old friends didn't respond with smiles of their own. Even in the fading light, Smoke could see sorrow etched on their weathered faces. Something else was there, too. Something in their eyes.

Something that resembled rage.

"What's going on?" Smoke said.

By now, Sally was off the buckboard and at Smoke's side. Pearlie Fontaine, Smoke's friend and right-hand man on the Sugarloaf, had been waiting on the porch, too. He now stood with the others and spoke first.

"Smoke, I'll take care of the horses and the buckboard. Why don't you head inside. I've got a pot of coffee going. Have some supper left, too, if you're hungry."

"Thanks, Pearlie, but it was getting so late by the time we

left town that we grabbed a bite at the café. What's going on here?"

Pearlie looked to Nighthawk and then Audie before heading to the horses. "I'll get these animals squared away."

Smoke handed him Drifter's reins, but kept his eyes on the two visitors.

Age had taken some of Nighthawk's height, but not much. Smoke knew that an enemy only underestimated the deadly and taciturn Crow warrior to their detriment. He was as tough as they came. Smoke doubted anyone would actually take him lightly. Even in his seventies, he was a large, powerfully built man who appeared and moved as if he were twenty years younger.

His close friendship with Audie was a study in contrasts. Audie was a diminutive man, approximately four feet tall, who grew up in the hallowed halls of the prestigious universities back east. Since he had been a professor, many didn't understand why he'd left that life behind so many years ago to head out west and learn the ways of the mountain men.

But that's exactly what he'd done, and now that tough, rough-hewn life was every bit as bred into him as within Preacher himself. Audie had been described as a lot of trouble in a small package. He and Nighthawk were inseparable.

Smoke had had a few adventures with them, back in the old days when he was under the tutelage of Preacher. Now it was great to see them, but one look into their eyes told Smoke it was not under good circumstances. They weren't here simply to pay him and Sally a friendly visit.

Sally interrupted the tense silence and asked, "Are you hungry?"

"No, ma'am," Audie said. "Perhaps we should . . . talk inside."

"Of course," Sally said.

She waited until the two visitors turned to the door before exchanging a curious glance with her husband. Smoke shrugged as he took her hand and led the way into the main house.

"How about that coffee Pearlie mentioned?" Smoke said.

"No, thank you," Audie said, presumably speaking for Nighthawk, too. "Smoke, it might be best that you sit down for this. You've no doubt already surmised that the news we bring is not pleasant."

Smoke nodded. "Sorta figured that, Audie. Let's sit around the kitchen table." Smoke cut to the front of the procession and swept his hand toward the table. "Make yourselves at home. I think I'll go ahead and have some of that coffee."

"I'll get it," Sally said with a soft smile.

Smoke nodded and then joined his visitors in sitting.

"All right," he said, once situated, "go ahead and speak your piece." He kept his eyes trained on Audie, knowing he would be the one to elaborate. To say Nighthawk was a man of few words was an understatement.

The old professor sighed, looked to Nighthawk, and then back across the table at Smoke. "There is no pleasant way to say this, so I must be blunt. Preacher is dead."

Sally gasped loudly. She dropped the coffeepot, but was able to catch it before it clattered onto the stove top. She forgot about what she was doing, placed it down, and hurried to Smoke's side. "He's d-dead?"

"I'm afraid so, ma'am," Audie said.

Nighthawk offered a simple nod, but his eyes revealed the fact he was contemplating it all and mourning the passing of his old friend.

"Dead? I figured Preacher would outlive us all. Thought he'd see a hundred and maybe more," Smoke said.

"And you might have very well been correct," Audie said, "had it not been for that murderous bunch that took him out up in Montana."

Smoke's neck muscles tightened. He gritted his teeth and balled his fists. "Are you telling me Preacher was murdered?"

Nighthawk nodded slightly, adding, "Umm."

Sally fell into the chair beside Smoke and wrapped her hands around his arm. Her shoulders shook as her body was wracked with sobs. Smoke pulled free, but only long enough to wrap his arm around her. He held her a moment and let her cry. He understood her sorrow. Perhaps soon he'd feel it, too.

But right now, another emotion had seized him.

Raw, powerful anger.

He knew it wouldn't release its grip, either, until he'd cleared out every last varmint responsible for Preacher's death.

He gave Sally a few minutes and then said, "Might be best you go in there. I have some things I need to discuss with Audie and Nighthawk."

"You mean how you're going to hunt down the guilty and make them pay?" Sally said. Her words were edged in steel. When she ventured a look at Smoke, he realized she wasn't upset about the proposed plan. She wanted justice every bit as much as he did. Even under the grave circumstances, he couldn't help but offer a slight grin.

"That about sums it up," he said.

"I'll stay."

Smoke swallowed the lump in his throat and nodded. There was no sense in arguing with that woman when she'd made up her mind about something.

"All right, Audie. Start at the beginning and tell me everything," Smoke said.

"I wish we had more to tell, but we are still trying to piece it together ourselves," Audie said. "What we do know—having received word through the usual chain that news travels through on the frontier—is that Preacher had wandered into a settlement called Desolation Creek, up in Montana Territory. We don't believe he had any particular business there. He was simply . . . passing through. But for whatever reason, he ran afoul of a local criminal figure—a Venom McFadden, I believe."

"Venom?" Sally said, jerking her head back. "What kind of name is that?"

"I'm afraid I don't know the details on that, ma'am," Audie said. "Nor do I know the specifics of what happened to Preacher. We've heard tell that this McFadden character has a tight grip on the town and the valley in which it lies. He's exercising control over everything and everyone. A real hard case, it seems."

"The outlaws are in control?" Smoke said, scratching his chin and shaking his head. "I reckon that didn't go over too well with Preacher. He's never been one to sit by and let owlhoots run roughshod over innocent folks."

"Indeed," Audie said.

"Umm," Nighthawk said, his jaw set hard, his hands resting atop the table in tight fists.

"I'm afraid this challenge ultimately proved too much even for Preacher," Audie continued. "He was shot, from what we understand."

"How long ago was this?" Smoke said.

"I'm not certain, but I'd estimate a month, perhaps a little longer," Audie said.

Nausea roiled deep inside Smoke's stomach. He hated to think that Preacher had been gone that long and he hadn't known. Of course, news didn't travel very fast on the frontier, and he understood it had likely occurred even longer ago than a month. The time that had passed didn't change anything, though. He'd ride into Desolation Creek and make McFadden and his men pay. If by chance they'd already bled that town dry and moved on, he'd find them, wherever they'd gone. They could run to the ends of the earth, but they'd never escape Smoke and the retribution he was set to deliver. He had a debt to pay. He'd settle Preacher's account.

In lead.

"I hope you didn't just drop by to give me the news," Smoke said.

Smoke could feel Sally's eyes on him, but he kept his own trained across the table.

For the first time that night, Nighthawk's lips turned upward slightly. A brief twinkle was in his eyes and Smoke realized the old Crow was thinking about the same thing—justice.

"Hardly," Audie confirmed. "We are riding up to Montana Territory just as soon as we leave here.

"And we intend to bring hell down on Venom McFadden."

CHAPTER 4

Alonzo Caballero wasn't sure how much more he could take.

His nerves were already shot and it wasn't even eight o'clock in the morning. Of course, they tended to stay frayed, keeping the man on edge these days. How could they not? Venom McFadden had him and that whole town right in the palm of his hand, and nobody could do a blasted thing about it.

Alonzo tried to forget about that and go on about his business as usual. The store would open soon. He needed to restock the candy jars between now and then. He'd been selling a lot of peppermint sticks, as of late, and that fact didn't surprise him. With all the tension in Desolation Creek, parents were probably trying to distract their children as much as possible. Heck, even quite a few adults had been enjoying the sugary treat. It was a small reprieve from their troubles, at least, but far from a solution.

The way Alonzo saw it, there wasn't a solution to the dire situation the town faced. McFadden had Desolation Creek in a death grip, and he was going to choke it slowly until he'd extracted every last cent from it. Then he'd move on to another town and, no doubt, start the process all over again.

There had been a few quiet rumblings from the town's citizens about mounting a rebellion. Nothing much had come from them, though. People were too afraid to face McFadden or that bunch of vipers he surrounded himself with. Alonzo had made a few threats, but never to McFadden's face. He wasn't a gunman. He wasn't capable of defeating any one of those men. At least not on his own.

But if people would band together, well, maybe there was a chance. Folks had seemed too afraid to talk about it much. The newspaperman seemed ready to act, and would join Alonzo, but what could two men do against an army? And that's what McFadden had—a platoon of gunhands patrolling the town and making every man, woman, and child bend to his will.

It wasn't right. It couldn't stand. But under the circumstances, what could Alonzo do?

He brought one of the peppermint sticks to his nose and took a moment to savor the scent. He would eat the candy if he could afford it. With as much as McFadden had leached from the store recently, funds were mighty tight. Alonzo needed every penny just to live on and stay in business.

The candy sure smelled good, though. It made him smile for a moment before he dropped the stick in the jar and reached for more to put in with it. But he dropped them as a loud crash startled him. Red-and-white chips littered the floor as several of the sticks shattered upon hitting the wooden puncheons.

"Darn it," he said.

He forgot all about the candy as the realization of what was occurring swept over him. His breathing grew shallow as he swiveled his head toward the store's entrance.

Five men walked through the broken door, which hung limply from its busted hinges. Venom McFadden was in the lead, with one of his kill-crazy lackeys, Chuck Hicks, strolling close behind. The other three men stood at a respectful distance, but, obviously, they were ready to step in if their leader gave the word.

McFadden stopped a few feet from Alonzo and smiled.

Alonzo couldn't resist the urge and crossed himself while muttering a prayer under his breath.

McFadden looked exactly how Alonzo had always pictured Satan himself—handsome enough to charm the unsuspecting, but with cold, calculating eyes and a hint of cruelty lurking just behind those dark pupils.

He had perfectly manicured black hair, which was showing a hint of gray around the temples. His teeth were whiter than any Alonzo had ever seen and almost too straight. He moved with a natural, athletic grace and carried himself as if he owned the whole world.

Well, he did own *his* world, Alonzo thought grimly. In Desolation Creek, Venom McFadden was lord and master. Only a fool opposed him.

With a swiftly beating heart, Alonzo realized he'd been that fool.

"Good morning, Al."

Alonzo cleared his throat. He tried to calm his nerves, but it was an exercise in futility. "T-the s-store isn't open yet."

McFadden chuckled. "We know, Al." He jerked a thumb over his shoulder. "That's why we kicked the door in."

The other men laughed.

McFadden's tone seemed friendly enough, and anyone who didn't know better might mistake him for a cordial fellow just walking around town, ready to visit with his neighbors.

Somehow that made him seem worse to Alonzo. Shouldn't monsters look terrifying? Wouldn't they have ghastly appearances?

But here this man was—with his natural good looks, fancy black suit, matching vest, and stark white shirt beneath it— looking more like aristocracy than an outlaw.

Perhaps he truly was *El Diablo*—the only explanation that made sense.

"Pass me one of those peppermint sticks, would you, Al?" McFadden said.

Alonzo thought of protesting, but knew it wouldn't do any good. Perhaps if he cooperated, the encounter would be over with soon.

He tried to keep his hand as steady as possible while passing the jar to McFadden. He wasn't successful and the snickers from the other men stung his pride. He couldn't do anything about that, though. He couldn't do anything about any of it.

"Thank you very much, Al," McFadden said as he removed a stick. He brought the candy to his lips and sucked on it. "That is mighty good. What about cherry? You have any cherry candy?"

Alonzo placed the jar back atop the counter and tried to calm his racing mind long enough to consider his inventory. "N-no cherry, Mr. McFadden."

He was ashamed to use such a formal title, showing respect to that monster. He wished he had more courage. He wished he could be as brave in front of McFadden and his men as he had been when talking to the other citizens.

"That's a shame. But this will do." He took another pull off the peppermint stick and then said, "Say, I heard something about you."

Alonzo's back stiffened. The portly man brought a thick hand to his head and instinctively wiped the sheen of sweat that had beaded atop his bald head. "What is that?"

McFadden shrugged. "Heard some, well . . . sort of nasty things, Al. The type of things a friend wouldn't say about another friend."

Alonzo gulped. "Sir, I did not—"

The outlaw leader held up a hand to cut off further protest and then said, "Now, I didn't want to believe it, because I know you and I are pals. Right, Al?"

"Yes, yes," Alonzo said. "We are amigos."

McFadden spread his hands. "That's what I thought. But these things are very troubling. Instead of gossiping about it and dragging other folks into it, I thought I'd come see you directly. To straighten this out. Because we're . . . *amigos*."

"That's right," Alonzo said with a newfound hope. "We can talk about these things."

"Exactly." McFadden came alongside the storekeeper and put his arm around him, as if they were old pards from way back. "I'll go ahead and tell you what I heard, assuming there are no ladies in here." He made a show of turning a full circle to survey the store, keeping his arm on Alonzo's shoulder and guiding him into the spin as well. "This isn't the kind of thing womenfolk should hear."

Alonzo swallowed hard. Of course, he remembered most of what he'd told some of the others in town. Why had he been so foolish?

I should have kept my big fat mouth shut!

"Rumor is, Al, that you cursed me. Called me a low-down, dirty skunk, among other things. Being a religious man, I'll not repeat those things here. Truth is, they hurt me pretty bad. And I think they hurt the Lord, too." McFadden used the hand he had draped across Alonzo's shoulder to tap the crucifix the store owner wore.

"I am sorry for this," Alonzo said. He didn't even bother to hide the fear in his trembling voice. There was no use. McFadden could feel his body shaking. He couldn't fool anyone.

"Oh, I forgive you," McFadden said, putting his free hand over his heart. "It's the Christian thing to do. But Chuck here, well, I'm not so sure he's feeling very religious."

"C-Chuck?" Alonzo said, looking toward the gunhand.

The man's lips were peeled back in a cruel smile, revealing his jagged yellow teeth. He looked like a wolf about to consume a stray sheep.

"That's right," McFadden continued. "You see, we also heard you said that Chuck is fast, but perhaps someone is faster. Maybe someone could draw on him and win." He let the statement hang in the air, smiling at Alonzo's labored breathing before adding, "Did you say that, Al?"

"I did not . . . It's just that . . ." Alonzo pushed away and stepped back to sum up McFadden. He wasn't suddenly brave. He was angry. He could not stand the indignation any longer. He practically spat out his next words. "You come into our shops and take what you want! You do not pay. You do not treat us kindly. You rob and use. That's it!" He slashed his hands in the air as his nostrils flared. He narrowed his eyes and leveled a stubby finger toward McFadden. "We cannot live like this! The people here have families to feed. The town cannot survive this way."

McFadden snorted, shaking his head and looking toward his men. "You hear that, boys? You think someone is your friend and then . . . well, this. There's no loyalty anymore."

"Loyalty?" Alonzo said, his voice rising and his cheeks burning a bright red. "You speak of loyalty when you plunder this town and abuse its citizens? You think you know loyalty?"

"That sure hurts, Al. You know, when I heard what you'd said, I didn't believe it. I said Al is my amigo and he wouldn't talk behind my back. But what do you know? As sure as I live and breathe, you said it." He shook his head as he bowed it. "And now you're saying even more. Outright nasty things. Just goes to show, you can't trust anyone these days." He clicked his tongue several times and then lifted his gaze again. With a wide smile plastered across his face, as if inviting someone to Sunday dinner, he said, "Say, I've got an idea. You thought maybe you could beat Chuck on the draw. Let's test it. What do you say, amigo?"

Suddenly Alonzo lost some of his starch. "T-test it?"

"That's right," McFadden said. "A good ol' quick-draw competition out in the street. If you win, I'll leave you alone forever. You'll never hear from me again. If Chuck wins, well . . . I suppose that don't matter none to you, being as you'll be dead and all."

Alonzo's brain was having trouble processing all he was being told. His jaw hung slack as he looked at the men before him. Finally he mustered enough wits about him to say, "But I do not even have a gun. I don't have one!"

"Why, that's no trouble," McFadden said with a dismissive wave. "Sam over there is a nice guy. He'll loan you one. Isn't that right, Sam?"

"Be happy to," one of the gunmen said with a smile. "It's a good one, too." He pulled an ivory-handled Colt from his holster and walked to where Alonzo stood. He continued to smile as he shoved the gun in the front waistband of Alonzo's pants.

"Careful now," McFadden said. "We don't want to shoot anything off that he might need."

This drew uproarious laughter from everyone present, save for Alonzo, who didn't find a thing funny about his predicament.

Behind him now, McFadden raised his booted foot and drove it hard into the shopkeeper's backside. "Go on. Out to the street."

Alonzo's eyes burned with tears. He sniffled, but felt foolish for showing such weakness before these men. How could he help it, though? He was marching to his death and he knew it.

"Come on out, everyone!" McFadden yelled, once they'd all stepped into the bright morning sun. "We're going to have an old-fashioned duel right here in the street!"

A few people were milling about. The blacksmith put his hammer down, wiped his brow, and left the anvil he'd been working on. "What is this?"

"Just a little argument between Alonzo and Chuck," McFadden said. He aimed a pointed stare at the man and said, "You wouldn't poke your nose where it doesn't belong, would you?" Beside him, Chuck's hand fell to the butt of the gun he wore.

The blacksmith gulped and stepped back a few paces. Then, as if he couldn't live with himself, he shook his head and started forward again. "No, this ain't right."

"Stay b-back, blacksmith," Alonzo said, trying to gather as much bravado as possible. "This is between me and . . . Chuck."

He cast telling glances to everyone who'd gathered on the boardwalk, making sure everyone understood.

He didn't have a fighting chance. He was about to slide into eternity. It was simply his time. At least he could keep his friends safe. There was no reason for anyone else in town to meet such a tragic fate.

"You see?" McFadden called loudly. "Alonzo called Chuck out. He wants it this way."

Alonzo choked down the rising bile in his throat and said a silent prayer. He thought of the crucifix around his neck and drew a small measure of comfort from it. At least on the other side, he'd be free of men such as Venom McFadden. At least there would be no more devils.

He stood in the center of the dusty street. A slight wind blew around him. He started to whimper, but caught himself.

No. I'll go out fighting at least. Fighting, not crying.

A few paces away, Chuck Hicks stood. He'd been in plenty of situations like this one, even some against real gunfighters. He was calm, cool, and collected.

It was simply Tuesday morning for him.

Sure, Chuck was fast, but even gunfighters made mistakes sometimes. Chuck wasn't invincible. *Maybe,* Alonzo thought. *Just maybe I can . . .*

He pawed for the gun handle centered on his belly. It hadn't even cleared the waistband before he heard the loud report of gunfire only feet away.

Alonzo had the strange thought that the wound didn't

hurt. He knew he'd been shot. He felt a warmth, followed by a wetness, but it didn't hurt.

It was the last thought he ever had.

"It was a fair fight," McFadden said.

There was no need to state such a thing. The law in Desolation Creek wouldn't do a thing.

"Now I want you all to know," he said, turning a slow, measured circle in the center of the street, addressing those gathered as if giving a political speech, "that ol' Al here left me his store."

There were several shocked gasps from the onlookers, but no one stepped forward in protest.

"Right before we went outside, he put his arm around me and said, 'Amigo,'—that's what he called me, his amigo—but he said, 'If anything happens to me, I want you to have my store. You're the only one I trust to run this place besides myself.' I was rooting for poor Al. But he went and did a foolhardy thing, calling out Chuck like he did. It's a shame."

McFadden grabbed the lapels of his black jacket and smiled proudly. "So, now I'm in the mercantile business. Y'all come on by later and have a look-see at the stock. I'll cut you a good deal." He winked.

He strolled toward Chuck as the horrified crowd dispersed. Leaning in, he said, "Fetch the undertaker. Tell him I want Alonzo displayed for a bit. He can prop up the casket right there in front of his shop. Serve as a warning to the others."

Chuck smiled gleefully. "I'm on my way now."

McFadden nodded and slapped him on the back. Then he turned and appraised the store. He smiled, laughed, and clapped his hands together.

"I own a store now. How about that?"

CHAPTER 5

Smoke rode into Big Rock alone, just as the businesses and shops were opening for the day.

He'd thought of setting out for Montana Territory at first light, but then decided against it. He wanted to get up there to settle the score with Venom McFadden as soon as possible, but there were a few things he needed to take care of first.

He looped Drifter's reins around the hitching rail in front of Longmont's Saloon and looked around the street. An elderly couple walked along the other side, waving to Smoke as they passed. He feigned a smile and waved back. No sense in looking sour even if he wasn't in a jolly mood.

Images filled his mind of Preacher lying dead in a muddy Montana street, leaving a bitter taste in his mouth. His nostrils flared as he took a deep breath. He stood silently for a moment until his anger was under control. He needed a clear head, and riding into Desolation Creek filled with pure rage wouldn't cut it. Preacher had taught him better than that. Whatever he did, he needed to be calculated about it.

He exhaled loudly and then strode into the saloon.

No business was being done at this hour and Louis Longmont was sitting at his private table, with a steaming cup of coffee and a book open before him. As if sensing Smoke, he looked up and smiled.

"What do you say, my friend?"

Smoke nodded. "Morning, Louis." He didn't say "Good morning," because it wasn't. "Mind if I join you?"

"You don't even have to ask. Sit down, I'll get you some coffee." He motioned to an empty chair at the table as he stood and walked behind the bar. "Be back in a minute."

He disappeared through the doorway that led to the back and then reemerged moments later with a steaming cup. He placed it in front of Smoke and then took his seat.

"Didn't think we'd see you back in town so soon, after that little contretemps yesterday."

"Didn't think I'd come," Smoke said. He started to say more, but then stopped short and picked up the cup to take a sip. The warmth felt good against his lips. He smacked them and then set the cup down.

"I get the feeling this isn't a social visit," Louis said, arching an eyebrow.

"Preacher's dead," Smoke said flatly.

"What?" Louis sat back and drew in a sharp breath. His eyebrows rose in a mixture of surprise, confusion, and disbelief.

Smoke nodded. "Killed up Montana way."

"Smoke, I'm—"

Smoke nodded again and interrupted in a voice as hard as flint, "I'm riding up there."

Longmont chewed on the information for a moment before asking, "You need help?"

If Smoke had needed the help, Louis Longmont would be a good one to ask. A former gunman, Longmont had gotten out of that life and now enjoyed a more peaceful existence managing his own saloon. Sure, some danger still occurred every now and then, but for the most part, it was a lot less dangerous than his former life.

"Not in Montana," Smoke said. "I'm heading up there with Audie and Nighthawk, Preacher's old trapping pards. They're the ones who delivered the news."

"I see," Longmont said before taking another pull of his coffee. Once the cup was back on the table, he said, "Are they in town with you? I haven't seen them in quite a while."

This drew a short but genuine laugh from Smoke. "No, and thank goodness. Audie attracts enough attention, being a little fella like he is, but Nighthawk, well . . . folks around here might get a bit scared to see that giant ol' Crow warrior walking the streets. Especially after the trouble we just had."

Longmont laughed now, too. "Only thing worse would be if a blue-belly soldier was with him."

There'd been some trouble a while back with a band of renegade Cheyenne, led by a blood-lusting butcher named Black Drum. There'd been even more trouble with the supposed army soldiers who'd flooded the valley to "protect" the good citizens of Big Rock. That was all in the past, though. A lot of powder had been burned, and blood spilled, to resolve those issues, but at least both threats had been stopped.

Returning to the matter at hand, Smoke said, "I'm going to be gone for a while. Pearlie is staying at the Sugarloaf and I have two hands working there, both good men. But—"

"Sally," Longmont said.

Smoke nodded. "Sally."

"I'd be happy to look in on her, Smoke. I'll keep a sharp eye out and make sure nothing happens to bother her."

Smoke took another gulp of coffee, nearly downing the entire cup in that one swallow. Standing, he offered his hand. "I'm obliged to you. Hopefully, we won't have much trouble and I'll be back in no time."

Louis stood, shook his friend's hand, and chuckled wryly.

"I hope that's the case, Smoke. I'm not sure if you've noticed, though, but trouble just has a way of following you."

Smoke grinned.

"Come to think of it, I have noticed that. More than a few times."

"Howdy, Smoke. Surprised you're back in town so soon."

Monte Carson stood up from behind his desk and waved Smoke toward him. Smoke sat and then took off his hat, scratched his head, and settled in the chair. He squared the hat atop his head once more and said, "Monte, I'm riding out for a while. Can't say how long I'll be gone."

The sheriff arched an eyebrow as he studied his guest. The bright morning sun filtered in through the window, illuminating the wanted dodgers tacked to the wall behind him.

"Sounds like trouble," he said after a long moment.

"It is. Up in Montana Territory. Preacher's dead."

"What?" The lawman looked and sounded as shocked as Louis Longmont had been.

Smoke nodded.

"What on earth could do that old mountain man in?"

"Not what," Smoke said. "*Who*. Seems he rode afoul of some outlaw."

"Someone killed Preacher?" Monte said, his jaw falling slack.

Smoke went on to tell him what little he knew of the events and of Venom McFadden.

"I don't like it, Smoke. This Venom feller must be something if he was able to get the drop on Preacher. That old pelican still had every bit of the bark on him."

"I'm not sure exactly how it happened, but I aim to figure it out," Smoke said. "Right before I blow them all to pieces."

"Smoke, I'm sorry," Monte said. "I know how much Preacher meant to you. Is there any way I can help? You know I'll do it, after all you've done for this town. Big Rock owes its whole existence to you."

Smoke brushed off the comment the same way he did anytime Monte said something to that effect. It seemed as if the sheriff never missed an opportunity to let Smoke and others know that Big Rock only existed because Smoke had gone to war with Tilden Franklin and won. And there was some truth to that, though Smoke didn't like to rehash it all.

"I'd be obliged if you'd check in on Sally. Pearlie will be there, along with two other hands. They're good men. Everything should be fine and I'm not expecting trouble. At least not here."

There would be plenty of shooting in Montana, though, Smoke thought with a grim smile. Might not be enough bullets left over for anyone to raise a ruckus around Big Rock.

"Of course," Monte said. "Be honored to."

"Like I said, I'm obliged." Smoke stood and extended his hand.

Monte did the same.

"When are you heading out?"

"Tomorrow morning," Smoke said. "I'm going to drop by the mercantile and get outfitted, then spend one last night in my own bed."

And with Sally nestling in my arms, as close as I can get her, Smoke thought, though he kept that notion to himself.

"Don't worry," Monte said, slapping Smoke on the back. "Big Rock and the Sugarloaf will be well cared for while you're gone."

Smoke had no doubt the sheriff was right. Things ought to be right peaceful around this valley, he thought.

Because I'm taking all the destruction with me up to Desolation Creek, Montana.

CHAPTER 6

The sun was just cresting over the eastern sky as Smoke stepped out onto the porch and surveyed the scene before him. The ranch looked beautiful in those golden shades of the early dawn. He'd miss that view and the patch of land he called home.

He'd miss even more the woman who stood beside him.

He stopped and let Sally walk a few paces off the porch before coming up behind her and wrapping his arms around her waist. He leaned around, gave her a kiss on the cheek, and then rested his head against hers.

"I'll hurry back to you," he said.

"Smoke," she said, shaking her head and turning around until they faced each other. Putting a hand on his cheek, she smiled and gazed into his eyes. "I knew the kind of man you were when I married you. I know you have to go and settle this score. I'd never ask you to stay."

Smoke had no doubt the sentiment was genuine. Sally had stood by him through a lot of gunsmoke and violence. She wasn't above taking a hand in the shooting when circumstances called for it, though Smoke preferred her safe and sound, far from harm's way.

"Truth is," she continued, "I want to go with you. I'm just as angry over what happened to Preacher as you are."

Smoke nodded. "I don't doubt that, but someone has to stay here and run the Sugarloaf. We have a ranch to build, remember?"

"I'm not some dainty thing you have to protect."

"No. No, you aren't. But you are the woman I'm going to grow old with, and right now, you'll stay safe and sound here on the Sugarloaf with Pearlie. And at the first sign of trouble—not that I'm expecting any—you'll get Monte or Louis out here to lend a hand."

"Yes, *Daddy*," she said with a healthy dose of sarcasm in her voice. She laughed and gave him a hug, followed by a lingering kiss. "I'm not asking you to stay, but I am telling you to hurry back."

Just then, Pearlie walked out of the barn and came toward them, leading Drifter. He held out the reins and said, "All saddled up and ready, Smoke."

"Thanks, Pearlie. And much obliged for you taking care of things around here."

Pearlie nodded and then fell back a few paces, giving the couple one last moment of privacy.

Smoke gave Sally another kiss and lightly caressed her cheek.

"I'll be back before you know it."

"I'll hold you to that," she said.

Audie and Nighthawk had camped in a clearing not far from the ranch house. After living for decades in the mountains, both men preferred having the stars over their heads to a roof. They were packed and mounted and waiting for Smoke when he arrived at their camp.

As they were riding off the Sugarloaf range, Audie asked, "Is Sally worried about you?"

Smoke let out a short laugh. "Not hardly. Well, I'm sure she is, to a certain extent, but mostly she's mad I cut her out of this deal. I think she'd charge right in, guns a-blazin', if she could."

"We'll go to Desolation Creek, but I'm not sure guns blazing is the best way to handle this," Audie said. "Probably a good thing she isn't accompanying us."

"Umm," Nighthawk said.

"You're right, old friend. The female of the species often *is* the fiercest."

Not much more was said about Sally, a fact Smoke was grateful for. She was never far from his mind, but he didn't need to dwell on missing her.

Besides, as the days passed on the trail north, he found it hard to think about anything besides Preacher lying in the street, shot all to pieces, his lifeblood being soaked up by the thirsty, uncaring ground. True, Smoke hadn't actually witnessed the grisly scene, but his imagination conjured up realistic notions that haunted his dreams and some waking moments.

He also considered this Venom McFadden character. He had to be one tough hombre to get the drop on Preacher. Many a man had tried that very thing and they'd all ended up in early graves.

Until McFadden.

It stuck in Smoke's craw and he was more than ready to settle the score. That would come soon enough, he told himself. What he really needed was a plan and he had plenty of time to think of one as they rode along.

Colorado faded into Wyoming Territory. The majestic Rockies tapered off into distant low-rising hills. A sharp wind blew across the high plains, but, thankfully, it wasn't cold. Smoke remembered how bitter the region could be in the dead of winter, when that wind cut right through a man and chilled him to the bone. He was grateful to be making his trek in more pleasant conditions.

If only his reasons for heading up that way were pleasant.

He thought of Preacher covering that same trail on his way to a rendezvous. Those trappers worked hard, but knew how to let loose, too. Those old rendezvous had turned out to be wild times and Preacher had enjoyed a great many of them. Smoke smiled, taking some solace in the fact that his friend was now enjoying the Big Rendezvous in the Sky, reunited with some of those pards who had gone on before him.

Smoke was thinking about that, in fact, the day Audie said, "I've been trying to think of an adequate way to handle this, but so far, I'm at a loss. I suppose we might not know until we arrive and survey the town, gaining a clearer understanding of what the situation is."

"Umm," Nighthawk said with a nod.

"Reckon that's about right," Smoke said. "My anger tells me to ride in and settle things quickly. Hit fast and hard. But Preacher taught me better than that."

"Indeed he did," Audie said. "So, how do you want to handle this? I believe you've had more experience with this sort of thing than Nighthawk and I. True, we have been in some scrapes in our day, but you, well . . ."

Smoke chuckled. "Yeah, I'm no stranger to trouble, that's for sure. As far as a plan, I'm not sure I have the answer yet. We still have a few days to figure it out. And like you said, we might not know every detail until we've gotten a good lay of the land up in Desolation Creek."

"What a dreadful name for a settlement," Audie said. "Fitting, I suppose. Much like Venom's name. Or nickname, whichever it might be."

Smoke said nothing as he looked to the west, squinting to see if he could make out the mountains that rested somewhere just over the horizon. He couldn't see them, but he saw *something*.

He squinted even harder, leaning forward to gain every advantage he could.

"Something is kicking up a cloud of dust," he said, more to himself than his riding partners. "What on earth?"

That old familiar feeling spread across the pit of his stomach, right about the time he first heard the shots.

"Blast it," Audie said.

"Umm," Nighthawk added, his hand going to the stock of the Henry rifle that rested in the scabbard lashed to his saddle.

Smoke had his hand hovering near his rifle, too. Because to their left, coming over a low ridge, a whole heap of trouble loomed.

And it was heading straight toward them.

CHAPTER 7

Smoke didn't like charging into a shooting scrape without knowing who—if anyone—needed to be shot at. But it only took a quick glance through the spyglass he'd pulled from his saddlebags to figure out which side he was on.

A buckboard was jolting down the low-rising hill, going so fast that he feared the wheels would come right off or the whole thing would topple over. Two figures were hunkered as low as they could get on the front bench. One was handling the team, pushing the two horses to give every ounce of speed they had. The figure next to him was fumbling with a rifle and not having much success in sending lead behind them.

Smoke looked just in time to see the passenger's hat fall off to reveal long, flowing blond hair that whipped around the woman as the wagon gained speed. A bullet plunked right into the wood mere inches from where she sat, blasting splinters into the air and causing her to let out a curt scream.

Behind them, four riders barreled down the hill, sending a volley of shots toward their prey.

Well, there was no doubt about it now, Smoke thought.

He didn't like the odds and he sure didn't like someone shooting at a woman. He dug his spurs into Drifter's flanks, causing him to gallop toward the action at a ground-eating clip. Audie and Nighthawk followed.

Smoke waited until he was a tad closer before putting the reins in his mouth and raising his rifle to his shoulder. It wasn't easy to draw a steady bead while galloping that swiftly, but Smoke had been in enough of these situations and had gained plenty of experience. He squeezed off a shot and was rewarded by the sight of a pursuing rider throwing his arms in the air before pitching off his horse. His foot remained caught in the stirrup and he bounced along the ground for a few yards before coming free. His body lay lifeless in the grass.

The riders were aware of Smoke's presence now. They spread out and turned their attention to him, Nighthawk, and Audie.

They fanned out, too, and galloped past the buckboard with Smoke on one side and Audie and Nighthawk on the other. They were close enough for pistols now, so Smoke shoved his rifle back into the sheath and drew his Colt.

Three riders remained and one of them was charging straight at Smoke.

Smoke nudged Drifter to his left and barely avoided a bullet. He sure felt the wind-rip of it, though, as it sizzled past his ear, so close he could hear the wicked whine of its passage as well. He was unscathed, thankfully.

The rider who'd fired the shot wasn't as lucky. Smoke's gun belched flame and a second later the rider's head snapped back as a "third eye" appeared dead center in his forehead. He stayed atop his mount for a few seconds longer, a ghastly display looking as if a lifeless, hollow-eyed rider had appeared from hell itself. He finally passed Smoke before toppling from his horse, never to move again.

Two dozen yards away, Audie and Nighthawk were engaged in their own battles with the remaining two riders.

Gunsmoke billowed across the plains as the sound of rapid shots mixed with the thundering hoofbeats of the charging horses.

Smoke sent Drifter in that direction, raising his gun to tip the odds in Audie and Nighthawk's favor, but he couldn't get a clean shot. The two riders were so close to his friends that it made gun work too risky.

Based upon the amount of shots Smoke had heard, he suspected the four had empty guns. Or perhaps Nighthawk preferred hand-to-hand battles versus gunfights. Whatever the reason, he launched off his horse and crashed into one of the two riders. The giant Crow warrior and the unknown gunman landed on the ground with a hard thud. Nighthawk was on top. He sent several savage blows to the man's head and Smoke could hear the gruesome sound of bones crunching even over Drifter's drumming hoofbeats.

The sudden display of savagery gave Smoke and Audie the advantage they needed.

The other rider remained atop his horse, momentarily stunned by the violence taking place before him. It was the last mistake he ever made. When he came back to his senses, he tried to level his piece at Nighthawk, but it was too late. Smoke had swung Drifter into a tight arc and came up in front of the man. His gun boomed at the same time as Audie's, and the two shots rolled into each other, sounding like one.

One slug tore into the man's chest, while the other punched into his gut. He tried to lift his gun hand again, but his strength failed him as the life drained from his body. He slid off the horse, landing in an ungainly heap in the grass.

A few feet away, Nighthawk's quarry had managed to roll free and was now staggering to his feet. The man spat blood. A deranged fire burned in his brown eyes. He looked miniature compared to the Crow he was facing off with, but that was just about everyone who stood close to Nighthawk, Smoke thought.

The man reached for the knife tucked into the waistband of his buckskins and held up the blade with a taunting sneer. "I'll cut you, you no-good Injun!"

He bent slightly at the waist and moved sideways on his feet, ready for the melee. Smoke thought of ending the fight, but quickly realized there was no need. Nighthawk wasn't in any danger.

The big Indian's movements were so fast that the naked eye could barely follow them. He pulled his own knife from a sheath somewhere on his side and flicked his wrist. The blade swooshed through the air, covering the four feet between the two men in a mere second, before driving deep into the other man's chest.

The opponent gasped loudly and staggered closer. His arm stiffened and he dropped his own weapon. He hiccupped and gurgled before falling forward, face-first onto the ground.

"Umm," Nighthawk said.

"Indeed," Audie said from the back of his horse. "A most unpleasant surprise for that lout, but it appears as if the young travelers are unharmed."

Smoke maneuvered Drifter around to see that the buckboard had stopped at the bottom of the hill. The man who'd been driving it was hurrying toward them, with the rifle in hand. The woman remained with the wagon.

The fella was breathing hard when he arrived. "Are . . . they all—"

"It's over," Smoke said with a nod. "Is she okay?" He jerked his head toward the woman.

"She's fine," the man said. "I'm much obliged to you gents. Gee, I can't thank you enough!"

The relief momentarily vanished as his eyes left Smoke and Audie to settle on Nighthawk. Smoke noticed he gripped the rifle a bit tighter, but to his credit, he didn't gasp or outright run away.

Eager to ease the sudden tension, Smoke said, "Name's

Jensen. Smoke Jensen. These are my friends Audie and Night-hawk. I'm glad we came along when we did."

The introduction seemed to make the young man a bit less nervous, but he still kept a tight hold on the rifle.

"I'm Brett Cummings. That's my sister, Amy."

"And just who are—pardon me—*were* these *gentlemen*?" Audie asked, looking at the bodies that littered the prairie before him. His voice dripped with scorn as he used the term "gentlemen."

By now, Nighthawk stood over the body of the man he'd just killed. Brett watched in horror as the Indian pulled the knife from the corpse and swiped the blade against the dead man's clothes. The blood smeared on the tattered buckskin shirt. The blade was clean when Nighthawk returned the weapon to its sheath.

As if finally remembering Audie's question, Brett tore his eyes away and leveled them back at Audie. "Bandits, I suppose. They were hiding around one of those little hills over yonder and tried to surround us when we came down the road. I lit out of there, but they were about to overtake us. That is, until you three showed up. Again, I'm much obliged. They would have stolen our entire load." He swallowed hard, his face turning slightly pale, before adding, "And done who knows what to my sister."

"We're glad to help," Smoke said. "Speaking of your sister, we best get on over there to check on her."

"Oh, yeah. Yeah. Of course," Brett said.

He walked alongside Smoke and the others as they headed toward the buckboard.

"You mentioned those owlhoots wanting to take your load," Smoke said. "Just what are you hauling?"

The young man looked up at Smoke with concerned eyes, probably fearing Smoke and his riding partners might have the notion of picking up where the now-dead thieves had left off. He must have realized Smoke would find out sooner or later, so he said, "Some food. Drink. A few other items to sell. My folks run a trading post about ten miles up the trail. That's where we were hoping to make it to, so we could get a little help, but I didn't really figure we'd get there. Not until you three came along."

"Glad to help," Smoke reiterated.

They arrived at the buckboard and Smoke took stock of the young woman who waited there. She couldn't have been older than nineteen. Her hair was blond and shiny and she had high cheekbones, which rose prominently just below her ice-blue eyes. She was a pretty girl and Smoke shuddered to think what the hard cases had in mind for her. Thankfully, the outlaws would take that secret to their graves.

"Thank you, all of you," she said.

"Umm," Nighthawk offered.

"My friend is correct," Audie said. "We don't take pleasure in such displays of wanton violence, but I'm afraid it could not be avoided in this situation. Those brigands were set on plundering you both. I doubt anyone will mourn the passing of such villainous men."

"You say the trading post isn't far from here?" Smoke asked Brett.

"Just about ten miles, if even that."

"We'll ride the rest of the way with you, just in case there's more trouble." Smoke doubted there were more members of the gang lying in ambush, but he'd feel better escorting the youngsters safely home.

Brett looked to be twenty-three or twenty-four, and, in reality, Smoke couldn't be considered an elder when compared to the man. However, Brett was evidently inexperienced to the harsh realities of the frontier. In that regard, Smoke was decades ahead of him.

"Thank you!" Amy said, clearly relieved at the news. "There's been so much trouble around here lately. Seems as if everyone's gone crazy."

"Trouble?" Smoke said.

She nodded and then shrugged. "I have no idea what's going on."

"I'll tell you what's going on," Brett said. "All the hard cases passing through and causing trouble on their way up to Montana. I bet that's what those fellas lying over yonder were doing. Probably just waylaying us to get supplies to outfit them for the rest of their trip."

Smoke had a pretty good idea why there'd been such an influx of hard cases traveling north, but he decided to hold that discussion for a later time. Brett and Amy were already shaken up enough, and he couldn't blame them. Had Smoke, Audie, and Nighthawk not come along, they'd most likely be dead by now.

Or wishing they were.

"Is there any law around here? Might need to report this," Smoke said.

"Ha!" Amy said with a snort.

Brett chuckled. "What my sister means is Slade's Gulch—where we'd picked up these supplies—is about thirty miles that way." He jerked his head in the direction they'd come from. "Not much law there, to speak of."

"We're on our own around here," Amy added.

Smoke nodded. "Even so, we best take care of these bodies and round up their horses. Looks like you're the proud owners of four new mounts."

"I'm much obliged, sir, but . . . well, you fellas did all the . . . uh, work." Brett looked somewhat sheepish as he admitted it. "I think those animals are rightfully yours."

Smoke couldn't argue the point, but he wasn't interested in the horses. He doubted Nighthawk and Audie were, either. They'd set out on their trek for vengeance, not profit. Besides, he didn't want the extra animals slowing them down the rest of the journey to Desolation Creek. The Cummings family probably didn't make a lot of money with that remote trading post. The horses might be a major boost for them.

"You keep them," Smoke said. Something final reverberated in his tone and neither Brett nor Amy argued with him. "We best get busy with those bodies."

"I'll help," Brett said, grabbing a shovel from the buckboard. "It's the least I can do."

The four men completed their grim task without incident and then headed for the trading post. It wasn't much, just a log cabin, an outhouse, along with a smokehouse, small stable, and corral off to the side.

A thin wisp of smoke curled from the cabin's chimney and Smoke caught the aroma of something mighty pleasant.

Nighthawk sniffed the air. "Umm."

"You said it, old friend. I'm famished as well," Audie said.

Amy and Brett looked to the visitors with a hint of confusion. Brett next spoke. "I'll get these horses unsaddled and rubbed down. You fellas want to put your mounts up?"

"Reckon we'll just hitch 'em to the rail," Smoke said.

A rest might do the horses some good, but he wanted to get the lay of the place first. He had no reason not to trust the Cummingses, but it never hurt to keep a quick escape possible until one knew exactly what they were walking into.

Thankfully, inside the trading post, he found a friendly space that matched the friendly face behind the bar.

"Afternoon," the tall, broad-shouldered man said.

"Afternoon," Smoke replied.

The man's gaze moved over to Nighthawk and concern registered in his eyes. Smoke waited for the speech about not serving his kind, but a sharp stare was all they received.

That stare softened, however, when Amy hurried past and up to the bar. "Pa, these men saved us!"

"Saved you? Are you hurt?"

He hurried the length of the bar to the opening and then

rushed to his daughter. His eyes traveled down, and then up, before his breathing returned to normal.

"I'm not hurt, Pa."

"Brett?"

"He's fine. Taking care of the horses."

"We need to unload the wagon first."

"Not those horses. The four these men gave us."

By now, a woman had entered from the back storeroom and was at her husband's side. "What's this I hear about needing rescuing?"

Even though the woman was half a head shorter than Amy and a bit thicker, they obviously were mother and daughter.

"Just what's going on here?" the man said, scratching his heavy, stubble-clad jaw.

Amy went on to tell them about the harrowing ordeal back on the trail. Once she had finished, the woman threw her arms around Amy and hugged her tightly. The man thrust out his hand toward Smoke.

"I'm much obliged to you men for what you done. I can't . . . well . . ." His voice trailed off as he evidently tried to control his emotions. He then shook his head and said, "I never should have sent them. Not with all the trouble that's been going on around here. What was I thinking?"

"Herb, this isn't your fault," his wife said.

He just shrugged and scratched his jaw again. He then shook Audie's hand and Nighthawk's.

"You boys sit down and let us get you something to eat. Whatever you want to drink, too. It's on the house."

"That's not necessary," Smoke said. "We can pay—"

"We won't hear of it," the woman said.

"Greta, go on and get them some stew," Herb said. "Go on and help your ma, Amy."

Smoke studied his host as he walked to a nearby table. Herb Cummings had some extra weight on him, but he appeared strong as an ox, too. His thick, dark, curly hair was receding, giving him a large forehead. His eyes were kind, yet tired, and Smoke figured the family worked mighty hard to keep the trading post going.

Smoke casually surveyed the rest of the room before sitting down.

A man sat alone at a table, shoveling stew in his mouth, dripping more back into the bowl than he got through his lips. He had a hard look about him, and the dirty range clothes he wore hadn't been washed in probably a month. He hadn't been, either.

He'd taken the farthest table, his back against the wall, a fact that Smoke noted. Thankfully, he had Audie and Night-hawk to keep watch, but Smoke felt exposed sitting in the center of the room. It was the only space available, though.

Besides the unkempt fella, three young men, who appeared to be cowboys, were at a table. They had beers before them and had turned around to listen to the story of the attempted holdup, but soon they returned their interest to their card game. Two looked to be twenty-one at the oldest, while the other was probably pushing thirty-five. They were talking quietly, minding their own business, and their presence didn't bother Smoke.

However, Smoke remained watchful of the lone, dirty fella in the back.

"You gents want beer? Whiskey? Both?" Herb Cummings asked.

"I appreciate the offer," Smoke said. "But I could sure use some coffee, if you have any."

"We always keep a pot on the stove. I'll bring you some. How about you two?"

"Umm."

"I have to concur with Nighthawk," Audie said. "Coffee for me as well."

Herb arched one of his bushy eyebrows before nodding and walking away, wearing a puzzled expression.

"Umm," Nighthawk said, casting his eyes slightly to his left toward the lone man at the table in the back.

"I agree with that, too," Audie said in a low tone. "He's trouble. We've seen enough of it in our lifetimes to recognize it easily. I suppose the same is true for you, Smoke."

Even though the older men had decades on Smoke, Audie's assessment was certainly true. At his relatively young age, Smoke had already experienced more than a lifetime of trouble.

Thinking of age, Smoke took a moment to silently marvel at Audie and Nighthawk. Much like Preacher—or, like Preacher *had been*—the two moved far easier than most men of similar years. The way Nighthawk had bounded off his horse and wrestled that outlaw to the hard ground would have been impressive for a man forty years his junior. And Nighthawk hadn't so much as grunted in pain. He didn't move stiffly now, either, as if the stunt hadn't fazed him.

"I can spot trouble, all right," Smoke said. "Spotting something else, too. Does that feller look familiar to you?"

"Umm."

Audie reached high, making a show of stretching, and then popping his neck by turning it side to side. Once he'd accomplished his goal of getting a better look at the man, he said, "My goodness, Nighthawk is right! He resembles one of those brigands we sparred with back on the trail."

Smoke nodded. "Spittin' image of the one Nighthawk got."

"It's not far-fetched to surmise *he* is waiting *here* for them," Audie said with a shake of his head.

"Umm," Nighthawk added.

Audie burst into laughter, evidently a tad louder than he'd anticipated. He put a hand to his chest, calming himself, and then said in a quieter tone, "That's right, my friend. He'll have a long wait indeed!"

The women came back with bowls of stew and a plate of corn bread, while Herb brought the coffee. Once the food and drink were placed in front of the men, Herb said, "You gents let us know if you need anything else. What I said earlier is true—your money is no good here and I can't thank you enough. I'm going to help my boy unload that wagon, but just holler if you need something."

"We're in your debt," Smoke said.

"Don't talk like that," Greta said. "We are in your debt!" She flashed them a lingering smile before scurrying off with her daughter to tend to various chores around the trading post.

Smoke dug into the stew and smiled as the warm, savory flavors filled his mouth. It sure beat the trail food he'd lived on since leaving the Sugarloaf. He also took the opportunity to take another gander around the trading post.

The cabin appeared nice and sturdy. It wouldn't surprise Smoke a bit if Herb had built the thing himself. He looked like the sort of brawny man who was good with his hands.

A few bottles of whiskey and a wooden keg of beer were behind the bar, but there were also items for sale such as jerky, sugar, coffee, and other supplies a traveler might need. Smoke wondered how much business they got around here. Obviously, enough to keep them open. He figured the cowboys engrossed in the poker game probably lived in these parts, working at one of the spreads nearby. Wyoming Territory was prime cattle country. There weren't many towns, though. That might change one day as settlers poured into the area to take advantage of the good grazing lands. Until then, the ranchers had much of the rugged, untamed land to themselves.

The stew hit the spot and the corn bread was perfect. When Mrs. Cummings came by to refill the coffee cups, Smoke commented that she was a fine cook. She smiled at the praise and walked away in even better spirits than before.

All the while, Smoke kept a casual yet watchful eye on the man who sat alone at the table. He'd had more than a few shots of whiskey, but so far wasn't showing any signs of being drunk. He sure looked unhappy, though. His scowl grew as the hour wore on.

Upon his return, Herb shot the lone man a look, too, but didn't say anything. Instead, he stopped at the table where Smoke, Audie, and Nighthawk sat. "Mind if I take a seat?"

"Help yourself," Smoke said, motioning toward the empty chair to his right.

Herb sat and rubbed the back of his neck with a wince. He then rotated his arm in its socket and massaged his shoulder before saying, "I think age is catching up with me. Used to be that I could unload supplies all day and barely notice I was holding anything. Now I get sore as can be if I lift too much."

"Umm."

Herb looked across the table to the big Indian and raised his eyebrow once again.

"Exactly, Nighthawk. I figured you were a bit sore from that rather nasty tumble you took off the horse." Audie looked to Herb. "You should have seen it. Nighthawk decimated one of those bandits by tackling him right off his mount. Quite impressive."

As Audie was taking a sip of coffee, Herb said, "That's actually why I wanted to talk to you all. I can't tell you how much I appreciate what you did. My son and daughter owe you their lives! I'm in debt to you, too."

"Not at all," Smoke said, waving the notion off. "We just happened to come along at the right time." He took a sip of his own coffee before sending a pointed glance in Herb's direction. "Your son mentioned a lot of trouble passing through this way, heading up to Montana. You been having a lot?"

Herb sighed heavily as he nodded. "Sure have. Word's gotten around that some character up in Montana is hiring gunhands. Sounds like he's trying to build an army. More than a few have passed through here. Most have kept to themselves and paid their way, but we had a couple get out of line. Had to run 'em off with my scattergun. You better believe I've been keeping that Greener within close reach since then."

"Can't blame you there," Smoke said.

"Yeah, things have been a mite tense around here. Desolation Creek isn't too far over the border and we're only a few days' ride from there. I'm not sure what's going on up that way, but I'd just as soon it came to an end, that's for sure," Herb said.

"Guess you see a lot of travelers," Smoke said.

"Sure. A fair amount. Other than that, the boys that ride for the local spreads come in once or twice a week for a drink and maybe a friendly game, like those over there." He looked toward the cowboys playing cards. "That's the kind of trade I want. I've had enough of these worthless varmints riding the outlaw trail."

"Say, maybe you saw one of our friends come this way. He's an older fella, but spry for his age." Smoke went on to describe Preacher.

Herb scratched his jaw and then shook his head. "Can't say I've seen him. You meeting up with him?"

"No," Smoke said grimly. He took another sip of coffee to keep from explaining further.

Thankfully, Herb didn't press it. Instead, he turned his focus back to the lone man sitting in the back and said, "Truth is, I don't like the looks of that hombre right there. He's making the missus nervous. Not sure I want him around my daughter, either."

Smoke could understand why. The man just had a hard look about him.

As if on cue, the man stood and staggered toward Smoke's table.

And he looked mighty angry as he arrived.

CHAPTER 8

"Hey, barkeep," the man sneered. He used the back of his hand to wipe his mouth and then said, "What direction did that little girlie of yours come from?"

Herb's jaw clenched. He cleared his throat and slowly rose from his chair while keeping his eyes steadily on the angry man before him. "That *little girlie* is my daughter."

"Good for you, Pops. But I asked what direction she came from."

Smoke's hand was already resting on the butt of his gun. He assumed Audie and Nighthawk were ready for trouble, too.

Still tense, Herb said, "Their comings and goings aren't any business of yours, mister. You best settle your bill and ride on out of here."

"Pa," Amy said from behind the bar, the concern thick in her voice.

"Go on to the back," he said, waving her away with one hand.

The man watched Amy with a leering eye as she did what

her father had told her to do. This made Herb even angrier, as evident by his balled fists.

Smoke couldn't blame the trading post's owner. The stranger had been acting mighty suspicious and now his haughty, angry attitude was even worse. Plus, with all the outlaw trouble in the region, a man would feel he had to protect his family, even if it meant driving off a paying customer.

Evidently, the cowboys had noticed that a confrontation was brewing, because they'd stopped their card game and were watching intently as the scene unfolded. Their hands rested near their sidearms, too, and Smoke figured they'd back Herb's play if it came down to it.

The rude man's lips curled back to reveal jagged, tobacco-stained teeth. Smoke nearly shook his head in disbelief at how ugly the fellow was. A chunk was missing from his right ear. He had a scar over his left eye that cut his brow in half. His hat and clothes were just as tattered as he was. He stank something awful.

Unfortunately for Smoke, the man stepped even closer. Smoke wondered if that was by design—smell so bad that you cause your opponent to wince, then use that brief second as an advantage to draw on them. He almost laughed grimly. This hombre wasn't smart enough to come up with something like that. It was far more likely the man just plain stank to high heaven.

"I'm meetin' up with my brother and some pals. They should have been here by now. That little girlie of yours see anything?"

"She doesn't know a thing about your brother," Herb said. He jerked his head toward the door. "Now pay your bill and hit the trail, mister. We don't want any trouble around here."

Chairs scraped loudly across the wooden floor as the cowboys stood up and stepped closer. The rough man looked over his shoulder to see he was badly outnumbered and then turned his gaze back to Herb. He held his left hand up as if surrendering.

Smoke wasn't fooled by it. He kept his eyes trained on the man's right hand and was ready for it when he went for his gun.

Smoke sprang from his chair while drawing his own Colt. He flipped it around with one fluid motion, now holding it by the barrel, and then brought the butt down on the man's rising wrist.

The hard case howled in pain. His fingers opened and his gun fell to the table with a loud thud, knocking over what remained of Smoke's coffee.

Smoke wasn't finished.

He raised his arm and slashed it across his chest until his gun handle connected with the stranger's face. The man took the blow with another shriek and staggered backward, past where Nighthawk sat and onto the closest empty table behind him. His knees gave way and he crumpled to the ground, but he wasn't out. He was conscious for the further humiliation of Nighthawk hoisting him up by his collar and then shifting, until one hand held the back of his shirt and the other held the waistband of his britches.

Nighthawk charged for the door, while the man protested and cursed, kicking his legs and trying to hit the big Crow warrior. His arms only found air as he was helplessly carried through the room. He resembled a sniffling child, throwing a temper tantrum on his way to the woodshed.

The cowboys were laughing. Smoke had a hard time not joining them, but he knew it would only make the situation worse. He might as well have, though, he decided, because the foul stranger would not let the indignation go. He'd suffered too much embarrassment and his pride would overrule what little common sense he might have.

Nighthawk used the stranger's head like a battering ram to open the front door and then gave the fella a good toss. Without a word, Nighthawk shut the door and returned to his chair, sat down, and finished the hunk of corn bread he'd been working on, as if nothing had happened.

Herb's jaw hung loose for a moment as he stared at Nighthawk. Finally he shook his head and said, "Well, I'll be. How about that?"

The cowboys voiced their various exclamations of agreement before taking their seats once more.

"Mister, you are welcome here anytime. Any time at all. You remember you have friends right here. All of you," Herb said.

"Umm."

"I second that, Nighthawk," Audie said. "We are obliged to you for the hospitality, sir."

Smoke was half-listening to the conversation and keeping one eye on the door as he picked up the man's discarded gun and tossed it to Herb.

"Wonder if he'll come back for it?" Herb said. "I'll tuck it behind the bar just in case."

Smoke figured they wouldn't have to wait long for the man's return. In fact, he assumed the fella was somewhere still close by, stewing about what to do. If he had any sense at all, he'd be saddling his horse and lighting a shuck out of there. Smoke suspected that was just wishful thinking, though. That hombre wasn't the logical type.

That hunch proved correct mere seconds later.

The front door swung open to reveal the disgraced man standing in the threshold, a shotgun in his hands and at the ready.

Herb was behind the bar and, thankfully, Amy and Greta were in the back room, busy tending to various jobs. That left Smoke with a wide-open shot. He stood, his Colt seemingly materializing in his hand as if by magic, sending his chair crashing to the floor behind him.

His gun roared. The man in the doorway stumbled a bit, but stayed on his feet. He only received a second slug punching into his chest for the effort. He triggered both barrels of the Greener while falling backward, but the loads sprayed harmlessly into the ceiling, sending pellets and wood chips down in a shower on his twitching, jerking body.

He was dead when Smoke, Audie, and Nighthawk reached him.

The smell of acrid gunsmoke hung heavy in the air. Smoke's ears were ringing and he knew everyone else's were, too.

"Is everybody all right?" Herb asked, running from around the bar to survey the scene.

"Umm," Nighthawk said.

Audie laughed. "Yes, everyone but that poor fellow. Oh, friend, sometimes your sense of humor is too much." He then looked grimly to the sprawled-out body of the downed ruffian and added, "Of course, no disrespect to the recently deceased."

Smoke barely heard what was said behind him. He inspected the body of the man he'd just killed and clicked his tongue in frustration. That was the second time that day he'd been forced into gunplay.

He knew it was only a harbinger of things to come.

There would be a lot more powder burned and lead flying up in Desolation Creek.

He just prayed they would come out on the right side of it all.

CHAPTER 9

Venom McFadden looked at himself in the full-length mirror and smiled.

"Not bad," he said aloud. "Not bad at all."

He leaned in, inspected his black string tie, then straightened it.

His white shirt was crisp. His vest was perfectly fitted. He cut a dashing figure, if he did say so himself. He tore his eyes from his reflection long enough to grab the black coat that hung from the tall, freestanding rack and shouldered into it. He then looked at himself once more. Tugging on the bottom hem of the coat, he smiled as he realized he'd achieved perfection.

"Even better," he said.

He grabbed his matching hat, but stopped before squaring it atop his head. He thought it over, then tossed it onto the large four-poster bed behind him. His hair just looked too good to wear a hat today. Perfectly in place. Not a single strand sticking up.

He continued smiling as he walked down the long hall and toward the staircase. Desolation Creek had been good to him. It had been almost too easy, he marveled. He'd suspected all along that the town would fold and give him his way. He'd selected it, after all. It was isolated. There wasn't much law, to speak of, save for Marshal Ted Parker, and he was too drunk to care about much one way or another.

Yes, McFadden had known the town would be easy pickin's. He just hadn't known how easy.

He was still smiling to himself when he sauntered down the stairs and strolled to his left into the large, high-ceilinged room that made up the ground floor of the Dead Moose Saloon. A long bar, with plenty of polished brass and a slick top, was against the far wall from the staircase. At least two dozen tables and chairs were placed around the spacious floor. A roulette table and a faro layout were in the very back of the room. No gambling took place this early in the day, however. In fact, no patrons were there at that hour.

The bar was far from empty, though.

Two tables were occupied, eight gunmen spread out, eagerly awaiting their orders for the day.

McFadden strolled past, flashing them his wolfish smile and heading straight for the bar.

"Good morning, Mr. McFadden," Sam Hawkins, the barkeep, said. He dutifully put a cup atop the bar and then held up the coffeepot he'd retrieved from the bulging-bellied stove. He filled the cup and stepped back a few paces.

"Good morning, Sam. Thank you." McFadden raised the cup in a toast, took a sip, then nodded. "It's good, Sam."

Sam looked pleased and then shuffled off to return the pot to the stove. He was wide and short, with pasty skin and a balding head that seemed to perpetually sweat. He'd come with the bar, McFadden having taken over the property through *interesting* means after coming to town. He'd kept Sam around because he was a darn good bartender and made one great cup of coffee. Plus, he was too much of a coward to ever challenge McFadden.

Sam Hawkins was a follower—just like everyone else in Desolation Creek.

Well, almost everyone.

There was that little matter of the newspaperman Darnell Poe.

The morning sun shone brightly through the large, square windows set on either side of the batwing doors. A few rays even poked over those doors and tumbled in beneath them as McFadden turned and leaned his back against the bar.

He took another drink of the steaming hot coffee and then looked over his men, who waited patiently. "I'm going to take a trip over to the newspaper office," Venom said.

"Poe, huh?" Hal Taggart said.

Taggart was McFadden's right-hand man and gave the orders when Venom's attention was pulled elsewhere.

"That's right. Seems as if he's been talking. Now he claims this town would be better off without me."

The men laughed.

"Can you imagine that?" McFadden continued. He swept his hand across the room and said, "I've brought prosperity to this once–dried-up town. But some people just don't see it that way."

"And it's our job to make them get it, right?" Taggart asked.

"Exactly."

"No reason for you to trouble yourself with this, boss. Me and the boys can handle it. Trust me." The words came from Chuck Hicks.

McFadden looked at Hicks. He liked the young man well enough. Hicks was an outright mean, nasty fella. He had cold, angry eyes, always resembling a coiled rattlesnake just waiting to strike. He simply lacked the brains to work for himself. He'd always be a hired hand, for however long he had left in his life. Eventually he'd go up against a man who was faster. Hopefully, McFadden thought, by then he'd have gotten all he needed out of young Hicks. If not . . . hired guns were a dime a dozen.

"I said I'm going to the newspaper office," McFadden said coolly before taking another sip of coffee.

Taggart gave Hicks a stern stare. The younger man swallowed hard. Recognition flashed in his eyes and McFadden doubted he'd ever question him again.

"I'm sorry, boss," he grumbled.

"It's all right," McFadden said, holding up a hand. "You're eager to spare me any unpleasantness and I appreciate that. But I need to make an appearance and talk to Poe, man-to-man. You know, it could be beneficial to have a newspaperman on our side. There's a lot of power behind the press. I get him on my side, and then, well . . ." He trailed off with a shrug.

"Might not be a bad idea for some of us to pay a visit to the marshal, too," Taggart chimed in.

McFadden looked at him. "Oh?"

Taggart was a strong, powerfully built man who was in his forties, but looked a tad older, thanks to his graying hair. He'd started as a cowboy and had worked his way up to ranch foreman before realizing he could make more money outside of the law. He'd left honest employment behind. He didn't have much choice, seeing as how he'd siphoned off a few cows here and there during his droving days. After he got caught, it was either stay and face the consequences, or flee and find work elsewhere.

He'd fled.

He brought with him a strong work ethic and good organizational skills. The other men respected him and he was a skilled second-in-command for McFadden.

"He dropped by here earlier," Taggart said. "Wanted to talk with us about some complaints he's gotten from a few citizens and . . . whatever." He waved it off and shook his head as if it were the most ridiculous thing he'd ever heard.

"Complaints? Well, then, I guess we'll stroll over to see good Marshal Parker right after we talk to our newspaperman," McFadden said. He pointed to Chuck and two others. "You two, come with me. The rest of you, make the rounds and visit all the businesses in town. It's my favorite day." McFadden smiled. "It's collection day."

The paper's office was a new building that still smelled faintly of cut lumber, though the ink of the printing press, which rested in the back room, was starting to become the dominant scent.

Darnell Poe was in his thirties, nice-looking, and didn't much look like a newspaperman to McFadden. Weren't they supposed to be old and stodgy? Veteran journalists with world-weary eyes? Poe had too much spring in his step. McFadden supposed newspapermen had to start somewhere. Give him a few years and those handsome looks would fade and the cynicism would set in.

It was more than his good looks, though, that McFadden found vaguely unsettling.

Poe was cautious around McFadden, but he wasn't afraid. Venom knew, because he could sense fear in the people around town. That terror drove him. It fed him, in a way. In Poe's presence, though, he starved.

That made McFadden as angry as it did curious.

Perhaps it would require a demonstration to get Poe in line. Of course, McFadden could always have Hicks or one of the others simply shoot Poe and that would be the end of it. But a newspaperman as an ally was too good a prospect to pass up.

He'd thought about simply killing Poe and running the newspaper himself, or having one of his underlings do it, but neither he nor they knew the first thing about writing, let alone actually *printing* a paper. He could bring in someone with experience from Denver or Salt Lake City, but that would take too long. It was best to let Poe stick around.

For now.

He'd have to earn his right to keep breathing, though. He needed to prove himself useful.

"And to what do I owe the pleasure of your visit this morning?" Poe said, looking irritated as he glanced up from his desk when McFadden and his men entered the office, jingling the bell above the door.

That right there was enough to make McFadden seethe with rage. Everyone else in town would have shrunk a bit or at least gulped.

Not Darnell Poe.

He was too calm. Collected. Defiant almost.

McFadden hated defiance.

Poe slid off the stool he'd been sitting on and stepped around from the tall desk. McFadden's eyes quickly scanned him. He knew Hicks was doing the same. Poe didn't appear to be armed. If he did have a gun on him, he couldn't reach it quickly.

Poe stopped, only a few feet from McFadden.

"No reason to be unfriendly," McFadden said. "This is a social visit."

"A social visit?"

"Yes," McFadden said with a nod. "I'm here to extend an invitation. I haven't seen you in the Dead Moose and I want you to know you're welcome. First drink is on the house, in fact. You'll have a line of credit, of course."

"Free drink and credit?" Poe said, a hint of sarcasm in his words and the smile that accompanied them. "Why so generous, McFadden?"

Venom spread his hands. "Why not? I offer this to all my fellow businessmen in town."

"I'm not a businessman," Poe said. "I'm a journalist."

McFadden laughed. "You're telling me you don't want to turn a profit?"

"I pursue the truth, not wealth."

McFadden studied Poe, taking a long, hard look into the man's eyes. He found only sincerity, causing McFadden to shake his head. "You can't spend truth."

"There's more important things in life than money."

This drew a genuine laugh from McFadden. "A righteous crusader." He let the statement fester for a moment before adding, "Is that why you're trying to stir up the town's people against me?"

"I don't have to stir up anyone," Poe said. "They're already riled. What did you think would happen? You extort money from them. You're slowly taking over every business in Desolation Creek. You're heavy-handed—"

He stepped closer, about to say more, when Hicks lurched toward him with his right hand falling to the butt of his gun.

McFadden held up his hand. Hicks was breathing heavily as he thought it over, but eventually nodded and moved back a tad. He still stayed at the ready, just in case his boss required him to shoot the arrogant newspaperman.

"I'm trying to build this town into something. I'm bringing prosperity to Desolation Creek," McFadden said. His voice was still measured, but it had risen slightly. He hoped the red-hot anger he felt simmering inside wasn't visible on his cheeks. There might be a time to fly off the handle and give in to the rage. Now wasn't it. There was still a chance Poe would see the benefits of throwing in with him, or at least supporting him subtly from afar.

It didn't seem like that would happen anytime soon, though.

"Prosperity?" Poe said. He laughed and then added, "Look around, McFadden. The only one getting rich is you." His eyes shifted to Hicks as he said, "Sure, the outlaw trash you hire as gun-wolves make a little money, but the rest of this town is drying up and about to wither away." He was looking back to McFadden now, without a hint of hesitancy

or trepidation. "You're not just holding this town back. You're killing it."

McFadden couldn't keep his anger in check now. His neck muscles bulged as his nostrils flared. He raised a finger to Poe and closed the gap between them, standing so close that his hot, coffee-laden breath gusted into the journalist's face as he said, "I've been patient with you, Poe. I know what you're doing, trying to stir up folks around here, but it won't work. Look around you. You're alone. It's just you in this little office, churning out that rag you call a newspaper. It's by my good graces that you've been allowed to operate this long, but my patience is wearing thin. Your paper—and you—can be ended."

He lowered his finger and relaxed his posture. He took a deep breath. Poe had never so much as flinched, to his credit.

McFadden sure didn't like that.

He turned and strolled casually toward the door, stopping to look over his shoulder.

"Or," he said with a smile and more pleasant tone, "you can join me. Maybe even write a nice, friendly story to help folks see the benefits of having me around." He turned to face Poe, once again, from across the small office. "I'm expanding. Be hiring a lot of folks. Creating jobs. Everyone will win. You think it over, Poe.

"Before it's too late."

CHAPTER 10

The Absaroka Mountains rose majestically around Smoke, Audie, and Nighthawk. The men were settled into their camp for the night. They'd stopped to build a fire a few miles back, bacon and biscuits having served as their supper, before moving on to bed down in another spot. Now a deep darkness overtook the valley and Smoke felt the mountains more than he saw them. The country was wild and untamed, and even though he missed the Sugarloaf, something about this vast, untamed land still called to him.

That love of the wild places was one of the things he had gotten from Preacher, all those years ago when Smoke—then called by his given name, Kirby—and his father, Emmett, had ventured west on a vengeance trail and run smack-dab into a crotchety old-timer in greasy buckskins. It had been Preacher who had dubbed Smoke by that name, because of his speed with a gun. Over the years, Preacher had given him much more than that nickname.

"I sense you aren't asleep, Smoke," Audie said quietly from his bedroll.

"I'm not."

Audie sighed. He allowed a heavy silence to stretch the moment out before saying, "We all miss him. Even when we weren't with him—which was often in our travels—you still knew he was out there. A force for good in this universe. His death has left a void. He will never be replaced."

"Umm," Nighthawk added from his buffalo robe.

Smoke only nodded, though the other men couldn't see the gesture.

Somewhere in the distance, a wolf howled. Straight above, in the dark blue canopy stretched tightly overhead, stars shone and winked. Smoke wondered if Sally was already asleep or maybe reading in bed by lamplight. She might be on the porch, gazing on the same stars he was.

Smoke almost chuckled to himself. More than likely, Sally was spittin' mad and wishing she could ride into Desolation Creek herself to dole out a little justice on Preacher's behalf.

Audie's calm voice once again cut through the quietness of the night.

"'Thou know'st 'tis common; all that lives must die, passing through nature to eternity.'"

"Umm."

"You're correct, my friend. That is from *Hamlet*. Fitting in such a time as this. Preacher has simply gone the way so many before him have. The way we all must go. It does not make his passing any easier, though."

"He was one of a kind, that's for sure," Smoke said. "And I reckon I know what you mean, about that void in the universe now that he's gone."

"Grief is a powerful force," Audie said. "It reminds me of another quote. 'To weep is to make less the depth of grief.'"

"Umm."

"I do say, old friend, you're on a roll tonight. That is indeed from the Bard of Avon himself."

Smoke rose slightly and propped himself up on his elbows, casting a glance at his friends. The starlight was just bright enough that he could make out their forms, but not many details. He knew they couldn't see him, either, but they wouldn't need to, to know how gravely serious he was when he said, "I'm not in a weeping mood. There might be a time for that. But right now, crying isn't what will ease my grief. We owe Venom McFadden and all those riding with him, and I'm ready to settle the accounts."

"Umm."

"Me as well," Audie said. "But just how are we going to do that? We haven't discussed strategy."

"I know," Smoke said. "Been giving it a lot of thought, though, and I think it came to me back at the trading post."

The Cummings family had been gracious hosts, extending an invitation for Smoke and the men to stay as long as they'd like. They'd spent one evening there, but hit the trail early the next morning. Smoke was just glad they'd come along when they had, or that whole family might have been wiped out by owlhoots.

That detour had slowed them down, but it was worth it, as it had saved good folks from bad men. It had also given Smoke a notion on just how he wanted to handle things in Desolation Creek.

"They mentioned hard cases have been riding through on their way up to Montana," Smoke said.

"Indeed," Audie said. "Seems as if McFadden is collecting undesirables in Desolation Creek and building an army!"

Smoke nodded. "The way Herb made it sound, half the gunslicks in this neck of the woods are looking to cash in on what McFadden is doing."

"That means the odds against us increase with each passing day," Audie said.

"Umm," Nighthawk added.

"Oh, I know you aren't afraid, old friend. Neither am I. And Smoke isn't, either. But it doesn't make our job any easier."

"Umm."

Audie laughed as if he'd just been told the funniest joke he'd heard in a long while. "You're absolutely correct! Since when has that stopped us before?"

"Sounds like McFadden has an army, all right, but let's use that to our advantage." Smoke sat up all the way and leaned a bit closer to the other men. Audie and Nighthawk caught the movement and matched it, eager to hear the plan.

"If we ride into town like we're hunting trouble, it won't take long before McFadden shoots us in the back or sics his whole army on us. We're good, but no one can handle odds like that. I figure that's how they did Preacher in. There was no way he was bested in a fair fight."

"Umm."

"Nighthawk is right," Audie said. "A fair fight for Preacher would have been a dozen or more men against him. They had to come in an even greater force. Or ambushed him, though I suspect that old mountain man would have been difficult to ambush."

Smoke nodded again. "We obviously don't want that happening to us. Let's ride in separately. Maybe even find work. Take a few days to learn the lay of the land. Might be that we can pick 'em off, one by one or a few at a time. Evens the odds a little. McFadden has a weakness. Everybody does. This will give us time to see what it is. We can figure out how to strike from there."

"Umm."

"I agree," Audie said. "This is the wisest course of action." He looked to his old friend and said, "Though we are more than capable, I'm afraid our advanced age makes us appear past our prime."

"Umm."

Audie chuckled. "Speak for myself, eh? Ha! I just mean to imply we probably can't find work as gunhands in this Venom character's army. But certainly there are other jobs around Desolation Creek to be had. Smoke, I assume you're going to go right into the belly of the beast."

"Sort of the way I had it figured," Smoke admitted.

He was faster on the draw than most men and had an almost supernatural aim. If he really wanted work as a gunman, he would have no trouble finding it. McFadden would have a lot of use for a man of Smoke's skills.

"Umm."

"This plan has my vote of confidence as well," Audie said.

"Sounds good. Guess we'll ride in separately. I'll give it a couple of days and come in last," Smoke said. "I want Venom full of holes, as much as you two, but there's no use in rushing it. Our best bet is to play it smart and see the hand we're dealt."

"Very wise. As the French author Eugène Sue wrote, 'Revenge is very good eaten cold,'" Audie said in agreement.

Smoke stretched out once again and took one last gander at the stars before closing his eyes.

It was as good a plan as they were going to come up with and it gave them time to learn just how strong a hold McFadden had on Desolation Creek.

Now the only other part of the plan Smoke had to figure out was how to keep innocent citizens safe while he was pretending to be an outlaw. It would take some quick thinking and creativity on his part, but it wouldn't be the first time he'd had to rely on his brains as much as his guns.

He could do it.

Or, rather, Buck West could.

CHAPTER 11

Smoke was thankful when the time to ride into Desolation Creek finally came.

Solitude did not particularly bother him, and he was a man accustomed to loneliness as he'd experienced it at various times in his life. He'd drifted through plenty of valleys and had ridden the high country with nothing but his thoughts. There were times he'd enjoyed the peace and quiet.

Right now, though, he was itching to handle the business that brought him into Montana Territory. He wanted to deliver justice for Preacher. Every day Venom McFadden spent walking the earth was one day too many. The time to settle the score was now.

Ordinarily, Smoke could have used the extra couple of days to plan just how he was going to go about this vengeance mission. The problem was, he couldn't rightly know without having the lay of the land. So, he'd simply waited patiently, planning what little he could.

Now, as he aimed Drifter down the center of Main Street, he breathed a sigh of relief that the waiting had come to an end. True, he wasn't ready to pull iron and start delivering hot-lead justice to the hombres who had it coming, but at least he was starting the process. He'd learn about McFadden soon enough.

And when he did—once the time finally came—heaven help the outlaw.

On first glance, Desolation Creek seemed like many other frontier settlements Smoke had been in. False-fronted buildings lined the street, some with overhangs that covered the boardwalk. An apothecary, a store advertising the latest in women's fashion, and a dry goods shop were located nearby. A three-story hotel, the Absaroka Saloon, the post office, and a marshal's office were across the street.

Other businesses were farther along, but Smoke decided to rein up at the Absaroka, like most newcomers would. It would be a good place to gain some information, more than likely.

Once Drifter was secured to the hitching rail, Smoke ambled up the steps, scooted his boots across the boardwalk, and pushed through the batwing doors.

The Absaroka wasn't much of a saloon.

Straight ahead, against the back wall, was a bar made of planks that rested across three spaced-out barrels. A few tables and mismatched chairs, scattered around the knotty wood floor, stood between Smoke and the bar. The place smelled musty, with the scents of stale beer, cheap tobacco, and body odor mixed in for good measure.

Smoke swiveled his head from left to right and saw that only one other patron was there, which wasn't too odd, since it was before noon. An old, skinny man who looked like a prospector sat at one of the tables; though at the man's obviously advanced age and frail condition, Smoke wasn't sure how much prospecting he actually did these days.

Other than that, just a tall, lanky man stood behind the bar. He looked shocked to see Smoke.

"Howdy," Smoke said as he edged closer. He leaned on the bar and gave a friendly nod.

"You, eh . . . need something, mister?"

Odd way to greet a customer, Smoke thought, but he didn't react. Instead, he asked, "How's the beer?"

"Warm," came the answer from the old miner sitting at his table.

Smoke smiled and then said to the bartender, "Reckon I'll have a warm beer."

The barkeep studied him for a moment before nodding. He grabbed a mug from the shelf behind him, held it to the barrel, and filled it. Placing it before Smoke, he asked, "You new in town?"

Smoke fished out a coin, dropped it on the counter, and raised the glass. "Just got in."

"So, that's why you're here," the bartender said with a snort.

He palmed the coin and turned away, taking the stained once-white towel from his shoulder and using it on a few freshly washed glasses that were waiting for him on the shelf. Smoke was about to ask just what the gent meant by that comment when the prospector stood and shuffled over to the bar. Sidling up next to Smoke, he said, "Don't mind ol' Earl. He's just upset because the Dead Moose done stole all his business."

The bartender didn't even turn around, just threw his arm back and gave a dismissive wave accompanied by another grunt.

"Dead Moose?" Smoke repeated. "That another saloon here in town?"

He put the mug to his lips and pulled in a sip of beer. He fought the urge to spit the flat, hot, bitter liquid out. His brain fired to life, shouting commands for his throat to swallow the beer. He'd done some hard things in his life. He'd had his back to the wall more times than he could count, with insurmountable odds stacked against him. Through sheer toughness, skill, a little bit of luck, and a fierce fighting spirit, he'd always prevailed.

Until now.

This might be the one obstacle I can't overcome, Smoke thought.

He steeled himself, tried to swallow, but couldn't.

For the love of all that's sacred, I've got to get this beer down!

He tried again, this time finding success. He made a mental note not to drink any more of the straw-colored liquid.

Come to think of it, Smoke thought, taking a quick glance in the mug after he set it down, there might have been chunks of straw floating in that.

Evidently, he hadn't hidden his opinion of the beer good enough, because the frail old prospector cackled and said, "Told you it was warm. But that ain't the worst of it! I suspect it's really horse piss."

The barkeep shook his head angrily as he walked away and around from the bar to wipe down a table that didn't seem dirty. He grunted loudly the whole time.

"You see, he cain't get no good beer," the miner said. "Not since McFadden got a hold on the distributors and all."

"Shut up, Hodges," the bartender said, his deep, anger-filled voice filling the small space.

Hodges waved the command off and lowered his voice as he leaned in closer to Smoke. Talking from the side of his mouth, he said, "McFadden owns the other saloon here in town. That dang Dead Moose. Few months back, we had three watering holes to choose from. Well, McFadden done ran the Gold Strike out o' business and is working on this fine establishment here!" He slapped the bar, causing the planks to bounce. A bit of beer sloshed over the mug's rim and splashed on the bar's top. It would not be missed.

"Just go on down to the Dead Moose," the barkeep said loudly. "They have a better selection. It's not like I'll be open tomorrow, anyway. Man's got to have enough sense to know when it's time to quit."

He walked to the back corner where a doorway was and stepped through the threshold, disappearing into the back room.

"I don't blame him for being all fired up and angry," Hodges said. "I'd be, too, if I was being run out of business. Heck, I'm mad that my favorite waterin' hole is closing! I just don't see how he can stay afloat much longer."

Smoke nodded and turned slightly, propping his elbow on the bar and looking at his talkative companion.

Hodges was a short man, probably about sixty, but maybe north of there, with good-humored ice-blue eyes. He had a white mustache that matched the stubble on his cheeks. He wore clothes that probably had been tattered from hard work and had scarred, calloused hands.

"This McFadden just in the saloon business or is he running other things here in town?" Smoke pressed.

He hoped he wasn't asking too much, too soon, but Hodges seemed eager to talk and Smoke needed information. Besides, if Hodges had been one of McFadden's allies, he'd be over in the Dead Moose. Smoke figured the old miner was stubborn, with an ornery streak in him a mile wide. Already Smoke knew he wasn't the sort to give in to bullies.

The smile faded from Hodges's face and he arched one of his bushy eyebrows. "Say, you ain't here to ride for him, are you?"

"Just passin' through," Smoke said. "Might stay, might not."

Well, it wasn't exactly a lie. If fate smiled on him and he could take McFadden out quickly, there was no way Smoke would stay in Desolation Creek. He doubted that would be the case, but he didn't need to lay his cares out for Hodges. So, he left the explanation at that and waited.

Hodges sized him up for another moment and then nodded. "Guess there ain't no harm in talkin'. You'll find out what's what, soon enough, if you stick around this town, that's for sure.

"To answer your question, young fella, McFadden wants this whole dang town and he darn near has it. Why, he took over the general store a week or so back after the owner—poor Alonzo—met an untimely demise. He'd already taken over a few other businesses. About the only one he doesn't have a hand in is probably the newspaper and that's just 'cause it ain't selling enough copies to be profitable."

Smoke nodded, remaining casual in his stance. He thought of lifting the beer to his lips once more, but then decided not to bother. Hodges didn't seem to miss much, so Smoke had no reason to even go through the motions.

Smoke still wasn't ready to reveal his true intentions regarding his reason for visiting Desolation Creek, so he asked, "And what did you say this fella's name is?"

"McFadden. Venom McFadden."

The barkeep popped his head around the corner, keeping his body shielded behind the wall of the back room. "Don't you talk too loud, you old goat! They're liable to tie ropes around this place and yank it down with us in it!"

"Oh, I ain't skeered of them," Hodges said, waving the bartender off.

Earl grunted yet again before disappearing once more.

Smoke waited a second and then said, "Is there any law in this town? Seems like the sort of thing a marshal or a sheriff would be interested in."

This elicited another cackle from the old man. "*Law?* Well, we have Marshal Parker, but he ain't gonna do a dad-blasted thing! He's every bit as old as me and twice as drunk." He swiped his hand through the air as if batting down the suggestion. "No, sir, Marshal Parker ain't gonna do nothing but sit in that office, collect his salary, and keep his head down. Guess you have to give him credit for bein' smart at least."

"What about a county sheriff?" Smoke asked.

"This is a big county, boy, and he ain't got the deputies or resources to make it out here very much. Probably just be shot down if he did come, anyway."

A moment of heavy silence passed before Hodges said, "Yes, sir, we're all on our own. Ain't nobody comin' to help. I'd drink to that, if I had a drink." He eyed Smoke expectantly.

Smoke smiled and slid his beer across the bar's top toward the miner.

"You mean it?" Hodges asked with a grin.

"Oh, it's the least I can do," Smoke said.

Hodges smiled as he reached for the mug. "Figure we're all dyin' of something. Might as well keep drinkin' this poison." He took a sip and grinned even wider. "Thanks. Say, you're okay, mister. What did you say your name was?"

Smoke hadn't said, and Hodges knew it, but Smoke went ahead and played along. "West."

"West?"

"Buck West."

The old-timer thought for a moment, scratching his chin and pinching his lips, but then shrugged, as if the name didn't mean anything to him.

"Well, I best be getting on. I might stay a night or two. Be nice to sleep in a bed," Smoke said. "Where's the livery stable?"

"Keep going down Main Street," Hodges said. "You'll pass the Dead Moose on the corner. Can't miss it. It's big and fancy. Just beyond that, across the street and on the edge of town, is the stable."

"Much obliged," Smoke said over his shoulder as he walked toward the batwings.

"I got a feelin' about you," Hodges called out.

Smoke stopped walking. His spurs jingled as he turned around to face the crusty old miner once more.

"You ain't just passin' through," Hodges said. "I'm not sure what you're doin', but you sure ain't just passin' through. Whatever you aim to do, I reckon I'll sit back and enjoy the show."

He raised the beer in a toast.

"I got a feelin' it's gonna be quite a show, too. Better than them acting troupes that used to come through town."

He took another sip.

"Yes, sir, one heck of a show."

CHAPTER 12

Hodges had been right—there was no way to miss the Dead Moose.

The structure was massive, sitting on its corner lot, towering above the other buildings and looking impressive with the fresh coat of blue paint and ornate bright white trim work around the windows and along the roofline.

A few men loafed on the porch, one sitting in a chair that was tipped back, his booted feet propped on the railing that ran on both sides of the building's angled porch. One had his hip on the railing, while another just stood casually by, with his thumbs hooked in his belt.

They gave Smoke cold, hard stares as Drifter slowly walked by. Smoke didn't turn his gaze away, as if scared, but he didn't look too menacing, either. No reason to stir up trouble just yet. The time would come for that. If these men worked for McFadden—and he suspected they did—they'd get what was coming to them soon enough.

The blacksmith shop and the stable were located across the street from the Dead Moose, and a little farther on. Smoke dismounted in front of the big livery barn and stretched, taking his time and moving casually. He could feel the stares from across the road. He guessed a couple of the men had even moved, trying to get a better view of him as he looped Drifter's reins around the provided hitch rail.

He sauntered inside the stable with a smile.

Gunhands were a predictable lot. They were already sizing him up, trying to figure out what to make of his presence and determine whether or not he posed a threat.

They'd have their answers before long.

Inside, the familiar scent of hay, manure, and leather greeted him, along with an equally familiar voice, as a short, broad-shouldered figure stepped out of one of the stalls and strolled toward him along the stable's center aisle.

"Good morning, sir, are you inquiring about a place for your mount while in Desolation Creek?"

Audie had traded his well-worn buckskins for a homespun work shirt and a pair of canvas trousers held up by suspenders. He had high-topped work boots on his feet, instead of moccasins. The pitchfork he held in his hand, resting the end of its handle on the hard-packed dirt by his feet, was taller than he was.

Smoke nodded and said, "That's right, mister," not calling Audie by name in case others were around.

Audie smiled. Keeping his voice low, he said, "Good to see you, Smoke. I had a feeling you'd make your presence known today."

"We're alone?" Smoke said quietly.

"We are, although I cannot guarantee McFadden's men aren't outside, listening in. You no doubt saw them as you rode by the saloon."

"I did," Smoke confirmed, keeping his voice low and stepping deeper into the dim, high-ceilinged barn so that no one outside could hear the conversation. "I see you found a job easily enough."

"The livery owner was delighted when I applied. Apparently, quite a few folks got out of town while they still could, once they realized that McFadden was bent on taking over. It's left him and other business proprietors shorthanded when it comes to workers."

"Things are that bad?" Smoke asked.

"Worse," Audie said. "The dreaded Venom McFadden has this town in the palm of his hand. He's squeezing everyone. The citizens are outright terrified."

"That's the impression I've gotten, too," Smoke said. "Hold on."

He stepped outside and made a show of stretching and yawning. Sure enough, two of McFadden's men had moved positions and were keeping a watchful eye on him, a fact neither tried to hide. No one had crossed the street, though, so he and Audie still had some privacy at least.

Smoke paid the gunmen no attention as he collected Drifter's reins and led him inside the barn doors, which Audie had opened wide. Once inside, they led Drifter to a stall and continued the conversation.

"They haven't shown much of an interest in me," Audie said. "I suppose I don't look all that threatening to men of their ilk."

Smoke had to smile at that. The man's diminutive appearance did work to his benefit. Enemies only underestimated Audie to their detriment.

"What about Nighthawk?"

"Oh, he's in the thick of it," Audie said. "Would you believe my old chum is working at the Dead Moose? Why, they have him perched there nightly, watching over the proceedings with a scattergun."

Smoke chuckled at that. The presence of Nighthawk would certainly deter trouble. Only the bravest—or dumbest— of cowpokes would stir anything up with the giant Crow close by.

"Have you talked with him much?" Smoke said.

"No," Audie said with a shake of his head. "We were waiting on you to arrive and get a look around before comparing notes."

"Have you seen any sign of Preacher's horse or Dog?" Smoke asked.

"Neither is here at the livery," Audie said.

Smoke tugged at his earlobe and then scraped his thumbnail along the line of his jaw as he thought. Preacher hardly ever went anywhere without the rangy gray stallion called Horse and the big, wolflike cur known only as Dog. If he had been just drifting when he rode into Desolation Creek, his old trail partners would have been accompanying him. They ought to still be around here somewhere. He would keep his eyes open for them. Preacher would want them cared for.

"I'm going to get settled in at the hotel and then stop in for a drink at the Dead Moose."

Audie set a bucket of feed and a bucket of fresh water in the stall with Drifter.

"Where are you staying?" Smoke asked.

"Right here," Audie said. "Home, sweet home. There's a room in the back that comes with the job."

Smoke had figured as much. He also suspected Nighthawk had a room at the saloon, though it was possible they were making the Indian sleep off-premises somewhere. Probably a shack out back.

"Why don't we meet here tomorrow night? There's plenty of reasons why we might be visiting the livery stable, so no one will think suspiciously of it if they see me coming around."

Audie agreed.

Hopefully by then, they'd have a plan and could start settling old accounts.

Preacher's accounts.

* * *

"Will you be staying with us long, sir?"

The man behind the hotel counter looked nervous, and with good reason, Smoke thought. With all the gunhands riding into town to work for McFadden, decent folks were on edge.

"I'm not sure," Smoke said.

He finished signing his name—or rather, Buck West's name—in the ledger and then slid the leather-bound book back across the desk. The man read the name and said, "Welcome to Desolation Creek, Mr. West."

"Thank you."

"Are you . . . here on business or just passing through?"

"Not sure yet on that, either."

Smoke left the statement purposely vague. If he was going to hire on as one of McFadden's men, too much friendliness might raise suspicion.

"I see," the man said.

He was of medium build, with dark hair that had been combed over and plastered to his head with grease, causing it to lie flat. He seemed to possess naturally nervous eyes, as if he saw the entire world as suspect. That natural inclination was no doubt heightened because of the current events.

"I can put you in room six, sir," he said. "It's on the second floor."

To Smoke's right was a staircase, lined on one side by a wooden banister and a red-and-white–floral wallpaper that ran on the other side. From what Smoke could tell looking at the building from the outside, there were only two floors, and there didn't seem to be any rooms on the first one. Smoke didn't point that out, though, and simply accepted the offered key.

"Much obliged."

"We have a small dining room through there," the man said, pointing to the doorway cut out in the wall just before the staircase. "Dinner is served until eight."

"I'll keep that in mind," Smoke said, picking up his saddlebag and slinging it over his shoulder. Next he took the rifle he'd rested against the counter. The sight of the gun caused the attendant to gulp before he returned his eyes to Smoke once more.

"Enjoy your stay."

Smoke nodded, turned to walk away, but stopped. "You know where a fella might get work around here? Thinking about hiring on with someone for a spell."

He didn't want to make the man even more nervous, but he also needed all the information he could glean. *Don't worry,* he thought, *you won't have to be scared much longer. McFadden won't be alive to terrorize you or anyone else.* Of course, Smoke couldn't say that aloud, even though he wanted to.

"I'm afraid most businesses around here are barely hanging on as it is," he said. "All except . . . the Dead Moose." He stated the name as if it left a sour taste in his mouth, but quickly straightened up and cleared his throat. He probably didn't want to anger Smoke, in case he became one of McFadden's hired hands.

"Appreciate it," Smoke said.

He went to his room, dropped off his gear, and took a quick look around. It wasn't anything fancy—just a small, square room, with a squeaky bed, a nightstand with a kerosene lamp, and a table beneath the window that held a washbasin. He made use of that water, cleaning the trail dust and grime from his face, as he peered through the sheer curtains that covered the window.

There were a few people milling around on the street below, but no one would mistake Desolation Creek for a bustling city. Smoke wondered how many people had made a beeline out of the settlement. He couldn't blame those who had. There was bravery and then there was foolishness. Going up against a ruthless outlaw with an army full of gunwolves was downright foolish for most people.

Of course, that was exactly what Smoke was going to do,

but not before he got the feel of the situation and evened the odds a little.

"Might as well get to it now," he said to himself.

He finished washing his face, toweled off, and then stepped into the hallway, locking his room behind him. He dropped the key in the pocket of his vest and set out for the Dead Moose.

A wry smile curled his lips upward.

It was time to meet Venom McFadden.

CHAPTER 13

By the time Smoke strolled into the Dead Moose Saloon, the establishment was doing a fair amount of business.

Several men had bellied up to the bar and a few of the tables were occupied. Two saloon girls were making the rounds, being sure to lean over the tables in a way that revealed the plunging décolletage of their red dresses, giving the onlookers a full view of their ample cleavage. Several cowpokes were so enamored by the creamy swell of the women's breasts that they didn't even notice Smoke as he walked by.

Others noticed and kept their eyes trained on him, their hands falling to their right sides as their backs stiffened a bit.

Those reactions were not lost on Smoke.

He passed a table full of six men engaged in a card game and went straight for the bar.

The faro and roulette tables were to his left, and toward the back of the room, though they weren't open at the moment. Other than that, a lone man sat at a table, occupying that corner of the room all by himself, and Smoke wondered if that was McFadden.

Smoke positioned himself at the very end of the bar, just past the curve, where he could keep his eyes on the front door and the other patrons. The only person behind him was the lonely figure at the table, but Smoke couldn't do much about that. He doubted there'd be any gunplay. As far as anyone else knew, Smoke was just looking for a drink, the same as any other man there.

The bar was a far cry from the one he'd leaned against earlier in the Absaroka. It was sturdy, slick, and glossy, with plenty of polished brass. There was even a rail that ran the entire length for weary cowboys to rest a foot on. Spittoons sat at well-placed intervals. A large mirror, surrounded by smaller shelves that contained bottles of various liquors, hung behind the bar. A beer keg rested on a stand next to that. It almost seemed too fancy for such a small frontier town and it immediately told Smoke a lot about its proprietor.

McFadden had grand aspirations. He thought of himself in a mighty high manner.

"What'll it be?" the bartender asked.

What Smoke really wanted was hot coffee, but he figured Buck West would ask for something a little stronger. Smoke didn't want anything too potent, though, so he simply said, "Beer."

Couldn't be any worse than the sip of beer he'd endured at the Absaroka, he thought.

He was right.

The beer was cold and didn't taste half-bad.

The bartender went on seeing to the needs of other patrons and Smoke casually watched the room. One table held the two men who'd kept a watchful eye on him earlier, when he was at the livery stable, and their eyes returned to him now. He acted as if he was paying them no attention.

He saw the perch where Nighthawk would sit—a wooden ladder-backed chair on a square platform about as high as a stage some saloons had for dancing girls—but it was empty now. Evidently, the old Crow wouldn't be on duty until later in the evening.

Smoke continued to watch the room, gleaning little insights here and there and tucking them away for later. Some might prove useful; some might not. One thing was for sure—he already knew who fancied himself a gunman.

Chief among them was the slender, dark-haired fella who occupied a table with the two men who'd watched Smoke.

This man had cruel eyes and a smirk to match. His movements were light and graceful. Smoke had the impression he was lightning quick with the ivory-handled six-chambered revolver that was lashed down around his thigh.

There was always one, Smoke thought.

His thoughts were interrupted when the bartender trudged toward him. The squatty man stopped, shifted on his feet, and said, "You want another?"

Smoke nodded.

When the bartender returned with a fresh beer, Smoke said, "This is quite a place you have here. You the owner?"

The pasty man snorted. "Hardly. This is Mr. McFadden's place."

"He's doing well for himself," Smoke said, raising the glass and bringing it to his lips. He took a sip, wiped the foam from his mouth with the back of his hand, and said, "Yes, sir, doing pretty well."

"I'd say so," the bartender said. "Owns half the town."

"You don't say. He might be the man I need to see," Smoke said. He grinned. "I'm a little light on funds."

The bartender scowled.

Smoke shook his head. "I can pay for my drinks," he said, feigning offense. He fished two coins from his vest and tossed them on the bar.

The bartender hurriedly palmed them, as if they might disappear at any moment.

"I ain't looking for a handout, neither. I'm just saying, I

could use a job before I ride on. I might see this McFadden fella."

The bartender's back stiffened. "It's *Mr.* McFadden and you don't just *see him*. Not without an appointment, anyway."

"Busy man?"

The bartender studied him a moment and then ignored the question, instead posing one of his own. "Just what is your line of work, mister?"

Smoke shrugged. "This and that."

The barkeep's eyes instinctively fell to where Smoke's gun hung on his hip, though the view was obstructed by the bar. He looked back to Smoke. It was evident he was thinking hard. A bead of sweat had formed on his brow, though Smoke didn't know if that was from nervousness or just the man's natural state. Finally he jerked his head forward, indicating the direction behind Smoke.

"I don't know if there's any openings. Taggart would. He runs things for Mr. McFadden."

Smoke turned around to see the broad-shouldered, stocky man who occupied the table near the back. He was busy writing in some kind of book. Looking back to the bartender, he said, "Taggart?"

"That's right. Hal Taggart. If there's a job, he'll know."

"Much obliged," Smoke said.

He left the beer atop the bar and turned toward the back of the room. He could feel the bartender's eyes on him as he moved, but he didn't think he was in any real danger.

He walked slowly and casually, thinking of just how he wanted to play things with Taggart. When Smoke was about four feet from the table, Taggart looked up with cool blue eyes.

"Can I help you with something?"

"Figured maybe I could help you," Smoke said.

Taggart's eyes narrowed, and for a moment, Smoke thought the conversation would end before it had a chance to get going. Taggart sighed, set down his pencil, and leaned back, crossing his arms across his chest with a sigh.

"Well, go on. Explain."

Smoke's lips turned up in a half smile as he stepped closer. "Mind if I sit?"

"Be my guest."

The chair scraped loudly against the floor as Smoke pulled it back. He lowered his frame in it and sat there as relaxed as possible. To onlookers, he would appear as casual as an old man sitting on the bench outside the barbershop. And there were certainly onlookers. The young fella Smoke had identified earlier—the one who fancied himself a gunfighter—was keeping his eyes trained intently on Smoke. The bartender kept casting glances their way, too.

Smoke wondered if they sensed the truth about him. While he looked at ease—and to a certain extent, he was—he could be out of that chair in a crouch, iron drawn and at the ready, on a moment's notice.

"I've heard this is Venom McFadden's town," Smoke said.

It wasn't a lie. Talk about Desolation Creek had reached him back in Colorado, thanks to Audie and Nighthawk. It was the topic of conversation at the Cummingses' trading post back in Wyoming, too. Smoke guessed he wasn't the first would-be gunhand who'd ridden into town looking for work.

If he had his way, he'd sure be the last.

"It is Mr. McFadden's town," Taggart conceded with a slight dip of his head. "That ain't up for debate."

"He must be doing all right for himself," Smoke said with a grin.

"He's a very prosperous businessman."

"A real civic leader, huh?" Smoke said.

Taggart tensed, uncrossing his arms and shifting in the chair.

"Didn't mean any offense," Smoke said, holding up a

hand. "I'm just saying I heard he employs men of my talents, pays good wages, and rewards loyalty."

"That so?"

Smoke nodded. "That's so."

Taggart cleared his throat and said, "And just what is your talent?"

"I'm wearing it on my hip."

This drew a chuckle from Taggart. "What's your name, son?"

Smoke didn't like being called "son," but he let the comment slide. While he was a young man, his wisdom and experience had made him a man folks respected back home in Big Rock. He sure wasn't looked at as a not-yet-dry-behind-the-ears kid, though Smoke wasn't the type to put on airs. Still, it bothered him to be spoken to in such a way by a man of Taggart's ilk. Anyone who sided with and rode for the likes of Venom McFadden was trash, plain and simple. For now, Smoke would play along. He had a mission to accomplish, after all.

Remembering Taggart's question, he said, "West. Buck West."

He could tell Taggart's mind was racing. "Buck West" had made a little bit of a reputation as a gunman and owlhoot while Smoke was using the name several years earlier. At the time, fake wanted posters, put out by crooked lawmen in cahoots with Smoke's enemies, had offered rewards for Smoke Jensen, dead or alive, so he'd had to adopt a new identity for a while.

Some time had passed since then, however, and Smoke wasn't sure if what little reputation the name carried still lingered in folks' memories.

"You've heard of me?" Smoke asked with a smirk.

"You ask like I should have."

Smoke shrugged. "I've been around."

"Huh," Taggart said. He let that offering hang in the air a full minute before adding, "You got anyone after you?"

"Why do you care?" Smoke said.

Taggart's eyes narrowed. "I don't give a darn about you, kid. I just want to make sure you ain't leading a posse in here. That could be bad for business. And bad for your health."

Smoke shook his head. "Anyone who's ever tried coming after me isn't alive to continue the hunt."

"That a fact?" Taggart said, a slight trace of mockery in his tone.

"That's a fact," Smoke said.

"Well, you're a braggadocious cuss, I'll give you that."

Again, Smoke didn't like being spoken down to, like he was some little kid with a wooden pistol outside his house, playing gunfighter. He resisted the urge to argue, though, realizing all that mattered was settling the score on Preacher's behalf. That would only happen if Taggart believed the man before him was a hired gun and outlaw named Buck West, who was looking for work.

"I'm not bragging," he said flatly. "Just stating a fact. I make my living with a gun. I'm fast and accurate. *Deadly* accurate. I thought Mr. McFadden was a man who could use that sort of talent, but it appears you've everything shored up." He rose from the seat. "I'll be riding on."

"Now hold on, just hold on," Taggart said. "No need to get a burr under your saddle."

Smoke gave him a hard stare.

Taggart must have read the steel in Smoke's eyes, because he waved a hand at the chair, saying, "Please sit. It might just be that we have an opening."

Smoke nodded and did as asked.

"Maybe," Taggart continued. "But you're going to have to prove your worth."

Smoke's shoulders twitched. "Just tell me what I have to do and I'll do it."

That wasn't entirely true, of course, and for a moment, Smoke was worried the man would give him an order he could not comply with. He would do a lot of things while posing as Buck West if it served the greater good, but he'd never hurt innocent folks. Preacher wouldn't have wanted that. Smoke would never do it, either.

"We'll get to the job talk," Taggart said. "*If* you're as good as you say you are."

"Go on," Smoke said.

"You say you're fast."

"I am."

"The fastest?"

Smoke shrugged.

He probably was the fastest, at least that he'd ever seen, but he sure didn't go around bragging about it. First of all, he wasn't looking for a reputation. He was just fine living in obscurity with Sally and Pearlie on the Sugarloaf. Ranching was the life for him, not drawing a gunfighter's wage. Secondly, a man brags about how fast he is, and every prideful fella that fancies himself a quick draw wants to challenge him. Eventually you slip up or meet that person who actually is faster. Either way, it wasn't a life—or death—Smoke wanted.

Of course, Buck West wouldn't have such a practical view of his abilities. So, Smoke shoved his personal feelings aside and said, "Some say."

Taggart studied him another moment and kept his eyes trained on him while calling loudly, "Hicks, come here a second."

Smoke knew who Hicks was before he even looked around.

The one he'd already noted. The tall, loose-jointed one with the cool eyes.

Sure enough, it was him. He walked straight for Smoke, his spurs jingling slightly in the hush that spread across the room. A cruel smile curved his thin lips.

And his hand hovered right over the butt of that fancy gun on his hip.

CHAPTER 14

"Hicks, I want you to meet Buck West."

Taggart swept his hand across the table at Smoke.

Hicks said nothing, but kept the half sneer plastered across his darkly tanned face. Now that Hicks was closer, Smoke suspected the man had some Indian in his blood, but he wasn't certain.

What he was certain about was Hicks's temperament—this was a cold-blooded killer who took delight in gunning men down. That much was evident just by looking into his serpentine eyes.

"West is looking for work. Thinks we might have a spot for him," Taggart continued. "Says he's fast and accurate."

"He's fast?" Hicks said, never taking his eyes off Smoke.

"What he says," Taggart confirmed.

Smoke wanted to bolt out of that chair and knock the little grin right off Hicks's face. He'd encountered men like this before. He knew exactly who he was dealing with. Well, almost exactly. Just how fast was Hicks? Was he the one who'd gotten the drop on Preacher? Just the thought made

Smoke's blood boil. Was that arrogant, insolent face the last thing Preacher had seen before dying?

Suddenly Smoke didn't give a shucks about the plan. He wanted to kill Hicks right now, followed by Taggart and the whole lot of gunmen who sat at the table across the room.

That wouldn't deal with McFadden, though. Who knew where the man was? Smoke didn't even know what he looked like. He could easily get out of town, never to be seen again.

Plus, Smoke might just get killed in the process.

Starting the ball now wasn't wise and wouldn't avenge Preacher. Not fully, anyway. So, he choked down his bitter anger and worked hard to keep his face impassive.

"Crew's full," Hicks said dismissively. "We don't need him."

Taggart laughed. "I'll be the judge of that. I call the shots on Mr. McFadden's behalf, and don't you forget it."

Clearly, Hicks didn't like being dressed down in such a way, but he must have respected Taggart, because he nodded and kept his mouth shut as he continued to eye Smoke.

"I want to see how fast he is before I send him riding out—or hire him on."

"If I draw on him, he won't be alive to do either," Hicks said.

The muscles in Smoke's right hand involuntarily twitched. He wasn't certain he wanted to shoot Hicks—not until he knew whether or not he'd been there when Preacher was gunned down. But he sure wouldn't mind drawing his Colt and bringing it down over the grinning weasel's head. Might teach him some manners.

"I'm not talking about drawing on him," Taggart said, a hint of impatience creeping into his cadence. "I'm talking about a friendly competition. We can do it out in the street."

"A competition?" Hicks said, finally shifting his focus to his boss.

"That's right. We can use . . . coins. I'll toss 'em up and

say when. You two will draw and fire. We'll see just how Mr. West's skills match up to yours."

"I'm game." Hicks looked back to Smoke. "What do you say?"

Smoke shrugged. "Why not?"

"Now we're talking," Taggart said. He eased his large frame out of the chair and turned to face the front of the saloon. Projecting his voice, he said, "Sam, bring me some coins."

"But Mr. McFadden—"

"He won't mind," Taggart said. "Anyway, I make the rules when he's not here. Now bring me some coins."

The barkeep looked nervous as he complied, but soon Taggart took the handful of jingling coins as everyone in the saloon watched in silence.

"We're going to have us a little shooting contest, boys. Come on."

The whole place erupted into cheers and conversation. That little frontier settlement hadn't witnessed much entertainment and everyone was eager to have a break in the mundane day. They let Taggart, Hicks, and Smoke get out the batwing doors and then filed outside after them. The crowd fanned out on the boardwalk, some even crossing the street and lining up near the empty lot beside the livery stable.

Audie must have heard the commotion, because he moved up closer to the stable's open doors and peered out, hanging back just enough to stay in the cool shadows inside the barn, but still able to see. Smoke noticed him, but pretended that he hadn't.

"You gents stand right here," Taggart said.

Smoke and Hicks stood even with each other, about six feet apart, in the street. Taggart was off to the side, close enough to toss the coins into the air, but far enough to be out of the line of fire.

Smoke took out his Colt and shoved a cartridge into the sixth chamber he usually kept empty. Hicks did not, telling Smoke a vital fact—the man walked around with six at the ready. Smoke would certainly keep that in mind.

"The rules are straightforward. Draw when I say. Speed counts, but it ain't worth nothin' if you can't hit what you're aiming at. You two ready?"

Both competitors nodded.

Smoke was confident enough in his speed and marksmanship that the contest didn't bother him. The thought was swirling around his brain, though, that this might be some sort of setup. Were Taggart and Hicks the type who would kill him without even knowing anything about him? Based on how bad he'd heard McFadden's gang was, he couldn't rule out the grim possibility.

His concern ebbed when movement registered to his left, and he realized Nighthawk had appeared, joining the onlookers. That giant Crow was hard to miss. He towered over everyone. Smoke was thankful to have friends present, realizing he no longer had to worry about a bullet in the back while he took part in Taggart's little game, not while Audie and Nighthawk were nearby. They would act to save his life in the event of a double-cross, even though it would ruin the plan they had put in place.

Taggart bounced the first two coins in his hand a few seconds before tossing it out and high into the air, saying, "Draw!"

Smoke moved with lightning-fast speed and his usual accuracy. He wasn't tense, wasn't nervous. Just letting instinct take control of his muscles and guide him as he performed one of the actions he was best at. His shot sounded a fraction of a second before Hicks's did. Both coins bucked in the air, being propelled upward an extra foot at the bullets' impact, before falling to the street. Tiny plumes of dirt swirled upon their landing. Taggart ran to the fallen targets, while the shooters pouched their irons. He whistled.

"Both hits. But West was a mite faster."

"That's a lie!" Hicks said, stepping closer to Taggart.

The foreman cast a look of stinging rebuke Hicks's way, causing the younger man to fall in line with a grumble.

"Let's try two now," Taggart said, collecting more coins from his vest pocket and jingling them in his hand.

He got back in place and gave the shooters a few moments to prepare. He then tossed the four coins sky-high. This time, it was an even draw, Smoke's and Hicks's shots blending together in a single peal of gun thunder. And again, the coins were launched higher into the air upon the bullets' impact. They fell to the dusty street with dull thuds.

"Can't get more even than that," one of the men in the crowd said.

"That's good shootin'," another muttered before sipping the beer he'd brought with him.

"All right, I need some help. Who wants to lend a hand?" Taggart asked.

A short, skinny man stepped forward. "I can."

"You can't throw these coins high enough, Lambert," Taggart said.

The crowd laughed, causing the man's cheeks to glow red. He didn't protest, though, stepping back into the crowd without another word.

"Collins, how about it?" Taggart said, noticing a man across the street and wagging a finger to motion him out.

Collins was about Taggart's height, with powerfully built arms.

"Sure," he said with an impassive shrug.

He met Taggart in the middle of the road, collected some coins, and then took his position across the street, not far from Smoke.

"Watch my lead, we move at the same time. Let's try three coins now."

Collins nodded.

Taggart let the shooters prepare, a smile across his face as he drew the moment out to heighten the anticipation. His arm lifted swiftly, Collins in lockstep with him, and Taggart yelled, "Draw!"

Smoke cleared leather a second before Hicks did. To on-lookers, it looked as if he barely moved his gun once it was aimed; yet all three coins bucked upon being dinged by the bullets.

Hicks hit his marks, too, but was still a tad behind Smoke as he slid his gun back into its worn leather holster.

There were astonished gasps from the onlookers, as well as some whoops and hollers.

"I'm afraid West is the winner," Taggart said.

"That can't be!" Hicks argued.

Taggart spread his hands. "He had the best two out of three."

Hicks started to speak, but simply huffed and blustered for a moment. He turned and glared at Smoke before turning back to Taggart. "Four. Try four." His right hand fell to the butt of his gun. "I'll hit 'em all."

"No, you won't," Smoke said.

Hicks turned around and angrily barreled toward him. "What did you say?"

"You won't hit 'em. Not right now," Smoke said casually.

"And why not?"

"You need to reload," Smoke said. "We both do."

The crowd laughed, causing Hicks's face to turn even redder.

Smoke paid him no attention, already thumbing fresh cartridges into his Colt's cylinder.

Hicks hastily did the same and then replaced the gun in the holster.

"You sure you want to do this?" Smoke said.

"And just why wouldn't I?" Hicks growled.

"Well, you're angry. It's liable to cloud your judgment, throwing your speed and accuracy off."

"I don't . . . I don't need a lesson from the likes of you!"

Smoke shrugged. "Just offering you a bit of friendly advice . . . *son*." He'd thought of not adding that last word, but just couldn't help himself. He smiled faintly as he kept his eyes forward, listening to Hicks huff in anger a few feet away.

"You got enough coins, Collins?" Taggart called across the street.

Collins took stock of his supply and then nodded.

"All right. Let's get to it," Taggart said. He gave several fake tosses, keeping the competitors guessing. Collins did the same. Hicks nearly took the bait, but Smoke didn't so much as flinch. He waited patiently, listening for Hicks to make the call rather than focusing on his movements.

"Draw!"

Smoke's Colt was out, aimed, and roaring at astonishing speed. He blasted the coins, his shots once again booming down Main Street a second faster than his rival's. Both men once again hit their mark, though.

"You all saw it," Hicks said. "I was faster."

A few of the men who'd been seated with Hicks in the Dead Moose nodded their agreement.

"That's right," one of them said. "You won that one. It's even now. Two to two."

"That's a dern lie," Collins said. "This feller here had his iron out before yours even cleared the leather."

Hicks stomped toward him. "You want to say that again?"

Smoke suppressed a chuckle as he thumbed fresh cartridges into his Colt once more. Hicks was already riled up. No sense in sending him into a full-fledged rage. He might goad his buddies into turning their guns on Smoke. Smoke could take a few of them out, but he'd probably go down in the process.

Is that what had happened to Preacher? Had he incurred the wrath of the hotheaded gunman, only to be cut down in an unfair fight?

Smoke made a vow to find out exactly what had happened

to Preacher. He couldn't worry about that now. He needed to stay loose and keep his wits. Hicks was coming unraveled enough for the both of them.

And that gave Smoke the advantage—not that he needed it. He was simply faster than Hicks, plain and simple.

"It's a tie," Hicks said again, turning a circle so as to address the whole crowd. "You all saw it. We go one more time to determine the winner."

"You want to try with five coins?" Taggart asked.

Hicks was reloading when he said, "Five."

"West, that okay with you?"

Smoke nodded and got in position.

"Collins, you got enough?"

"Need a few more."

Taggart counted what was in his hand before calling for the bartender. "Sam, go fetch us some more."

Progress was halted while the portly bartender scurried inside. He returned a few moments later, nearly stumbling off the boardwalk, running into the street. He stopped at Collins and dropped a few coins in his palm before running the best he could to Taggart. Poor guy was winded in his haste to please the boss. He then took his place safely in the crowd, away from the line of fire.

"Okay. Five coins," Taggart said. "This determines the winner."

"Just get to it," Hicks said, and sneered.

The scene played out much as before, but to Hicks's credit, his speed was even with Smoke's. The five shots rolled into each other, nearly ringing out as one, before the coins rained down onto the street.

"Well, I'll be," Taggart said. "We might just have us a tie." He cast an arched eyebrow to Hicks, clearly not believing his own words, as he squatted on his haunches to survey the targets. "Except," he said, picking up a coin and standing up, "you missed one."

He held it up for Hicks to see and then waved his arm, letting the onlookers get a good look at the undented coin. There were gasps and murmurs.

"That's bull—"

"You missed, Hicks. Collins, how about over there?"

Collins smiled as he picked up the five coins and bounced them in his hand. "Five hits!"

The crowd clapped, save for those who were clearly friends of Hicks.

"Well, that settles it," Taggart said. "West won, fair and square."

"That's not—" Hicks stepped forward, but stopped as his boss moved toward him, a stern look on his face. "We have use for a man of Mr. West's skills, Hicks. Let this go. That's an order."

Hicks's neck muscles bulged as his nostrils flared. He finally turned away and stomped off, grumbling as he approached Smoke.

Smoke finished reloading and slid his gun back into the holster. He'd filled all six chambers.

When in Desolation Creek . . .

Hicks looked as if steam were about to billow from his ears. Smoke nearly snickered at the mental image, but stopped short of actually laughing in the man's face.

"This ain't over, West. Ain't over by a long shot."

"Well, maybe you have better luck with long shots than you do close-range ones," Smoke said, unable to help himself.

That angry look returned to Hicks before he trudged away, cursing enough for a month of Sundays. Smoke watched the man walk up the steps leading to the boardwalk and into the Dead Moose.

By now, Taggart was at his side.

"That was fine shootin', West. Mighty fine." He scratched his jaw and said, "You know, come to think of it, I think we can use you. Go on in and have a drink. First one's on the house. Then get some rest. We'll call on you tomorrow. I have a feeling Mr. McFadden will want to meet you."

Smoke smiled, more to himself than Taggart.

"Good. As it just so happens, I want to meet Mr. McFadden, too."

CHAPTER 15

Smoke awoke the following morning with an empty, gnawing loneliness clawing at his insides.

He rolled over in the bed, looked toward the window, and tried to find comfort in the sun's warm rays that filtered through the sheer curtains.

It didn't work.

He sat up and shook his head, trying to clear the cobwebs. He wondered what Sally was doing. She was no doubt up and already working, tending to the various chores ranch life required. He also wondered if she was sick with worry. She had faith in his abilities, but still, it was awfully trying to be separated, knowing Smoke's quest was a vengeance one.

Smoke smiled. Most likely, more than anything else, Sally was spitting mad that she wasn't here with him helping to find justice for Preacher.

He told himself to stop worrying about that and focus on the task at hand. He needed to finish this business with McFadden so he could get out of Desolation Creek and back to the Sugarloaf, where he belonged.

He sprang from the bed and pumped his legs a couple of times to loosen up the natural stiffness he felt after sleep. It hadn't been a particularly restful slumber, unfortunately. Dreams of Preacher had haunted him.

Today he aimed to find out exactly what happened to the old mountain man. Where was he buried? What had happened to Horse and Dog? Smoke hadn't seen a cemetery yet, but that wasn't unusual. A church was outside of town, perched atop a hill, and in all likelihood, the cemetery was behind it.

Smoke wondered if that church was even open for worship these days. McFadden didn't strike him as the devout type, based on what Smoke knew about him. One way or another, Smoke would find out where Preacher's earthly remains were and how he'd ended up in that condition. The trick would be to do it in a way that didn't arouse suspicion.

Smoke took his time scrubbing his face at the washbasin, getting the sleep out of his eyes, and letting the water wake him up. He glanced out the window and saw that the streets were starting to come to life, though it still wasn't a particularly busy town.

Hopefully, that would change once the citizens were free of McFadden and his men.

Smoke finished washing up and then got dressed. He lined his gun rig up around his waist, buckled it, and checked the cartridges in his Colt. He dropped the gun in its holster and then drew again, repeating the process several times before stepping into his boots. He locked the room and headed downstairs.

Coming off the stairs, he could see the clerk watching him closely from behind the desk. Smoke nodded to him and then stepped through the doorway that led to the dining room. He found a table in a corner, where he had a view of both entrances—the one to his right, where he'd entered from the hotel, and the one straight ahead that led to the street. With his back to the wall, he relaxed a bit, though still kept a watchful eye.

There were only two other patrons, an elderly gentleman and his wife, working on their breakfast at a table close to the window. Their conversation stopped and the man's eyes lingered on Smoke as he found a table and sat down.

Smoke wasn't surprised.

By now, word would have gotten around about that little contest in front of the saloon yesterday. Word Smoke had hired on with McFadden might also be making the rounds by now, especially in a town that small. Smoke couldn't blame the man for the disapproving scowl he wore as his eyes lingered on him for a moment longer than politeness dictated. That couple might even be victims of McFadden in some way. It stood to reason that everyone in Desolation Creek was, in one way or another. Working for McFadden— or pretending to work for McFadden—would certainly earn Smoke the scorn of those around town. He'd just have to accept that and live with it long enough to keep his masquerade going. Folks would change their tunes, once they saw why Smoke was really there. It didn't matter much, anyway, Smoke thought. He wasn't there to make friends. Still, he didn't cotton to the idea of good, decent people being afraid of him.

A young woman came by the table, approaching with a hint of hesitation in her movements. She was tall, slender, and pretty in the light blue dress she wore. She had somewhat mousy features with brown hair put up in a bun.

"Good morning, sir. My name is Clara. Would you like coffee?"

"Yeah," Smoke said, fighting the urge to use proper manners and put the poor girl at ease. For now, he needed people to be afraid of him. Anything else might stir McFadden's curiosity.

Or Taggart's, more than likely.

Smoke was starting to think Venom wasn't around all that much.

"Get me some eggs, bacon, and biscuits if you got 'em. And keep that coffee coming."

"Yes, sir," the woman said, scurrying away. She returned a few moments later with a steaming cup of coffee and placed it in front of him before retreating again. Smoke appraised the delicate china and thought it was probably the fanciest cup of coffee he'd had in a good while.

The elderly couple had gotten up, finished with their meal and not willing to linger, now that McFadden's newest thug was dining in the establishment.

So, Smoke drank his coffee as he sat in the room alone, nothing but his thoughts to keep him company, not that he'd figured on chatting with the couple, anyway. Being alone was best, he decided. It gave him time to figure out a strategy.

He'd spend today getting the lay of the land and learning more about McFadden's operation. That night, he'd meet with Audie and Nighthawk at the livery stable to compare notes.

His food was delivered and Smoke ate most of it in peace, until he caught sight of a big figure in the doorway. Smoke's right hand hovered nonchalantly near his gun as a thought struck him.

He didn't need to only watch out for McFadden's men—say Hicks or someone else angered by his presence—but also for vengeful citizens. He hadn't heard of any taking the law into their own hands and ambushing McFadden's men, but if they got fed up enough, there was no telling what they'd do.

Smoke couldn't blame them, either. Tyrants can only suppress freedom for so long before people get sick enough that they rise up. The citizens of Desolation Creek had just as much of a right to take on McFadden as Smoke did. More, actually. They lived under his tyrannical rule. The trick was not getting caught in the crosshairs if such an uprising did begin.

Smoke filed that thought away for later and decided to explore the possibility that there might be folks fed up enough to fight. Maybe they could help Smoke, Audie, and Nighthawk when they made their move against McFadden and his gang.

Right now, though, he was relieved to see it was only Taggart coming into the dining room. The big man moved a bit stiffly and slowly, probably from years in the saddle, punching cattle, and sleeping around campfires. He stopped in front of Smoke's table and said, "The boss wants to see you."

"Now?"

"I'm here, ain't I?"

Smoke looked at the breakfast he had left and thought about his options. McFadden wouldn't like being kept waiting and Smoke needed to play along.

For now.

At least he'd finished most of his food. He stood, grabbed a remaining hunk of biscuit, and popped it in his mouth before washing it down with one last swallow of coffee.

"All right. Lead the way."

He grabbed his hat from the tabletop, slapped it on his head, and followed Taggart.

It was time to finally lay eyes on McFadden.

Venom McFadden sat alone at a table near the rear of the Dead Moose Saloon, his back to the gaming tables and his eyes forward, surveying his kingdom. He was dressed somewhat like a dandy, not exactly what Smoke had imagined.

Come to think of it, Smoke wasn't sure what he'd imagined. With a name like Venom, he was thinking of a roughhewn man with disdain permanently etched across his face. McFadden, though, resembled a gambler, with his crisp white shirt, fancy, clean black vest, and matching hair that was perfectly in place. All that was missing was the deck of cards spread out before him. Instead, only a cup of coffee rested on the table before him.

Smoke watched the steam rise and curl from the cup and wished he'd had more. That little china cup hadn't held much and Smoke had made the young woman refill it three times. Even then, it wasn't enough.

"Ah, the famous Buck West," McFadden said, not bothering to stand. "Sit." He swept his hand over the table and Smoke walked across the saloon's floor, his boots clunking loudly with each step and his spurs singing their jingling tune. He took the seat directly across from McFadden and nodded.

What had McFadden meant by that "famous" comment? Had McFadden heard of Buck West's exploits? Smoke didn't mind if he had. They would only bolster the reputation he was trying to sell.

"Word around here is that you put on quite a show yesterday. I heard it was some fine shooting."

Smoke only nodded again.

"A man of many words, eh?" McFadden said with an amused smile.

"Just waiting for you to get to the point," Smoke said.

He was pushing it a bit and he knew it. He wanted to see what sort of temper the man had swarming just beneath the surface.

It was slight, but Smoke's keen eye caught it—a quick flash of anger in McFadden's eyes, less than a second of unbridled rage, fading as quickly as it had appeared.

"Watch it, son," Taggart said, standing a few feet away, behind Smoke and slightly to his left.

"Didn't mean any disrespect by it," Smoke said. "I signed on to work, though, and I'm eager to get started and earn some pay."

McFadden pursed his lips together and bobbed his head slowly. "I like that. Ready to hit the ground running."

"That's right," Smoke said.

"Well, you'll get your chance this morning. I need to know, though, before we continue this . . . little arrangement. Do you have any qualms about following orders?"

"What are the orders?"

"Whatever Mr. McFadden says," the gruff voice of Taggart said immediately.

McFadden held up a hand to calm his foreman, but kept his eyes trained on Smoke.

"I'm trying to build something in this town. Something big. Something prosperous. Not all the good people of Desolation Creek see it that way, so it will be your job to . . . persuade them." He let the statement hang in the air a moment before saying, "Will that be an issue?"

"Can't say that it will be, as long as this prosperous thing you're building is *prosperous for me*."

McFadden laughed. "Good. I think we see eye to eye. Sometimes examples have to be made. It's for the greater good."

Smoke took the moment of silence that followed to think of Preacher. He fought the urge to ball his fist, stand up, and stove McFadden's arrogant face in. He was fast enough to draw and take out Taggart, but that shot would no doubt arouse others who worked for McFadden. They might even be in the saloon, upstairs in some of the rooms, asleep or awaiting orders.

Now wasn't the time.

"Just make sure you are the one giving the examples and not the example itself. Have I made myself clear, West?" McFadden continued.

"I reckon so," Smoke said.

"That's 'yes, sir,' West," Taggart said.

"I reckon so," Smoke simply said again.

He could only play along so far. McFadden smirked. "That will do. Now you're going to go with Hicks and a couple of others to visit Darnell Poe. He's the newspaperman. It seems he thinks Desolation Creek would be better off without me. I want you to convince him otherwise."

"Just how much convincing does he need?" Smoke said.

"I said *convince him*, don't kill him. I have plans for him. Understand?"

"I reckon."

Taggart grunted again, but Smoke didn't pay him any attention.

"This won't be a problem, will it, you working with Hicks?" McFadden said.

"I hold no ill will toward the man," Smoke said.

"Well, that's mighty charitable of you. I'm not sure young Hicks will feel the same way, but I admire your Christian attitude."

Smoke stood without acknowledging the sarcastic remark.

"We'll get the job done," he simply said.

"Good. I pay well, but I expect results. Now go on. You'll find Hicks and the others waiting for you outside."

Smoke thought once more of just getting it over with and shooting McFadden right then, but better judgment won.

It was tough, though.

It was only eight in the morning and already he wasn't sure how much more of this sickening charade he could take.

Sure enough, Hicks and two other men were waiting outside.

One was short, squatty, and built like a bull. The anger in his eyes told Smoke he had the temperament of a bull, too. He had a scar over his left eye, a gash in his cheek, and several missing teeth revealed by the harsh smile that stretched his thick lips.

The other one was taller and didn't have an ounce of fat on his body. Rather than looking lean, he looked as if he'd missed a few meals and Smoke almost told him he'd be happy to buy him breakfast, but he figured such sentiment wouldn't be appreciated.

"You ready?" Hicks said.

"You bet," Smoke said, plastering a cocky grin on his face.

"Just get one thing clear," Hicks said. "We're working together because the boss wants it. That sure don't make us pards, though. Understand?"

"Wouldn't have it any other way," Smoke said. "So, are we done talking? The boss gave us a job to do and I don't like to keep him waiting."

Smoke hated even saying those words: "the boss." Venom McFadden sure wasn't his boss, but such talk couldn't be avoided right now.

Hicks hissed for a moment before spinning around on his boot heels and stalking off down the street. Smoke waved his hand for the other two to go and said, "After you, gents."

The walk only took a minute. Smoke noted how the town's folks gave them a wide berth. He was barely into his little ruse and already he'd had enough. He was thankful when they reached the newspaper office, ready to be away from the scared, intimidated faces on the street. That relief was short-lived, though, when he realized the unpleasant task he had to do.

"Hold up," Smoke said as the other three reached for the door.

"You giving orders now, West?" Hicks said as he turned around to glare at Smoke.

The other two snorted their contempt.

"I just want to be clear before we go in," Smoke said. "Boss said we weren't to kill Poe."

Hicks laughed, but it was devoid of all humor. "What's the matter, West? You got a weak stomach or something? Ain't ever killed a man?"

"I follow orders," Smoke lied. "Best you do the same."

The sneer left Hicks's face, replaced by unyielding rage. He closed the gap between him and Smoke, leaving only a few inches. "You just started with this outfit and you sure don't call any shots. When Mr. McFadden and Taggart ain't around, I give the orders." He jerked his thumb back at his chest. "It might be, as I need to teach you a lesson right here and now."

"Do it, Hicks," one of the other men said.

"He thinks he's high and mighty, don't he?" the other said.

Smoke knew there was a plan to adhere to, but he could only take so much. "Hicks, you just try anytime you want. Be a shame to have to shoot you, though. It isn't that I've taken a shine to you. I sure haven't. But the boss might get a little testy if I kill one of his men without asking and then I'd be out of a job. I love money more than I hate you, so why don't we put this little squabble aside and do the task assigned to us? Any account between us can be settled up later, once the boss gives the okay. Sound good to you?"

"Better than good," Hicks said, the cold, humorless smile coming back to his lips. "Just be clear, though, that you don't give me orders. Not now. Not ever."

Smoke didn't say a word and continued to stare into Hicks's coal-black eyes until the man turned around and turned his attention to the newspaper office.

"Let's go, boys. But remember what the boss said. We don't kill Poe today."

The other two men nodded while giving Smoke hard stares of their own.

Inside, the office smelled of ink and paper. There was a small lobby, with a waist-high wooden railing that separated it from the rest of the structure. A small gate swung in on hinges as Hicks pushed through it, on his way to the back, where Poe was busy working over a wide table. The newspaperman looked up, his spectacles sliding to the tip of his nose. The apron he wore had a few ink spots, breaking up the beige with black splotches.

"I won't bow to intimidation!" Poe said, standing up straight and walking around the table.

Hicks nearly stepped back, but caught himself in time, Smoke noted. He was used to people being intimidated by him. This Poe was a brave man and it had taken Hicks by surprise.

Without warning, Hicks rocketed both arms forward, his palms landing on Poe's chest and sending him back hard. He bounced against the table, causing a jar of ink to topple over. It splashed onto the floor as it trickled over the edge. A stack of papers was dislodged, floating to the floor, one by one.

Before Smoke could do anything, Hicks had his gun out. He brought the barrel down hard on Poe's head, just as the newspaperman was staggering upright from being pushed against the table.

He went down hard on the ground, groaning as a crimson streak flowed down a fresh gash on his forehead.

It took every ounce of strength Smoke had not to do the same or worse to Hicks. He needed to maintain his pose as a hired gun, but he sure wouldn't stand by while a man was beaten to death.

Thankfully, the violence ended as quickly as it had started.

Looking down at the groaning Poe, Hicks said, "This is Mr. McFadden being patient. Merciful, even. But it only goes so far. Know what I mean, Poe?"

When the newspaperman didn't answer right away, Hicks sent the tip of his boot into Poe's ribs.

"Know what I mean, Poe?" Hicks said louder.

"You . . . going . . . to make an example of me . . . the

way you did Alonzo? Or . . . like that old man?" Poe said through gritted teeth.

This had Smoke's attention.

Was the old man Preacher?

"Oh, not like them," Hicks said. "No, we'll make it worse for you. Alonzo died fast. One shot was all it took. The old-timer, well, we had fun filling him full of lead, but he probably died after the third or fourth shot." Hicks laughed and said over his shoulder, "You remember that, boys? How he flopped around in the street like a fish on dry land?"

The other two laughed.

Smoke nearly jerked out his Colt and laid waste to the three outlaws, but managed to keep a tight rein on his temper.

"In your case, Poe, we'll drag things out. You see, a lot of folks don't know this about me, but I'm just as good with a knife as I am a gun. Been a while since I cut a man up. I'm about due." He kicked Poe again and waited for the loud groaning to end before saying, "You don't stop riling up the townsfolk against us, I'll be back with my knife. Trust me, you'll wish you met the same fate as Alonzo or that old man." He kicked Poe one last time for good measure. He started to walk away, but turned after making it a few feet.

"Can you hear me?"

It took Poe a moment, but he finally nodded.

"Good. Mr. McFadden wants two things from you. Stop agitating the folks and print a good story about him. One that puts a real shine on him. Who knows? You might just get paid. Even if you don't, well, I figure not having your insides cut out of you is payment enough."

The other two hard cases laughed.

"You've been warned," Hicks said before leaving.

Smoke let the other two men file out before he joined them outside. He hoped his anger didn't show. His blood felt as if it had heated near boiling point.

"Well, you were useless in there," Hicks said to Smoke. "Guess I need to tell the boss we don't need you."

"I didn't see them doing anything," Smoke said, looking at the other two. "How could we? You went off half-cocked like that."

"You telling me how to do my job, West?"

"No. I'm just saying leave some for the rest of us."

Smoke shook his head angrily and walked off, using the excuse to put some distance between him and Hicks.

Because if he didn't—if he was around the man another second—he'd put a bullet between Hicks's beady eyes.

CHAPTER 16

Thankfully, Smoke didn't have to pretend to do any more of McFadden's bidding that day. He passed a few hours nursing a beer in the Dead Moose, so as not to raise any suspicion on his whereabouts. When it was clear his services were not needed further, he went back to the hotel and had an early supper. After that, he spent some time in his room, lying on the bed and turning everything over in his mind.

He still didn't know exactly what had happened to Preacher, but he'd learned enough to know Hicks was definitely behind it. The way it sounded, Preacher being filled with so much lead, a lot of others had their hands in it, too. Of course, it all came down to Venom McFadden, who, no doubt, had ordered the execution.

Fine by Smoke. He had a bullet for every one of 'em and knew Nighthawk and Audie would feel the same way. No sense in sparing any of McFadden's army.

The sun had settled low by the time Smoke stepped back into his boots. He left his room and strode casually down the stairs and through the hotel's lobby. Outside, he took a minute to breathe in the fresh air before stepping off the covered boardwalk and crossing the street.

He continued to move at a measured pace. A few people noticed him and eagerly stepped aside and averted their eyes. That was just fine with Smoke. The fewer people noticing he was out and about, the better.

He had the perfect cover, though—visiting the livery stable to check on Drifter. It wasn't necessarily a lie, either. He missed his old friend and was eager to see how the big stallion was getting along.

None of McFadden's hired hands were out and about, so Smoke made it to the livery stable undisturbed and unnoticed. That far down Main Street, past the soft glow of the lamppost lanterns, the deep purple curtain of gathering darkness was thicker, except for the lights spilling through the windows and entrance of the Dead Moose.

Smoke paused for a moment in front of the stable to listen to the lively yet tinny piano music pounding from the Dead Moose. Through the windows, he could see figures flicker across the yellow light, but couldn't make out any details. He wondered if Nighthawk would be able to get the time off for the clandestine meeting.

He opened the small door next to the larger barn doors and stepped inside, closing it behind him. He moved into the shadows to his right. He didn't anticipate any trouble, but with as tight a grip as McFadden had on Desolation Creek, nothing could be ruled out.

"I assume you're here to check on your mount," Audie's voice said.

The light inside the stable, coming from two kerosene lamps that hung on separate posts, wasn't too bright. Smoke gave his eyes a few seconds to adjust to the faint glow. Once they had, he called out, "Just checking on Drifter."

"Well, come right along, sir. You have the entire place to

yourself, save for this Indian gentleman. He also is checking on his mount."

Smoke smiled and stepped out of the shadows, his boots crunching on a few strands of loose hay that littered the floor. "Glad to see you could make it, Nighthawk."

"Umm."

"I agree," Audie said. "It is indeed a fortuitous occurrence that your shift does not start until ten. That gives us more than enough time, I'd say."

Smoke nodded. "Yeah, we best keep this quick."

"Umm."

"Same here!" Audie said. "Everyone I've encountered is talking about that show of marksmanship you put on in the street yesterday, Mr. West. It was most impressive."

"Just doing what had to be done," Smoke said, keeping up the pretense that he was Buck West, even though Audie had said they were alone in the stable. Smoke didn't trust that there were no spies lurking around outside. "How about you two?"

Audie's shoulders rose and fell. "Nothing much, to speak of, though I have learned more about what happened to an old friend of ours."

Smoke and Nighthawk looked at him expectantly.

"It seems as if he rode into town and was here less than a day before he ran afoul of Venom McFadden. Evidently, he quickly realized the good citizens of this community were living in oppression and decided to do something about it.

"He raised some disturbance in the saloon, but was bested in fisticuffs when McFadden's men ganged up on him. From the way I hear it, it was not a fair fight at all."

"Umm."

"That's what I said, Nighthawk. There must have been an army of those miscreants if they were able to drag Preacher away. But that's exactly what they did. Drug him into the street and emptied their revolvers into him."

Nighthawk bowed his head in reverent remembrance of his friend. Audie saw the gesture and nodded, following suit.

"Any idea where he's buried?" Smoke asked, his voice tight now from the strain of the emotions roiling inside him. He couldn't keep up the pose any longer. The story of Preacher's death had affected him too deeply.

Audie looked up once more. "The cemetery up the hill by the church. Unfortunately, his grave is unmarked. Laid to rest in a pauper's plot, with not so much as a cross to mark the final resting place of his earthly remains."

Smoke chewed on the information for a moment. He wasn't at all surprised that Preacher had tried to step in upon realizing the evil Venom McFadden was capable of. Preacher was never one to sit idly by while good folks were victimized. Far from it, in fact.

What did surprise Smoke, though, was that Venom's men were able to dispose of him with such apparent ease. He shook his head. Guess everyone slows down at some point, he thought.

Even ol' Preacher.

Smoke's time would come one day, and he hoped death found him peacefully on the Sugarloaf. But that wasn't today.

Today Smoke had a job to do and its name was vengeance.

"As much as I want to pay McFadden back tonight, I reckon we best wait a few more days. Being on the inside of his operation, I might find ways to whittle down the odds."

"Umm."

"Yes, I agree," Audie said. "You look for ways in the Dead Moose, Smoke will look for ways inside the inner circle, and I'll keep making notes about McFadden's comings and goings." He patted the pocket on his shirt, causing a folded piece of paper inside to rustle. "I can see a lot from the loft of this stable. How many men McFadden has coming and going, when they make their collections, and when he rides out. I've noticed he takes a trip every day or at least every other day, riding north."

"You saddle his horse for him?"

"No," Audie said. "And thank God for it. I'm not sure I could stomach the encounter. No, McFadden has his own stable just behind the Dead Moose a ways." He shook his head and rolled his eyes. "He's a very important man, you know."

Smoke chuckled grimly. "He'd best enjoy it while he can."

"Umm," Nighthawk added.

"My goodness, old friend! You really want to do that?"

"Umm."

Audie whistled. "Taking his head clean off with a tomahawk, eh? I don't doubt you would."

"How about we meet back here in two days?" Smoke suggested. "Let's change up the time a bit. Say five o'clock?"

The other two men agreed.

"Maybe by then, we'll have tipped the odds and can hash out a plan." Smoke drew in a deep breath. "And then we strike."

CHAPTER 17

The following morning, Smoke was eating breakfast, when Hal Taggart appeared in the hotel dining room. This time, he didn't even bother coming in all the way, but merely poked his head in through the arched entrance from the lobby, having entered from the hotel side of the building.

"Mr. McFadden wants to see you, West."

The young woman waiting tables nearly dropped the tray she held at the mere mention of McFadden's name. Taggart chuckled, apparently finding her fright amusing. Smoke wanted to teach him a lesson right then and there, but choked down his anger and got to his feet.

"As a matter of fact, I was about to head that way."

He'd been smart enough to start breakfast earlier this morning, suspecting Taggart might drop by, so he was pretty much finished with the meal. He picked up the coffee cup from the table and downed what was left of the strong black brew.

"Why don't we just have a standing appointment?" Smoke said. "I'll head to the Dead Moose every morning after breakfast, about this time."

Taggart grunted. "You sure seem like you want to run things around here. Like maybe you're already too big for your britches."

When Smoke looked at him with a puzzled gaze, Taggart went on, "Hicks told me how you acted yesterday. Sounded like you had a notion of taking control. Funny thing is, Hicks has been with us a lot longer than you have. You might do well to consider yourself on a sort of . . . *probationary* period."

That was a mighty big word for an owlhoot such as Taggart, Smoke thought. He let the comment roll off him with a shrug. "Hicks is a stupid fool. As for me and you, I was just trying to save you the trouble walking down here every morning. But suit yourself."

"I will do what suits me. And Mr. McFadden. Now come on."

Smoke smiled to himself as he followed Taggart out of the hotel.

"I'll catch up with you," he said. "Forgot my hat."

Taggart seemed annoyed, but didn't protest as Smoke hurried back inside. The truth was that Smoke had intentionally left his hat. He'd figured out quickly that McFadden's men were under the impression they didn't have to pay for their meals or anything else they took in town. Smoke, however, had no such notions and he couldn't even pretend he did after seeing how scared that girl had been. So, he quietly left some cash on the table, giving her a little something extra for having to put up with the trouble.

He doubted she'd talk and the risk of McFadden finding out was low. If he did, Smoke could just say he was unaware of the arrangement and didn't want to get kicked out of the hotel. Either way, it didn't matter much. McFadden wouldn't care about it soon enough.

He wouldn't care about anything.

Smoke walked down the street, not getting in too much of a hurry, and came up beside Taggart.

"Mr. McFadden has a job for me, huh?"

"Why in the world would he want to see you?"

Smoke remained silent until they reached the Dead Moose. McFadden was on the front porch, standing atop the stairs, where the building formed a corner, just in front of the bat-wing doors. Four other men were there, the two from the newspaper office the day before and two more Smoke had never met.

Hicks was nowhere in sight, a fact that didn't bother Smoke one bit. He had woken up in a particularly foul mood after a night of tossing and turning. He missed Sally, he was angry over Preacher's demise, and just generally not in the mood to put up with nonsense.

And Hicks was pure nonsense.

"Good morning, Mr. West. How are you on this fine day?" McFadden said.

Smoke simply nodded and said, "Looks like we'll be busy today."

"Busy indeed," McFadden said. "You see, you and these fine gentlemen here are going to take a trip up north. I've been surveying some land up there that I want to acquire. I need your help securing it."

Smoke had a pretty good idea where this was going. McFadden needed the ruffians' help in *stealing* the land from whoever was already on it.

Sure enough, as McFadden laid out the plan, Smoke realized his hunch had been correct. Once McFadden was done, he said, "Can you do that?"

"Sounds simple enough—go and rough up some home-steaders until they decide to pack up and leave," Smoke said.

"*Rough up* sounds so coarse. How about we say . . . *persuade*? *Reason with?*"

Smoke chuckled. "You're the boss."

"I certainly am. You'll ride up there with Boyd, Carter, and the two Cole boys here. Carter is in charge of this little excursion. You men understand?"

The thugs all nodded and grunted.

"Good. Try not to kill anyone. That might get the attention of the sheriff or, heaven forbid, a U.S. Marshal. We're out of town limits on this one, so there are other lawmen to consider beyond our beloved drunken marshal," McFadden said.

The men laughed.

Come to think of it, Smoke thought, he'd seen neither hide nor hair of the marshal. Could the man sober up enough to be a potential ally when the time came to turn the tables on McFadden? Surely, he had some resentment for being put on the sideline the way he had been. Maybe that anger could fuel a desire to fight. Smoke made a mental note to check into it discreetly later on.

For now, he had a job to do and he didn't look forward to doing it. If there was one bright spot, it was the no-kill order McFadden had given. Looking at the bunch he was about to ride with, though, Smoke wasn't sure they'd follow it.

Carter was of medium height, with dark blond hair and a bushy beard that hung low off his chin. He had blue eyes and Smoke supposed he'd be considered handsome if he cleaned up a bit and didn't look so dadgum mean. His eyes held a certain contempt that he shared with the other three who were tackling the mission.

The Cole brothers were large framed; one was clean shaven, with a receding hairline, and the other a bit stronger, with a perfectly bald head, but a thick black beard, which started around his ears.

Boyd was the smallest of the bunch, but appeared every bit as mean. His brown hair looked as if he'd dragged a comb through it. His cheeks were freshly shaven.

They went to the livery stable, retrieved their mounts, and saddled up. The riders fell in line with Smoke in the rear. The others seemed eager for him to be there, as if it showed his lowly status as the new man to the crew. Smoke was just fine with that. He preferred to keep a watchful eye on the hombres and was thankful not to have his back to them as they rode the ten miles or so out of town.

They arrived at a homestead nestled in the foothills of the mountains. The one-story house was plain, with a gray barn out back, a small corral, and an outhouse.

A wisp of smoke curled from the house's chimney and there were other signs that the inhabitants were home.

Smoke didn't like that.

He'd been hoping to find the place empty, but fate had other plans.

His mind raced as he considered his options. His best bet was to simply let the situation unfold. He had no desire to intimidate these homesteaders, but what could he do without ruining his masquerade as a hired gun-wolf? Unless McFadden's men forced him to act, he'd keep his gun in its holster. If they started the ball by trying to kill a homesteader, well, Smoke would dance to whatever song they played.

It didn't take long before he realized that was the direction the encounter was heading. The tension was palpable as the riders came onto the property. A certain uneasiness, which Smoke had experienced many times before, was in the air.

Something to do with death.

Smoke hoped this time his instincts were wrong.

But as the minutes wore on, he realized they were unfortunately accurate once again.

The Cole brothers rode their horses close to the house, veering to the left to circle it, while Boyd went right. Carter stayed in the yard, high atop his mount, and lit a cheroot as he watched the house. Once he had his smoke going, he inhaled loudly, held it, and then exhaled, resembling a storybook dragon as smoke streamed from both nostrils.

"You inside," he finally called, "come on out! We'd like to have a word with you."

There was no response, but Smoke saw slight movement from a curtain in the front window, to the right of the door. A moment later, Boyd's horse came trotting back into the front yard. "Few horses gone. I think ol' Newt done skedaddled. Kids probably with him."

Carter grunted. He watched the window for another moment and then said, "Someone's inside."

"You think it's her?" Boyd asked.

"Sure do."

By now, the Cole boys had circled around the entire house and were back among the others. The bald, bearded one scowled at Smoke. "You gonna do anything, or just sit there on your horse looking stupid?"

"Best I can see, there's not much to do right now," Smoke said. "Boyd told us the horses were gone. Looks like we came at a bad time."

"They ain't all gone," Boyd said, putting a plug of tobacco in his mouth. His cheek bulged as he smiled to reveal dirty teeth. "I think the girl is here."

Everyone but Smoke laughed.

"So, we ride on to find the menfolk," Smoke suggested. "Or leave them a little message so they get the point when they come back. Maybe bust up his barn a little."

"Oh, we'll leave a message, all right," Carter said. "Won't have anything to do with the barn, though."

The other men chuckled again.

"Y'all heard what Mr. McFadden said. I'm running this little operation," Carter continued. "That means I get the first go at the girl."

The Coles and Boyd clearly didn't like the edict, but none protested.

"West, go on in there and fetch her," Carter said, motioning for Smoke to ride up to the house. "You prove your worth and we might just give you a turn at her. When we're done, of course."

The men laughed again, apparently finding this all uproariously funny.

Smoke needed to stall as he determined a plan. He knew

he'd not let harm come to that girl. "What if this is a trap? You said there's menfolk around here, right?"

"Yep. Newt Simmons and his two boys, Paul and Jasper."

"What if they're lying in wait, ready to ambush the first hombre who walks through that door?" Smoke said.

Boyd spit a string of brown juice from his lips. "Sounds to me like you're afraid of a little girl. She ain't but fourteen, maybe fifteen. I think even you can take her."

The other men laughed once again.

Smoke wasn't sure what he wanted to do more: shoot them, or have a long, serious conversation as to what constituted humor. They seemed too easily entertained.

"Yeah," the beardless Cole boy said. "Go on and do what Carter done told you to do."

Smoke smiled. "Be glad to. Just spread out and cover me. Best y'all each man a post and make sure those men don't come back and get the drop on us."

"I know how to do things," Carter growled. "I don't need your help."

"Whatever you say, Carter," Smoke said.

The more Smoke thought of it, the more he realized it was best he was going inside first. He could at least talk to the girl and calm her fears before he sent lead at Carter and the others. He wasn't sure how he'd explain their deaths, but he'd worry about that on the ride back to town. Right now, he had to protect that girl and it sure didn't seem like he could talk the cutthroats out of anything.

Not with his mouth, anyway. His gun would have to do the talking from here on out.

He walked up the steps. His boots made heavy thuds on the porch. He couldn't just knock, behaving like he was a friendly neighbor coming over for a cup of coffee—not with Carter and the others watching.

He also couldn't assume that the girl wasn't waiting on the other side of that door with a shotgun, ready to blast the first man who came in. He suspected that's why Carter had sent him. Being the new fella—and the one who'd bested Chuck Hicks—had made Smoke an object of disdain in the group. He couldn't care any less. None of them had long to live, anyway.

"Oh, and West?" Carter called.

Smoke looked back to him.

"Don't even think about locking yourself inside there and taking the first turn. You're the last one hired on. You'll go last."

The other men laughed and hollered, clearly finding the comment hilarious.

"I heard you," Smoke said.

Smoke stepped back a few paces, lowered his shoulder, and charged the wooden door.

It splintered and flew back. He immediately went into a low crouch and rolled. He came up on his knees to see his hunch had been right. A scared girl was in the front parlor, her hands clutching a short, double-barreled shotgun. Besides the violent shaking that wracked her body, she appeared immobilized by fear. Tears streamed from her eyes.

Smoke made up his mind right then.

He didn't care if Carter and the others fell to their knees and begged forgiveness. He was going to kill 'em all.

"It's okay," he said, keeping his voice low. He rose quickly and got out of the doorway so that Carter and the others couldn't see or hear what was coming next. "I'm a friend. You're safe."

He kept his hands out and made soft patting motions, trying to show he wasn't a threat. With that gut-shredder pointed at him, he didn't want to spook the girl into jerking the triggers. The way she looked, it wouldn't take much.

Unfortunately, his words didn't appear to be registering, and he wasn't a bit surprised.

"I have a wife, Sally. A ranch back in Colorado. I'm . . . a lawman," Smoke lied.

It wasn't necessarily true, as he had no badge. But he was

bringing the law to Desolation Creek, so he figured that counted enough.

"A l-lawman?" she finally said.

"Yes, ma'am. Those men outside work for Venom McFadden. Do you know who he is?"

She started sobbing loudly at the mere mention of the name.

"What's taking so long, West? You better not be having a go at her!" Carter yelled.

"Where's your pa? Your brothers?"

"Up in the h-hills," she said through tears.

"You got a spot you can hide?"

"Maybe . . . under . . . th-the . . . bed."

Smoke nodded. "That's a good spot. Now you're thinking. Go. Quickly. I'll take care of them."

But instead of moving, the girl released a bloodcurdling scream that made Smoke's ears ring. She dropped the shotgun as she began to shake even harder, and Smoke realized why—Boyd was coming into the house.

Smoke's instincts took over and he moved without even thinking about what he was doing. He stooped down, scooped up the shotgun from the floor, and aimed the deadly twin barrels toward Boyd. The Greener boomed in Smoke's hands, the thunder deafening in the confined space.

The load of buckshot cut Boyd nearly in half. Blood splattered on the wall and threshold behind him as his body flew backward and then hit the floor. It twitched several times before going completely still.

"What happened?" Carter yelled.

Smoke turned, grabbed the girl, and got her on the floor, his body covering hers, just as a thunderous volley of shots came from outside. Bullets flew through the open door and chewed into the wall. The window fractured into a dozen pieces as bullets came through it. Pictures fell, a piano across the room splintered as small holes appeared, and a vase shattered in half.

Then the shooting stopped and Smoke realized they were reloading. He had to move, and fast.

"Get to that hiding spot!" he yelled, getting off the girl and helping her to her feet. "Stay low. Go! Go!"

She had barely cleared the room when the shooting started again. But instead of running down the hall toward the bedrooms, she ran straight back to the kitchen.

"Oh, no," Smoke said, realizing she was going for the back door.

He put his back to the wall beside the window, switched the shotgun to his left hand, and palmed his Colt. He left the cover long enough to send a few shots outside, but he didn't have time to aim. Maybe that would at least cover the girl's retreat. He just prayed the owlhoots didn't realize she was coming out the back way. If they did, the poor girl would have more trouble than she could handle.

If there had been any chance they weren't going to notice her, she ruined that and made sure they did. She began yelling hysterically the minute her feet hit the patch of dirt just outside the back door. "Pa! Pa! Help me!" The plea sounded like the scream of a wild banshee and Smoke knew the poor girl had lost control. He couldn't blame her.

It was only a matter of time before Carter and the others realized she was outside. There was nothing they could do for Boyd. He wouldn't be chasing that girl, or anyone else, ever again—not that Smoke figured there was much honor among the group. They probably were just fine with Boyd being gone, as they didn't have to cut him in on anything they helped themselves to.

Smoke stayed low as he dashed through the parlor and into the kitchen. He proceeded through the back door cautiously, in time to see Carter ride around the house, coming from Smoke's left.

Carter sent a shot toward Smoke, but he wasn't fast enough. The bullet hammered into the wooden doorjamb just as Smoke jerked back. It had been close, but Smoke was alive and upright, unfazed by the narrow miss.

Carter's luck wasn't as strong. He yanked back hard on the reins, but his horse couldn't slow down in time. He finally came to a halt right in front of the doorway. Carter realized his vulnerability and tried desperately to thumb off another shot.

Smoke was quicker, though. His Colt was holstered now and he held the Greener steady against his shoulder. It bucked once, sending its load up toward Carter.

Carter tried to deflect the oncoming barrage by twisting the reins and spinning his terrified horse, but the gesture was only partially successful. He took a heavy number of pellets in his side, groaning loudly in agony as the metal balls bore into his flesh. Blood started to flow from the tiny holes in his old, faded blue Union Army shirt.

He fell off his horse, but managed to land on his feet and stay upright. He used the mount as cover, sliding his arm around the animal's neck and thumbing off two shots in Smoke's direction.

Smoke had discarded the empty Greener and was now going to work with his Colt. He didn't want to hit the horse. The animal stayed in place, though, being kept there by Carter and the tight grip he had on the reins.

Smoke wondered how long Carter could last. Surely, he'd pass out from the blood loss soon. Smoke couldn't wait him out, though. The girl was somewhere out there, still screaming, with the Cole brothers after her.

Then fortune smiled on Smoke. Behind the horse, Carter shifted, one of his legs now exposed. Smoke dropped to one knee, took aim, and sent a slug into Carter's knee. He howled even louder and dropped the reins as he toppled off his feet. The horse wasted no time getting out of the fracas. It galloped away quickly and out of Smoke's sight.

Carter wasn't dead yet, but he was clearly in agonizing

pain. His leg and side were losing blood at a rapid rate. His eyes rolled back in their sockets, and for a moment, Smoke thought Carter was about to expire, but then he caught a second wind and tried to stagger to his feet.

"I'll . . . kill you," he growled. He was only able to get on his knees, but that was enough for him to raise his arm and draw a bead on Smoke.

Smoke's gun roared twice. Carter fell back, never to move again.

The girl had reached the barn and Smoke caught sight of her just as she disappeared through the open doors. The Cole brothers were off their horses now, giving chase on foot, and right on her heels. Smoke took a few seconds to reload his Colt and then took off after them.

He reached the barn in time to hear the girl plead for mercy. He barreled through the door, but saw only one of the Cole boys with the girl.

He sure felt the other one, though.

A piece of wood crashed into the back of Smoke's skull, sending him to the ground. The barn began to spin. He felt as if he might lose consciousness and yelled at himself— whether aloud or in his head, Smoke didn't know—to fight through it.

White spots dotted his vision. He felt a wave of nausea wash over him. He swallowed hard and stayed still for a moment. Thankfully, the room stopped spinning, but the back of his head hurt real bad. He couldn't worry about that now, though. His life—and, more important, the life of that girl— depended on his ability to stay in the fight.

"Shoot him!" one of the Cole boys yelled at the other.

The clean-shaven one clawed at the gun he wore, but Smoke had his wits about him enough to realize the Coles weren't gunmen. They probably relied on their large frames to intimidate people. They used brute force to get their way. Their gun instincts were awful and they were slower than molasses. That gave Smoke all the time he needed to draw and shoot.

Except . . . where was his gun?

Smoke saw the revolver lying on the hay-strewn floor of the barn and realized he'd dropped it when he took that knock to the head. It was probably six feet away from him and he knew there wasn't time to reach it before Cole put a slug in him.

So, he shifted his focus, surged up onto hands and knees, and launched himself toward his adversary. He wrapped up the man's legs in a diving tackle and knocked him off his feet. Smoke swarmed up the man's body, drove his knees into his chest, and kept him pinned to the dirt floor.

Cole brought his gun up and tried to take aim, but Smoke put both hands on it and wrenched hard. The gun came loose and Smoke held on to the barrel, raising it like a club. He brought the butt down, but Cole jerked his head to the side, avoiding the blow. He twisted his body.

Normally, Smoke would have been able to retain control, but still feeling woozy from the hard blow to the head, he lost his balance and fell on his side. Cole lifted his heavy, booted foot and smashed it down on Smoke's wrist, causing his hand to go slack and release the gun.

Cole picked it up and rose unsteadily on his feet. He was panting as he cocked the hammer. "You betrayed us, you son of a—"

He intended his gun to have the final word, but it only clicked harmlessly on an empty chamber. This only confirmed Smoke's suspicions that the Coles weren't gunfighters.

It also gave him the time he needed to roll to his right, toward a row of stalls, and reach for the pitchfork that rested against a wooden post. He took hold of it and came to his feet, going low as if in a fighter's crouch. Cole was still struggling with his gun, and it evidently wasn't just an empty chamber that had kept it from firing.

The old, rusty weapon was plain broken.

He pitched it aside and growled, lowering his head and charging Smoke like a bull. Smoke had plenty of time to sidestep the attack. But instead of moving completely out of the way, he leaned into the charge, holding tight to the pitchfork and using Cole's momentum against him.

The man screamed as loudly as the girl had earlier as the prongs sliced through his clothes and bore into his skin. The sharp tool drove deep in his chest, causing a wet gurgle that made Smoke wince as blood began to well from Cole's mortal wounds. He staggered back, the wooden handle of the pitchfork protruding straight from his chest. He looked down in a state of disbelief. He opened his mouth to speak, but no sound came forth, only blood. He walked forward and then collapsed.

Smoke hoped the girl hadn't witnessed that, but if she had, at least she was alive. He aimed to keep her that way, too.

The other Cole forgot about the girl and ran toward his brother. "Shane! Shane!"

Oh, so that was his name, Smoke thought.

He didn't have time to think anything else, because the remaining owlhoot was turning his sights on Smoke, and he was beyond enraged.

In a blur of speed, Smoke reached his fallen Colt, brought it up, and triggered a shot. Flame lanced from the gun's muzzle as a slug whipped across the open space. The last outlaw's head snapped back.

He died quickly, pitching backward to land with his arms flung out to the sides. His legs were drawn up crookedly. They didn't even twitch.

Smoke reached the hysterical girl just as the swift rataplan of thundering hooves came from outside the barn.

CHAPTER 18

"You say you're some sort of lawman?" Newt Simmons asked.

He was a trim man, with callused hands and stark lines born of hard times etched into his face. He had dark hair, dark eyes, and a no-nonsense disposition.

Smoke didn't know if that was his normal demeanor or a result of what had taken place. Smoke figured he wouldn't be in a good mood, either, if ruffians had tried to attack his daughter and shot up his home, so he couldn't fault the man.

"Something like that," Smoke said. "I'm working to take down McFadden."

They were standing in the backyard, staying behind the house in case McFadden sent other men to check on the progress of the brutal mission. It had been a few hours since the gang had set off to intimidate the Simmons family, and either McFadden or Taggart was possibly growing concerned by now.

"What if he's one of 'em, Pa?" a teenage boy said.

He was tall and awkward the way boys his age are. He

also seemed angry and eager to prove his mettle, also the way boys that age are so often apt to do.

"I understand why you'd be suspicious," Smoke said. "It's a pretty far-fetched–sounding story, but I'm telling you the truth. Your daughter is safe, isn't she?"

Simmons scratched his jaw as he thought it over. Finally he nodded and said, "I reckon that makes sense."

Smoke looked at the bodies—all four now covered in blankets and lined up beside the barn—and then back at Simmons. "I need to take at least one back. I'll be needing their horses, too."

Simmons nodded. "You don't want to take 'em all?"

"No. Boyd was nearly cut in half by that scattergun. I can't transport him. I'll say the others are in the same condition. I'll take Carter with me and maybe that will suffice." He couldn't very well take one of the Coles. The last thing Smoke wanted to do was explain how he got that pitchfork wound.

"I'll help you bury the others and then I need you all to get out of here. Do you have anywhere you can go?"

The man nodded. "My sister lives just fourteen miles or so north. She'd put us up."

"Do it," Smoke said. "That buys me some time to explain all this. I'll only need a few days. And I appreciate your help and silence on this."

"*You* appreciate *me*?" Simmons said, smiling for the first time since riding in. "Mister, I can't even think about what would have happened, had you not been here. Millie would be—" He choked up a bit and swallowed hard. "Well, I'm forever obliged."

He extended his hand and Smoke shook it.

"We just went to do some work up in the hills," Simmons explained. "Millie stayed here to tend to the household chores and—"

"We best get them buried," Smoke said, cutting the man off. Poor fellow already felt guilty enough for putting his daughter in danger, even though it wasn't his fault. Folks should be safe in their own homes. Of course, with the McFaddens of the world around, things didn't always work out like they should, though.

"We'll handle that," Simmons said. "You get on back to Desolation Creek before McFadden feels the need to send more men. I don't want anyone else poking around out here."

"And you'll hide out at your sister's place until it's all clear?"

"You bet," Simmons said. "Just do me a favor. When the time comes, send word to the Allen home and I'll come running, ready to fight. It's high time we gave that snake, Venom McFadden, what's coming to him."

They gathered the horses, put them on a line, and then hoisted Carter's body over one. He lay across the saddle on his stomach, his arms and legs dangling off either side. With a grim look on his face at the distasteful task, Smoke tied the corpse in place.

Smoke shook Simmons's hand again, smiled at Millie, touched a finger to the brim of his hat, and then mounted Drifter. On the way back to town, he figured out the story he was going to tell.

They had ridden up to the Simmons place to find the man and his sons waiting. They had picked off Boyd, Carter, and the Coles, while Smoke managed to avoid getting ventilated. He'd put a slug in Newt, but left the youngsters alive. Last he saw them, they were all rushing out of there. Smoke stayed around to bury his pards there, since they were so chewed up by the scattergun, except for Carter, and then headed on back to town.

It wasn't a great story, but it was as good as he could come up with. It couldn't be *dis*proven by the evidence left at the little ranch. Not without digging up the carcasses of the dead gun-wolves, anyway.

Smoke wasn't sure what McFadden wanted with that

piece of land. It was nice, sure, but there were plenty more like it around the valley. Maybe he wanted all of them and the Simmons spread was just first on the list. McFadden certainly wouldn't be the first ruthless land baron to terrorize homesteaders.

McFadden might move in on the land and that could complicate things, since it still belonged to Newt Simmons, who was very much alive. Smoke couldn't worry about that, though. Besides, he planned to stop McFadden for good before the crazed outlaw had time to enact any such plans.

And in a way, today's events had turned out to be a blessing rather than a curse.

He'd made a new ally. He'd also taken out four of McFadden's men, thereby whittling down the odds just a bit. Maybe there would be a chance to take out a few more before he worked his way up the chain to McFadden.

Smoke contemplated it all on the ride back to Desolation Creek. He came into town, with the livery stable as the first structure he saw. Audie was standing outside of it, looking the opposite direction intently. Something had captured his interest.

"What is it? A pretty woman?" Smoke asked with a chuckle.

He climbed off Drifter, jerked his thumb over his shoulder to indicate the empty horses and fresh corpse, and then said, "We need to talk."

"I'll say we do!" Audie said, finally turning his head to look at Smoke. He didn't seem the least bit interested in the strange cargo Smoke had led into town. "A stagecoach just arrived. One of the last ones McFadden is allowing in! It's the talk of the town."

"He's shutting down the stage line?"

"That's the rumor."

Smoke shook his head. "He's raising the stakes for some reason. We need to move quickly. We might not have as much time as we thought."

Audie was so upset about something that the need for discretion had slipped his mind. He used his young friend's real name as he began, "Smoke, about that stage—"

Smoke looked around to make sure no one was close enough to hear the conversation, then interrupted, "Audie, something happened out at that homestead."

"Smoke," Audie said slowly, "I'm sure it is engrossing and I look forward to hearing about it. But first, you need to know something. That stage came in."

"Yeah, so you told me," Smoke said with a shrug. "The last one before McFadden shuts down the line. I'm not surprised there's still a crowd hanging around the station."

"You remember asking me if I was enamored by a pretty woman?"

"Yep," Smoke said with a smile.

"Well, there *was* a pretty woman on that stage. Quite beautiful, in fact." Audie still looked halfway stunned. "And her name is Sally Jensen!"

CHAPTER 19

"What?" Smoke said, leaning closer in an instinctive attempt to hear his old friend better.

Surely, he hadn't heard correctly the first time. His ears were playing tricks on him, or maybe he just missed Sally so bad that he was imagining things. Either way, his brain was trying to make him think Sally was close by.

That was the last thing he actually wanted, of course. She didn't need to be in the very spot where all the turmoil was about to begin.

And once Smoke, Audie, and Nighthawk began their assault on Venom McFadden and his hired guns, that's exactly what would happen. Revenge was coming to Desolation Creek.

"I'm afraid it's true," Audie lamented. "The stage arrived in town a short time ago, as I said, and it was Sally who stepped off it. The rumor floating about town is that McFadden allowed one last trip to be made because the stagecoach carried such *beautiful cargo*." His eyes narrowed into a hard stare. "I assume such comments will only earn McFadden a greater portion of your wrath."

Audie was right about that, Smoke thought, though he wasn't sure how much more rage he could muster. He was already a burning inferno just below the surface, especially after hearing Hicks brag about how they had gunned down Preacher in cold blood.

Smoke sighed. "We've got to wrap this thing up quickly. I was already thinking that way, even before Sally showed up. The citizens get more and more afraid of McFadden with each passing day. Soon they won't have any will to fight."

"Do they possess such a will now?" Audie asked. "I've heard rumblings around town, but few are eager to commit to a cause. Not aloud, anyway. This McFadden scoundrel has spies everywhere, it seems."

Smoke suspected that was the case and was eager to wrap up the current conversation for that very reason. He was also eager to talk to Sally and find out just what in the blazes she thought she was doing. Sometimes that woman had a way of driving him plumb loco.

"I think we can get a few people on our side," Smoke said after giving Audie's question some thought. "The newspaper fella seems eager to take a stand. I met a man today who wants to pitch in, and he might just be able to get a few other homesteaders to come along, too."

"It's not an army, but it is a start," Audie said. "Perhaps we can get even more people for the cause. Strengthen our position. As the Bard himself said, 'Robust grass endures mighty winds.' As of now, I fear we are not robust enough."

"Hopefully, in a few more days' time, we can change that," Smoke said.

In his estimation, that still sounded too long, but he needed to be patient and only strike when he'd tipped the odds in their favor.

Smoke left Audie to care for Drifter and then made his way purposefully down Main Street. He couldn't outright run and draw the attention of everyone, but he wasn't able to just casually meander toward the stage, either. The thought of one of McFadden's snakes slithering close to Sally made his blood boil.

The crowd had started to disperse by the time Smoke reached the parked stage. He'd held out hope until the last minute that Audie had made a mistake.

That hope quickly vanished, however, as he stopped a few feet from Sally. He fought hard not to show his reaction to the onlookers . . . not that any of the men were looking at him.

All eyes were on *her*.

And how could they not be, as beautiful as she looked, with her abundant curls and gorgeous dark eyes? Those curls were pinned up in an elaborate arrangement, and a dark red hat with a feather in its band perched on them. She wore a red-and-white–floral print dress, tapered at the waist to show off her figure before spreading out and falling all the way to her ankles.

She was a sight for sore eyes, and had Smoke not been in the middle of dismantling an owlhoot gang, he would have already taken the woman into his arms. It killed him that he couldn't do that now.

It also killed him that McFadden himself was approaching, his serpentine eyes trained on Sally as he bowed slightly.

He's no aristocratic gentleman, Smoke thought. He figured his nostrils were flaring. As angry as he was, he wouldn't have been a bit surprised if steam was billowing from his ears.

"Welcome to Desolation Creek, Miss . . ."

"Miss Jenkins," Sally said. "Sally Jenkins."

Smoke now had to fight a smile. She hadn't changed her name much, but it would do, he supposed.

He inched a bit closer until he could see her left hand. Sure enough, she wasn't wearing her wedding ring. He didn't know if that was good or bad. The sight of it might help keep the men at bay, but it also might ruin whatever role she was playing. He finally decided it was best she hid it. Knowing McFadden and his men, it wouldn't make one bit of difference. Married or not, if they wanted her, they'd come for her.

The mere thought made Smoke want to jerk out his pistol and go to work, right then and there. He could kill McFadden before anyone knew what was going on. He would get a few others, too. But the ones behind him would pose a problem.

And he didn't want lead flying around anywhere in the vicinity of Sally.

No, he had to stick to the plan, even though it wasn't much of a plan yet. He wouldn't settle for only getting a few, even if he could do it and get him and Sally out of there before getting themselves killed.

He wanted the whole gang taken out.

Every last one of them.

Those thoughts flashed through Smoke's mind in a mere couple of heartbeats as he considered his options and decided on his course of action. Meanwhile, in response to McFadden's greeting, Sally went on, "Thank you." She extended her hand and allowed McFadden to kiss the back of it.

Congratulations, McFadden. You just earned an extra bullet right there. Dirty son of a . . .

Smoke pushed the thought down and kept his expression neutral.

"My name is Venom McFadden," the oily man continued.

"Venom?" Sally said with feigned shock, pressing a hand to her chest as her eyes went wide.

Smoke had to hand it to her, she was really selling it.

"A mean-sounding name, I know, but I assure you that I'm quite harmless," McFadden said with a chuckle. "My Christian name is actually Vernon, but my younger brother couldn't say it correctly. He was just a tot, learning to talk, and it always came out *Venom*. The name just sort of stuck."

He shrugged and offered a good-natured yet dishonest smile.

Sally laughed. "I suppose that's a good reason to have such a cruel-sounding name."

"Ma'am, you won't find a cruel bone in my body," McFadden assured her.

Smoke suppressed the urge to roll his eyes and spit in disgust into the dirt at McFadden's feet.

"What brings you to our fair city?" McFadden asked.

A few in the crowd hung around, but most who didn't work for McFadden were eager to get out of there. They no doubt tried to stay out of the man's sight as much as possible—probably out of a sense of self-preservation. A group of gunhands stayed close by, though, obviously eager to gaze upon the pretty woman who had suddenly materialized in their midst. It was evident, though, that none of them were dumb enough to swoop in and try their hand at impressing her. McFadden had first pass at Sally.

Or so he thought.

"Just passing through, really," she said. "Needed a fresh start, if you know what I mean."

"Oh, I do indeed. We all need one from time to time," McFadden said. "How long are you planning to stay?"

"I'm not sure," she said. "I planned on staying a couple of days at least, looking around and seeing if this town suits me." She stopped talking, did her best to look a tad sheepish, and then added, "That is all right, I suppose?"

"Of course, of course," McFadden said, plastering that politician's grin on his face.

"Are you the mayor or something, Mr. McFadden?"

He puffed out his chest slightly.

Oh, she's good, Smoke thought, stifling a grin at the way she was pulling McFadden in like a well-hooked trout.

"No, I am not, but I can see how you might get that impression." He shrugged. "Not a bad idea, actually." He looked at Taggart, who stood nearby, and repeated the word "Mayor."

Taggart nodded.

"Miss Jenkins, I don't mean to presume, but I would like to extend an invitation. I own the Dead Moose Saloon, just down the road there. I own a good deal of this town, in fact. If you're looking for work . . . well, I could find you a position, of course." He smiled and held his palms up, spreading them as if to dismiss any improper notion Sally might get. "I don't mean to presume your occupation, and, of course, I'm only referring to acting as a hostess of sorts. A friendly face to greet all those thirsty customers as they enter."

"Well, thank you, Mr. McFadden," she said. "I will certainly keep that in mind if I decide to stay in Desolation Creek."

"Please, call me Venom," he said, his rakish smile making Smoke momentarily daydream of crashing his gun's butt across the outlaw's skull. "And as you make up your mind, we have plenty of rooms on the top two floors of the Dead Moose. Of course, I don't mean to imply anything improper, Miss Jenkins."

"Of course not," Sally said. "I appreciate your kind offer, but I'll be perfectly comfortable in the hotel tonight. As for tomorrow . . . well, we'll see when the time comes."

McFadden continued to grin as he nodded.

"Yes, we will."

"You left with four men," Taggart said with a grunt. "Yet you rode in alone, unless you count poor Carter. What's going on, West?"

The crowd had dispersed. Sally had sauntered off toward the hotel after briefly locking eyes with Smoke and giving him a slight nod of acknowledgment. No one had seen the small interaction. It had been all Smoke could do not to whisk her away from McFadden and his men, but doing so would have created more problems than he needed.

And, in all likelihood, could have gotten them both killed.

McFadden had disappeared inside the Dead Moose, uninterested in Smoke's presence. Taggart, on the other hand, had wasted no time in approaching. Smoke told him then where to find the riderless mounts and Carter's body. They'd walked down to the livery stable together, and Taggart evidently didn't like what he saw.

"They were waiting for us," Smoke lied.

"Who?"

"That fella you sent us up to see. Think Carter said his name was Simmons or something like that."

Taggart nodded. "That's right. What do you mean he was waiting for you?"

Smoke gave him the rehearsed version of the day's events. He kept his tone flat and emotionless, as a hardcase gunman would. He had no ties to the Coles, Carter, or Boyd. He made it sound as if he was sorry to see them cut down, but wasn't particularly bothered by it.

He wasn't sure if Taggart believed him. Apparently, he wasn't as good an actor as Sally was.

Taggart scratched his jaw. "Pretty lucky for you, huh? You got out of there alive."

Smoke balled his fists and stepped closer. "That wasn't my first shooting scrape, Taggart. If you're saying I had a hand in this, then you—"

"Easy, son," Taggart said.

The comment went all through Smoke, but he let it go without a retort.

"And what did you say happened to Simmons?" Taggart asked after a moment of heavy silence.

"Like I told you, we swapped some lead. I put a bullet in him, I know that. Not sure if he lived or not. Last time I saw him, he and his boys were running into the hills to the west of the house. Probably have a cave up in there they hide in or something."

"More than likely," Taggart said, nodding. "Too bad about

Carter and the others. They were decent hands, although those Cole boys could be a little surly." Taggart shrugged it off. "You know, we might send someone up there to have a look-see. Just to make sure."

"Have at it," Smoke said. "It's like I told you."

"I'm sure it is," Taggart said. He thought for a moment and then continued, "Just don't go leaving town or nothing. Mr. McFadden might want to talk with you."

"I aim to stick around."

"Now that we're down four men, there's a bigger piece of the pie to be had."

A cruel smile curved Smoke's lips. He nodded and turned away, dismissive of Taggart, who snorted as if he didn't like Smoke's attitude—but wasn't going to do anything about it.

Now that McFadden was down four men, Smoke mused, the odds were actually a mite closer to even.

He was keeping his eyes open, too. Before sundown tomorrow, he was hoping he could whittle down the odds a little more.

He had a feeling that time was running out. They needed to strike quickly.

But first, he needed to see a lady at the hotel.

The beautiful Miss Sally *Jenkins*.

CHAPTER 20

S moke was almost to the hotel when a figure stepped off
the boardwalk and approached him. His hand instinctively fell to the butt of his gun and remained there even
after realizing it was Hodges, the old miner he'd encountered when he first rode into Desolation Creek. He hadn't
seen him since that day in the Absaroka Saloon.

Smoke didn't think the old-timer would draw on him—
and didn't want to shoot him even if he did—but he couldn't
just stand there and let himself get ventilated, either. He was
walking a fine line. Working for McFadden—or *pretending*
to—put a target on his back if folks got fed up enough to act.
That was just another reason why he needed to move things
along and make a move against the outlaws. This double life
was wearing thin already, and Smoke needed to settle the
score for Preacher before something else tragic happened.
He didn't blame the folks of Desolation Creek for being
angry, that was for sure.

And it was evident the crusty old man was angry.

"Easy there, boy, you gonna shoot me like you've done
others?" Hodges glared at Smoke, practically spitting the

words out. Obvious contempt twisted his weathered, lined face.

"I haven't killed anyone," Smoke said. "Not in Desolation Creek."

That was technically true, Smoke thought. He'd killed four men just that day, but that had happened outside of town. He just hoped that little incident wouldn't come back to haunt him.

He studied the old man for a moment and then relaxed a bit. Hodges wasn't armed, as far as Smoke could see. Of course, he might have a gun tucked away somewhere, but Smoke doubted there was any real danger.

"What about homesteaders?" Hodges said. "You ain't shot anyone in town, but that don't mean you didn't plug some poor family just tryin' to make a livin'. Or did you burn them out?"

Smoke wanted to tell the man that all was not as it appeared. Maybe he could even recruit him to the cause. The miner clearly had starch in his britches, confronting a hired gun like this right in the street where McFadden or his men could see it. Smoke liked Hodges's grit.

Then another thought suddenly occurred to Smoke—word must have gotten around that McFadden was intimidating homesteaders up north of town. Maybe Hodges knew something about why McFadden wanted that land. He'd have to look into that later. Right now, he had to maintain his false identity, end this encounter quickly, and get on up to the hotel to see Sally. As much as he hated treating the old man so harshly, Smoke knew that a hardened outlaw would do such a thing. Right now, Smoke had to be Buck West.

"What I do for Mr. McFadden is none of your concern," Smoke growled.

"So, there it is," Hodges said, shaking his head. "I wanted to hear it for myself. Confirm the word that's going around. Thank you for that at least." He shook his head ruefully. "Can't believe you're working for that low-down, dirty skunk. When I talked to you in the Absaroka, I thought there was something different about you. Guess it goes to show a feller never knows." He turned and walked away, still muttering to himself.

Smoke filed the information away to use later and marched into the hotel. Once inside the lobby, he was glad to see the clerk was not behind the desk. That freed Smoke up to have a look at the registry book, which lay atop the polished wood. He marched across the lobby, as if he owned the place, and grabbed the book, as if he had every right to view it.

Just like Buck West would.

Sally Jenkins was the last guest to sign the register. He took note of the room number, thankful it was only one door down from his, and then put the book back the way he'd found it. He walked up the stairs and strolled casually to his room. He couldn't discount the notion that McFadden might have posted men around the hotel to keep watch on the beautiful stranger. He also couldn't discount the notion that McFadden might send his gun-wolves to burst in at any moment and take Sally by force, insisting she stay at the Dead Moose.

They'd try, anyway. Smoke would never let that happen, even if it meant revealing his true identity. Thankfully, though, it appeared that the hallway was empty.

He went to his room first, resisting the urge to rush to Sally.

He looked around and made sure everything was undisturbed. Best he could tell, no one had been in the place since he'd left that morning.

He took a few minutes to pour some water in the washbasin and scrubbed trail dust and grime off his face. Smoke wouldn't have been surprised if a few specks of blood were mixed in with the soiled water as well. He felt better after cleaning up.

It was time now.

He opened his door slowly, moved to the side, and cautiously poked his head around the jamb to check one direction. He then shifted his body and checked the other.

No one.

He didn't think McFadden would try anything against him tonight. McFadden couldn't be sure that he wasn't telling the truth about what had happened out at the Simmons ranch. Smoke was sure Taggart would have filled him in on that by now.

But he couldn't guarantee McFadden wouldn't make a move. Letting his guard down might mean death and he would not leave this world before dispensing justice on Preacher's behalf.

He sure wouldn't exit the world—leaving Sally at the mercy of Venom McFadden.

Confident that no one was lurking in the hallway, Smoke took a couple of long strides to Sally's room and rapped his knuckles gently against the door.

She must have been waiting for him. She opened the door quickly and stepped aside. He moved in, shut the door quietly behind him, and then took her in his arms.

The two hugged for a long moment, swaying slightly, Smoke kissing the top of her head and breathing in the scent of her hair. She lifted her head and he pressed his lips against hers. The kiss was long and deep, leaving them both breathless. He pulled away enough to say, "I've missed you."

"Oh, Smoke. I've missed you, too. So much."

They kissed again. Smoke gave her one more peck atop the head and then said, "Okay, now that that's out of the way . . . what on earth are you doing here?"

She stepped back a few paces, offered a cute smile, and shrugged.

"Try again," he said.

"I just missed you so much, Smoke. I couldn't stand another moment away from you!"

A half smile tugged at his lips. "Sure. Try again."

She blew out a lungful of air and then waved him off.

"Fine. I'm mad! You rode away without giving me a chance to come with you. I want justice for Preacher just as much as you do! I didn't appreciate being cut out of the deal."

Smoke chuckled. "That's more like it. That's the Sally Jensen I know. Nice touch with the Jenkins, by the way."

"You like that?"

"Not at all," he admitted. "What I'd like is for you to be back on the Sugarloaf with Pearlie. This is a dangerous situation, Sally. You shouldn't be here."

"I've been in dangerous situations before," she reminded him. "Besides, I might be of some use. I can get a job at that saloon and—"

"I don't think so," Smoke said, shaking his head. "Absolutely not."

"So, what? I'm just supposed to jump on the next stage out of town?"

Smoke gave the question some consideration and then said, "That's what I'd like, yes, but we have a problem."

"What's that?"

"Rumor around town is that McFadden is shutting the stage line down. No one in or out," Smoke said. "Afraid your only option is to stay here." He gave it some more thought and then said, "Reckon the safest place for you to be is with me, anyway."

She nodded. "I agree."

Smoke shook his head again before leveling a finger at Sally. "You are trouble. Nothing but trouble."

"I can't deny it," she said.

She rushed into his arms again. As irritated as Smoke was, he couldn't resist her, and returned her embrace.

"So, what do we do next?" Sally asked after the hug had ended.

Smoke gave her a pointed stare. "*We* don't do anything. Audie, Nighthawk, and I will figure it out. You're going to stay safe and out of harm's way. Stay in your room as much as possible. Time your meals in the dining room for when

I'm in there. We can't exactly sit at the same table, but I can at least keep an eye on you and make sure you're safe. Under no circumstances are you to poke around McFadden or his men."

"Yeah, I wasn't supposed to leave the Sugarloaf, either, and we see how well I listened."

Smoke opened his mouth to respond, but closed it and only offered a headshake. No sense in arguing with her. Sometimes he thought that only fed her need for trouble.

"If I don't go to the saloon—at least to look at the job firsthand—McFadden might get awfully suspicious," she said. "This way, I can at least do it all on my terms, instead of waiting on his men to burst in here, throw me over one of their shoulders, and haul me to the Dead Moose!"

Smoke couldn't argue that point, actually. It made the most sense. He'd prefer Sally was at home on the Sugarloaf, tending to the ranch with Pearlie, but nothing could be done about that now. He had to play the hand that was dealt to him.

The dealer was just lucky she was so blasted pretty. He couldn't be mad at her even when she dealt lousy cards!

"Tomorrow," he said. "Maybe you'll learn something valuable we can use when the time comes."

"The time to move against McFadden?" Sally said.

"Exactly."

"And when will that time come?"

Smoke shrugged. "We're still working on that. All the pieces aren't in place, but I think they're coming together. Until then, you and I both just need to lay as low as possible and stay out of trouble."

Upon further reflection, though, Smoke wasn't sure that was possible. He wasn't convinced Sally could stay out of trouble.

And come to think of it, neither could he.

CHAPTER 21

Smoke awoke the next morning with a feeling of uneasiness swirling in his stomach.

Perhaps it was that Sally was so close, yet not in his arms. Or it could be that a low-down, mean-as-a-snake varmint had leered at her the day before, with clear intentions of getting to her. Of course, it might be that Smoke had ridden into town with Audie and Nighthawk, intent on dispensing justice in Preacher's name, but did not seem any closer to their goal than when they'd arrived.

He was ready for action, that was sure. It felt as if he needed to move quickly. He had already been feeling that call, but Sally's unexpected arrival had certainly increased it. Who knew what the day held, he thought as he stepped out of bed and stretched. Maybe today would finally bring the event that would tip the scales in their favor. He assumed Audie and Nighthawk were just as ready as he was.

He cleaned up, got into his clothes, and checked his gun before buckling the belt around his hips. He waited until the time he had agreed on with Sally, then strolled downstairs and into the dining room.

Sure enough, she was already there, sitting at a table beside the window, a teacup in her hand as she peered outside. She felt his presence and turned her head to smile and nod at him, but then turned her attention once again to the window. Her polite greeting was the sort she would have given any stranger and held no real indication that they were acquainted.

More than acquainted, if you wanted to get right down to it.

With a little bit of luck, and the Good Lord on their side, they'd be back at the Sugarloaf soon enough, with all this mess behind them.

The serving girl dropped by Smoke's table, not even asking what he wanted, simply bringing a cup of steaming hot coffee and a plate of eggs, potatoes, bacon, and a biscuit. He nodded and took a sip of the coffee without saying a word. He wondered what Sally thought of his rudeness. Surely, she understood.

She also probably realized why the girl was nervous in Smoke's presence. It was only natural, after all, to behave that way around killers.

And while Smoke couldn't deny the fact he was a killer, he certainly wasn't one in the vein the town had him pegged for. Soon enough, they'd see the truth for themselves. If things went as planned, he'd go from villain to hero, but he didn't care about that. This was all about justice.

Preacher would be avenged.

Smoke ate his meal uninterrupted, except for the refill on his coffee. When he was finished, he stood, grabbed his hat, and casually walked out of the dining room, but not without one last look at Sally.

Nothing suspicious about that, he told himself. She was pretty enough that *any* man would look at her whenever he got the chance.

He took his time walking to the Dead Moose. Folks gave him a wide berth, though something seemed a bit different than his earlier encounters with them. Was it just his imagination or were there more whispers? It was almost as if something was in the air. A tension brewing.

Smoke made a mental note to check on that later. It wasn't necessarily anything tangible, rather just something he noticed in a few folks' eyes. He was careful to watch his back. He couldn't rule out the notion that someone—maybe Darnell Poe—had it in mind to ambush a few of McFadden's men. And as far as the townspeople were concerned, he was a member in good standing of that vicious gang.

Smoke realized he had a lot to watch out for that day. He didn't want to be ambushed, no matter how well-meaning the citizens of Desolation Creek were. He needed to be on alert for any opportunity to swing the odds in his favor. And now, he had to make sure Sally was protected.

She was going to see McFadden about that job today and the thought of her even stepping foot in the Dead Moose didn't sit well with Smoke. Sally wasn't some prim-and-proper, dainty woman who was offended at the presence of whiskey. Heck, she was probably tougher than a good number of the men in that saloon.

No, he was bothered that she'd be so close to McFadden. He was as dangerous a man as Smoke had ever encountered. He claimed the job was merely as a hostess—Sally walking around to catch the attention of the cowboys and other patrons, freshening up drinks, and just being present and pretty. Smoke didn't particularly like that, but given the circumstances, Sally was right. It might be helpful to have someone like her on the inside. Nighthawk was already there, but the more eyes and ears they had in that place, the better.

What bothered Smoke was the idea that McFadden might have *other notions* regarding her employment. He might also think he was entitled to certain *privileges*.

Smoke's nerves were drawn tight by the time he arrived at the Dead Moose. He did his best not to show it, but the situation only got worse when he learned what his assignment was for the day.

"Collections," Taggart said. "Think you can handle that without getting everyone around you shot up?"

The man was clearly still annoyed by the events of the day before. Smoke wouldn't be a bit surprised to learn Taggart had sent someone out to the homestead to verify his story. Let them, he thought. They wouldn't find much to disprove it.

Smoke glared at him, the way arrogant Buck West would. "I gave as good as we got yesterday. Maybe if you hired more capable men, this wouldn't be an issue."

Taggart's back stiffened at the comment, but he finally waved off the suggestion. "Easy, son. Don't take it personally. I'm sending two men along with you, but you shouldn't run into any trouble. Folks around here will pretty much do whatever we tell them to." He chuckled at the callous comment.

Smoke didn't.

He was relieved that neither of the two men picked to work with him was Hicks.

"This is Chip Dover and Don Haines," Taggart said as two men stood from a nearby table, pointing to each of them in turn as he stated their names.

Chip was the taller of the two, but Haines was broader. Both looked as if they'd lived rough lives, with angry eyes and scars on their faces. Haines had a pocked face and a slash beneath his left eye. He reminded Smoke of a bulldog used for fights. Dover, on the other hand, seemed a tad different, as if his eyes didn't miss a thing. He appeared cold and calculating, so Smoke wasn't surprised when Taggart continued, "You're running today's show, West, but don't go getting any ideas about your place in this organization. You're still the low man around here. They're going to keep a watchful eye and report back to me."

"This an audition?" Smoke said.

"Something like that," Taggart agreed. "You still need to prove yourself."

Smoke almost smiled. So, that was it, huh? He was on probation after yesterday's events out at the homestead.

"So, go on," Taggart said. "Go get what the boss likes best. Money."

The morning passed slowly and Smoke hated each stop worse than the previous one. He was tired of playing the villain, sick of people practically cowering in fear when he entered a room. Of course, under the circumstances, he couldn't blame them. They worked hard for their money and there he was, taking it by force to give it to an arrogant, evil man who thought he was entitled to whatever he wanted on the earth.

It made Smoke plain sick.

When he arrived back at the Dead Moose, he was tired of feeling that way.

"You get it?" Taggart asked, standing up from the usual back table he occupied and shuffling his boots across the hardwood floor.

Smoke tossed the sack a few feet, Taggart reaching up and snatching it from the air. He jingled it, then frowned and cocked his head to the side as he asked, "Is it light?"

"It's all there," Smoke said.

"Easy, son. Just joshing with you."

Smoke thought about pointing out that he hadn't reacted to the initial comment, but let it pass. He was sick of dealing with the likes of Taggart.

"There any trouble?" Taggart asked Dover and Haines.

"Nah," Haines said with a nasally voice. Smoke assumed he spoke that way because his nose had clearly been broken multiple times. It was as crooked as could be. "Ain't nobody gonna say anything to us."

"I hope you're right," Taggart said. "I'm not so sure now."

Smoke wondered what that little comment meant, but

didn't have time to ponder it further. He was taken aback when he spotted movement in the back of the room.

Sally.

She was emerging from a room in the rear of the saloon, past the gambling tables, and she looked stunning.

A little too stunning.

The dress she wore was a bright red. The plunging décolletage would certainly grab any man's attention, and her pushed-together, bolstered bosom would only add to their lust. Smoke tried hard not to react, but he figured every other man would react the same way, so it didn't really matter. He quickly recovered, but Taggart had seen his look and turned around.

"Dress fit okay?" he drawled in his usually gruff manner.

"Yes, Mr. Taggart."

"I'll say it does."

Those words came from Hicks, who had just sauntered through the batwing doors. Smoke's hand fell close to his gun, just in case.

He didn't like any man leering at Sally in such a way. He downright hated it with Hicks.

"I'm going to go to the bank, count this money, and get it stashed away," Taggart said. He raised his voice. "Miss Jenkins is only to look at, boys. Am I clear?"

Haines, Dover, and Hicks all nodded.

"West?" Taggart said. "Am I clear?"

Smoke managed a nod and kept his face passive, as if he didn't have a care in the world and none of this meant a darn thing to him.

"Good," Taggart said. "When I get back, we'll talk about tonight. In the meantime, you boys get yourselves a drink. I'd say you've earned it."

Despite not having lifted a finger that morning that Smoke knew of, Hicks included himself in the offer of a free drink. He sat with Haines and Dover at a table while the barkeep brought over three glasses and a bottle. Smoke bellied up to the bar and leaned against it, occupying the back, side position he preferred, which gave him a good view of the whole room, save for the gambling tables and that door Sally had emerged from. He'd look back there occasionally, too, although he wasn't really expecting trouble.

But as it so often did, trouble found him, anyway.

Twenty minutes had passed, with Hicks making comments here and there to Sally, who lingered near the bar. She wasn't close to Smoke, but she was close enough in case trouble came.

She's probably watching out for me, Smoke thought, *while I think I'm watching out for her.*

They both let Hicks's comments roll off their backs, but soon the arrogant gunman would not be denied. He stood up and carried his glass with him, not at all unsteady on his feet—despite downing half a bottle of the amber liquid.

"Honey, don't you play hard to get with me. I saw the way you looked at me when I walked in."

The glass clanked loudly against the bar's top as he practically dropped it down. A drop of whiskey sloshed over the side. He smiled playfully as he moved his fingers to it, flicking it at Sally.

She laughed slightly, but wasn't overfriendly.

"What's the matter, darlin'? You don't want to have a drink with me?"

"I need to stay sober," Sally said with a smile. "I have a long night ahead."

"I'll say you do," Hicks said. "Long night ahead with me. Ain't that right, boys?"

Haines and Dover cackled right on cue.

"That's right, Hicks," Haines said. He raised his glass in a toast.

Smoke studied Sally and saw that her breathing pattern changed slightly. She was getting nervous.

Smoke was just getting angry.

"Leave her alone, Hicks," Smoke said, never even shifting his eyes to the other man. He lifted the beer he'd been slowly nursing and sucked in a small drink.

"What was that?" Hicks said, pushing off the bar and walking toward Smoke with his chest puffed out.

"You heard me," Smoke said, not bothering to hide the annoyance in his voice. It felt good not to be acting for once. He'd done so much of it since arriving in Desolation Creek that he felt like one of those thespians Audie always talked about, except Smoke's part hadn't been anywhere near as elegant as something Shakespeare created.

"You know, West, you've been giving orders since you rode into this town and I don't like it. I get the impression you don't know your place." He stepped closer, keeping his eyes trained on Smoke. "Maybe I oughta teach you."

Smoke let go of the beer, leaving it on the bar, and turned around, finally looking at Hicks.

"You heard Taggart," he said. "Hands off the lady."

"Oh, that's what this is about?" Hicks asked. "You're following orders? Were you following orders yesterday when you got four good men killed?"

Obviously, Hicks and Smoke had drastically different definitions for the word "good," but Smoke didn't bring that up.

"We rode into an ambush, plain and simple. I tried to save 'em, but . . ." Smoke shrugged.

"Kinda funny, you ask me. They're all dead, but you"— Hicks poked Smoke in the chest—"made it back just fine."

It took every ounce of willpower Smoke possessed not to grab the man's hand and twist it until his wrist snapped. Might be best if he did, Smoke thought, as it would take Hicks's gun hand out of commission. Starting a fight might draw the ire of Taggart and ultimately McFadden, though. Smoke wasn't anywhere close to being afraid of the men. He needed to stay inside the gang, though, as it would be easier to tip the odds in his favor that way. He could do more good by remaining in the inner circle.

It looked as if Hicks might not give him that choice. His

eyes were burning with fury. He'd been looking for a reason to go after Smoke, and now with Taggart gone, he'd found one.

"Those men were my friends," Hicks said.

Chairs scraped loudly on the floor as Haines and Dover stood up. They stepped closer, but stayed behind Hicks. From the corner of his eye, Smoke could tell Sally was bracing herself for what was coming.

Tension and the threat of violence hung heavy in the air. Smoke had been in enough fights to know he was about to be in another.

"They were my friends," Hicks repeated. "And you just left them there to die."

He was fast, but Smoke was still a mite quicker. With his left hand, he managed to block the punch that Hicks threw just before it crashed into his nose. Hicks was temporarily stunned, shocked someone could match his speed. He wouldn't let that throw him off for very long, though, so Smoke had to act swiftly. He jabbed his right fist into Hicks's gut, causing the man to double over, and giving time for Smoke to send another fist crashing into his face.

Hicks was down and writhing on the floor, but the display of fury wasn't deterring Haines and Dover. They charged Smoke, Haines hitting him first and wrapping him up in a diving tackle. Smoke landed flat on his back, the bulldog of a man on top of him, pinning him to the ground. Dover was coming, too, intent on kicking at Smoke while Haines kept him on the floor.

Desperate to gain the upper hand, Smoke brought his leg up until his knee rammed hard into Haines's groin. The ox was tough enough to absorb the first blow, though the pain registered in his eyes as he gasped. He shifted his weight, letting a little pressure off Smoke, but he was still on top of him. Smoke followed it up with a second blow. He watched as Haines's eyes rolled up in their sockets. The man's face turned green and he pitched to one side. Smoke eagerly shook free and came up on his knees just as Dover launched the first kick.

Smoke grabbed his foot. Dover danced about on the other one, unstable and out of control, before Smoke twisted hard. Bone crackled loudly and Dover howled in pain as Smoke released his hold.

Dover staggered back a few paces before crumpling to the floor.

The fight wasn't over yet. Hicks rose and spit blood, huffing and puffing as his hawkish eyes zeroed in on Smoke. He went into a fighter's stance, bobbing and weaving as he sidestepped, all while glaring at Smoke. He sent a right toward Smoke.

Smoke could have easily dodged the punch, but he knew that's what Hicks was expecting. Smoke didn't take the bait. Instead, he leaned into it, but lowered himself, taking the hit on his shoulder. It didn't have much impact. The uppercut Smoke drove into Hicks's chin did, however.

The owlhoot's head snapped back, but he didn't go down. Instead, he charged at Smoke like an enraged bear, roaring in anger as he approached. He was in a wild frenzy, which gave Smoke even more of an advantage. He stepped aside, grabbed Hicks by the hair, and sent him crashing into the side of the bar. His body jerked as his head hit the hardwood. He fell to the floor with a heavy thud.

Haines, Dover, and Hicks were all down, but it looked as if the fight was just getting started. By now, five other men were rushing into the Dead Moose, evidently having seen parts of the scuffle through the bottom or top gap of the batwing doors.

I should have known, Smoke thought. *There's always gunhands loafing around outside.* They were eager to back Hicks's play, too, having known him far longer than they'd known Smoke.

One rushed past Sally in an attempt to get to Smoke. He didn't make it very far. The woman snatched off his hat and then raised her arm. She nodded in satisfaction as the bottle she'd snatched off the bar shattered on the side of his head. He stayed on his feet long enough to flash a shocked expression at her, but then it was lights out. His knees gave out and he fell to the floor as a trickle of blood ran down his forehead and into his left eye.

That left four for Smoke to deal with.

And one had a knife.

"That's not good," Smoke said aloud. He backed up a few paces, but remained in a fighting stance. "I don't suppose you want to put that knife down, huh?"

"Nope," the hard case said.

"I can't appeal to your gentlemanly nature?" Smoke said.

"Oh, no." The man spat a strand of brown juice from his bulging cheek.

"Aren't there rules?" Smoke implored.

"In this fight? Ain't no stinkin' rules!"

"Well, I tried." Smoke didn't say another word, instead drawing his Colt and cocking it.

"Hey, I ain't got no gun!" the man said, stopping dead in his tracks and looking slightly sick as he gulped, accidentally swallowing part of the tobacco he'd had plugged in his cheek.

"No rules, remember?"

"Get him!" one of the other men shouted.

They all drew their guns and Smoke realized it was about to turn into a gunfight when a thunderous boom interrupted the proceedings. The glasses and bottles behind the bar rattled. A picture on the wall shook. Acrid smoke clouded the air, causing a haze to settle in. One of the men erupted into a coughing fit. The others all turned to see the source of the sudden eruption.

Nighthawk thudded loudly down the stairs. The double-barreled shotgun looked tiny in his enormous hands. The boom still echoed off the walls.

"Umm," he declared as he glared at the combatants.

"We better do what he says and stop this ruckus, boys," Smoke said. "I think he means it."

The others looked confused, but no one dared turn their anger on Nighthawk. Even Smoke had to admit the giant Indian looked intimidating as he stepped off the bottom stair. He still towered above them all, even though he was now on level ground.

One fella coughed, looked around, and then tried to stand straighter. "I don't take orders from no Injun."

"Umm."

The man looked puzzled at Nighthawk and then at Smoke.

"Today," Smoke said, "I think we all take orders from an Injun."

The man gulped and dipped his head slightly.

Smoke caught the brief tug of Nighthawk's lips and knew the Crow warrior was finding the scene quite amusing. Taggart sure didn't when he arrived a few seconds later.

"What in blazes is going on here?" he yelled.

By now, Hicks was scrambling to find his footing as he pulled himself off the floor. He let out a lungful of air and then groaned. He was still wobbly as he stepped toward Taggart.

"It's West!" he said, his voice sounding stronger than his body looked at the moment. "He went plain loco and attacked us."

"That isn't so," Sally said.

All eyes turned to her.

Smoke kept his gun hand free and ready just in case. He noticed Nighthawk preparing for battle, too, shifting the shotgun in his hands in case he needed to bring the barrels up quickly. He still had one load in there, and at that range, it would take out two or three men.

"Oh, is that so?" Taggart said.

"As a matter of fact, it is. He"—she leveled a harsh glare at Hicks, then looked back to Taggart—"was about to put his hands on me. Mr. West stepped in and stopped him. Then the others attacked Mr. West."

Taggart studied her a moment before turning his gaze to Hicks and then Smoke. "You some kind of knight in shining armor, West? You stick up for women, do you?"

Smoke didn't answer the question directly. Instead, he said, "You told us she was off limits. Simple as that."

"You always follow orders?" Taggart said.

Smoke shrugged. "Let me make it simple, Taggart. I like money. McFadden has money. I stay in good with him, I make money. Pretty easy, really."

Taggart smiled. "I can respect that." He looked at Hicks and sighed. "Boy, sometimes I swear you don't have a lick of sense. You're fast on the draw, but you don't have the brains to go along with it. Let me make this clear." He stepped even closer, leveling a finger at Hicks and raising his voice as he continued, "The boss has his sights on this woman and that means she's off limits to the likes of you and me. You understand that?"

Hicks was clearly incensed over the public dressing-down, but he didn't overreact. Instead, he said, "Sure. Whatever you say, Taggart. Just keep West away from me until we can settle this. Then we'll see just how fast I am."

He stomped off through the batwing doors without another word.

Smoke was glad to see him go, but he knew the fight had only made things worse. Now he'd have to watch his back even more closely.

"All of you simmer down," Taggart said to the men. "Get a drink. Play some cards. Just do something until Mr. McFadden needs us." He shook his head with another exasperated sigh and muttered, "I swear, sometimes it's like raising kids."

He came up beside Smoke and continued in a lower tone, "Go on back to the hotel and stay out of sight for a while. Let Hicks settle down."

"I'm not afraid of him," Smoke said, thinking of how an outlaw like Buck West would respond.

"I don't care about that," Taggart said, his cadence hardening. "The boss has plans for both of you. And after we lost four men yesterday, well, I don't need you two killing each other. Now do as I told you. I appreciate you stepping in and stopping Hicks. I reckon you've earned a day of loafing."

Smoke nodded and started to walk off, not thrilled to be leaving Sally behind. At least Nighthawk was there. Thankfully, fate smiled upon him when Taggart said, "Hold up."

Smoke stopped and turned to face the man.

"Miss Jenkins isn't really needed until business picks up tonight, and I think it would be best to keep her out of sight for a while and let all these men settle down. Walk her to the hotel with you. But don't you dare get any notions about moving in on her. You got that, West?"

"Of course," Smoke said. He looked at Sally. "Miss Jenkins?"

She had been standing close enough to hear the conversation. She nodded and hurried past Taggart. Once both of their backs were to the others, Smoke and Sally smiled.

Well, that had worked out quite nicely indeed.

CHAPTER 22

"I heard something you might find interesting."

Sally was talking quietly from the side of her mouth as she and Smoke walked to the hotel.

Smoke kept his eyes peeled for Hicks or any of his cronies. Thankfully, they reached the hotel without incident and quickly ducked inside. They were on the second floor when Sally finally elaborated.

"I overheard Taggart and McFadden talking," she said. "They're worried the town is going to rebel. Evidently, that newspaperman is really stirring things up."

"Did they say when?" Smoke asked.

They stopped in front of Sally's door. She opened it and Smoke looked inside, making sure no one was waiting for her. It was clear.

"As far as I could tell, they don't know, but they think soon. They were talking about sending you, Hicks, and the others out to make a show of force. They want folks afraid. Smoke, I'm afraid something terrible is about to happen."

Even as low as she was keeping her voice, Smoke could hear the worry that infused her words.

"I know," he said. "Me too."

"When are you going to . . ."

Smoke looked up and down the hallway in both directions and then whispered, "Tomorrow at the latest. I need to meet with Audie and Nighthawk. I'll be doing that later today."

He wanted to kiss her, but knew it wasn't wise. Their conversation could have been innocent, but a kiss definitely wouldn't be. While Smoke didn't see anyone lurking about, it wasn't out of the realm of possibility that they were being watched right now. McFadden was a paranoid man who retained power by controlling every element of his environment that he could. He could have any number of people working for him, doing his bidding.

"Good night, Mr. West," Sally said with a sly half smile.

"Good night," he said, tipping his hat.

It took every ounce of strength he had to turn around and leave her in that room, but he did so, knowing she would be relatively safe stashed away there in the hotel. He was pondering if hardened outlaws who work for low-down, dirty skunks would tip their hats to a lady when he heard heavy footsteps coming up the stairs.

He moved quickly to the other side of the hall and poised his hand over his gun. A moment later, he saw a long shadow cast on the floor at the top of the stairs just before the large frame of Taggart climbed into view. It took Taggart a moment to realize he was being watched.

"Easy there, West. I'm just coming to let you know the boss wants to see you."

Smoke stood. "Nothing personal. After that little scrape with Hicks—"

"I understand," Taggart said, a wry grin parting his lips. "You ain't dumb, that's for sure. I suspect Hicks is so spittin' mad at you that he would ambush you, if it wouldn't get him in trouble with Mr. McFadden."

"You're probably right."

"He might do it, at that," Taggart continued. "But not to-night. Mr. McFadden needs every man he can get."

"Thought I had the night off."

This seemed to anger Taggart as he stiffened a bit and scowled. "Plans changed. You're wanted back at the Dead Moose and I suggest you don't keep the boss waiting."

"I'm coming," Smoke said.

He followed Taggart down the stairs and into the hotel lobby. Two guests were there, chatting with the clerk behind the counter, then falling silent the minute they saw Taggart and Smoke.

Smoke wondered what was going on. Was something brewing in Desolation Creek? He thought of Sally upstairs and prayed she would stay there. It was the safest thing she could do, but that didn't always mean anything with her. If Smoke knew that woman—and he sure did—she would be right in the middle of whatever trouble erupted.

If trouble erupted.

As of now, he was hoping it would not. His gut told him that it wouldn't be a quiet night, though.

Smoke studied the faces he saw in the street. There were people out and about, going on with their normal business, but most averted their eyes.

A few ducked into doorways, while some turned their backs and continued their conversations. Smoke had no idea what they were talking about. Maybe Taggart's and McFadden's paranoia was rubbing off on him, he thought.

They reached the Dead Moose, where the throng of assembled gunhands was even bigger than it usually was. Men stood on the porch, leaning on the rails, while others took spots on the two loafer's benches that were positioned on either side of the angled door. They all gave Smoke hard stares as he walked up the steps and followed Taggart through the swinging doors. Smoke had to smile. By now, they'd all heard of the fight between him and Hicks.

Thinking of Hicks, Smoke swept the room with his eyes, but didn't see him. No one else was in the saloon, except for McFadden and the barkeep.

McFadden sat at the table usually occupied by Taggart and leaned back as Smoke approached. Taggart took one of the other chairs to his boss's side. Smoke wasn't offered a seat. Why give such a courtesy to a mere hired hand?

"I heard you had a little boxing match in my saloon earlier," McFadden said. His voice was neither angry nor jovial. His face was just as impassive.

"Is that what this is about?" Smoke said. "Getting onto me like a child for causing a ruckus?"

"Easy, West," Taggart snorted.

McFadden chuckled. "I don't care, but I do hope Hicks isn't busted up too badly. I think we'll need him. Sooner rather than later."

"Something going on around town?"

"We'll get to that," McFadden said. "Right now, though, I want to be crystal clear on something." He leaned in, resting his palms on the tabletop and sending a very pointed stare toward Smoke. Once their eyes were locked, he said, "Whatever animosity exists between you and Hicks will just have to wait. If you two want to shoot each other, then have at it, but only when I'm done with you. I thought we were clear on this, but it apparently bears repeating."

"I didn't shoot him," Smoke said. "Just gave him a good walloping."

"West, how many times have I gotta tell you to watch your tone with Mr. McFadden?" Taggart said.

"It's fine," McFadden said. "It's fine. I'm just trying to figure out if I can trust you to do what you're told, West."

"I've done everything you've asked of me so far," Smoke pointed out. "I'm not interested in your plans, but I am interested in your wages. As long as the money keeps coming, I keep working."

McFadden nodded as he leaned back once again. "I can respect that." He looked to Taggart and jerked his head in the direction of Smoke.

On cue, Taggart fished a small bag from his vest pocket and tossed it toward Smoke, who caught it one-handed. He smiled as he looked down, bouncing the bag, listening to the jingle. "Much obliged."

He pocketed the cash and then waited. McFadden continued a few seconds later. "Something is going on here in town. I want you on patrol tonight."

"Anywhere in particular?" Smoke asked.

"Just make yourself visible. *Very visible*, if you know what I mean. I don't think this town is stupid enough to try anything, but I'm hearing rumors that Darnell Poe is stirring things up even more so than before. We might need to remind them who runs things around here."

"You want me to make an example of anyone?" Smoke asked. He needed to know where McFadden's mind was and just how far he was willing to go tonight.

McFadden shrugged. "If it comes to that."

Smoke fought hard to restrain his anger. He needed more information and flying off the handle wouldn't help matters any. He asked bluntly, "You want me to take out Poe?"

"Absolutely not," McFadden said, his voice rising slightly. He gave himself a moment to regain his composure. "I still want a newspaperman on my side. He's no good to me dead. Who knows how long it would take to bring in someone else who knows about the printing and all that? No, make sure Poe stays upright. Knock him around if you have to, but no guns."

McFadden steepled his fingers in front of his face and went on speaking. "Not with him, anyway. Some of the others, well, as long as it isn't that pretty little gal who came in on the stage, I'm just fine with whatever you want to do, West." He smiled coldly, reminding Smoke once again of a snake.

Taggart chuckled.

Smoke nodded.

They wouldn't find it so funny before too long, he thought.

"The others will be out and about, too," McFadden said. "Just keep clear of Hicks. If you do see him, well, I don't want any fireworks between the two of you tonight. Understand?"

It bothered Smoke, the way he was being talked down to, but he simply nodded and said, "Anything else?"

"No, I guess that about covers it. I've given the orders to the others, but I wanted to see you by yourself." McFadden rose to his feet. "I have a notion about you, West. You see, I think you could go far. Do big things. You're smart. Quick on the draw, too. It isn't just anyone who can get the best of Hicks.

"But I want to know, right here and now, how willing you are to use that gun of yours when it comes down to it. You won't back out on me, will you, West?"

"I ain't backing out of anything. Like I said, you pay"— he patted his pocket, making the fresh coins he'd deposited jingle—"I work."

McFadden searched Smoke's eyes for a moment. A heavy silence settled over the room. Finally the boss outlaw nodded. "Good. Then get to it. You're on duty until sunup. Can you handle that?"

"Don't worry, I won't be falling asleep on the job, if that's what you're worried about." Smoke nodded to the two men and then walked outside. Hicks was out there now, standing with the others, but he turned away on seeing Smoke.

Suppressing a grin, Smoke meandered down the front steps and across the street. He made a show of going slow, just out for a stroll to keep a watchful eye on Desolation Creek. He needed to talk with Audie, though he didn't want to rush it.

He cast a few hard stares to two riders who trotted by. It worked, as the men quickly averted their eyes and gigged their horses to go a tad faster. He then looked in the livery stable and called loudly, "How many are in there?"

He disappeared through the doorway.

Inside, Audie stood waiting.

"I thought you might come by."

"What's going on?" Smoke said.

"Trouble, that is what. That chatter around town sure is increasing. Tension is brewing. I can feel it."

"Me too, and McFadden just confirmed it. He's sending us out in force tonight. He suspects something is coming," Smoke explained.

"Is the shooting about to start?" Audie asked.

Smoke shrugged. "I'm not certain, but it sure seems like something is going to happen. This town is awfully beat up. Not sure they have much fight left. Of course, the opposite might be true. Could be that they're fed up and ready to take McFadden down, once and for all."

"We aren't quite ready yet," Audie said, a worried expression shading his face. "We want the town on our side, but we haven't organized anything. Launching an assault on Venom McFadden and his men without proper planning might be a death sentence to all involved."

Smoke nodded. He'd been thinking along those lines, too. He was pretty sure he could round up some resistance among the town's citizens. He had a hunch Darnell Poe would fight. If he could get word to Newt Simmons in time, he'd probably join in, too. It was possible he'd even recruit some other homesteaders in the country north of town.

It would take some time to get word up there, though, and if the powder keg was about to blow, Simmons might not be much help. Smoke needed to find a way to get out there and talk to him.

"Think you could take a little trip tomorrow?" Smoke

said. "It's possible we have some allies, but we need to get word to them."

"I'd be neglecting my duties here at the stable, but I suppose that doesn't matter. It isn't as if I actually want or need this job."

Smoke chuckled grimly. "The way things are going, there might not be a stable left before too long. I have a feeling McFadden is mean enough to burn this whole town to the ground before he gives up."

"Indeed," Audie said. "His cruelty is only growing, as it does with men of his ilk. Yes, I'll take a ride tomorrow. Who is it that I am searching for?"

Smoke told him the general description of where Simmons could be found.

"I hope he's rounded up some others who are willing to fight," Audie said. "They could possibly tip the odds in our favor."

"Might be that they can," Smoke admitted. "Either way, we'll have to play the hand we're dealt." He drew in a breath. "And something tells me we'll be playing it mighty soon."

CHAPTER 23

The streets were devoid of chatter, but thick with tension as businesses started closing for the night.

Smoke felt a bit like a marshal or deputy, patrolling the way he was, only he sure wasn't walking the boardwalks to keep the good citizens of Desolation Creek safe—at least . . . not in their minds.

In reality, that was exactly what Smoke was doing. He gave a few gruff snorts and hard stares to folks he encountered. He tried to look as intimidating as possible, a feat that was not hard for him, since he was a seasoned warrior well beyond what his relatively young age would indicate.

He still hated every minute of it, too. He was tired of folks being afraid of him. He longed to be back in Big Rock, where he could smile and chat with the folks on his trips into town. He could sure go for a cup of coffee with Louis Longmont and Monte Carson right about now.

His thoughts were torn from those homesick feelings when he came upon Hicks leaving the general store.

"They locking up for the night?" Smoke said.

For a moment, he thought Hicks wouldn't answer, but the gunman finally said, "They are."

"You making sure they aren't of a mind to cause trouble?"

"Well, why else would I go in there?" Hicks said. "Ol' Miss Betty has to be at least sixty and I sure ain't looking for a romp in the hay with her."

The two men with Hicks laughed.

"She is about sixty," Smoke agreed. "Which means she isn't a prime candidate for an uprising against Mr. McFadden. Why are you wasting your time with her?"

Hicks bristled at the question. He stomped loudly across the boardwalk until he stood half a foot from Smoke. Raising a finger, he said, "You listen, and listen good, West. I don't answer to you. If anything, you answer to me. You're the last one to sign on with this outfit and that means you ain't got no clout. You understand that?"

"*Ain't got no?* Man, you speak about as bad as you fight," Smoke said.

Hicks's body tensed. He balled his hand into a tight fist, and Smoke was ready for him to throw a punch, but the man caught himself and lowered his arm.

"Stay out of my way, West. When we've done what needs doin' around here, we'll settle this up. Don't worry about that."

"Hicks, I haven't worried one second about you." Smoke strode along the boardwalk, not altering his course. Hicks stepped out of the way, but not before Smoke's shoulder bumped his. Once Smoke's back was turned to Hicks and his cronies, Smoke smiled. Sure, all he had done was ruffle some feathers, but it brought a little bit of entertainment to what was shaping up as a long, boring night of walking the town.

The night came alive with more excitement soon enough. It was about thirty minutes later when Smoke was walking behind the buildings on the east side of Main Street that he encountered three men. He saw them before they saw him, allowing him to duck behind a stack of crates and crouch low. For a moment, he thought they were some of McFadden's army of gun-wolves, but he soon realized they were townies having some sort of clandestine meeting.

Smoke remained absolutely still and listened closely, but they spoke in hushed tones and he couldn't make out what was said. Whatever it was, it was urgent.

His mind raced with options. Should he continue to play the part and try to scare the men into submission for the time being? He feared anything the town was planning might be too haphazard to actually work. Scaring them might buy him, Audie, and Nighthawk some more time.

While Smoke was ready to move the plan along, he didn't want to do it to the detriment of success. Audie was going to travel up north tomorrow. Perhaps Simmons and some of the other homesteaders and small ranchers would come back with him and help.

That left another option. Smoke could reveal his true identity and let the townsfolk know what he was up to. Maybe they'd agree to let things lie—at least for another day or two. That carried an awful lot of risk, though. Word would no doubt spread through the community and might even make its way to McFadden. That would put him—and Sally—at risk.

Of course, a third option existed: He could throw in with whatever the citizens were about to do. It was risky without proper planning, but it might be possible. He, Audie, and Nighthawk had gone up against stacked odds before, always coming out on top. Each situation was different, though, and McFadden had raw ambition combined with a cruel streak that made him unpredictable.

Smoke didn't have time to weigh the options any longer. Two of McFadden's men came around a corner, suddenly appearing behind the buildings a few feet ahead of the con-

spiring citizens. Smoke didn't think anyone could see him
behind the crates, but he might have to make his presence
known. McFadden's men—Smoke couldn't see who they
were in the dark—were coming on quickly. The citizens noticed them at the last possible minute and tried to dart into
the closest alleyway. McFadden's men called out and one
reached for his gun.

Smoke kicked over the crates, the crash drawing the gunhands' attention. "It's just me," Smoke said. "Buck West."

He wasn't sure that would keep them from opening fire,
especially if they were friends of Hicks. The fellow still
pulled iron, but he didn't level it at Smoke. Instead, he said,
"They're up to something. Time we put a few in the ground
to make this town see who they're dealing with."

Smoke recognized the man as he stepped closer. His
name was Isaac Jennings. Smoke hadn't had any run-ins
with him. Smoke couldn't recall the other man's name. He
was tall, hadn't talked much so far, and seemed to wear a
permanent frown. He held up a club of some kind; Smoke's
eyes narrowed at the sight of the knotty, rough wood.

With an ugly grin, the man said, "I'll take care of 'em
with this. Bash their hard heads in right on Main Street.
Leave 'em layin' there. That will get everyone else in line.
It's what Mr. McFadden said to do."

Smoke's pulse quickened. Things were escalating and he
felt as if he was losing control. "The boss really said to kill
them?"

"Not them exactly," Jennings said with a shrug. "Just told
us to put a few down before sunup. Make folks watch."

"Yeah, and said we get to choose how we do it," the other
one said, tapping the wooden club against his palm and con-
tinuing to grin for the first time since Smoke had met him.
His jagged yellow teeth made Smoke wish he hadn't smiled.

"You're better off with the frown," Smoke said.

"Huh?"

Smoke didn't explain. Instead, he moved at a lightning-quick pace that stunned both of the other men. He grabbed the gent's arm, wrenched it hard, and grabbed the club as it slipped from his fingers. He lifted the nasty-looking instrument up high and brought it down on the man's head with terrific force.

The man's hat protected him from the full force, but the blow still stunned him. The follow-up Smoke sent across his face did the trick. He stumbled back before falling to the ground, out cold.

"What the—" Jennings exclaimed, trying to claw his gun out of the holster on his hip.

Smoke was quicker. It wasn't even close. He thrust the club forward, ramming it into the man's stomach hard and knocking all the wind out of him. As the man doubled over, Smoke used his free hand to flip his hat off and then raised the club and slammed it against his skull with a sharp crack.

Smoke didn't know if he'd killed Jennings with that wallop, and didn't really care one way or the other. There wasn't time to check. He simply dropped the club, gathered up Jennings's fallen gun, took the other man's weapon, and tossed them both into a barrel that rested against a nearby building. A pair of soft splashes told him the barrel was partially full of rainwater.

Smoke hurried down the alley in search of the three citizens who had fled. He slowed, though, realizing he needed to proceed with caution. As far as the town knew, he was an enemy, one of McFadden's hired killers. He sure didn't want to get cut down by someone who didn't understand his true intentions.

As he approached the mouth of the alley, Smoke remained in a crouch. The sun hadn't retreated all the way below the horizon, so he still had quite a bit of light, even if it lessened with each passing minute. He had enough, though, to see what was going on. He only had to scan the street for a moment before he spotted Hicks and his two friends holding their guns on the three citizens.

"Just where do you hombres think you're going?" Hicks asked with an arrogant smile on his face.

"H-home," one of them said. He was an older, slender gent with silver hair. Smoke realized he was the town's barber.

"H-h-h-home?" Hicks said, making fun of the man's nervous stutter.

The men stood motionless, afraid to move because of the three guns leveled squarely at them. Finally one of them said, "We can move about this town as we please!"

Smoke could hear the man's voice cracking with fear, despite trying to sound resolved. He'd about seen enough. Smoke would never let three innocent people get gunned down, and as Hicks and his cronies lifted their guns slightly, it appeared that was about to happen.

Before Smoke could intervene, a group of citizens came around a corner and marched determinedly down the street, coming in behind the three men being terrorized by guns. Smoke let out an audible hiss as he realized what was taking place.

The town was making its move.

The mob was probably two dozen people strong. A few carried torches. In the lead, unsurprisingly, was Darnell Poe. The sleeves were rolled up on his white shirt; his usual printing apron was gone. He wore an angry expression, punctuated by fiery eyes.

He stopped in the middle of the road, a couple of yards from the others. The three citizens seemed to relax a little, upon looking over their shoulders and realizing they weren't alone.

"Well, well," Hicks said. "What do we have here?"

"We're taking our town back," Darnell Poe said, his voice loud and full of defiance.

A few behind him cheered.

Smoke was busy trying to count the number of townspeople who had gathered. He compared that number to

McFadden's army. The town had a small edge, as far as numbers went, but that was negated by other factors. As far as Smoke could tell, not everyone in the citizens' brigade was armed. Some wore six-chambered revolvers. A few had Greeners and a couple clutched repeating rifles. Some only held rusty, single-shot rifles, which wouldn't do much good up against McFadden's gang of hired guns. The other residents weren't armed, except for a few clubs, rakes, and hoes scattered among them.

Poe himself held a Henry rifle, and if the resolve on his face was any indication, he was ready to use it.

Hicks laughed. "Ain't this a hoot? We got ourselves an uprising here. A regular ol' mutiny."

His two friends laughed.

"What if I told you, Jennings and Howell were waiting just around yonder, ready to cut into you all, right here and now?" Hicks said. He raised his voice. "Ain't that right, Jennings?"

Nothing but silence.

"Jennings?"

Smoke couldn't help but smile. He wasn't sure when—if ever—Jennings would answer. The other feller must be Howell and he wasn't in any better shape.

Smoke had managed to whittle down the odds, all right, but they were still stacked high against him and the citizens.

And it was only getting worse.

Behind Hicks, more of McFadden's men marched in a solemn procession down the street, some even taking to the boardwalks on both sides, others looming tall on their horses as they came into view.

The whole scene looked eerie, Smoke thought, with the glare from the torches flickering in the air, casting macabre, dancing shadows around them.

The tension was palpable as the two sides faced each other, with only a few yards separating them.

"You know, the boss said he wanted you alive, Poe," Hicks said. He shook his head and chuckled. "He's convinced he needs a newspaperman on his side."

"He's wasting his time." Poe's jaw tightened.

"He'll get what he wants," Hicks said. "He always gets what he wants. That's good news for you, right? Means I won't kill you. Not yet. The bad news is . . . well, when I'm done with you, you'll sure wish you was dead." Hicks made a show of looking at the others in the crowd. "The rest of you darn fools will be."

Smoke had to hand it to the citizens. Even though they were afraid, they didn't shrink back, but stood tall and proud under Hick's hard gaze. That show of defiance made Hicks's lean face suddenly twist with rage.

"Kill as many as it takes!" he called to his companions. He aimed his Colt squarely at the silver-haired barber. "And I'll start with you!"

"Ah, well," Smoke said, standing upright and getting ready.

"Ah, well" was right.

Things were breaking loose right there on Main Street of Desolation Creek.

CHAPTER 24

Smoke's Colt roared and bucked in his hand.

He held his breath, praying he hadn't accidentally hit a citizen. His aim didn't cause the concern. It was as accurate as always. It was the townie who'd lunged for Hicks in an admirable attempt to save the old barber, just as Smoke triggered his shot.

Thankfully, the citizen lowered his head as he rammed hard into Hicks's chest. They both staggered back and Smoke's bullet smashed into a wooden post on the porch behind them. His shot had drawn the attention of the other gunmen, though, and several of them were eager to return fire. In the commotion, Hicks managed to scramble away and disappear into the crowd.

The street lit up with gunfire, the muzzle flashes competing with the torches. Some of those shots from McFadden's men were aimed in Smoke's direction, at the mouth of the alley where he had been concealed until the ball opened. Slugs hummed around him like angry hornets.

Smoke fell to the dirt and rolled to the side, going under the raised building to his left and coming to a stop a few feet in. The building's porch cut his view off, so he bellied forward until he was just beneath its edge, still concealed by the overhang.

McFadden's men continued to pepper the alley, where he'd just been, with gunfire. The roar was loud. To his right, he could see bullets chewing away at the ground, sending dust and dirt into the air in miniature geysers. Some bullets thudded into the two buildings on either side of the alley, causing wood splinters to rain down as the slugs chipped away at their facades.

Smoke drew a bead and thumbed off a shot. He was rewarded when one of McFadden's men toppled from the horse he was sitting on, going to the ground in a tangled mess of arms and legs.

That revealed Smoke's position, though, so he had to roll again to avoid the bullets that flew his way. Thankfully, McFadden's men didn't have the luxury of shooting at him for very long. By now, the townies had joined in the fight. They spread out, some scattering onto the boardwalks along both sides of the street, while others dove behind water troughs. A few took cover in unlocked buildings. A handful broke into the nearby alleys.

All of them poured hot lead at McFadden's men.

The gun-wolves scrambled for cover, too, as both sides exchanged fire. Smoke stretched out on the ground, trying to figure out his best move.

Both sides of the fight represented a potential threat to Smoke. The townsfolk thought of him as one of McFadden's men. McFadden's bunch didn't yet realize that Smoke had fired that first round, moments earlier, but if he just darted out from the building, they might mistake him for a citizen and blast away.

He twisted his neck and looked over his shoulder, seeing that the building was raised the entire way. He carefully turned around, avoiding a few wooden blocks that held the foundation up, and snaked his way to the back gap. He took a careful look and saw that the alley behind the building was clear. He eased out and stood, keeping his gun at the ready in case anyone surprised him.

He turned to his left and saw the bodies of Jennings and Howell still lying there, motionless. Jennings didn't appear to be breathing; Howell's chest rose and fell in heavy, strained efforts. Smoke realized that the clubbing might yet do him in.

No time to dwell on it, he decided. He drew a deep breath, exhaled, and then darted across the side alley's opening and to the cover of the next building. He repeated this process several times until he came to a row of three connected buildings. He went for the middle one and tried the back door. It was locked, but it only took two swift kicks before it splintered on its hinges and gave way.

Smoke dropped low as he went through the opening.

The room was empty of any occupants, as far as he could tell in the bad light.

He kept to a crouch and picked his way carefully through the back room, avoiding several crates and barrels of merchandise. He then stepped through another doorway and took a moment to study his surroundings.

The store was deserted, too.

He went to the front and peered out the window. He was behind McFadden's men now, just as he wanted.

It was time to even the odds a bit.

Two gunhands were on the building's porch, both kneeling as they took potshots at the citizens who were holding their positions down the street. Smoke put his hand on the doorknob and readied himself. He threw the door open, the sudden movement catching the men's attention.

One spun around, ready to fire, but held it when he saw Smoke.

"West! Where have you been? The whole rotten town is rising up against us."

Smoke cocked his gun, the metallic noise jarring and causing the man to tense.

"Hey, you can't—" He raised his gun, but Smoke fired first. The man dropped to the wooden planks and rolled until he fell into the street. By now, his compadre had realized the attack was behind him and spun around to go on the offensive. He sent two shots toward Smoke, both missing, since Smoke had already ducked back into the shop.

"What's going on?" one of McFadden's men yelled.

"It's West! He's with *them*!" the man on the porch called back.

Smoke grimaced as he moved low along the inside wall beneath the large glass window beside the door. He'd hoped his true allegiance wouldn't be revealed just yet, but that cat was out of the bag now.

He stood up, his gun blasting, spouting muzzle flame as he fired two shots through the glass.

The window shattered with a loud clatter. Two deep red rings appeared on the gunman's side. He spun around to face Smoke and tried to bring up his gun.

Smoke's third shot punched dead center into his chest. His jaw fell slack. His eyes looked hollow as he stumbled backward. He fell off the porch, flat on his back, his lifeless hands dropping the gun they'd held.

Smoke ducked and fed his Colt fresh cartridges.

Bullets tore into the front of the store.

Once he had all six in the wheel, he raised his hand and sent a few wild shots outside, not expecting to hit anything. He replaced those rounds and thought about what to do next.

The Colt was good, but a rifle and scattergun would be even better. He needed to get to his hotel room. Plus, he wanted to tell Sally to lay low and stay off the streets. It would be slow going to reach the hotel and he'd have to cross the street, but there wasn't any other way.

He retreated deeper into the store, through the back room, and out the door he'd come in. To his right was clear, but two of McFadden's men approached from his left, hurrying along the back of the buildings, probably trying to sneak up on the citizens from behind.

"It's West!" one said.

Evidently, they'd heard the earlier warning, because they both leveled their guns and blasted away. Colt flame bloomed like crimson flowers in the shadows.

Smoke dropped to the ground and rolled, coming up on one knee and returning fire. One man instantly flew backward as the bullets hammered him off his feet.

Smoke sent a slug toward the other man, but it missed, instead pounding into the building behind the target. This allowed the man to take aim. He never had a chance to fire, though.

Smoke heard the shot just before he saw his would-be killer grab the side of his neck. Blood poured between his fingers. He gurgled loudly before stepping back and hitting the building behind him. He slid down the wall and died in a sitting position.

Audie came into view, waving at Smoke with the hand that wasn't gripping a long-barreled revolver.

Smoke reloaded his Colt, taking every opportunity he could to make sure he had a full cylinder, and then sprinted toward Audie.

"Much obliged," Smoke said.

"Of course, friend."

"Have you seen Nighthawk?"

"No. I'm sure he's on his way, though." The professor turned mountain man let out a grim chuckle. "So much for all our plans and preparations. Events have seized the bit in their teeth, as so often happens."

"Have you seen Sally?" Smoke asked, in no mood to debate philosophy.

"No, indeed. Not a sign of her."

"Thank the Lord," Smoke said. "She must be staying put."

He wasn't sure he believed that himself, though. Knowing Sally, he figured she'd be running toward the fracas, eager to pitch in. He needed to reach her before that happened— and get those guns in his room.

"I need to make it to the hotel," he said.

"I'll cover you," Audie said.

The two were talking loudly as gun thunder continued to roll down Main Street, making the town sound like the Fourth of July. The bright flashes added to what might have been a holiday atmosphere, under other circumstances.

No one was feeling particularly festive, though.

"Are you ready?" Audie asked.

"Let's do it," Smoke said.

He thought of saying a silent prayer as they set off, but decided against it.

The time for praying had ended.

The time for shooting was now.

Somewhat to Smoke's surprise, he and Audie made it to the hotel without incident.

Shots continued to ring out along the street as he entered the building. Audie stayed outside, promising to keep a sharp eye out for Venom McFadden. He and Smoke had a notion that McFadden might try to run out of town. It would be just like a low-down, dirty skunk to take off for the tall and uncut when the shooting started, hoping the hired men would sort it out. He'd probably ride back into town if and when the battle was won in his favor.

Neither Smoke nor Audie would let that happen if they could help it.

Inside, the clerk huddled in fear behind the desk. Smoke left him there and ran up the stairs. He came onto the second floor just as Sally was rushing along it toward the stairs, Smoke's rifle and Greener in her hands.

She stopped short and offered a smile. "I was just . . . uh, bringing these to you."

"To me, huh?" Smoke said.

"That's right," she said with a nod.

He couldn't help but grin back. "I'll bet."

"You know me, just supporting my husband."

He reached out and took hold of the weapons. Upon second thought, he handed the Greener back to her. "You stay in your room. Better yet, my room. Our room."

She accepted the gun as she said, "What about the role you've been playing? McFadden will be furious if he finds out you're not really on his side."

"None of that matters now," Smoke said. "After tonight, with a bit of luck and the Good Lord on our side, McFadden won't be in charge of this town." He let his eyes fall to the gun she held, before matching her gaze once more. "Anyone tries to come in that room besides me, Audie, and Nighthawk, you give 'em both barrels."

"I can do that," she said, though she didn't look excited about the prospect.

Smoke knew she meant it, too. Had he not shown up in time, she would have charged into the fray, emptying both guns and most likely going after McFadden all by herself. He was just glad he reached her when he did.

"Have I ever told you, you're hard to handle?" Smoke asked.

She laughed. "Come back to me in one piece tonight and you can handle me all you want."

Smoke reared his head back. "Well, I'll be!" He grinned. "That's a mighty good incentive. I'll be back soon."

He leaned in, gave her a quick kiss, and then headed down the stairs. She stood at the top and called after him, "You come back to me, Smoke Jensen! I mean it."

He stopped midway down, turned, and said, "I will, Sally. Always."

The tender moment was cut short before the two could say another word. A bloodcurdling scream rang out from somewhere nearby, putting a frightened expression on Sally's face and causing Smoke to lift the rifle and work its lever, throwing a cartridge into the chamber.

He listened.

Another scream followed.

It was close, Smoke realized. Very close.

Someone was in trouble in the hotel's restaurant.

And Smoke was going in to help them.

CHAPTER 25

The young woman was terrified.

Smoke had seen her scared before, scared by his presence each morning when he had his breakfast, but now she was even more afraid. Three of McFadden's men had taken up residence in the dining room and were using the barrels of their rifles to break the panes of glass from the windows and clear away the jagged edges left behind.

One of the men started shooting. Another raised his rifle to his shoulder and drew a bead on somebody outside. The third looked around as Smoke charged into the dining room.

"It's West!" he yelled. "He double-crossed us! He's one of them!"

Smoke didn't like this. Word had clearly spread among McFadden's ranks that Smoke was on the side of Desolation Creek's citizens. He had no notion of keeping up his masquerade beyond that night, but being able to sneak among the gunhands and wreak havoc from *the inside* sure would have been nice.

No use crying about that now, though. There wasn't time. The man dropped his rifle, pulled his Colt, and fired just as Smoke ducked back through the doorway. The bullet struck the frame around the entrance and chewed splinters from the wood. Smoke eased back a few steps up the stairs and leaned against the wall that separated the hotel lobby from the dining room.

"Smoke!"

He looked up to see Sally still at the top of the staircase. She motioned with the Greener and Smoke nodded, placing his rifle down. She tossed the scattergun down to him. Smoke caught it deftly, then readied himself and moved quickly.

He faced the wall and jumped sideways, his body flying past the open threshold. He only had a second to take stock of the room. Thankfully, Clara was still huddled in a corner, well out of harm's way. Smoke triggered one of the barrels. The buckshot caught the man at close range as he had been storming toward the doorway. He screamed in agony as his body was nearly blasted in half.

Smoke kept flying until he landed hard on his shoulder and slid, going right past the doorway and behind the small stretch of wall on the other side.

Smoke's ears were ringing. Gunsmoke was thick in the air.

Shots blasted into the hotel lobby. The portion of wall he ducked behind offered some cover, but it was only about three feet in length. They'd get him eventually. He quickly thought over his options. He could go through the lobby's front door, run down the boardwalk, and enter through the dining room's door, but that would expose him to the bullets that were flying outside. And there were a lot of them, from the sound of things. It was like war had broken out in Desolation Creek. Smoke supposed it had.

Slugs continued to punch into various places in the hotel's lobby. The red couch on the other side of the room was chewed up. The pillows were now ribbons. Feathers floated down in an almost peaceful white rain. Two paintings on the wall across the room tumbled to the ground as their frames splintered.

Smoke peeked around the corner long enough to take a quick account of the room. The girl was still clear of a potential shotgun blast.

One of McFadden's thugs wasn't.

The gun roared and tried to come out of Smoke's hands, thanks to the awkward angle at which he held it while still trying to maintain his cover. He let it fall. It was empty now.

The buckshot tore into the man's legs. He howled in pain as he crumpled to the ground. Now on his knees, he raised his rifle and tried to lever a shot, but Smoke was quicker. His Colt bucked twice against his palm. The man went down, with a bullet in his forehead and one in his cheek, right under his eye.

Smoke hurried across the threshold, back to the wall that ran the length of the stairs. There was more cover there, and Smoke needed it, as the remaining gunman turned his rifle's attention to him.

The slugs punched into the wall, but didn't break through. Smoke looked at his own rifle and decided against it. The Colt would be best now. He was thinking of how to play his hand when he heard the man call out.

"Come on, West. Toss your guns out and step through the door, nice and easy."

The young woman screamed again.

"You hear that, West? I got her. Gun to her head. I'll put a bullet in her brain."

Smoke sighed.

Darn it all.

He looked up to Sally, conveying with his eyes that he had to comply.

She was having none of it. She hurried past him. He reached for her, but was too late as she walked just beyond his reach.

"Wait!" she called. "Don't shoot. It's me."

She put her hands up and stepped slowly into the doorway.

What on earth was she doing? Smoke wondered. His heart raced. He was nearly gripped with panic, but fought it off, realizing that wouldn't help Sally. He needed to maintain a clear head. As soon as he had his opening, he'd strike. What he'd do, exactly, remained to be seen. Surely, an opportunity would present itself.

"Mr. McFadden wants her," Sally said to the gunman. "Don't hurt her."

"What?" the man said.

Smoke now realized what Sally was up to. If he hadn't been so annoyed that she'd put herself in harm's way once again, he might have even smiled.

"You heard me," Sally said. "The boss said he's taking what's his. That's why he left me here in this hotel. I'm to keep an eye on her."

"He wants her?" the man said. "I thought he wanted you."

"He does," Sally said with a smile. "This whole town belongs to him."

She eased into the dining room and sauntered closer, as if she didn't have a care in the world.

"You want to kill her and answer to McFadden?" Sally said. "I sure don't want to be around if you do."

The man gulped. "None of that matters now," he said, his resolve clearly weakening.

"You think Mr. McFadden will lose?" She snorted. "I haven't been in this town long and I know him better than you do."

Smoke was grinning now. Sally could have been an actress! She sure sold it good.

He also used that time to thumb fresh cartridges into his Colt. Once he had a full six, he closed the loading gate and prepared.

Inside the dining room, the man finally nodded.

"Okay, but I'll still kill West."

Sally shrugged. "Go ahead. It's not him the boss wants.

It's her." Sally reached out and grabbed the terrified girl's wrist, dragging her closer as the confused gunman let go of her. Sally shoved her hard, sending her to the floor out of the line of fire, before joining her. She yelled, "Now, Smoke!" and then fell on top of the girl, shielding her.

Smoke stepped into his room, gun ready.

McFadden's hired man yelled in defiance as he tried to level his gun, but Smoke was already in motion.

He used his left hand to fan the hammer, sending four quick slugs into the stunned man. Small holes appeared in his torso before blood began to well. He fell to the side, against a table, pulling it down on top of him as he crashed to the ground.

Smoke spun a circle to make sure there were no more threats. Seeing it was clear, he quickly reloaded and then retrieved the scattergun.

"There are more loads in my saddlebags upstairs," he said, handing the weapon to Sally. "Go! Take her. Lock that door and move something in front of it!"

The scared girl kept thanking them both.

"I love you, Smoke," Sally said as she passed him.

"I love you, too," he said with a soft smile. "Now go on."

He grabbed his rifle and watched the women as they hurried up the stairs. He wanted to stay with Sally, but he was needed outside.

Where the war was taking place.

Acrid gunsmoke billowed down Main Street, filling Smoke's nostrils and nearly making him cough. The air was hazy with swirling clouds. He could practically taste the burned powder.

He looked around for Audie, but didn't see him.

Shots continued to ring out. From the sound of it, he judged fighting had broken out all throughout Desolation Creek. Bodies littered the road and the boardwalks.

One shot nearly hit Smoke.

He dove off the boardwalk and took cover behind a trough. A few more slugs thudded into it. Water began to pour out on the other side, spraying from the trough in .44- and .45-caliber–sized streams.

Smoke raised his head just enough to see where the shots were coming from. Evening had settled down over the town, and with the battle raging, no one had lit the lamppost lights. The rolling clouds of gunsmoke further hampered visibility.

Smoke caught a break, though, when he saw two muzzle flashes from the boardwalk across the street. At least two men were over there behind the railing with their rifles steadied on the water trough. Smoke sent four shots their way, two where he'd seen one flash and then two where he'd seen the other. Still, the shots continued from their direction.

Smoke wondered how he could take those would-be killers out. He raised his head again to sneak a peek. He looked just in time.

A giant, hulking figure materialized on the opposite boardwalk, barely visible through the smoky haze. A loud, violent snap resounded, even over the gun thunder. A faint whimper followed next, more snapping, and then one body flew off the porch and into the street, landing in an ungainly heap.

Smoke's eyes went wide as he watched the hulking figure's arm rise. He made out the faint outline of what appeared to be a tomahawk. It slashed downward just before Smoke heard a terrified shriek followed by a wet gurgle.

No more shots came from over there. The menacing phantom disappeared just as quickly as he'd materialized.

Smoke smiled and tipped his hat, though he knew the figure didn't see the gesture.

Nighthawk was on the move.

Smoke took advantage of the lull to dart away. He ran quickly toward the Dead Moose. He prayed he wasn't too late. The last thing he wanted was for Venom McFadden to get away. His operation was done here in Desolation Creek. The people clearly weren't afraid of McFadden anymore and tyrants thrived on fear. Without it, they were nothing.

But Venom could move on to another town.

Smoke wouldn't let that happen.

Even more than that, Smoke still needed to avenge Preacher. The old mountain man's death could not go unpunished.

A moment later, he finally found Audie.

The little man was pinned down behind a wagon that had been rolled into the center of the street. It gave Audie good cover as he fired on the Dead Moose, but he couldn't leave his position. Plus, he was vulnerable from the direction Smoke now came. Audie seemed to realize that, because he spun around and brought his rifle to bear.

"It's me," Smoke called from the boardwalk.

Audie nodded and then went back to the fight in front of him. Shots were whipping out of the Dead Moose and chipping away at the wagon, as well as spraying the buildings all around. Suddenly Smoke realized he and Audie weren't alone. He watched as citizens swarmed the area and took up positions. Some were hiding behind troughs, some on the roofs, and a few scattered along the boardwalk.

"Stop right there, West!" a man yelled just as Smoke was about to make a dash for the wagon where Audie was holed up.

Darnell Poe came into view. He had his gun trained on Smoke and he looked eager to pull the trigger.

"I'm not Buck West and I'm not with McFadden," Smoke said. "Not really, anyway."

"It's too late to save your skin now, West," Poe said. "You must think we're plain stupid."

"He tells the truth," Audie yelled from behind the wagon.

More shots came from the saloon. Some of the citizens returned fire.

Smoke didn't like being so exposed; right now, though, McFadden's men weren't his biggest concern.

"We're just supposed to believe that?" Poe said.

"I'm not sure about this one." Hodges, the old miner Smoke had met in the Absaroka Saloon upon entering town, stepped forward and studied Smoke.

"What do you mean?" Poe asked.

"Well, I ain't been too sure what to make of this feller ever since I met him," Hodges said. He spat a measure of tobacco juice. "There's somethin' different about this one. I'd bet my gold claim on that."

"That claim has never paid off," Earl, the Absaroka's barkeep, said.

Hodges cackled before offering, "I'm just sayin' I got a hunch about this young man. He ain't halfway bad."

Smoke nodded in appreciation of Hodges's support.

Poe was not convinced. He jabbed the barrel of his rifle toward Smoke and said, "Start talking, mister. You got about one minute to convince me you don't deserve a bullet."

"Look, I can't explain it all now. We've got to get McFadden! But you gents remember an old mountain man who rode into town not long ago?"

"Sure do," Poe said. "*Your boss*, McFadden, had him filled full of lead!"

"That was my . . . friend," Smoke said, struggling with the right word to describe what Preacher had been to him. No reason to elaborate now, but Preacher was certainly more than just a friend. Smoke would certainly never forget his own father, Emmett, but Preacher had been a second father to him. "I'm here with Audie over there. And Nighthawk. We've been working to dismantle McFadden's gang from the *inside*."

"Nighthawk?" Poe said.

"Big Indian fella," Smoke explained. "Been sitting shotgun over in the Dead Moose."

"I don't frequent that establishment," Poe said.

"He's been in there, all right," another citizen chimed in.

"He's also been in this battle," Smoke explained. "Turning the tide."

"I ain't seen no Indian," Hodges said.

"You'll only see Nighthawk if he wants to be seen," Smoke said. "Trust me."

"Mister, I'm not so sure we can trust you," Poe said.

"We can!" a new voice said.

Smoke and the others looked to see Newt Simmons making his way through the crowd. "This man was at my place the other day. McFadden sent men to scare me, trying to get me off the land. Some wanted to . . . They wanted to . . . violate my girl. This man stopped them."

"That true?" Poe said, cocking his head to one side as he studied Simmons.

"Wouldn't have said it if it wasn't."

Poe thought it over for a moment and then nodded. "What's your name?"

"Smoke Jensen," Smoke said, seeing no reason not to reveal his true identity.

"Smoke Jensen?" another man in the crowd said.

"I've heard of you," someone else said.

Scratching his snowy-white bearded chin, Hodges said, "From down Colorado way?"

"That's right."

"Heard tell of you, too," he said. "Word is, you've been in a fight or two. People say you can handle yourself."

"Let's stop jawing and find out," Smoke said.

That brought a grin out of the old-timer. "Young feller, I like that idea."

Poe still seemed hesitant, but he didn't try to stop Smoke as he ran toward the overturned wagon, where Audie was pinned down. A few shots came from the Dead Moose, but none of them came close to hitting him.

"I trust Mrs. Jensen is doing well," Audie said as Smoke dropped to a knee beside him.

"Don't worry about her," Smoke said. "She'll outlive us all."

Audie grinned. "I have no doubt."

"Is McFadden inside?" Smoke said, jerking his head toward the saloon.

"I'm not sure, as this is the closest I've been able to get. They started shooting the moment they caught sight of me. Guards posted everywhere, it seems."

"That makes me think McFadden is inside," Smoke said.

"Me too," Audie agreed.

Their conversation was curtailed when more shots burst forth, this time coming from *above*.

"The roof!" Smoke said, shaking his head in frustration.

The Dead Moose was the tallest building in town. From that angle, the shooters had a nearly perfect view. Judging by the shots he heard, and the puffs of smoke he saw when he snuck a glance, Smoke estimated there were two men up there, each one positioned to the side of the building's peaked roof, behind the false-fronted third floor.

The citizens unleashed a volley of fire at them, but the rooftop shooters had ducked by then.

"They can pick us all off from up there!" Hodges said before spitting.

"He's right," Poe said. "We need to get someone up on that roof, but how?"

Smoke was about to volunteer, when the situation was decided for them. A large figure appeared on the roof, causing the citizens to raise their weapons.

"Hold your fire!" Smoke said. "He's with us!"

The crowd watched as the rooftop silhouettes danced before them. The two shooters were clearly stunned as the figure loomed up behind them. They had no time to react—nor the strength to break his grip—when he grabbed them by their necks and bashed their heads together. He effortlessly picked one up and pitched him off the roof before repeating the process on the second shooter.

"Umm!" Nighthawk called loudly.

"Excellent!" Audie said, standing up and jogging toward the saloon. He stopped midway, turned around, and yelled, "Well, what are you all waiting for? You heard him. The saloon is clear!"

Poe exchanged a confused glance with Hodges and then Simmons before shrugging and racing to join Audie. Smoke passed them all and bounded cautiously up the steps, through the batwing doors, and into the saloon's main room.

A grisly scene greeted him.

A man lay facedown on a table, his arms and legs hanging off the sides, while a tomahawk stuck up, still embedded in his back. Three more of McFadden's men lay in various places around the floor. Two additional men were sitting in awkward poses on the staircase, their glassy eyes staring at Smoke and the other citizens as they poured in.

The coppery smell of blood filled the air, along with all the unpleasant odors of death.

None of the deceased were McFadden.

Nighthawk appeared on the second floor, peering over the railing and locking eyes with Audie. "Umm."

"Blast it all!" Audie said. "McFadden got away."

"Are you sure?" Poe said. "We need to search this place!"

"Yes, we do," Smoke agreed. "And we need to take account of the dead and wounded. I'm sure there are some folks who need to be patched up."

Poe nodded. "If McFadden got away, well—"

"We'll go after him," Smoke said, indicating Audie and Nighthawk. "We came to town to settle the score with that snake and we aim to do just that.

"Right now, though, there's a lot of people who need tending to."

The others agreed and the crowd dispersed, still being cautious in case McFadden had any sympathizers left behind. It would be a long night as they cleaned up the grisly aftermath of the battle.

Smoke would help, but he was eager to get back to Sally and then get a good night's sleep.

Something told him the fighting was far from over.

He'd pursue Venom McFadden to the ends of the earth if that's what it took to avenge Preacher.

CHAPTER 26

The following morning, Smoke awoke to find his body stiff, sore, and aching all over.

The morning sun was poking through the lace curtains. Sally was by his side, for which he was grateful, but his smile faded as the events of the previous evening flooded his memory.

It had been a long night. Desolation Creek had lost six citizens. While Smoke hated that, he also realized the death toll could have been much higher, especially when facing a gang as ruthless as Venom McFadden's. A few more folks had been wounded, and the town doctor had spent hours patching them up, but they were all expected to make full recoveries.

As for McFadden, he'd gotten away, along with Hicks and a few others in the gang. Ten had been killed. Three were wounded and in jail. It seemed as if McFadden wouldn't be running things in Desolation Creek any longer.

Smoke himself had managed not to get shot, so he took some consolation in that. He sure felt that move he'd made, though, jumping off the stairs and landing on his shoulder down in the hotel's lobby. Even his legs were sore as he stretched them out. He groaned.

"That bad?" Sally said.

"Worse," he said.

Her head was resting on his bare shoulder. Smoke liked the way her silky hair felt against his skin. He'd missed that.

He wasn't glad she'd pulled that little stunt, coming into Desolation Creek on the stagecoach, but he could admit it was good to see her. He just thanked the Good Lord she hadn't been hurt in last night's fight.

"You've been hurt worse," she pointed out.

"I was younger then, too."

"Ha! You aren't old."

He shrugged. That small movement caused him to wince yet again. "Surely, I won't still be involved in these sorts of scrapes when I'm older," he said. "If it hurts this bad now . . ."

"I'm not convinced you'll ever stay out of trouble for very long," Sally said. She rolled off of him and propped her head up on her elbow, gazing into his eyes.

He smiled. "I'm not sure you're one to talk."

She laughed again. Her smile faded as she put her fingers to a black-and-purple bruise that ringed his shoulder. She traced it lightly. "You *are* banged up."

"I'll feel better when I get out of bed and walk it off. Look at us, lying in bed like we don't have a care in the world, and the sun's been up for an hour or more, by the looks of it."

"We're not on the ranch, remember. We could pretend this is a trip. You've taken me to Montana for some rest and relaxation. We can sleep late, take all our meals at the restaurant, and go shopping."

Smoke sat up with considerable effort. He caressed her face. "I have to—"

"Go after Venom McFadden. I know."

He nodded.

"I wouldn't expect anything else," she said.

"Sally, do you—"

"No. Don't stay. Go. He has it coming after what he did to Preacher." Her jaw tightened with determination. "Besides, we know all about men like him. If you don't stop him, he'll do all this again to some other town. His kind won't stop until they're in the ground. Finish it." She scooted up in the bed until she could kiss his lips. "Just hurry back."

"Yes, ma'am!" he said.

A smile turned her lips upward. "I suppose you're too sore to . . ."

Smoke's grin stretched from ear to ear.

"It's darn near miraculous!" he said.

"What is?"

He winked and said, "I'm feeling better already!"

"Mr. Jensen! Mr. Jensen!"

Smoke and Sally turned to see Darnell Poe hurrying along the boardwalk toward them.

"Good morning," Smoke said, keeping his arm around Sally's waist.

"Good morning," Poe said. He was holding a writing tablet and pencil. The first page was folded over and the second page was already halfway full. "Just going around town and getting the lay of things, now that the sun is up."

"This is going to sell a lot of papers," Smoke said. "Even though most folks lived it, I reckon they'll want to read all about it."

"Oh, you can believe that!" Poe said. "This is a new day in Desolation Creek and much of the thanks for that belongs to you and your friends."

Smoke shook his head. "We played a small role. It was the citizens who rose up and took their town back."

"You're being modest, Mr. Jensen." The newspaperman looked to Sally. "You deserve a thanks as well, Mrs. Jensen."

"Me?"

"Yes, ma'am. I spoke to young Clara in the hotel's dining room. She indicated you saved her life!"

Sally looked bashful as she shrugged. "Just helping out."

"Well, I'd love to get your side of the story. Could I drop by sometime today or tomorrow? I'd love to interview you while the events are still fresh in your mind. That is, unless you two will be leaving. With your work done, I don't suppose you'll stay around Desolation Creek."

"We aren't pulling out just yet," Smoke said. "At least Sally isn't. I'll be hitting the trail just as soon as I can."

"Hitting the trail?" Poe said.

"That's right," Smoke said. "I came to town to deliver justice to Venom McFadden."

"I'd say you did that last night and then some!" Poe said.

"Not yet. He's still breathing."

"Oh," Poe said, clearly surprised by the statement. "Yes, yes. I see."

"Good day, Mr. Poe," Smoke said.

It took Poe a few seconds to respond. "Good day, sir." He nodded to Sally. "Ma'am."

Smoke guided Sally around and the two set off once more, on their stroll toward the edge of town. Everyone they passed had a spring in their step. Folks looked Smoke in the eyes and greeted him with smiles. Despite bullet holes everywhere, serving as reminders of the previous evening's carnage, they seemed to have a new lease on life. Being free of a tyrant will do that to folks, Smoke realized.

They reached the Dead Moose and saw the porch free of the usual gunmen who loafed about. Normally, they'd be hanging around, while Taggart sat inside, determining assignments for the day. The foreman was among those who'd escaped, though word around town was that he had taken a bullet in the process. Taggart might be bleeding to death somewhere, Smoke thought.

Good riddance.

As for the Dead Moose, it looked odd, appearing so life-less and still. Smoke smiled in satisfaction. For all he cared, the town could raze the place. Someone would take it over, though, repair all the damage, and turn it into an honest business. It was still a nice building and there was no sense in letting it go to waste.

"Good morning," the familiar voice of Audie called out.

"Umm," Nighthawk added.

Smoke and Sally looked to see the old mountain men coming from the stables across the street.

"Good morning," Sally said.

Smoke nodded. "You still working the livery stable?"

Audie chuckled. "I told the proprietor I'd help out today, but that is all. He needs to find someone else."

"Really? I figured we'd hit the trail before it gets cold," Smoke said.

"Umm."

"Nighthawk is right," Audie said. "I'm afraid the town is almost completely devoid of ammunition. Whatever you have is what we're working with. Beyond that, there aren't even sufficient supplies to take with us on the journey. The store doesn't even have coffee."

"Is there another town we could stop at along the way?" Smoke asked.

"Umm."

"Exactly. Nighthawk did some scouting this morning. McFadden's tracks aren't hard to read, since he left so hastily. He had no time to conceal them. They go north," Audie explained.

Nighthawk nodded.

"Sugar Creek is the closest town, to the east."

Nighthawk nodded again.

"Thankfully," Audie said, "supplies are being sent over this afternoon from Sugar Creek. We should have enough to outfit ourselves and we could leave tonight or at first light in the morning."

"*Sugar* Creek?" Sally said in astonishment. "That's a far cry from *Desolation* Creek. It sounds a lot better!"

"Yes, ma'am," Audie said. "Certainly more hospitable."

Smoke thought it over. "I guess we have no choice but to wait."

"Indeed," Audie said with a ring of disappointment.

"Might be best," Sally said. "You need to rest up and let your bruises heal."

"Hey, I'm already feeling a mite better after . . ." Smoke stopped speaking and cleared his throat before adding, ". . . stretching this morning."

Sally sucked in her bottom lip just as her cheeks took on a soft red hue.

The shipment of goods from Sugar Creek arrived that afternoon, just after four o'clock, and it took some time for their unloading and stocking in the store.

After having killed the owner, McFadden had laid claim to the store, though he had no legal right. He'd done that with several businesses around town. The store's deceased owner had a cousin in town, so it was decided he was the rightful heir.

"I will give you this merchandise for free," Juan said in heavily accented English.

He was a short man, slightly portly, with dark skin and combed-back black hair.

"I'm much obliged," Smoke said, "but I prefer to pay my way."

"No, no, señor, your money is no good here," Juan said, slashing his hands across his belly to indicate he would not hear of it. "You helped save this town!" He leaned in, stretching his short body across the counter, getting closer to Smoke. "Besides, McFadden left much money in the register and the safe. I had to blow the safe open, but . . . well, much money, señor." He smiled devilishly.

Smoke chuckled. The way he saw it, whatever cash McFadden had left behind didn't begin to cover what he owed. Still, Smoke didn't like the idea of taking anything for free. He didn't feel entitled to any special favors just for doing what was right.

"It would mean a great deal to me if you'd let me pay," Smoke insisted.

Juan stepped back a few paces and shook his head in frustration. "I see you are a very stubborn man, Señor Jensen."

"You aren't the first one to accuse me of such."

After another moment, Juan spread his hands and sighed before speaking quietly and swiftly in Spanish. Smoke didn't know everything that was said, but he caught enough to realize Juan wasn't happy.

"I give you better prices," Juan said. "And I won't take no for an answer."

"Fair enough," Smoke said. "I'm much obliged." He offered his hand.

Juan smiled as he shook it.

Audie and Nighthawk appeared, bringing a few items to the counter.

"Beyond that," Smoke said, "we'll need that ammunition I told you about, some jerky, bacon, and coffee."

"*Sí*, señor," Juan said.

He got busy behind the counter. It took him a while to fill the order, as he was still learning where everything was.

"Next time you come back," Juan said, "I will have more items. This store will be big. You will see. It will grow."

"I have no doubt," Smoke said.

"I wish you much success on your mission," Juan said. "May *El Señor Dios* guide your path and return you safely to your bride."

"I'm much obliged for the sentiment," Smoke said. "And I'll take all the prayers I can get."

He thanked the new shopkeeper once more and then he, Audie, and Nighthawk carried the supplies outside. Once they were on the boardwalk, the sight of three rough and burly men walking their horses down the center of Main Street greeted them.

"That's quite a trio," Smoke said.

"Quite a trio indeed!" Audie said.

"Umm," Nighthawk added.

"Maddox! Hargis! Jedidiah!" Audie called.

The three men stopped their horses and turned their heads in unison to see who'd shouted their names.

One laughed. "Well, if that don't beat all! Ol' Audie and Nighthawk."

"Indeed," Audie said, stepping forward. "What brings you gentlemen to Desolation Creek?"

"I reckon we're here for the same reason you are," the man said. "To kill whoever done kilt Preacher!"

CHAPTER 27

The six men were clustered around a table at the Absaroka.

Earl seemed thrilled to have more than just beer behind the bar, and Smoke suspected he'd gotten his new stash of liquor by raiding the Dead Moose. No harm there, he figured. The spirits weren't doing McFadden a bit of good.

And with the Dead Moose temporarily in limbo, business was good inside Earl's place.

Old Hodges looked happy to have drinking companions. He'd raised his whiskey in a toast upon seeing Smoke and the others enter. Smoke had smiled back.

"First drink is on the house for everyone today," Earl said as he deposited a bottle and glasses on the table.

"I'd be obliged for a cup of coffee if you have any," Smoke said.

"I think I can work one up. Yes, sir," Earl said.

The usually grumpy man had an outright skip in his step as he made for the bar. It matched the overall chipper and festive mood that had settled over Desolation Creek.

The others, except for Nighthawk and Smoke, all poured splashes of whiskey into their glasses and downed the shots.

"Mighty good," one of the men said, wiping his mouth with the back of his hand. "I do believe I'll have another."

"Smoke, meet our friends," Audie said. "This is Hargis."

Hargis was a big man who wore a shaggy black buffalo coat that was just as matted as his long, graying hair. His thick beard hung to his chest. He had very broad shoulders, which made him seem a tad younger than he probably was, though the deep lines on his weathered face spoke of his real age.

"Good to know you, Jensen. Heard a lot about you," Hargis said with a nod. He followed the statement by taking another shot of whiskey.

"And this," Audie continued, "is Jedidiah."

Jedidiah was tall and lean, with an almost skinny face and short white hair, along with a matching trimmed beard. He looked more like a farmer than a mountain man, Smoke thought, but the old man's eyes held a lot of experience and wisdom.

"And I cannot leave out Maddox," Audie said.

Maddox was of medium build, with shoulder-length dark hair that was just starting to gray. He had a beard—though not quite as bushy as the one Hargis wore—and was easily the youngest of the trio, though he still had a good thirty years on Smoke.

"Seems like a lot has happened in this town," Maddox said, his gruff voice sounding as if he'd swallowed some gravel.

"A considerable amount," Audie said. "Let me start at the beginning."

He recounted the events that had transpired and then leaned back in his chair, shaking his head in frustration. "McFadden got away, but not for long."

"Because we're going after him," Hargis said.

"Indeed."

"Word's been spreading about what happened to Preacher," Jedidiah said. "Lots of folks are mighty mad. We might even run into others ridin' the same vengeance trail."

"Surprised we ain't already," Maddox said. "We rode up here just as soon as the news reached us."

By now, Smoke had his coffee and was working on it as he listened to the conversation. Earl had brewed it just the way Smoke liked it, strong enough to get up and walk around on its own hind legs. The steaming liquid helped ease the aches of his body even more.

"We ain't got much daylight left," Maddox said. "You boys reckon on setting out in the morning?"

"At first light," Smoke said.

He didn't want McFadden's trail to grow cold. Even more, he wanted to finish his business and get on back to the Sugarloaf as quickly as possible.

"Any idea where they're going?" Jedidiah asked.

"No, but I don't think they'll go far," Smoke said. "I think his boys are busted up pretty bad and McFadden isn't the type to go anywhere without protection. He hides behind other men. They'll need to lay low somewhere. Maybe there's a hideout north of town. Whatever the case, I don't think we'll have any trouble finding them. Considering all of us, I suspect we could track just about anyone or anything."

The mountain men all guffawed.

"Ain't that the truth!" Hargis said. "McFadden sure picked the wrong bunch to get on the wrong side of." The men laughed some more before Hargis's smile disappeared, replaced by a wistful gleam in his eye. He raised his glass. "To Preacher."

The others followed suit.

"To Preacher," they said in unison.

"And," Hargis added, "to finding the low-down varmint who did him in . . . and making him pay."

* * *

The following morning found Smoke hesitant to say goodbye to Sally yet again.

He'd gone so long without being with her that the thought of separating once more was not appealing. He had a job to do, though. The sooner he did it, the sooner they'd be back home on the Sugarloaf.

As they stood in the center of the boardwalk, Smoke debated internally. Should he put Sally on a stage back to Colorado? Now that McFadden was gone, nobody remained to hinder the travel. Yet that notion didn't exactly sit well. A lot of dangerous country lay between Desolation Creek and Big Rock. Sally would be safe there at the hotel until he returned to escort her home.

"You going to drag this out all day," Sally said, "or are you going to get on Drifter and move on down the road?"

He chuckled. "Trying to get rid of me?"

"No. Trying to get you back home quicker."

He put his hands around her waist and reeled her in for a kiss. He lingered for a moment, holding her and whispering, "Be right back."

"I know it," she said.

They kissed again before he stepped off the boardwalk and mounted the waiting Drifter.

"I suspect this will all be over in a few days," he said. "Until then, you stay put here in town. Enjoy the break from ranch life and stay out of trouble!"

"Me, get into trouble?" she said with a dismissive wave. "Perish the thought."

"Uh-huh," Smoke said.

He touched the brim of his hat and then gigged Drifter down the road, taking one last look at Sally over his shoulder. Then he put his eyes forward, realizing he needed to shift the focus of his attention. Longing for her might get him killed. He had a job to do and it was time to finally rid the world of Venom McFadden.

Up ahead, in front of the livery stable, Smoke saw Audie, Nighthawk, and the others atop their mounts, waiting for him. He was almost to them when Darnell Poe appeared, stepping out of one of the stores, his pad of paper and pencil still in his hands.

"Mr. Jensen, are you riding out to find McFadden?"

"I am."

Poe kept pace with Drifter as he stared up at Smoke. "Can I get a quote before you go?"

"Not sure what to say," Smoke admitted.

"Well, are you taking anyone with you? Any townsfolk coming along for the trek?"

Smoke shook his head. "McFadden is out of Desolation Creek. The remaining fight is between us"—Smoke pointed his chin at the awaiting party—"and him."

"I see," Poe said.

Smoke stopped Drifter and took a closer gander at the Dead Moose. Three men were outside of it, loafing much the way McFadden's men had done. For a moment, he thought there would be trouble. The men stretched and moved on, apparently realizing the saloon was closed. He watched them meander down the road. One gave him a hard look and Smoke wondered what it was all about. He didn't recognize these gents as residents of Desolation Creek.

Poe noticed him watching the men and said, "Word has gotten out that this town is open for business once more. Outsiders are already coming in!" He seemed excited at the pronouncement.

Smoke had some reservations. He'd seen men of that ilk before. They'd just chased them out of Desolation Creek, in fact.

He told himself to forget it, though. It was just his imagination. He was after McFadden and that was what mattered.

"Good morning, Mr. Poe," Smoke said, nodding before nudging Drifter toward Audie and the others.

"Gentlemen," Audie said, "are we ready?"

There were grunts and nods. They were properly outfitted, confident in their abilities, and eager to dispense justice.

For Preacher.

Without another word, the six men pointed their mounts north and left Desolation Creek behind.

It was time to finish this.

CHAPTER 28

"Hello in the barn!" Smoke yelled.

He waited a moment before Newt Simmons poked his head out of the open doors. The man smiled at his visitors, stepped out fully, and offered an inviting wave. "Come on in, Smoke."

Smoke rode in first with his compadres following.

"Good to see you," Simmons said with a wide grin. "What brings you out this way?"

"Well, we're on the trail of Venom McFadden," Smoke said. "Tracks lead north. Thought we'd drop by and find out if you've seen anything."

"No, I can't say as I have," Simmons said. "Of course, if he took off the night of the battle, I was in town, so I wouldn't have been here to see him go by."

Smoke rested his hands on the saddle horn and leaned forward. "I wondered about that," he said. "We were going to send for you and ask for your help when we made our move against McFadden, but things kind of got ahead of us. You were on hand for the trouble, anyway."

Smoke was just curious about that, not suspicious. Simmons had fought and risked his life alongside the townspeople and had proven to be a valuable ally.

The man thumbed his hat back and said, "Pure happenstance. The youngsters and I had gone into town to pick up some supplies. Didn't want to, you understand, since I knew it would be putting more money into McFadden's pockets to do business at the store, but there were things we needed. I figured we'd stay over until the next morning." Simmons shook his head. "When all the mayhem broke, I was sure regretting that decision, but it worked out all right. And if McFadden and some of those gun-throwers of his rode by here that night while they were getting away . . . well, I'm glad the kids *weren't* home."

"That's mighty true," Smoke said. Something occurred to him. "You're not missing any horses or anything else around here, are you?"

"You mean anything that McFadden and his bunch might've stolen?" Simmons shook his head. "Not a thing. If they were in a hurry, they must've passed us by."

"That was good luck for you," Smoke said. He lifted his reins, ready to turn Drifter and ride on.

Simmons went on, "Come to think of it, I did see some riders going south yesterday, like they were headed *into* Desolation Creek."

"Must be the three men I saw earlier this morning," Smoke said, more to himself than the homesteader.

"Oh, there were more than three," Simmons said. "Probably seven or eight. Looked like cowboys. They didn't pay me no never mind, so I didn't pay them much attention, either."

Smoke wondered why so many people were headed into town. Poe mentioned that word was getting around, but it couldn't have spread that quickly. For all that most folks in those parts knew, Venom McFadden was still ruling Desolation Creek with an iron fist.

"They're probably with one of the spreads around here,

looking to blow their wages, now that town ain't such a bad place," Simmons said. "You know how their type can be."

Smoke wasn't so sure about that, but his concern, right now, was finding McFadden. It didn't make sense that McFadden would send new gunhands into Desolation Creek. His stronghold was broken. Folks weren't intimidated by him the way they had been. He'd be better off setting his sights on a whole new town.

Besides, Smoke thought, McFadden seemed to have left most of his fortune behind. He probably didn't have the cash to hire more men.

"Much obliged for the information," Smoke said.

"I didn't help much," Simmons pointed out. "Wish I could do more. Shoot, after all you did for us—"

"It wasn't anything," Smoke said, eager to steer around the praise. He touched the brim of his hat before pulling on Drifter's reins and swinging him around.

The group rode farther north, stopping occasionally to study the tracks and look for signs. Nighthawk left the group several times to scout ahead. He returned to let the group know they were traveling in the right direction.

The first day passed without incident and the men rode on even after the sun set. They made camp, had supper, and then got back on the trail bright and early the following morning.

It was on the afternoon of that second day that they came to a small, ramshackle saloon nestled against a low, rising hill.

A wisp of smoke curled from the building's chimney. The air carried the faint smell of food.

"Might be as the folks here know somethin'," Hargis said.

Nighthawk was off his horse, studying the ground and moving along as he took stock of the tracks. "Umm."

"Really? They were here?" Audie said.

Nighthawk nodded. "Umm."

"You think one remains?"

The Crow nodded again.

"There's more than one fella inside," Maddox said, leaning his head toward a wagon that was parked near a rough-hewn corral. Inside the corral, two horses trotted a circle, seeming a mite uneasy.

Smoke felt that same uneasiness. He wasn't sure what was going on, but he made a note to keep his right hand near his Colt.

"I'll go in," he said. "Might be best if a couple of you waited out here."

"Umm."

"Nighthawk is right," Audie said. "Something is gravely wrong here."

"Why don't you three go in," Maddox said, pointing to Smoke, Audie, and Hargis. "We'll scout things out and be at the ready in case you need us."

Smoke liked that plan. It wasn't smart for all the men to go in and potentially be ambushed or waylaid.

They all dismounted. With the plan set, he led the group into the saloon.

Inside, the place was dirty and dim. It smelled musty and stale. Even the pot of stew—or what Smoke presumed to be stew—hanging over the fire in a stone hearth didn't help the odors any.

Another odor, which Smoke had encountered too often, was present. An unmistakable one.

The stench of death.

"How you boys doing?" a skinny, balding man asked. He was behind a counter that was nothing more than a few boards running over three strategically placed barrels. A few sets of antlers were mounted to the wall around the room. There were four tables scattered about, nothing more than knotty boards laid over barrels. The chairs looked home-made and didn't match.

The sod roof had a couple of holes in it, but even so, not

much light filled the squalid place. Smoke gave his eyes a moment to adjust.

"What'll do ya?" the man asked, not bothering to wait for an answer to his original question. "We got whiskey. Stew over the fire. My old lady's specialty. Coffee, if you'd like." His words ran together and he seemed slightly nervous.

Smoke, Audie, and Hargis took a few steps around the place and looked it over. The man behind the counter grew even more agitated.

"What are you lookin' for?" he said, a nervous laugh escaping as he spoke. He smiled, but it held no humor. "Ain't no mountain lions nor bears lurkin' in here, if that's what you're worried about."

"Came here looking for someone," Smoke said.

He pulled a chair out and took a seat at one of the crude tables, his back to a wall. Audie sat down, too. Hargis walked a few paces away and remained standing.

"Ain't no one here but me and you gents," the man said. "Of course, my missus is back there somewhere. I got two boys runnin' around out yonder. No one else, though."

He was too eager to volunteer the information.

"What about that wagon outside?" Smoke asked.

The man gulped. "Wagon? What wagon?"

"Horses in the corral, too," Smoke said.

"I, uh . . . I'm not sure."

Hargis grunted, bending down and retrieving something on the floor that had caught his eye. He stood, inspected what he held, and then showed it to Smoke. "Doll."

Smoke's heart slugged a little harder in his chest. The doll was tattered, made of an old flower sack, with yarn for hair. It had on a tiny homespun dress.

His hand fell to the butt of his gun.

Just then, two tall, lanky young men burst into the room from the back doorway.

"We did it, Pa. Just like you told us," one of them said.

He had dirty red hair and freckles. He wore tattered blue

army pants that were too big for him, along with a dirty, long-sleeved undershirt.

"Fine, fine," their father said. "Go on and help your ma." His eyes darted to Smoke and the others, letting his sons know they weren't alone.

The boys' eyes went wide as they realized they had visitors.

"Sure, Pa."

"What did they do?" Smoke asked when the boys had retreated back through the door where they'd entered. His voice was full of steel.

The man bristled behind the counter. "That ain't none of your concern," he said, still trying to plaster a smile on his face. "You boys just get comfortable. Rest a spell. You've prob'ly had a hard journey and need a few comforts." The man leaned over the counter a bit and smirked. "Might be I can even get you a woman. For a price."

"Thought you said no one else was here, save for your boys and missus," Smoke said.

The man straightened. "Yeah, yeah. That's right. Just mean if you were staying . . . well, I know where to send off for some, uh, hostesses. That's all I mean, mister."

Hargis looked as if he could fly into a rage. He tossed the doll. It landed on the counter, perfectly centered before the man. He swallowed hard once more.

"Who does that belong to?" Hargis growled.

"I don't—" The man's hand came up with a scattergun, but it wasn't any use.

Smoke, Audie, and Hargis all had their guns up and leveled before the saloonkeeper could even lift the barrels.

Their three shots sounded like one as their Colts roared.

None of the men missed.

The fellow was dead before his body thudded onto the dirt floor, kicking up a plume of dust and grass particles.

Smoke was on his feet. He spun around, keeping his gun

trained on the back doorway, while Hargis covered the front door in case anyone had it in mind to charge in that way.

"Umm," they heard.

Smoke lowered his Colt, and Nighthawk stepped through from the back, nodding slightly.

Smoke followed him into the back room. The two young men were sprawled across the floor, but their chests were rising and falling. It was the other three people in the room who drew Smoke's immediate attention.

A man, woman, and little girl were tied, sitting on the floor with their backs against the wall. Dirty clothes had been shoved in their mouths and held in place with wrappings. Nighthawk worked on freeing them. The woman looked terrified as he approached her, trying to scoot farther away, but being held in place by her daughter and then the corner.

Her husband, now free of his bonds and gags, told her, "It's okay, it's okay. These men are here to help."

"That's right," Smoke said. He squatted on his haunches and held his hands out so the family could see he was not a threat. "Are you all right?"

The woman cried loudly as Nighthawk took her gag out. Her brown hair had been tangled. Her cheeks were tear streaked. The panic in her hazel eyes subsided a bit, once her hands were free and she was able to hug her daughter. She clutched the little girl tightly.

"Thank you," she said. Her voice wasn't much more than a whisper. "Thank you."

The little girl was freed next.

"What happened here?" Smoke asked, standing.

The man tried to rise to his feet, but went back down quickly. He rubbed his ankles, trying to get the circulation flowing once more. He looked up at Smoke. "We are traveling down to her folks' place," he said. "They aren't in good health."

Smoke nodded.

"We stopped here for some dinner and . . . that man and his boys . . . hit me over the head. Then they . . . Well . . . We're right here."

Smoke's eyes moved to the woman for a second. The man shook his head. "They didn't do anything yet." He seemed as if he was getting choked up at the mere thought of what could have happened. Smoke couldn't blame him.

Hargis came into the room. He looked at the family, his eyes growing wide. "They hurt?"

"No, thank God," Smoke said.

Hargis looked angry. "Looks like they waylay folks around here. Unsuspecting travelers. Big trunk full of valuables and such."

Smoke exhaled loudly. He could only imagine what might have happened to the woman and that poor little girl, had he and the others not come along. His blood boiled, but it wasn't any use now. The way station's proprietor was already lying in the other room, expired.

"He mentioned his wife. Any sign of her?" Smoke said.

"Nothing," Hargis said.

"W-we d-didn't see a woman," the man said. He was able to stand now. He reached out, helped his wife and daughter up, and then threw his arms around them and embraced them tightly.

Smoke figured the man had lied about having a wife. Perhaps the promise of a woman's presence disarmed the travelers who stopped there.

"There was another man in here," the husband said. "T-they hit him, too. He was already in bad shape."

As if on cue, Jedidiah entered. "Found a feller you might know. His name is Taggart and he's asking to see you."

CHAPTER 29

Taggart was in rough shape.

As he lay on the ground, at the base of the hill behind the tavern, he could barely move.

He had a bullet wound and the white wrappings were now dark and sticky as the blood flowed once more on his side. A gash was torn into his head. A crimson streak trickled down into his left eye.

He looked awkward, with his big frame stretched straight out, but Smoke supposed the man was incapable of lying any other way.

Taggart tried to speak, but only a groan escaped his parched, cracked lips. He cleared his throat, gave it a few seconds, then tried again.

"West," he said, his voice surprisingly strong now. "Or . . . whoever you are."

Smoke nodded. "Smoke Jensen."

"Jensen, huh?"

Smoke only nodded again.

"We found him in a little cave over yonder," Jedidiah said. "Looked like someone just dropped him down there."

Upon closer inspection, Smoke realized that was most likely what had happened. Taggart's right leg was obviously broken.

"They did this to you?" Smoke said, jerking his head over his shoulder to indicate the tavern behind them.

"Yeah," Taggart said. "Except this bullet wound." He coughed before he could say anything else. He sucked in a lungful of air and hissed loudly. A wet rattle sounded in his throat. He didn't have long.

Even in the grim circumstances, he managed a slight smile. "You . . . or someone . . . in Desolation Creek . . . gave me the bullet."

"You expecting sympathy?" Smoke said.

"No sympathy," Taggart managed. He coughed again. He gagged so hard that Smoke thought the man would retch, but he kept everything down. "Did . . . you help the family? The ones inside?" A flash of panic made his face turn whiter than it already was. "They'll kill them!" His eyes closed. Smoke studied him more closely to see if his chest moved. Just when Smoke thought he'd expired, Taggart's eyes opened again and he inhaled loudly.

"The family is all right," Smoke said. "Do you know them?"

Taggart shook his head. "Never . . . saw them before. McFadden . . . left me here . . . Said I was . . . slowing him down."

Smoke wasn't surprised. Taggart had clearly been in no condition to travel, even before he'd been attacked at the tavern. Based on where that wound was, he'd been as good as dead before ever leaving Desolation Creek.

"The . . . skunk inside . . . or one of his boys . . . bashed me on the head. Drug me outside."

"Threw you into the cave?" Smoke guessed.

Taggart could only manage the slightest of nods. "Ain't no cave. Just a hole."

"And that broke your leg?" Smoke said.

Taggart didn't say anything, but it was evident that was what had happened.

"Took my money," he said, his voice but a whisper.

"Sort of like you took the citizens' money back in Desolation Creek," Smoke said.

Taggart's voice grew suddenly stronger as he said, "I ain't looking for sympathy, blast it! I'm done for. I know it. Fruit of my own evil ways. Just . . . save . . . that family."

"They're safe, Taggart," Smoke said. "The hombre who ran this place isn't, though."

"Dead?"

"Yep."

Taggart laughed morbidly. "I suspect I'll see him . . . soon enough."

"You finding religion on your deathbed?" Smoke asked. "Caring about that family and all?"

Taggart chuckled. "Funny . . . how dying . . . makes you change mighty quick."

Smoke didn't have a comeback for that. He figured Taggart was telling the truth. There was nothing like facing one's own mortality to help them see the light.

"Do another good deed," Smoke said as he stepped even closer. "Where was McFadden going?"

"Northeast of here," Taggart offered. "Hideout called Duggar's Canyon. It's known by men . . . like me."

"Northeast, you say?"

Taggart nodded. "Veer off the trail when you pass the two trees. They're . . . the gateway."

"How far are they, Taggart?"

Taggart's eyes were growing dimmer. His lips turned upward. "I was tired of working for others," he said. "Punching cattle. Drawing a cowhand's wage. Ain't never had nothing . . . to show for it. Now I done made money. Got . . . even less . . . to show for it."

One last breath escaped Taggart's lips. His body fell slack. He never spoke again.

"We'd best get the dead taken care of," Smoke said.

"And what about the boys?" Audie said, having come up behind Smoke to witness Taggart's last moments.

Smoke thought for a moment. "Not much we can do. Reckon we can burn this place to the ground so no travelers will stop here again."

Audie nodded.

It was indeed all they could do.

Smoke and the others helped the family recover from the shock of the ordeal and then helped them hitch their team.

"You sure you'll be all right?" Smoke asked the man.

"Her folks' place ain't far. We'll be fine."

"I wish you safe travels." Smoke extended his hand and they shook.

Smoke and the mountain men watched as the family rode away, their wagon wheels clicking loudly as the horses pulled the vehicle over the rutted road. The little girl, smiling as she held her doll, turned around on the seat and waved.

Smoke returned the grin and waved back.

By the time they mounted up and set off once again, they left a burning structure behind, along with two very confused and dazed young men. Their horses had been turned out, too, and their weapons confiscated. They wouldn't put up a pursuit; though Smoke figured they wouldn't have, even if they could've. It was evident their father had been the brains of that operation, and that was giving the backward family more credit than they deserved. The boys had simply been following his orders.

They rode until daylight failed them, stopping first to cook their supper and brew some coffee, then moving on several more miles to make camp in a different spot. The closer they got to McFadden and his remaining men, the more careful they had to be. Smoke wasn't willing to discount the possibility that they had lookouts on patrol or had posted a few men to lie in ambush.

So, they took turns keeping watch in the night, and the next morning, after setting out, Nighthawk frequently disappeared as he scouted on ahead to find signs of danger.

He never found any.

"I think McFadden is spooked," Maddox said.

"That would be my guess, too," Jedidiah chimed in. "Granted, I ain't never met the feller, but I reckon he's mighty rattled after that fight Desolation Creek put up." He cackled. "Sure wish I could've been there!"

"I don't doubt any of that," Hargis said. "But as a fact, I know the same as you gents, that you cain't never underestimate a man like Venom McFadden. I might not know him, but I sure know his kind. He won't go down quietly."

"You're thinking we'll have a fight on our hands?" Maddox asked.

"I expect," Hargis said. He looked to his left, to where his friend rode beside him, and grinned. "And I wouldn't have it any other way."

Late in the afternoon, the posse came upon two trees spaced apart, allowing enough berth for someone to pass between them. Their branches had grown in such a way that they touched in the middle, providing a natural canopy for anyone who traveled beneath them.

"Has to be them," Smoke noted.

"Umm," Nighthawk added.

"I've heard of this spot, too, old friend," Audie said. "Heard tell that it's used by a goodly number of outlaws. This is one spot, though, that you and I have never visited. Who knows what lies beyond this natural gate?"

"Umm."

Audie laughed and clapped his hands together. "Nighthawk, my dear chum, you never cease to surprise me. Yes, I love that quote, too. 'Boldness be my friend.' I suppose if there's one line from the blessed Bard that describes our many adventures, it is this one."

"Umm."

The riders had to pass beneath the trees, one by one. Smoke kept a sharp eye out, as it stood to reason that sentries might be posted at this point on the trail to Duggar's Canyon. There wasn't much cover, though, save for some tall, straw-colored grass, which blew in the slight breeze. They'd have to ride on before they hit thicker tree growth and then rocky hills, which would eventually give way to towering mountains.

They rode on for several hours before reaching the point where the trail narrowed and the cover increased.

"Umm," Nighthawk said.

"Thank you, my friend. We'll wait here," Audie said.

The men dismounted and found a cool, clear spring in a little natural alcove hidden among the growing hills. They watered the horses and waited on the old Crow to complete his scouting mission.

He returned two hours later.

"Umm."

"Eleven men? McFadden has that many left?" Audie said with a gasp. "Not staggering odds, by any means, but still more than I thought he had."

"Is it a box canyon?" Smoke asked.

Nighthawk nodded.

"This could be both good and bad," Smoke said. "There isn't a way for McFadden to escape on the other side. Of course, though, that means there's only one way in, too. McFadden and his men will easily see us coming."

"Surely, he has an escape plan," Maddox said, scratching his jaw and then spitting. "I know he can control who enters, but I'm not sure a fella like McFadden would leave himself cut off with no way out."

"Maybe he figures he'll never need to escape, because he's so well protected inside there," Jedidiah suggested.

"Either way, we can't go in through the front," Smoke said.

"Nighthawk," Audie said, "was there a way to sneak into the hideout, or are the canyon's walls too steep?"

Nighthawk smiled. "Umm."

"You sly old warrior, you!" Audie said. "You climbed down and snuck into their camp?"

Nighthawk grinned—or what passed for a grin with him.

"Then that's it," Audie said. "That's how we get inside."

Smoke thought it over. "Makes the most sense. We picket the horses and creep in on foot. If we wait for dark, we have better odds of not being spotted."

"Nighthawk wasn't seen," Jedidiah pointed out.

"That's true," Smoke said. "But that would be harder to accomplish with six of us."

Smoke wasn't sure how the giant Crow was able to do it in the first place. He wasn't hard to miss—except when he wanted to be. Nighthawk's ways were almost mystical.

"Umm."

"It makes sense they'd have a sentry or two on top of the rim," Audie said. "Very useful information."

"We'll take 'em out," Smoke said. "Even the odds a mite before we go down there."

Sitting on a log near the pooling spring, Hargis said, "We've got a spell yet before the sun goes down. I say we strike out when it's good and dark."

The others agreed.

Now all they had to do was wait a spell before delivering justice and retribution to Venom McFadden.

All in the name of Preacher.

CHAPTER 30

Three places along the canyon walls afforded the opportunity for Smoke and the others to descend into the outlaws' hideout.

They split into pairs, Smoke going with Hargis.

"I would gladly climb down there," Hargis whispered. "I'm itchin' for a fight. I expect you owe McFadden, though."

"I do," Smoke said. "And I aim to deliver."

"Wouldn't expect anything else," Hargis said. "I would give all my worldly possessions to be the one to put a bullet in that jasper. Preacher was a rare breed. Meant the world to a lot of folks and I'm one of 'em. Still, didn't have that relationship you did."

Smoke nodded.

"Go on," Hargis said. "I'll cover you. Might be down in a bit or might stay up top and give y'all some eyes from above."

Smoke hoped the big man would stay. He had little doubt Hargis could probably scale the canyon's wall, but it would be hard for a man of his considerable size. Plus, they did need a couple of men to stay on the canyon's rim and open up with their rifles when the shooting started. Strategically, it made the most sense.

There were a few lights burning in the box canyon below. As far as Smoke could see in the dark, the outlaws had built a sort of community down there, with multiple structures and a corral. One building toward the back looked like a cabin. It was the biggest one and Smoke assumed it belonged to McFadden. It made sense. McFadden was the sort who thought he was entitled to the best things in life—and he didn't care if he had to walk on or kill someone to get them.

None of the lanterns or torches below gave off enough light to reach the canyon wall. Smoke had plenty of darkness to conceal him as he began his descent, but that was a blessing and a curse. He could barely see a thing as he picked his way down. It was slow going. More than once, he stopped, holding tightly to the rocks and keeping his feet on the footholds the best he could, as noises below caused concern. At one point, two men strolled by directly under him, smoking as they talked. Neither seemed aware that about thirty feet over their heads was a man on his way to deliver justice and probably death.

Smoke took no pleasure in killing. Specifically, McFadden was the only man he wanted to see dead. The owlhoot had that coming for what he'd done to Preacher, not to mention countless other people he'd gunned down in Desolation Creek and probably other places. The world would be better off without him. Still, Smoke didn't have any bloodlust in his soul. He was simply doing what needed to be done.

He waited for the men to walk on, before beginning his slow descent once more. By the time he reached the ground, his arms were strained. The shoulder he'd landed on a few days earlier was throbbing once again. His legs ached. But he made it down undetected, so he'd fight through the pain. Once he finally made it back to the Sugarloaf, he was due for a good, long soaking in some of the hot springs that could be found around Colorado.

First things first, though.

Venom McFadden.

Smoke crept along the canyon's wall and stayed in the shadows. He stopped every few feet to peer into the center, trying to see if he could make out who was moving around, but there just wasn't enough light for that. He figured he would recognize McFadden's shape, though, and best he could tell, he was not among the men who'd congregated around a campfire. Smoke decided to keep working his way back until he reached the cabin at the rear of the canyon.

Perhaps he'd find Venom McFadden there.

And McFadden would find death.

"You feel bad the way we left poor ol' Taggart at that way station?" Jim Kent said.

Dave Lomax, his patrolling partner, shrugged.

They walked along the canyon's rim for a few moments before Dave answered, "Nah. He'd've done the same to us. Besides, he wasn't gonna live long. No reason slowing us all down."

"Maybe that feller who ran the place, or his wife, will doctor him up a bit," Jim suggested.

"Not much they could do for him," Dave said. "I bet Taggart done met the devil by now." He chuckled.

"Well, when it comes my time, I hope I ain't alone," Jim said.

The two men stopped walking. They looked down on the flickering lights below. So far, it had been a quiet night.

"You think anyone will come for us?" Jim said.

"Shoot, ain't no one coming," Dave said. "Nobody in Desolation Creek will chase us. They're just glad we're gone. They might alert some law—county or federal marshals. By the time they hunt for us, though, we'll have pulled up stakes and moved on to the next town. Ain't no real reason for us to be standing guard like this."

Jim thought about it for a moment. "I guess you're right." He watched the campfire far below for another moment before saying, "Sure do hate we had to leave. There were a couple of women back in town I wanted to take a pass at."

Dave laughed with a snort. "You see that girl in the hotel? The one worked the dining room?"

"Heck, yeah, I saw her," Jim said. "Shame we didn't get better acquainted with her, if you know what I mean."

"Maybe we'll ride back there one day," Dave suggested, "when folks've had a chance to forget what happened."

"By then, she'll be old, married, and used up," Jim said. Both men laughed.

"Ah, there'll be some young filly in the next town," Dave said. He turned and started to move off. "Gotta visit the bushes. Be right back."

Dave left the rocky rim and retreated into the brush and tall grass. He stopped in front of a tree, his eyes taking a few moments to adjust to the abject darkness that shrouded the wild country.

He was about to unbutton his trousers, when he realized something was wrong.

The tree was moving.

The tree shouldn't be moving.

"What the—"

It was too late. The giant Indian stepped closer, raising his tomahawk high and splitting Dave's head open before the man could even register what was happening.

Back at the canyon's rim, Jim turned around quickly after hearing a wet crunch. "Dave?" he called out. "You all right?"

The hairs on the back of his neck stood on end as he stepped into the tall grass. Something told him Dave wasn't all right. Something also told him he was being watched.

He took a few more steps, but the eerie feeling got the

better of him. He had just decided to turn and run, when the hand reached out and pulled him deeper into the night. Something flashed toward him.

He realized it was a tomahawk just before it smashed through his forehead.

Dave and Jim wouldn't be violating any woman in any town ever again.

Smoke approached the cabin with caution.

He kept low as he slipped around the back and surveyed the scene. There was no door, but there wasn't really a need for one, as the structure darn near bumped up against the canyon wall. Only the smallest of narrow walkways existed and Smoke had to shimmy his way through it just to reach the other side.

One door was in the front; the only windows were on either side of it. Whoever was inside was cut off.

He moved away and stayed in the shadows for a few moments as he thought of his plan. One way out was bad for McFadden—if he, in fact, was inside. One way in was bad for Smoke. That left a single entrance for McFadden to cover.

Smoke thought about waiting on him. The man had to come outside sometime. But there was no way to get word to his companions that he'd shifted the plan. Besides, they were hiding in the darkness, too. What if they were discovered? And by now, Nighthawk and Hargis had taken the sentries out, or had started to do so. Those men would be missed soon enough. No, waiting wasn't the best option.

Smoke needed to act.

Perhaps McFadden was already asleep. Maybe he was even wounded. Could be alone, too, though Smoke doubted that. He'd just have to sneak inside and see for himself.

Preacher, he mused silently, *I could sure use a hand here. Otherwise, I might be seeing you soon.*

* * *

Jedidiah stole along the wall of the canyon, careful to stay out of sight.

Ahead, four men were near the center of the circular area, gathered around a campfire. It sounded as if they were swapping stories, laughing loudly, and maybe had indulged in a little too much drink.

Good, Jedidiah thought. *Anything to tip the odds in our favor.*

It would be easy to jerk out the two pistols he wore and open up on the men right then and there. They'd be cut down in an instant. He reached for the guns he wore in cross-draw holsters, comforted by the familiar feeling of the smooth-handled Colts. He needed to give Smoke more time, though. They weren't sure where Venom McFadden was. He was the main target. The other drunken fools would be dealt with easily enough.

He released his grip on the guns. It wasn't time.

Yet.

His attention was pulled from the hombres around the campfire. What was that he'd just heard? It was faint but close.

He spun around, realizing he'd heard a boot scrape lightly on the earth's rocky floor. The more he thought about it, the more he wasn't sure if he'd actually heard it or just sensed it. Years of stalking the wild country had honed his skills. He was almost one with those untamed spaces. He could tell when humans were about, almost like a mountain lion.

He saw the man approaching in the darkness.

A sentry.

Jedidiah's mind raced. There wasn't any cover. No place to hide. He could crouch low against the wall and hope the man wouldn't bump into him, but the odds were mighty small. He could hide in the shadows and club the sentry over the head with his gun, taking him out of commission as silently as possible. That was the best way, he decided.

He retreated quickly, putting his back against the wall. Just a few more seconds and the sentry would pass right in front of him—if he didn't bump smack into him.

Jedidiah drew his gun and spun it in his hand until he gripped it by the barrel. He raised his arm, ready to strike.

The plan was as good as any he could come up with, and would have probably worked, had the light not approached.

Jedidiah gritted his teeth in frustration as he watched the flame dance closer and closer. A man had left the fire, holding a torch, and seemed to be walking right toward the hiding spot.

"Hey, Carl, you over here?" he said. "You gotta hear what Haycox just said. He was talkin' about—" The fire's yellow glow fell on Jedidiah's boots. Carl, about a yard away to Jedidiah's right, saw them at the same time.

"What the—"

Well, they had called the tune, Jedidiah thought. Now he would start the ball.

He went for his gun. The man holding the torch tried to do the same, but he had to shift the torch to his left hand before he could pull iron.

This gave Jedidiah all the time he needed. He'd already spun his own gun around, now gripping it by the handle and ready to shoot.

And that's exactly what he did.

Lead crashed into the sentry. He got a shot off, too, before falling down dead, but the bullet thudded harmlessly into the ground a few feet away from Jedidiah.

Jedidiah didn't waste time celebrating the victory. He swung his arm around to meet the torch-bearing man, who was rushing closer now. The cocking of his Colt sounded louder than it should have, echoing off the canyon wall, competing with the now-fading gunshot that rolled through the confined space.

That second shot seemed even louder.

* * *

Smoke was almost to the cabin's door, undetected, when the three shots rang out. He'd been moving slowly as the single burning lantern that hung on one of the porch's posts gave off enough light to make him visible.

It didn't take but a few seconds for the door to fly open and three men to pile out.

"Well, this complicates things," he said aloud.

"Who are you?" one man said, stopping on the porch.

"It's that damned West!" another said.

Smoke recognized the three from Desolation Creek.

They stayed on the porch, their guns still in their holsters, but clearly bracing for a fight.

"You betrayed us," one said.

"He wasn't ever one of us," another said. "He done played us."

"Look, my quarrel isn't with any of you," Smoke said. "I just want McFadden. You boys put your guns down and walk away, I'll let you live."

Smoke angled his body slightly. He was in a tough spot, needing to keep his eyes forward, but also watch his back. He only hoped Hargis could cover him from above with the rifle. In the darkness, that might prove a difficult feat.

The men laughed. The one in the middle said, "There's three of us and one of you. I know you fancy yourself fast, but do you really think you could take all three of us out?"

Smoke knew he could not get out of this without shooting. He decided on his target and prepared himself to draw. Still, he had to try one last tactic.

"I'll get one of you, for sure. Probably two. The question you boys need to ask yourself is which ones of you are prepared to die?"

They silently stared at Smoke. He could see their bodies twitching, just itching to draw.

The center man snickered again. "Nah. You know what I think?"

Smoke didn't say anything.

"I think," he continued, "that we'll cut you down where you stand before you even get a shot off. Ain't that right, boys?"

Smoke read the movement in their shoulders and knew it was time to make his move. His Colt was out and up in an instant, but he didn't draw a bead on any of the three men.

His shot hit the lantern and shattered it. The fire roared instantly, raining down on the unsuspecting men and stunning them so badly that they never got off a shot.

Smoke had already moved, going low and to the side, just in case they did.

He needn't worry.

The flames had turned into an inferno. The men danced around and howled as their clothes caught on fire. Two had the good sense to stumble off the porch and drop to the ground, rolling to smother the flames. The third continued his macabre dance as panic gripped him. He finally fell to the porch, but this only caused the flames to spread along the wooden puncheons.

The dry wood ignited quickly. The heat from the blast stung Smoke. The two on the ground were up now, leveling their guns as smoke still arose from their hair and charred clothes. The smell of singed flesh assaulted Smoke.

It only took one shot for each man to send them back to the ground. They never moved again.

The third man was still struggling with the fire, his screams growing louder by the second. He wouldn't be a problem anymore.

The fourth man, who appeared in the doorway, would be, however.

Venom McFadden.

CHAPTER 31

The rifle in McFadden's hands spit flame as he sprayed lead straight at Smoke.

Thankfully, Smoke had thrown himself to the side and rolled, sending a few shots of his own onto the burning cabin's porch.

They all missed, but so had McFadden's.

The outlaw lord darted off the porch and to his right, disappearing into the deep shadows along the canyon wall. Smoke sent a few shots after him, but wasn't surprised when he saw no indication that he'd hit his fleeing target.

The whole canyon was alive with gunfire now.

Every few seconds, eerie muzzle flashes lit up the darkness. The center area was lit fairly well, thanks to the glow of the campfire. The cabin was lit even better as it ignited like a tinderbox. As the flames grew, so did the illumination.

Smoke smiled.

McFadden couldn't stay hidden for very long.

Two outlaws ran toward Smoke, shooting as they came. He scurried toward the canyon wall and took cover behind a large boulder. A few bullets ricocheted off the top and chipped at the surface, but Smoke was well protected. He was drawing a bead on the incoming men, when a rifle's loud crack sounded from somewhere above.

The first man's skull exploded as the top half blew off. He continued to run a few seconds, his body not receiving the signal from his brain that he'd died. Then he stopped suddenly and fell face forward into the ground.

The rifle blasted again.

The second man's leg erupted in a sticky red flow. He howled in pain as he went down on one knee. His chest was the second part hit, the impact rocking him back. He cursed and growled as the third bullet smashed into his stomach.

He was finally down.

"Much obliged, Hargis," Smoke said, though he knew the man on the rim couldn't hear him.

The charnel smell of death already filled the canyon, but Smoke knew a lot of killing was yet to come.

Movement along the wall caught his eye. The cabin's fire had grown so large that its light now reached the farthest stretches of the canyon.

McFadden.

Smoke reloaded his Colt and then drew a bead. He sent three shots toward the running man, but they just whined off the rocks. McFadden threw one haphazard shot of his own in Smoke's general direction, but it didn't come anywhere close to hitting him.

Smoke stood and left the cover of the boulder.

McFadden was charging in the direction of the canyon's opening, no doubt thinking of an escape.

Smoke wouldn't let that happen.

So, he charged, too.

Straight into the heart of the battle.

Nighthawk found Audie in the canyon.

The diminutive man was pinned down behind an outcropping of boulders, trading shots with two outlaws who were inside the corral, using the railing as cover.

The giant Crow slid in beside the professor.

"Good to see you, old friend!" Audie said loudly, over the thunder of echoing gunfire. "What was that quote the Bard said, something about fighting?"

"Umm."

"Yes, yes. That's the one. 'Fight till the last gasp.' *Henry VI, Part One.* I believe it applies right now, wouldn't you say?"

"Umm."

More shots crashed loudly. Audie leveled his revolver and sent three bullets at his adversaries, but they only splintered the wooden railing.

"Blast it all!"

Nighthawk was up without another sound. He zigzagged as he ran toward the corral. The men inside noticed his approach and gasped in horror at the sight of a giant Indian charging them with a raised tomahawk. They stood up straight and tried to bring their guns around to meet him, but that only exposed them to Audie.

He stood, too, fanning the flame of his pistol as he threw bullets toward them.

One man's head snapped back as he took a shot right between the eyes. The other man caught lead in the neck. He dropped his gun and tried to cover the wound, but it was no use. He was already bleeding profusely and unstable on his feet. He fell next to his companion.

The horses in the corral were in a frenzy now, bucking wildly as they danced about, slashing the downed outlaws with their hooves.

"You saved me, Nighthawk!" Audie said.

"Umm."

"Don't give me that—you've already downed a few, I suppose. Can't have all the fun, now can you?"

All around, the battle continued to rage, but the shots

were decreasing. Enough of McFadden's men had been ventilated to quiet things down, but it was far from over.

Venom McFadden was still alive.

The fight wouldn't end until he'd met his Maker.

Smoke slowed his pursuit.

McFadden was running out of options. He only had a
couple of men left and they were exchanging shots with
Jedidiah and Maddox. It looked as if Nighthawk and Audie
were coming in to help, too.

One of those outlaws went down from a bullet fired from
up on the rim as Hargis continued to work the lever on his
repeater.

The jig was up.

If McFadden continued to run, the cross fire of the op-
posing sides would chop him down. If he turned back, he'd
face the burning cabin and then a dead end.

More than that, he'd face Smoke.

Apparently, he chose that option. He stopped altogether
and slowly turned to face the approaching enemy.

"You!" he said, his voice shaking with rage. "You're responsible for all of this!"

"No, McFadden," Smoke said. "You did this to yourself."

"Things were going good in Desolation Creek!"

"Good for you," Smoke said. "Bad for everybody else."

"But you ruined it!" McFadden went on as if he hadn't
even heard Smoke's response. He was shouting—partly in
anger and partly because of the still-ringing gunshots echoing from the canyon walls.

Smoke measured the angle of where McFadden stood
and where Hargis was. The mountain man could probably
end McFadden now, but he knew Smoke wanted the honor.

Smoke owed that much to Preacher.

As far as Smoke could tell, McFadden hadn't been
wounded. He looked to be in full health.

Physically at least.

Mentally, the man seemed unhinged.

A fiery rage, which burned in his eyes, marred his usual smooth, suave appearance. His cheeks glowed red. He was spitting as he talked. Smoke thought of a wild, snarling cur.

His string tie was undone, hanging limply around his neck. His trademark vest was gone. Spilled whiskey stained his shirt. His black pants were dirty and gray with trail dust. The black hair atop his head stood up in various places.

The flight from Desolation Creek had been rough for him.

Good, Smoke thought. McFadden had been undone. He now knew mental anguish.

He was about to know physical anguish as well. That is, if he lived long enough to feel it.

"The people of Desolation Creek were fed up," Smoke said. "People can only live under the rule of tyrants for so long before they rise up. They would have turned on you even if I hadn't ridden into town. That's all your doing, McFadden. Don't blame me or anyone else."

"Don't you preach at me!" McFadden spat. "I'm gonna kill you. You hear me? I'm going to take your life. You'll breathe your last breath because of me, and the buzzards will pick your bones clean."

"I'm right here," Smoke said. "Give it your best shot."

Instead of raising his gun, McFadden lunged for Smoke. In his deranged state, the outlaw wanted to try to choke the life out of his opponent.

He never had a chance.

Smoke evaded the attack and brought his own fist into McFadden's face as he passed by.

McFadden stumbled, dropping his gun. Smoke kicked it away before he could reach it.

Smoke pouched his own iron. If McFadden wanted a fight, he'd give him all he could handle.

McFadden planted his feet and bent at his knees, raising

his fists as he sneered. He bobbed and weaved, shuffling to his side. He tried to throw a right, but Smoke read it well in advance. He moved to the side and felt the swoosh of air as the fist sailed past his ear. McFadden tried for speed and immediately launched a left, followed by another right. Once again, Smoke was able to avoid them all.

McFadden wasn't so lucky.

McFadden doubled over and lurched forward as Smoke sunk a fist in his gut. It didn't last long, though, as Smoke's second blow connected with McFadden's jaw. His head snapped back with a loud pop. Smoke gave him a left to the face, followed by another right, and then one more left.

The man's face was bloody and swollen. Based on the look in McFadden's eyes, Smoke wasn't even sure if the man was aware of what was happening. He surprised Smoke when he said, "You . . . did . . . this. You . . . did it all."

"You killed my friend," Smoke said.

"Your . . . friend?" McFadden gurgled, and then spit a string of blood out. Smoke was pretty sure he saw a tooth fly to the ground with it.

"The old man?" McFadden finally said.

"His name was Preacher. And you're going to say it."

McFadden mustered a late surge of bravado and tried to stand upright. He grinned—or what passed as a grin—and shook his head. He looked grotesque, his cheeks puffed out, his mouth flowing with fresh blood.

Smoke gave him another punch in the face and then one to the gut.

McFadden doubled over and retched. He groaned and almost went down, but managed to stay on his feet.

Behind them, the fire continued to rage. The cabin crackled loudly as beams split. A crash announced the roof had collapsed. The heat was nearly overpowering. Cinders drifted in the air, along with the smell of charred wood.

"Say it," Smoke said again.

"P-Preacher," McFadden whispered.

Smoke nodded.

"His name was . . . Preacher," McFadden said.

His movements were painfully slow, but maybe in his deranged state, he thought he had a chance.

With clear, painstaking agony, he reached around and pulled a small pistol from the back of his waistband. Smoke watched, not in a hurry, before drawing his own gun.

"That's right," Smoke said, cocking his piece. "His name was Preacher."

The bullet bore into the center of McFadden's forehead. His eyes rolled up in their sockets. He stood there a moment, teetering, before his legs finally received the message and gave way. He pitched forward onto his face.

By now, the fighting stopped. The echoes of gun thunder faded in the canyon.

The other outlaws were just as dead as Venom McFadden.

CHAPTER 32

Smoke and the others had no desire to linger.

After the battle that had wiped out Venom McFadden and his men, they'd left the canyon, preferring to bed down somewhere else for the evening—away from the odor of fire and death.

They left the dead men where they had fallen, a feast for the scavengers that would return nature to its proper balance.

The following morning, Smoke and his friends were on the trail bright and early. They'd ridden along for a few hours when Smoke said to the others, "Are you headed back to Desolation Creek, or are you men setting off for the high country again?"

Hargis looked at the distant mountains. They called him the way they always did. Maddox and Jedidiah seemed lost in thought, too. Finally Hargis said, "Reckon I'll go on to Desolation Creek. I have it in mind to pay my respects at Preacher's grave."

"You know I do, too," Maddox said.

"Same," Jedidiah added.

"Did they speak words over him or just dump him in the ground?" Hargis said. "For all we know, that snake McFadden didn't even let the town have a proper funeral."

"I'm not sure," Smoke said. "But I doubt they did much, that's for sure."

"Ain't right," Maddox said quietly. "Just discard a man like that. A good man."

"You thinking on leaving him in Desolation Creek?" Jedidiah asked, turning his head to look at Smoke.

"I haven't even given his resting place much thought," Smoke admitted. "I've been so wrapped up in my thirst for justice that I haven't even gone by the cemetery."

"Smoke," Audie said, "have you considered transporting Preacher's remains? Perhaps his soul would like to rest on the Sugarloaf. You meant the world to him, after all."

"Umm," Nighthawk added.

"I was thinking along those lines, myself," Hargis said. "Reckon we'd all journey down Colorado way with you, if you want to move him."

"Be my honor," Maddox said.

Smoke gave the matter some thought for a few minutes. No one in Desolation Creek would object to him exhuming the remains. It wasn't as if anyone there had a connection to the old man. He knew Sally would be all for it as well. She'd keep his grave up with fresh flowers. Smoke would tend to it, too, keeping the grass trimmed down and the weeds away.

A part of him wondered if such things even mattered, one way or the other, to Preacher.

Preacher had never been confined to one place in life. Now that he was gone, it didn't matter where his body was laid to rest.

His soul would keep on wandering, trying to fill that thirst to see what was over the next mountain or down in the next valley.

"I'll think it over," he said. The recent violence had dulled his brain, and his body was achy and weary. "Right now, I'm just ready to get back to Desolation Creek, see Sally, and maybe take a good hot bath. Sleep in a bed one night and then pull up stakes just as soon as the sun comes up."

If he decided to move Preacher's earthly remains, it wouldn't take long to exhume him. Such an activity wouldn't slow him down any. The Sugarloaf was calling his name. He wondered how Pearlie was faring. Smoke suspected he was just fine. The foreman was more than capable. Business was probably going on as usual there at the ranch.

He also wondered what had transpired in Big Rock since the last time he'd been there. He'd spend a few days at the ranch on his return, but then he'd ride in to see Monte Carson and Louis Longmont and get caught up on all the news, if there was any.

The group rode until the sunlight failed them. The next morning, they were up and at their journey even earlier than the previous day. Smoke was thankful they didn't have too far to go.

They swung wide of the burned-out way station, not wanting to encounter any problems, though Smoke didn't think those two young men would pose a threat. Sure enough, Smoke and the others crossed the region without incident.

Smoke kept his eyes peeled, though, worried about someone else. As if sensing the extra attention he was paying their surroundings, Audie said, "What troubles you?"

"I was just thinking about Hicks. You know, we never found him."

"He'd be the one you had the shooting competition with in the street back in Desolation Creek?" Audie said.

"That's him."

Audie nodded. "True. He wasn't in the canyon, was he?"

"Nope."

Jedidiah said, "Always a chance he lit a shuck clean out of the territory. He might have wanted well clear of here before you cooked his goose!"

"I bet that's it," Maddox said. "He heard the name *Smoke Jensen* and then wet his britches before running off to find his ma."

The others laughed.

"I'm not so sure of that," Smoke said. "I don't doubt he has a self-preservation streak a mile wide. But something tells me he's not the type to let our beef go. I'm of a mind to think I'll meet him again."

"I hope not," Audie said. "I hope we're done with this mess altogether!"

The others agreed.

Smoke wanted nothing more than for that to be the case. Yet something told him they weren't out of the woods yet. He wasn't sure what it was, either. Venom McFadden was dead. Most of his men were gone, too. The others were scattered.

Why did he still have that troublesome feeling dogging his trail?

His gut told him more was coming.

And if he'd learned anything in his short but very eventful life, it was to always trust his gut.

Smoke's hunches proved correct sooner rather than later.

As they neared Desolation Creek and swung past Newt Simmons's place, Newt greeted them as he ran through his yard and to the road, waving his hands and calling for them to halt.

"Hello, Newt," Smoke said in a friendly tone. "You doing all right out here?"

Smoke knew the answer before it came. Why else would one of Simmons's sons be watching from the barn loft, a rifle in hand and at the ready? Smoke had a feeling other sentries were about, too. Trouble was definitely brewing out there.

"Far from it," Newt said. The words ran together. He struggled to catch his breath. He kept everyone waiting while he wheezed. He filled his lungs full of air, exhaled, and then said, "More men came to harass us. They want us off our land!"

Upon hearing the news, Smoke sat up straighter in the saddle.

"McFadden must have left a few strays behind," Hargis said.

"I'm sorry they did that," Smoke said. "The good news is that Venom McFadden is dead. Those men won't be back."

Simmons shook his head. "That's what I'm trying to tell you. It wasn't McFadden's men! And they were here yesterday. Came back this morning, too." He jerked a thumb over his shoulder. For the first time, Smoke and the others noticed the dead livestock. They were a ways out, but sure enough, the corpses of butchered cattle littered the pasture.

"Said they aim to have our land. It ain't just my spread, either. They've been going all up and down the valley. Gave us two days to clear out or said next time they'd just shoot us and take what they want, anyway."

"You didn't recognize these men?" Smoke asked.

"No. Had that look about them, though. Same look as McFadden's bunch."

"Hired guns." It wasn't a question. Travel around the frontier long enough and you learned the look of them.

Simmons nodded.

A few beats of heavy silence ticked off before Simmons said, "They did worse to Jackson, about a mile west of here. Done burnt his house down. He got his grandson out, but only by the grace of God. He said they just rode right up to the house, lit a few torches, and tossed 'em in through the window. His wife was in the garden or she would have most likely gone up along with the house!"

"Thought we were done with trouble around these parts,"

Hargis said before spitting a brown stream from his lips. "Guess we need to figure out who's trying to run these homesteaders off and why."

"It's not just us homesteaders," Simmons said. "There's something else."

A sour feeling started in the pit of Smoke's stomach before radiating upward. He felt bile rising in his throat and did his best to choke it down. He had a feeling about what Simmons was going to say and he didn't like it one bit.

"It's Desolation Creek. There's a new hard case running that town. And from what I hear, he's worse than Venom McFadden."

CHAPTER 33

"Someone new?" Smoke said.

Newt nodded. "A real cutthroat. They say he's already killed a few people there in town. He's moved into the Dead Moose and picked up right where McFadden left off." Simmons shuffled on his feet and sighed. "I ain't been in town yet, but that's the word I'm hearing from some of the men who have."

"Do they know who it is?" Smoke said.

Simmons shook his head.

Smoke looked beyond Simmons and to the loft, where the young man stood watch. His eyes then fell to the slaughtered cattle in the distance. It obviously wasn't the livestock this new tyrant was after, else he wouldn't be killing so many of them. He obviously wasn't a rancher intent on growing his spread, no matter who he had to hurt to do so. No, this person had other ambitions.

"Whoever he is, he's got the town locked up tight," Simmons continued. "Ain't letting folks in or out."

"Sally," Smoke said. There was no alarm in his voice. He wasn't full of panic.

He was full of anger.

Whoever this man was, he better have left her well enough alone.

Heaven help him otherwise.

"You fellas are welcome to stay here if you'd like, while you figure out what to do," Simmons said.

"Much obliged," Smoke said. "Guess we do need to figure out a plan."

"I'll tell you my plan," Jedidiah said. "We ride in, slapping leather, with guns blazin'! That's my plan."

"Ah, I understand the sentiment," Audie said. "But that won't do us or the poor people of Desolation Creek any good. We need to know how many men we're facing. Determine what the odds are."

"Umm."

"Yes, that's right, Nighthawk. Riders did pass by here on their way into town just a few days ago."

Smoke remembered, recalling what Simmons had said about quite a few riders passing by his place.

Where were they coming from? There hadn't been enough time for word to spread that McFadden had been pushed out of Desolation Creek. They must have been somewhere waiting.

Somewhere close.

A person in town had been lying low until the opportune time. But who could it be?

That was when a terrible thought struck Smoke. Had another hard case, every bit as bad as McFadden, been there the whole time, right under his nose, just waiting for a chance to strike?

He had a few ideas swirling in his brain, but he'd have to sneak into Desolation Creek to confirm his hunches.

And most importantly, he needed to check on Sally and get her to safety.

He fought the urge to give in to his anger. That wouldn't

help Sally. He needed to keep keen eyes and a clear mind. Rage would only blind him. There might come a time for it, but right now, he needed to take a levelheaded approach.

"We might as well rest our horses a spell," Smoke said. "We're much obliged for your offer to stay."

Simmons chuckled. "Truth be told, I'm glad to have the extra bodies around. I don't think those riders will be back to raid this place until the deadline they gave us expires, but you never can be too sure."

Smoke wished the men would come back.

He'd put them in the ground and even up the odds a bit.

As of now, the deck seemed stacked against them. Someone had a hold on Desolation Creek again. From what it sounded like, they'd turned the town into a prison. Smoke didn't know how many men were there or what kind of ammunition and weapons they had.

And Sally was right there, in the thick of it all.

"Well, that explains why we hadn't seen hide or hair of Chuck Hicks," Smoke said with a shake of his head.

The men were sitting out back of Newt Simmons's house. They had been invited inside, but none of them wanted to frighten Simmons's daughter. With all the menacing events going on around those parts, as of late, they thought it best to circle up outside and talk strategy.

They sat in the grass. The ground was hard, but it was still good to have a break from the saddle. Smoke just wished it had been under better circumstances. His return to Sugarloaf—and especially the chance to be back there with Sally—kept moving further and further away. It darn near seemed outside of his reach now. He wouldn't give up, though. He couldn't. Ever.

"You think it's this Hicks fella who is running the show in Desolation Creek?" Maddox asked.

"I do," Smoke said. "What I can't figure out is if he was

planning this all along or if the idea just sort of came to him."

"I suppose it doesn't matter," Audie said. "Except it could give us a better idea as to how cunning this man is. If he was lying in wait the whole time, with his men doing the same until they received word, it indicates we have a formidable opponent here."

"Exactly," Smoke said. "Could be that Hicks himself worked in secret to fan the flames of the town's rebellion."

"If that don't beat all," Jedidiah said.

The conversation stopped when Simmons approached. "You gents want some coffee?" He carried a steaming kettle in one hand and a few tin cups in the other. Behind him, his daughter had more cups. Simmons set the coffee in the middle of the circle and then distributed the cups.

"Much obliged," Smoke said.

The others voiced their appreciation, too. Once they were alone again, the six warriors continued their planning.

"So, how do you figure this, Smoke?" Maddox said. "I reckon we'll follow your lead. You've got the most invested here."

"Dang right," Hargis said. "Truth be told, now that the score's been settled for Preacher, what happens in Desolation Creek ain't none of our business. I'm in this to get your woman back, Smoke. And it sticks in my craw to see the townsfolk overrun again. Stepping in is the right thing to do."

His two riding partners nodded, and Maddox added, "It's possible this hombre Hicks had something to do with Preacher's death, too, so I figure the score's not settled completely until he's dealt with, too."

"You're right," Hargis said. "I didn't think about that. Well, one more reason to unleash a little fire and brimstone on the varmint!"

"I appreciate the help," Smoke said. "I have a plan in

mind. It's not perfect, but it's probably the best we can do on such short notice."

They all listened intently as he laid it out.

"That's the way you want to play it, huh?" Jedidiah said.

"It is," Smoke said with a curt nod. "Figure it's the only way we can."

The men drained the last of their coffee and started to stand.

Jedidiah smacked his lips, wiped his mouth, and smiled.

"Then let's get to it."

Night had fallen as Smoke made it to the outskirts of Desolation Creek undetected. At least, if anyone had detected him, they hadn't let on yet.

He left Drifter out of sight, and far removed from harm's way, covering the last bit on foot. He hoped his luck would hold out. He needed to move around without being noticed, gaining valuable information as to the current situation in town.

He came up behind the hardware store and cut through the small alley that led to Main Street. He stayed low and kept to the shadows. Two men walked by, within a yard of him, as he lurked just inside the alley mouth. They didn't notice that they were being stalked. They kept right along with their vulgar chatter, comparing notes on a whorehouse they'd both visited in Creede. Smoke watched them go and made a mental note.

Two.

He was keeping a tally of the gunmen he encountered. And he had no doubt these hombres fit the bill. Smoke had encountered enough of their kind to know.

They strutted down Main Street as if they owned it. Their arrogance was angering. The people of Desolation Creek had only had a couple of days of freedom before another tyrant with grand aspirations had taken over.

He fought off the anger he felt. He'd harness its power when the time came.

Right now, though, he needed to learn more.

And check on Sally.

The street was mostly empty. Smoke spotted a couple of other men, in the opposite direction, and he figured they were patrolling, too. Apparently, whoever was calling the shots had enacted some sort of curfew. Or perhaps the townspeople were just too tired and afraid—or both—to be out and about.

Whatever the case, it was eerily quiet.

Smoke cast his eyes in the direction of the hotel. He could see a lamp burning in the window of his room. That gave him a small measure of comfort, even though he didn't have definitive proof that it was Sally occupying the space. Someone else could have moved into that room since he'd left, though he found the notion doubtful. Sounded as if Desolation Creek was buttoned up tight once again. Folks weren't getting in or out. It stood to reason that the light was from Sally.

Maybe she'd managed to stay low and keep out of the mind of whoever it was.

If it was Hicks, as Smoke believed, he'd probably come for her sooner or later. He'd want to use her as leverage against Smoke. That was probably why he hadn't harmed her yet.

Assuming he had not.

Smoke watched as the other pair of guards, across the street, turned their backs. Then he darted from the alley and made it to cover on the other side.

He pressed his back against a building and listened. Nothing.

By now, both pairs of guards had crossed the streets at opposite sides. He got low, realizing the two he'd encountered moments before would soon pass him on this side as well. He waited.

Sure enough, they passed, this time talking about a whorehouse in Wichita.

He made a mental note that there were four guards so far and then thought about what to do next. He needed a friend in town. He had a few he could count on. Perhaps they could feed him information and make his job easier.

He thought of Darnell Poe. Who kept better watch over a town than its marshal and newspaperman? The marshal wasn't an option, given that Smoke hadn't seen him once since arriving in Desolation Creek. That left Poe.

Smoke moved closer to the mouth of the alley and looked across the street and to his right, toward the paper's office. It was dark. He tried to remember if Poe lived in the back of it, but could not. He wasn't sure he'd ever heard, one way or the other. Plus, from Smoke's vantage point, the building showed no signs of current life.

That left Hodges. The old miner was a salty fellow. He didn't miss much. He'd give Smoke the lay of the land if Smoke could find him.

He thought of the Absaroka. It was on the same side of the street that he was currently on. He could sneak behind the buildings and see if the saloon had a back door.

It was worth a try, so Smoke set off. He pictured the front of the street in his mind, counting the buildings as he crept along, until he found the one he was sure was the Absaroka.

He tried the back door and found it unlocked. He hurried inside, took careful time to close the door quietly, and then went into a crouch. He was relieved to see a few crates of liquor and barrels of beer, confirming that he'd indeed selected the right building.

The place smelled of alcohol. As he made his way through the back room, that odor got stronger, adding sweat and tobacco. He came to the door that led to the main part and stopped to listen.

He heard a few faint noises. A shuffle of a foot. Maybe

someone hitting their knee against the bar or tapping on the top with their fingers.

He nudged the door open quietly and took a peek.

Earl was behind the bar. Hodges sat at one of the tables. As far as Smoke could tell, the two men were alone in the saloon.

"It's Smoke Jensen," he called softly. "I'm coming in."

The announcement still spooked the two men. The bar-keep even reached for a scattergun under the counter, but stopped when he got a good look at Smoke.

"Thank heavens!" Hodges said, standing up and hurrying toward the bar.

Smoke moved around it now, keeping his eyes on the building's front entrance.

"What's going on here in town?" Smoke said in a low tone.

"I'll tell you what's going on!" Hodges said. "That scum Hicks!"

Smoke nodded at the confirmation that his hunch had been correct.

"He moved in and took over where McFadden left off, huh?"

"Best we can tell," Hodges said. "Truth be told, I don't know that much. I do know that he's wearing a marshal's badge now. He's got deputies, too. Plenty of 'em." The old-timer snorted. "Deputies! More like low-down owlhoots!"

"I saw four on patrol," Smoke said.

"He's got more than that," Earl said with a grunt.

"How many?"

"Why?" Hodges said, raising a bushy eyebrow. "You aimin' to do somethin' about all this?"

"That's the plan," Smoke said. "But I need information."

Hodges scratched his chin, then said, "I've seen eight at least. I think there's more, though. Down at the Dead Moose."

"That's his headquarters?" Smoke asked.

"I'm not sure what's going on down there," Hodges said. "I ain't been able to get close. I know for a fact that Hicks is keepin' hours at the marshal's office. I've seen him comin' and goin'. But I'm not sure what all is happening at the Dead Moose."

"Has Hicks given the town any sort of ultimatum?" Smoke asked. "Said anything about what his plan is?"

"Oh, he's been in here," Earl chimed in. "Said he doesn't mind me doing business, but I've got to pay for him and his deputies' protection! Reckon it's the same with all the other businesses in town."

"That's right," Hodges confirmed. "Ol' Venom McFadden wanted to have the only saloon in town, but Hicks doesn't seem to care about that."

"As long as he gets his cut," Earl added.

"Speaking of McFadden," Hodges said, "what became of him?"

"He's dead," Smoke said flatly. "Along with the rest of his men. All except Hicks, I suppose."

"And Hicks ain't alone," Hodges said. "He's got his own army, and those so-called deputies are every bit as mean as McFadden's bunch was!"

Smoke looked at Earl. "I'm guessing that amount he collects is pretty high."

"You better believe it!" Earl said. "I'm practically working just to buy more stock and pay him. I ain't got nothing left."

Earl let out a lungful of air and shook his head.

"That skunk gave a lecture about how it's our civic duty to pay taxes and—" He finished wringing his hands and then pushed them out, as if trying to shove everything away.

"What about my wife? Have either of you seen Sally?"

"She's fine," Hodges said. "I've been sneaking into the hotel to check on her. She hasn't been harmed."

"I'm much obliged to you for that," Smoke said.

"Least I could do after what you did for this town." He

gave Smoke a pointed stare. "I hope you're gonna do it again."

"That's the plan," Smoke said. "But I need to get the lay of the land first."

"I hope I helped."

"You did," Smoke told Hodges. "Both of you."

"Well, when the time comes, let us know," Hodges said. His grin was ornery.

"I'll help again . . . with gunsmoke."

Back outside, Smoke thought about what to do next.

He needed to get down to the Dead Moose to see how well Hicks was fortified. It might be that their best bet in getting to him would be on his way to or from the marshal's office.

Smoke had to laugh grimly at the idea of Chuck Hicks calling himself a marshal.

He looked up and down both sides of the street and found the four guards who were still patrolling. He remembered the plan he'd hatched back at Newt Simmons's place. Was it time to act?

After a few moments of careful consideration, he decided against it.

He needed more information first.

Then luck smiled upon him.

He spotted a figure carefully making his way down the street. Darnell Poe was going toward the newspaper's office. If Smoke could reach him undetected, he could sneak inside and get more information before striking.

It was slow going as he retreated deeper into the alley and then behind the building. He figured the best way was going all the way down, crossing at the very end of Main Street, and coming up behind the office. He only hoped Poe would still be there. Hopefully, he wasn't just dropping in to grab something he'd forgotten.

Smoke went as fast as stealth allowed. He went well past the buildings on Main Street until the darkness of the night covered his movements. The guards hadn't extended their patrol that far past the town's businesses, so he assumed he'd be able to make the crossing undetected.

He was right. He darted to the other side of the road without anyone shouting or alerting the others.

It was even slower getting back to the buildings and behind them. He hadn't seen Poe heading back down the road and he took some small comfort in that. It appeared as if the man was still at his office.

Five minutes after leaving the alley, Smoke approached the back door of the office.

It was locked.

He crept down the alley, took note of where the patrols were, and then hurried back. He'd have to knock, though he'd do it as quietly as possible.

He rapped his knuckles on the door and waited.

Nothing.

He did it again.

This time, he was rewarded when the door creaked open slightly. A nervous-looking Poe gasped when he saw his visitor.

"Jensen!" he said in a whisper. "Come in, come in."

He stepped back and held the door open long enough for Smoke to slide in. He shut it as quietly as possible and then turned to his visitor.

"What were you doing out there? Did anyone see you?"

Smoke shook his head. "Trying to figure out what's going on around here."

Two kerosene lanterns hung on the walls, across from each other, bathing the small workroom in a soft light. Papers were stacked neatly on Poe's desk. Another table— tall and resembling one a drafter would use—contained a copy of an unfolded newspaper, along with some pens.

"I'll tell you what's going on," Poe said. "Someone has taken over Desolation Creek!"

"Seems this town has a string of bad luck," Smoke said.

"You can say that again," Poe said. "Honestly, I'm not sure the citizens have any fight left in them. They were run ragged by McFadden. Which reminds me. Where is McFadden?"

"Dead," Smoke answered.

"Good," Poe said. "That's what he deserved."

"Along with Hicks, huh?"

"Hicks?"

"I heard he's the new *marshal* around here."

Poe nodded. "He is." He moved closer, a grave look on his face. "We have to be quiet. They might be listening."

Smoke nodded. "We can do something about this, Poe, but I need information."

"Whatever I can do," Poe whispered.

"I appreciate it," Smoke said. "Sure didn't take someone long to move in and take over in McFadden's absence."

"No, it didn't," Poe said. "And that someone was me."

Smoke cursed himself for getting distracted. By the time he saw the blow coming, it was too late. He hadn't even noticed Poe was holding a gun.

He took the blow on the side of his head and staggered. For a moment, he thought he'd be able to fight off the wave of pain and nausea that threatened to overwhelm him.

But the room started spinning even faster and he felt his legs give out.

For a second, he saw Poe standing over him, looking down and smiling in triumph.

That was just before Smoke's eyes closed and the world went black.

CHAPTER 34

Smoke awoke to find himself behind bars.

"Marshal," a man said, wearing an arrogant sneer and looking as if he'd just been told the funniest joke in the world, "your prisoner is awake."

Smoke groaned and tried to keep his eyes open, but even the dim light provided by the lantern outside of his cell made his brain hurt.

He slowly brought his hand up and touched the spot where Poe had delivered the brutal, treacherous blow. It was lumpy and tender. He winced.

When he heard boots thudding against the floor outside of the cell, he tried to sit up. It hurt to move, so he lay there another minute.

"Don't trouble yourself getting up," the cocky voice of Chuck Hicks said. "It's just me."

"I know," Smoke said through gritted teeth. "I could smell you."

Hicks lost his arrogant grin and scowled through the iron bars. Smoke smiled and managed to sit up.

"Well, would you look at that?" he said. "Making sport of you is good for the spirit *and* the body. Huh."

Hicks jabbed a finger between two of the bars. "You better watch yourself, Jensen. This is my jail. This is my town."

"No, it's not," Smoke said. "It's Darnell Poe's. For now."

"We're partners," Hicks said.

"That so?" Smoke managed to swing his legs off the uncomfortable cot. The iron squeaked with his movements. He almost hissed in pain as he forced his body to stand, but caught himself. He wouldn't give Hicks that satisfaction.

Hicks stood before the cell. A deputy was beside him, cradling a scattergun. Smoke recognized him as one of the men he'd seen riding into Desolation Creek that day he'd dropped by Newt Simmons's place, on his way to find McFadden.

"Poe is in charge and you know it. You're not smart enough to run anything."

Hicks's nostrils flared.

"I might take orders from him for now. But I'm second-in-command. Like Taggart was. How is poor ol' Taggart, by the way?" Hicks laughed. It was an ugly sound. "He wasn't feeling so well when he rode out of here."

Smoke shrugged. "He isn't hurting now."

"And McFadden?"

"You'll see him soon enough."

Hicks stepped even closer and put his hate-twisted face almost against the bars. "You're too stupid to realize the situation you're in, Jensen! You ought not be talkin' to me that way!" He made a show of looking around. "Your friends aren't here to back you up. No old trappers. No big Indians. And you're behind bars."

"Trust me, I've faced worse odds," Smoke said.

Hicks studied him for a moment before snorting in contempt. "I doubt you have."

He reached into his vest pocket and retrieved a key ring.

"This where you put the boots to me?" Smoke said.

He didn't show it, but he was ready for a fight. If Hicks and his deputy wanted a scuffle, he'd give them all they could handle.

"No," Hicks said. "We're just going out for a friendly drink. Poe wants to see you. At the Dead Moose."

Three other deputies spilled through the doorway that led to the main part of the marshal's office, each one holding a scattergun.

"Don't get the notion of trying anything funny, either," Hicks said. "We'll cut you down where you stand. At this range, these Greeners won't leave anything of you except a few chunks of meat."

"No, you won't," Smoke said. "I figure *your boss* wants me alive or I'd already be dead. Don't worry, though. I won't try anything. You're safe for now. I'm curious to see what Poe has in mind." He jerked his head toward the door. "Shall we?"

Hicks was grumbling under his breath when the gang led Smoke out into the office and then through the front door.

The street was deserted, with only the guards on patrol out and about.

Smoke had two deputies in front of him and two behind him, along with Hicks bringing up the rear. Smoke was still a mite unsteady on his feet, so the journey to the Dead Moose took some time.

Once they arrived, Smoke saw six men hanging around outside. They all leered at him with angry eyes. It was evident they wanted bloodshed, like ancient Romans waiting in the Colosseum for the gladiators to fight.

Smoke paid no attention to them as his captors prodded him up the stairs. He wasn't sure which of them he'd kill first, but there was a good chance it would be the hombre who kept jabbing the barrels of a shotgun into his back. That act had grown mighty old.

Smoke stepped inside and instantly noticed the last person he wanted to see there.

Sally.

To her credit, she didn't look terrified as she sat in a chair close to the bar, her arms pulled behind her. She appeared to be bound by ropes, although Smoke couldn't see the restraints.

"It's going to be all right," he told her. She returned the reassuring smile he gave her.

"Now, now," Darnell Poe said, standing up from the table where he was sitting. He picked up a shot glass and downed the liquor before approaching Smoke. "Don't make promises you can't keep, especially to such a pretty lady."

Smoke remained silent. Inside, he cursed himself for not seeing this in time.

As if reading his mind, Poe smiled and said, "I know what you're thinking. How did I miss this? Don't worry, it's not you. I'm just a great actor."

He turned and started pacing, apparently eager to captivate his audience with a monologue, as if he were on stage in some theater.

"I thought about joining a theater company once. They came through the tiny town in Kansas where I lived. Oh, it seemed so adventurous! I could run away from home and travel the world. In the end, I was too afraid. Too timid to take a chance."

He stopped pacing and leveled a hard stare at Smoke.

"But I'm not afraid anymore. Not of anything. Especially you. So, don't get any funny ideas. Perhaps I'll let you live through this."

Smoke doubted that. Why would Poe leave him alive? It didn't matter, anyway. Smoke sure wasn't about to sit there and take all this without putting up a fight.

Poe's steps were heavy as he came closer. "I need some information. Where are your friends, Jensen?"

"They left me," Smoke said.

Poe studied him a moment before snorting. "You expect me to believe that?"

Smoke shrugged. "Doesn't much matter what you believe. It's the truth. They had no reason to come back to Desolation Creek. Our business here was finished. I only came back for my wife. That's all I want now, Poe. Just let us ride on out. Truth be told, I don't care what happens to this town."

Poe laughed loudly. "You expect me to believe that, too? Oh, that's funny."

"Again, I'm just telling the truth. What you do with it is up to you."

Poe was starting to anger. He must have gotten used to people cowering before him since he'd seized power. "What happens with your life is up to me! Hers too. I'd change my tone if I were you!"

Smoke sighed. His patience was growing thin. He was also walking a fine line. He didn't want to send his captor into too much of a rage, as that might be bad for Sally. And the last thing Smoke wanted was for any harm to come to her.

But he also needed to string Poe along and buy some time. He wasn't sure what was going on with his plan. He just needed to have faith.

Poe walked behind Sally and stopped, putting a hand on her shoulder.

Out of instinct, Smoke's own hand fell to his right side, only to find an empty holster. Poe chuckled.

"We weren't stupid enough to leave you armed. I've heard about you, Jensen. More than that, I saw what you're capable of, just a few days ago. I must admit, that was something. And I'm not a man easily impressed."

Smoke didn't say a word as he continued to glare at Darnell Poe.

Poe waited, his eyes trained on Smoke, expecting him to say more. When nothing else was forthcoming, he said, "I'm going to ask you again, where are your friends?" He patted Sally's shoulder.

"I told you, Poe. They're on the trail. I don't know where they're going, though I suspect they'll head on to the Rockies."

"No, no, no," Poe said, starting to pace again as he shook his head. "I just can't believe that."

"Going to have to," Smoke said.

Poe stopped dead in his tracks. "I don't have to do anything, Jensen. Don't you forget that. This is *my* town. I call the shots. I sure don't take orders from a man like you!" He jabbed his finger angrily at Smoke.

"This is your town, huh?" Smoke said. "You were just waiting for something to happen to McFadden so you could take over what was rightfully yours. Is that it?"

"That's it," Poe said, smiling now as he resumed his pacing. He came to the window, looked out into the dark street, and then turned around again to face Smoke and the others. "Except I didn't *just* wait. I orchestrated things. Pulled the strings. I got folks riled up and willing to help." He laughed. "Isn't that wonderful, Jensen? That's my favorite part. They didn't know they were all part of my plan.

"I wasn't sure what to make of you when you showed up, but I had a feeling you'd be trouble. You played into everything so perfectly. I'm not even sure we could have run McFadden out of town if you hadn't been here.

"And the best part is, you chased him down and killed him for me! Now I don't have to worry about him coming back and starting some kind of war. You handled my enemy for me." Poe patted his hands together softly in mock applause. "Bravo, Jensen. Bravo."

He started pacing again.

Smoke rolled his eyes. He didn't know how much more of the speechifying he could take. He needed just a few more minutes, though.

His eyes fell to Sally. He tried conveying that she needn't worry. She nodded, a slight smile turning her pretty lips upward. Smoke realized she had faith in him.

He wouldn't disappoint her.

Not now or ever.

"Ah, isn't that sweet," Poe said, recognizing the silent conversation that was taking place between the married couple. "You're trying to comfort one another in your darkest hour."

"Poe, this isn't near my darkest hour. I've gone up against a lot tougher than you," Smoke said.

Poe's nostrils flared. His fists were balled. He inched closer to Sally. "You're making me angry, Jensen. You tell me what I want to know or I'll start taking that anger out on this pretty little lady here." He unclenched his fists and caressed Sally's face. She tried to scoot away, but the restraints held her in place. He smiled rakishly.

"That's right, darling. You and I might get really well acquainted here in a minute," Poe said.

"Poe, I told you," Smoke said, a hint of desperation in his voice. "They aren't here."

Poe turned his focus away from Sally and looked to Smoke, stepping closer. "Which direction did they pull out to?"

Smoke looked as if he didn't want to say. He sighed loudly.

"Where, Jensen?" Poe prodded, his voice loud now.

"Hargis and Maddox went on west," he said reluctantly. "Jedidiah said he was visiting his sister, up Dakota way. Audie and Nighthawk are on the trail back to Colorado. We're supposed to meet up at a trading post in Wyoming in a few days."

Poe studied him for a long, tense moment. "I'm not sure if I believe you." He walked back to Sally and stood behind her, this time putting both hands on her shoulders. "Guess we'll find out if you're telling the truth soon enough." He looked down with an evil grin before stooping lower and smelling Sally's hair. "Oh, the fun we will have."

"I told you the truth," Smoke said. "You don't have to do this."

"I know," Poe said. "I want to."

Smoke's jaw clenched tightly. "Tell me one thing," he said, still trying to draw the moment out. "I get why you want this town. Lot of money to be made. But why do you want the homesteaders' places up north? Why go after them?"

Poe stood up straight and laughed, forgetting about everything else at the chance to captivate his audience once more. "The town? Oh, Jensen, you're thinking too small. The town is just a bonus. It was the same way for McFadden. You see, the real money, well, that's up north.

"This is gold country, Jensen. There's about to be one massive strike up there. And when I hit it, I'll own it all. This town as well."

"You'll be the king of Montana, is that it?" Smoke asked.

"That's exactly it!" Poe said. "Now you get it! But you won't be alive to see it, I'm afraid." He looked over his shoulder to Sally. "You know, maybe she will be. I might keep her alive. She can be my bride—the queen of Montana." He turned and called out to Sally. "Would you like that, darling? You could be the wife of a very rich and powerful man."

Sally didn't say anything.

Smoke caught movement in his peripheral vision and looked briefly to his right, out the window. He smiled.

"You almost had it," Smoke said. "I've got to hand it to you, Poe. I mean, you really came close."

The humor drained from Poe's face. "What do you mean *almost*? I'm in control here, Jensen. I rule Desolation Creek."

"Poe," Smoke said, a hint of impatience in his voice, "I'll admit I didn't see you being behind all this. But I figured I'd be captured when I rode back into town. In fact, we were planning on that."

"What?" Poe said.

Smoke smiled, enjoying the chance to give his own mocking speech. "You see, you led me right into the belly of the beast and gave my pards out there a chance to see exactly what we're facing. How many men you have. Where you're headquartered. You played right into it. And I want you to know I appreciate that. You served us well."

The man was about to fly off the handle, just as Smoke wanted.

"What the . . . What do you mean?" Poe shouted.

It was then that Smoke saw the flicker of recognition in the man's eyes.

"Oh, sh—"

His words were cut off when both boarded-up windows on either side of the saloon's batwing doors splintered.

The shooting started.

And carnage broke loose in the Dead Moose.

CHAPTER 35

Gun thunder boomed out.

Three of Poe's men dropped to the ground as blood spread from their fresh wounds. They writhed in pain and shouted. Well, two of them did. The third was already dead.

Smoke used the distraction to race to Sally's side. He picked her up, chair and all, and carried her past the curve of the bar. He got low and worked on the knots of the ropes as shots continued to ring out.

"Smoke!" she said.

He kissed the top of her head. "Don't worry, this is almost over."

The saloon continued to fill with gunsmoke and death. Hargis's huge frame blocked the doorway. He fanned the hammer of his Colt, spraying lead at Poe's gunhands. The men were too stunned to mount much of a defense.

One twisted as a bullet smashed into his chest. He dropped his gun and groaned as the life drained from his body.

Another took a shot to his left eye, putting his hand there

as blood began to pour. A second shot punched into his neck, taking what few seconds of life he had left.

"Smoke!" someone yelled.

He'd just finished loosening Sally's bonds. He stood up cautiously and saw Maddox wading into the fray, having come in through the shattered window to the right of the batwings. He tossed a Colt into the air and waited while Smoke caught it. Next he tossed a rifle toward him.

Smoke nodded his thanks before turning to Sally. "Get in the back room and stay down!" He craned his neck to look over the bar and found what he suspected was there. "Wait."

He hopped over the bar, grabbed a scattergun that was beneath it on the shelf, checked the loads, and then passed it over to Sally.

"Just in case," he said with a wink. "Now go!"

She retreated through the door and Smoke smiled in satisfaction.

Now he turned his attention toward the raging conflict playing out in the saloon.

It was time to join the battle.

Nighthawk had taken position on one of the building's roofs across from the Dead Moose. When he looked down and straight ahead, he saw the saloon's angled entrance.

He had a good view of anyone trying to leave.

And anyone rushing to join the fight.

Like good hired hands, men flooded toward the Dead Moose, having heard the shots, eager to earn their pay and help their boss.

Nighthawk was thankful he'd brought his bow. He'd worried for a bit that he wouldn't have much call to use it. Finally, now was the perfect time.

His arrow swooshed down, hissing through the air, before driving into the first man's back as he hurried up the stairs that led to the saloon's covered porch. He arched in a strange angle and tried to scream, but couldn't. At last, he fell face forward and twitched for a few seconds before dying.

The two men behind him didn't have time to realize they were under attack from above, when Nighthawk sent another arrow toward them. It tore into one of the men's thighs. He shrieked in terror as he went down. He tried to spin around, but was blinded by the pain. On the ground, he finally managed to twist and face the other way, but all he got for it was another arrow, this one right in his center.

The other man had the good sense to get low, turning just as an arrow intended for him sailed closer. The movement threw off Nighthawk's aim, but not by much. The arrow still sliced into the hombre's left shoulder. To his credit, he was able to raise his other arm and send two shots up toward the neighboring building's roof. It didn't do any good. The bullets careened off the ridge, leaving chips in their wake, but not coming close to Nighthawk.

Nighthawk's next arrow got the man right in the heart. His arm lowered. He thumbed off one more shot as his muscles spasmed in their final throes. The bullet just thudded into the ground in front of him as he pitched forward, lying facedown in the street.

"Umm."

Nighthawk left his perch, eager to make his way down to join the fight on the ground level.

In the confusion of battle, Hicks managed to sneak out of the Dead Moose, leaving the shooting behind him. He nearly stopped in horror at the sight of the three bodies that littered the entryway. They all had arrows sticking up from them, causing a cold chill to trace his spine.

That blasted giant Indian was somewhere close by! He

waited for an arrow to streak out of the night and find him; thankfully, it didn't.

He cursed himself for showing fear.

There wasn't time for that. He needed to keep a clear head, too.

As always, he would live to fight another day.

Smoke Jensen would not.

He'd see to that.

Smoke overturned a table and took cover behind it.

Three men had come down the stairs, having heard the war from their rooms and eager to join in. They sent a spray of bullets toward Smoke, but they just ate away at the wooden tabletop. He raised his arm and fired blindly, not expecting to hit anyone.

He didn't have to.

Maddox was in the saloon, joining in the party, and he took care of the first fella who ran down the stairs.

The man's feet slid out from beneath him as he took a bullet to the stomach. He slid the rest of the way down, bouncing with each step until he landed at the bottom in an awkward, tangled mess. The one behind him couldn't stop in time. He tripped over his downed pard and stumbled out into the main part of the saloon. He fired his gun wildly, but accidentally hit one of his fellow gunhands, sending a bullet into the back of a man who was across the room and firing at Jedidiah.

The wounded man groaned before falling to the ground.

"Thanks!" Jedidiah said with a wave. He followed it up with a shot across the saloon that drilled into the unintentional benefactor's forehead.

That left the third man on the stairs, halfway up. He didn't know where to send his lead now, and that gave Smoke all the opportunity he needed. He stood, took aim, and slammed two slugs into the outlaw.

The man clutched his chest and fell forward, crashing into the banister. His body was too much and the wood splintered as he fell against it. He continued to plummet and landed on a table that rested against the staircase. It broke in half on impact.

"Smoke!"

At the sound of Sally's voice, Smoke spun around. She wasn't in the back room, like he'd told her to be.

She was behind the bar.

It was a good thing, too. A gunman had snuck up on Smoke and was about to pull the trigger, when Sally jumped up on the bar's top. She brought the bottle of whiskey, which she held, down hard, shattering it against the man's head. He was stunned and unsteady on his feet.

Smoke put a bullet into his midsection and he disappeared to the floor.

"Say, you're getting pretty good at that," he said, pointing at the broken, jagged bottle his wife held.

"Thanks," she said with a smile. "It worked for me back in Big Rock, and here in this very saloon, so I figured I'll dance with the one who brung me."

"You save me a dance," Smoke said. "Now get back to that storeroom!"

He turned to fire on a few more men who were on the saloon's floor.

The hulking giant Hargis blocked the front door.

Smoke Jensen was too close to the door that led to the back storeroom and to a rear door out of the saloon.

Darnell Poe had one option left for escape.

He heaved his body through the shattered window to the left of the angled entrance and landed on the boardwalk with a painful, jarring thud. Blood oozed from several cuts on his arms where the remaining glass in the window's edges had torn his clothes and raked across his skin. None of that mattered, though. Survival. That was all he cared about.

He scrambled off the porch, having to go under the waist-high railing, and ran across the street.

"That's him! That's Darnell Poe!"

The shout came from the old miner Hodges. He was running up the street, cradling a scattergun. He stopped and took aim.

The gun bucked and thundered. He was too far away to hit Poe, though.

Poe continued to run toward the livery stable.

How had this happened? His plan had been laid out so perfectly. He'd arrived in Desolation Creek just as McFadden had started squeezing it. At first, he'd been angry. That was his plan. He'd had his sights on this town. Then he realized how fortunate it was. All he had to do was wait and let McFadden do all the heavy lifting. He'd wear the town down and then Poe could strike. By that time, the townspeople would be too deflated to resist.

Curse that Smoke Jensen and his worthless friends!

They had no right to take what he'd worked so hard for!

He bounded into the livery stable, ready to find his horse and light a shuck out of there. He didn't see another option. Jensen and his crew had him beat. He hated leaving the town and all its money on the table. Even more, he hated missing out on that upcoming gold strike. Maybe he could live to fight another day, think of a plan on how to get to the homesteaders, and come back for what was rightfully his.

He wasn't so sure he'd survive that long.

By now, Smoke and the others had cleared out the saloon. They'd heard Hodges and were spilling into the street, giving chase.

"No! No! No!" Poe spat.

Perhaps he could hold them off. He had plenty of cover in the livery stable. Maybe there was a rifle tucked away somewhere.

He stood behind the door's threshold and sent a shot out to warn those outside. "Stay back!"

"It's over, Poe!" Smoke shouted. "Throw down your gun and come out peacefully. You don't have to die."

"You'll just cut me down!" he said.

He could barely see, as he was blinded by white-hot rage. His whole body felt warm. He was starting to sweat.

"You have my word, Poe. You surrender and you'll get a fair trial," Jensen said.

Poe took a moment to steel his nerves. He looked down at the gun he held and nodded.

He might go out, but he'd take a few of them with him.

And he'd start with Smoke Jensen.

Or maybe he could beat them. Shoot a few and the others would scramble.

It was worth a try. Anything was better than surrendering.

He'd never give up.

Smoke and the others watched as Poe came into view. He wore an evil sneer. He looked like a madman.

"This was supposed to be my town! That's my gold up in those hills!"

"Give it up, Poe. You're done. You don't have any more options," Smoke tried to reason.

He didn't think it would work, and his hunch was proven correct when Poe continued his deranged rant.

"I'm not going to be bested by some two-bit gunfighter like you, Jensen! You could have worked for me. I would have made you rich!"

Smoke didn't waste any breath arguing with the man.

"You think you can just ride in and take *my town*? Snatch what rightfully belongs to *me*? You and your stinking, shaggy mountain man friends. You're all trash! And that worthless Indian! A savage Injun!"

Smoke saw Nighthawk at the same moment the others did. The only one who wasn't aware of the Crow's presence was Darnell Poe, which was unfortunate for him.

He was right behind him.

Poe screamed in shock as his feet left the ground. He gasped in terror as he was spun around to face his captor.

"My name is Nighthawk."

The tomahawk split Poe's skull down the center. Nighthawk let go of the man's neck and stepped over the still-twitching but fading body.

He walked through the stable's door and toward his waiting friends.

"I do say, Nighthawk. Quite impressive!" Audie said.

The others nodded their agreement.

"Umm."

CHAPTER 36

"That's it," Audie said. "This horrid mess is finally over!" Nighthawk bent down and wiped the blood from his tomahawk on the shirt of one of the owlhoot corpses that littered the street. Satisfied that the blade was clean, he put it back in the loop on his waist.

"It ain't over," Chuck Hicks said, stepping out of the shadows of the Dead Moose. "Ain't over by a long shot."

Smoke sighed. "Hicks, look around. Poe is dead. McFadden is gone. Just give it up."

Hicks shook his head. "This ain't about them. This is about you and me finally settling this."

Sally pushed through the batwing doors, and when she saw Hicks slowly walking toward Smoke, she stopped short.

"Smoke!"

"Stay up there," Smoke said, raising his hand. "Stay away."

Sally clearly didn't like it, but she did as instructed.

"What do you say, Jensen? The first time we met was a little shooting competition right here in this street. How about we finish it? Only this time, ain't a bunch of coins being tossed around. I'm talking real stakes."

"You're outnumbered," Smoke said. "And I really don't want to kill anyone else today. Go on, Hicks. You don't deserve it, but you're free to ride away."

"Free to ride away?" Hicks laughed. "As if you give me permission to come and go. You measly son of a—"

He drew.

Smoke had already seen the play coming. His Colt was palmed and level just as Hicks cleared leather.

It was a single shot that drilled Hicks right in the heart. It echoed down Main Street and faded as Hicks took two steps forward.

"Jensen . . . you . . . you were faster."

Smoke nodded. "Enough."

Hicks's body went slack and crumpled. A line of blood trickled from his lips. He died lying on his back in the street, his glassy eyes staring up at the night sky.

"Is it really over, this time?" Sally cried as she ran off the porch and into Smoke's arms.

"It's over," he said quietly, kissing the top of her head. "It's over now."

"Maybe not!" Hodges called. "Look! Rider coming down yonder!"

He pointed to a lone figure who slowly came into view, as if materializing out of the night's darkness. His horse's hooves clumped loudly. A huge, shaggy, four-legged shape paced deliberately alongside. None of them—man, horse, dog—were in any hurry.

They passed the livery stable and approached the Dead Moose. The crowd parted. The rider reined his mount to a halt, looked to the bodies that littered the street, and arched an eyebrow.

"Heard tell there were some big doin's up this way," the

tough-looking old man said. He leveled a quizzical stare at Smoke. "What in the world you been up to, boy?"

"Preacher!" Sally said.

Smoke's jaw hung slack. "Preacher?" he said.

"Well, who else would it be?" Preacher said.

"Umm!"

"I'll second that, Nighthawk!" Audie said with a huge grin on his weathered face. "It's good to see you, Preacher! A sight for sore eyes."

"You're alive?" Smoke said, still in shock.

"Last time I checked," Preacher said. He grinned. "Of course, it could be that I died and I'm just too dern stubborn to stop walkin' around."

"If you're here," Hargis said, "then who's buried in the town's cemetery?"

A light of recognition flickered in Preacher's eyes. "If that don't beat all! You know, I've heard rumors there's been a braggadocious old coot masqueradin' around as me. Been tellin' stories to cadge free drinks and such, takin' credit for my doin's! I wonder if that's who's resting in my grave."

Smoke couldn't help but laugh, along with a clearly relieved Sally. "We sure are glad to see you," he said.

"You thought I'd really been kilt?" Preacher said. "Didn't you learn nothin' from that other time folks told you I'd crossed the divide when I hadn't? Son, I reckon I'll be roaming these mountains until Gabriel blows his trumpet!"

"And thank God for it," Smoke said. "Now that you're here, you might as well ride back to the Sugarloaf with us." He put his arm around Sally's shoulders and looked at the other mountain men. "All of you. I think it's time for a little reunion."

TURN THE PAGE FOR AN EXCITING PREVIEW!

Johnstone Country. Where Bullets Speak Louder Than Words.

Sheriff Buck Trammel is about to learn a cold hard truth about the Wild West: When you lock up the biggest, meanest crime lord in town, you'd better throw away the key. . . .

PRISON BREAK!

In the world of criminal lawbreakers in Laramie County, Lucien Clay was king. He terrorized the locals, robbed every business in the territory, and ruled the place with a merciless iron fist. Thankfully, he's behind bars now—along with a load of other prairie rats—thanks to Laramie's new sheriff, Buck Trammel. Unfortunately, Trammel can only enforce the law, while others specialize in working around it: namely, lawyers. And no lawyer is more crooked or corrupt than the belly-crawling snake Clay hired to get him out. By any means possible . . .

Their breakout plan is simple: The lawyer will wait until midnight. Then he'll break into the county jail to bust his client out. He'll scale the walls, kill the guards, ambush the deputies, and release the prisoner. There's just one catch: As soon as Clay is freed, the other convicts want out, too. Which sparks total chaos in the prison, creates a distraction for Clay—and unleashes the worst blood-soaked night of murderous mayhem Buck Trammel has ever witnessed. And will never forget. If he survives . . .

CHAPTER 1

Buck Trammel ducked his head back just as Verne Ayres cracked off another shot from his pistol. The bullet bit into the doorway less than an inch from where Trammel was standing.

"I already warned you once to stay out of here, Sheriff!" The wild-haired, old prospector punctuated his warning with another shot that split the batwing doors of the Tinder Box Saloon, forcing them open. "I told you I ain't comin' out of here 'til I'm good and ready. And I ain't nowhere near ready yet. This here party's just getting started."

Sherwood Blake, Trammel's chief deputy, tried to pull his boss back from harm's way. "You don't need to be here, boss. Your place is out there, keeping the people back. Let me and the boys handle this."

But the sheriff of Laramie County had no intention of going anywhere. "I was the first one here when it started, and I'll be the last one here when it's over. Where'd you send the others?"

"I have Johnny Welch and Charlie Root headed around to the back door," Blake told him. "The rest of our boys are tending to the crowd out front. Figured you wouldn't want anyone else to wander in here and get hurt."

"You figured right." Trammel lowered his Peacemaker as he stole a quick glance inside the Tinder Box Saloon. The place was being kept open while it was being redone by the new owner. Ladders and paint cans were set up throughout the interior.

He caught Ayres in the middle of reloading his pistol. The wild hair poking out from beneath the prospector's worn slouch hat was long and gray, matching his overgrown beard.

Trammel's curiosity was rewarded with a rushed shot from Ayres. "I see what you're doing out there. Can't say I ever put much stock in all the big talk I've heard about you these past few years. About how tough you are. How you always get your man. Like I always said, 'The bigger they are, the harder they fall.'"

Trammel had known of Verne Ayres, too, if only by his reputation as a talker and a drunk on the rare occasions he came down from the hills around Laramie. He had always been relatively harmless until that day. "This old fool has almost killed me twice. Where'd he learn to shoot like that?"

"No way of telling with Verne," Blake said. "He never tells the same story about himself twice."

"I can hear you boys plotting out there," Ayres hollered. "It's no use. I've got you right where I want you. Just let me have my celebration in peace and I'll be on my way."

The man could not only shoot but had excellent hearing. Trammel asked Blake, "Any idea what set him off like this?"

The deputy kept his head low but his Winchester ready as he whispered, "Heard from one of the fellas who ran out of there that Ayres was in the mood to celebrate a big strike. Said he'd finally hit the mother lode and was about to buy drinks for everyone in the place. But the bartender said something that turned his mood dark."

That was more than Trammel had known. He was on his way back to his office in City Hall when he saw customers running out of the Tinder Box like the place was on fire. Given that Adam Hagen was in the middle of changing the place from a brothel into a respectable hotel, Trammel had figured one of the workers might have accidentally started a blaze.

It was not until he heard the shots that he knew it was not as simple as that.

"Send someone to find the bartender and talk to him. I want to know why Ayres is so worked up. He might be able to tell us something that could calm him down."

"I'd be glad to, but we can't do that," Blake told him. "The bartender is lying behind the bar, right next to Verne. He was the first man Verne shot to start this whole mess rolling. The only one who got shot, too, near as I can tell."

Trammel figured bartending was getting to be as dangerous as enforcing the law in Laramie these days. The town was bursting at the seams now that Lucien Clay was in jail and Adam Hagen was buying up every property in sight. The town was filled with people looking for a new start and new ways to earn a living off the boom. "Verne must've found something big to justify this."

"He said he found gold," Blake reported. "Old Verne's been looking for a strike like this all his life, and now he's finally found it. Shame he won't be free long enough to enjoy it."

Both men ducked when another shot rang out from inside the saloon, punching open the batwing doors beside them once again.

"I can still hear you two schemin' out there plain as day. Do yourselves a favor and put the thought right out of your mind. There's no reason for anyone else to get hurt, including either of you. Just let me finish my drinkin' so I can get on back to my claim."

Trammel thought he might have a way to getting Ayres to lower his gun. "Is that what this is, Verne? A celebration?"

"It certainly is," Ayres shouted back. "And I don't appreciate it being ruined. Not by you and not by this sassy bartender, either."

"Help me, Sheriff!" a man cried out from behind the bar. "I'm hurt really bad."

He yelped when Trammel heard Ayres kick him. "And if you don't want to get hurt worse, you'll quit your belly-achin' and let me enjoy this here drink in peace."

Trammel was glad the bartender was still alive. He had to keep Ayres talking. "I thought this was a fight that got out of hand, not a party, Verne. That changes things."

"It does?" Ayres called back. "How do you figure it?"

"The bartender's still alive, so Blake and I don't have any reason to barge in there and take you in. It's just a misunderstanding between a bartender and a customer. Happens all the time."

"Then you boys have no reason to stay out there. Just go about your business and let me leave town on my own steam."

Trammel could not allow that to happen. "It's not much of a celebration with you sitting in there all by yourself drinking alone, now is it? If you promise not to shoot, the two of us would like to come in there and join you for a drink. It's been a while since we've had much cause for celebration around here, and we could use the excuse. Who knows? Your good fortune might rub off on us."

"Sure. And maybe you boys'll buy me a steak dinner with all the trimmings." The sheriff's hopes sank when Ayres laughed. "I didn't get this old by being that stupid, Trammel. You two are just fine right where you are. And the same goes for whoever you've got sneaking around behind this place, too. Prospecting's a lonely, thirsty business. I found this claim alone and I'll celebrate it alone. And I don't aim to allow you or anyone else to swindle me out of it, you hear?"

Trammel was about to ask him what he meant by swindling when he heard another voice come from inside the saloon. "You can hardly call it swindling if it's legal, Verne."

Trammel could not believe his rotten luck. It was the man who was renovating the Tinder Box into a respectable hotel.

Adam Hagen, his part-time friend and a full-time nuisance in Laramie. The last man in town who could end this peacefully.

"Speak of the devil and he shall appear," Verne seethed. "How'd you get in here, you snake? Slithered under the door, I imagine."

Trammel took a risk that Verne was distracted and peered inside. He found Hagen leaning against the doorway next to the bar. The doorway led out to the front lobby and the stairs up to the rooms.

As usual, he was wearing a red brocade vest and a gleaming Colt pistol on his right hip.

"I was upstairs reviewing plans for the place when I heard the shot," Hagen said. "How're you feeling down there, Tom?"

"My head is mighty sore, Mr. Hagen," the bartender replied.

"See what you went and did, Verne?" Hagen said to the prospector. "You let that nasty temper of yours get the better of you again. We talked about that the last time, or don't you remember?"

"I remember everything about you, you scoundrel. Every word you say is poison in my ears. And since this is my party, I say we talk about something different for a change."

Trammel saw Verne gesture toward Hagen with his pistol. "How about we talk about how you tricked me into signing over—"

Hagen drew his Colt and fired twice into Verne's chest.

Trammel had seen Hagen shoot enough times to know he could have cut him down from much farther away. Being as close as he was, there was no question Ayres was dead before he tumbled backward and stumbled over the fallen bartender.

Trammel quickly rounded into the saloon, followed by Blake.

On the other side of the hotel, Deputies Johnny Welch

and Charlie Root burst through the front door. Their rifles were at their shoulders and aimed at Hagen.

Hagen switched his aim to Trammel's chest. The smoking pistol hung there for a moment too long for the lawman's comfort. Given that Trammel was over six and a half feet tall, he was difficult to miss and impossible to mistake for anyone else in Laramie. Hagen had clearly seen Trammel and recognized him, too. But the thought of shooting him had entered his mind, if only for a moment.

Hagen slowly lowered his pistol and smiled at the sight of his old friend. "You ought to know better than to barge in on me while I'm working, Buck. I might've shot you in the heat of the moment."

Beside him, Deputy Blake thumbed back the hammer on his rifle. "All the more reason why you ought to tuck that iron away, Hagen."

The gambler's smile held. "What's the matter, Blake? Don't think I could get those two behind me before I took you, too?"

Blake did not budge. "You'll be dead before you try."

"Highly unlikely." Hagen holstered the weapon and held up his hands as he slowly stepped away from the bar. "Never let it be said that Adam Hagen is one to interfere with the law." He glanced behind the bar. "You can come out now, Tom. The bad man can't hurt you anymore."

Trammel motioned for Welch and Root to lower their Winchesters as a bald man popped up from behind the bar and pulled himself over it. He had expected to see a bullet wound but was surprised that all he had was a nasty gash on his gleaming head.

"I thought you were shot," Trammel said as the bartender moved to Hagen's side.

"He would've shot me if he had the chance." Tom pulled off his apron and held it against his bleeding wound. "Verne's pistol went off when he slammed me in the head with that old Navy Colt of his. He didn't shoot anyone."

"Thank heavens for that," Hagen said as he moved the bartender's apron and examined the gash for himself. "I imagined the worst when I heard the shot. Stands to reason why I was in such fear for my life."

Trammel knew that was a lie. He doubted Adam Hagen had ever been afraid of anything in his life. Not when he had a gun on his hip or a rifle in his hands.

Hagen sucked his teeth as he dabbed the apron at Tom's wound. "Verne got what he deserved for treating you this way. I'd be inclined to swear out a complaint against him if he was still alive, but I suppose he's beyond all that now."

"Yeah," Trammel said. "He's beyond a lot of things."

Hagen feigned insult. "That sounds like sarcasm, Buck."

The sheriff ignored him as he walked over to the bar and peered over the side. He saw Verne Ayres crumpled on the floor. Two neat holes still smoldering over his heart. His dead eyes fixed on the bare ceiling of the saloon. His new-found luck had clearly run out.

"Blake, you'd best get Tom over to a doctor to get that wound cleaned up. Doc Morrison's place is closest. Stay with him until he's been tended to, then get a statement from him for the record."

To his deputies still in the hotel lobby, he said, "Johnny and Charlie, I want you and the others to get statements from anyone else who was in here when it happened. I know the county attorney will want to have all the facts he can muster for his file. Tell everyone to stay outside until I tell them they can come in."

The deputies went off to carry out their respective assignments, paying Hagen particular attention as they passed him. Trammel knew his men did not trust the gambler, and they were right to be cautious.

He waited until Blake had helped the bartender leave before telling Hagen, "You and me are going to have a talk."

Hagen looked down at Trammel's pistol, which was still

at his side. "I put mine away, Buck. It's only proper for you to do the same."

Trammel tucked the Peacemaker into the holster under his arm.

"That's better. There are so many guns around town these days. It's getting so a man needs to shoot his way across the street."

Trammel ignored the exaggeration. "The town would be a whole lot quieter if you weren't armed."

Hagen gestured to the side of Trammel's nose. "That scar of yours seems to fade more with each passing week. You wear it well. Makes you look even meaner than you already did, not that anyone could ever accuse you of having a peaceful disposition."

Trammel fought the urge to touch the long scar that ran down his face along the side of his nose. He had received it when Major John Stanton had tried to get away from him a few months back. The assassin had fallen from a roof for his trouble and later died in prison of his injuries.

The scar served as a daily reminder to Trammel of how close he had come to losing his life.

"And that shoulder holster you still insist on wearing," Hagen remarked as he moved behind the bar and grabbed a bottle of whiskey. "When are you going to break down and wear your gun on your hip like a true Westerner? You've been out here long enough. Time to adapt a little to our ways."

"Like shooting harmless old prospectors in a saloon?"

"Calling Verne harmless is awfully generous of you, especially after how he brained poor Tom with that Colt of his." Hagen placed two glasses on the bar and picked up a bottle of whiskey. "I can't have my people treated so poorly. I wouldn't get anyone of quality to work for me if word spread that I let my employees get slapped around by some drunk."

"That isn't why you shot him, and you know it."

Hagen sighed. "But I suppose violence has a tendency to

follow us around wherever we go, doesn't it? Wichita. Blackstone, and now here in Laramie. The names of the towns might change, but the circumstances remain the same. You still have a position of authority and I'm still forced to dispatch undesirables."

Trammel watched him place two glasses on the bar as if he was about to perform a magic trick. There was always an elegant air about anything he did, but Trammel had known him too long to believe the façade. His fair hair had already begun to turn white in places, though he was just north of thirty. He kept his beard trimmed and close to his pale skin. He was a shade over six feet tall and managed to remain lean despite a strong appetite for hard drinking and late nights. His light eyes were set deeper than they had been when they first met back in Kansas. Harder, too.

Trammel thought the years had been kind to Adam Hagen in their own way, but not as kind as they might have been, and far kinder than he deserved.

"You didn't have to kill Verne, Adam."

"Of course I did." Hagen poured them a good amount of cheap whiskey. "I was in mortal fear of my life. He pointed his gun at me. I saw you watching the whole thing from the doorway. You saw it with your own two eyes. It's a miracle I wasn't killed."

Trammel did not look down at the glass Hagen slid toward him. "You could've just as easily backhanded him as shoot him."

"And risk poor Tom's life while a drunken lunatic was raving and pointing his gun all over the place? You think too much of my bravery, old friend."

Hagen set the bottle on the bar and reached for his glass, but Trammel grabbed his wrist before he could take hold of it. "You shot him for a reason."

The gambler's eyes narrowed with just a hint of spite. "I didn't claim to shoot him by accident, Steve. And we both know I don't like being handled, not even by my friends."

Trammel released him with a shove. "I heard what he said to you right before you shot him. Something about being swindled."

Hagen shrugged as he took his glass in hand. "The ravings of an old drunk blind with rage and riding high on glory. When Ayres wasn't up in the hills scraping at dirt, he was claiming someone swindled him. Before me, he accused Lucien Clay of robbing him blind, as if the old sot ever had anything worth stealing. You've been out here long enough to know how those old prospectors are. Always afraid that someone's trying to jump their claim on the off chance they manage to pull something of quality out of the ground. You've seen dozens of men like Ayres come and go. I'm from these parts, so I've seen hundreds. They're as common as horseflies in a stable."

He looked down at the body behind the bar and raised a toast. "To your memory, you old rat. I hope your find was as prosperous as you claim."

Hagen took a healthy swallow of whiskey but was careful not to drain the glass. Trammel knew Hagen was always measured in everything he did. How he drank. How he gambled. How he spent his money and how he made it.

And how he killed. Trammel had never known him to do anything without a reason. He never surrendered reason to emotion, not even when he watched Hagen wage a pitched battle with his family for control of their fortune.

But when Hagen found himself on the losing end, his family ran him out of Blackstone for his trouble. With his brother Caleb and Lucien Clay now in prison for murder, Laramie was left wide open for a man of Adam Hagen's cunning and resources. He was already well underway to building a new empire of whiskey and blood. A piece of a gold claim would only help him reach his aims that much quicker.

Trammel stood upright so his size advantage over Hagen was even more pronounced. "You're not leaving here until you tell me why Ayres thought you were swindling him. And if you lie, I'm going to lose patience."

"Look at you, rearing up on your hind legs like an old grizzly." Hagen set his glass on the bar and tried to rub some circulation back into his wrist. "City living hasn't softened you up as much as I'd hoped. How do you manage to stay so strong?"

"I was born in Manhattan, remember? Laramie barely ranks as a neighborhood where I'm from. Quit stalling and answer my question."

Hagen ran his tongue along the inside of his mouth as he thought it over. "Are you asking me as a friend or as the sheriff of Laramie?"

Trammel knew better than to corner Hagen. If he tried to make this official, he would spend the rest of the afternoon dancing around the question in a blur of words. Any one of the lawyers who had recently moved into town would trip over themselves to defend him in court. Trammel was more interested in the truth than a fight. "I just want to know the truth. Let's leave titles out of it for now."

Hagen considered it before saying, "Fair enough. In that case, I'll tell you. About a month ago, the newly departed Mr. Ayres down there found himself having a particularly bad run of luck at my blackjack table over at the Emerald Isle. You remember the dump. It used to be Lucien Clay's place before I took it over."

Trammel did not need to be reminded of it, nor of Hagen's rapid assumption of Clay's role as the biggest criminal of Laramie now that Clay was in jail for murder. Hagen might have changed the name and fixed up the place, but it was still a den of iniquity as far as he was concerned. "Go on."

"Ayres was convinced his luck was due to turn around. He practically begged me for some credit, but that was impossible since he was already into me for a considerable sum. Call me a softhearted fool if you wish, but there was something about his desperation that touched me." He tapped the center of his vest. "Right here."

"If you're pointing to your wallet, I'll believe it." Trammel could guess the rest and decided to save them both a lot of time by getting to the point. "You made him sign over his claim to you in exchange for credit, didn't you?"

Hagen held up a finger. "I only took half. I'm not entirely without scruples. And, as fortune would have it, Ayres wound up going on something of a winning streak. Not enough to entirely erase his debt to me, of course, but more than I had anticipated."

Hagen let out a dramatic sigh as he picked up his glass again. "But I still hold the note, and now that Ayres has departed this mortal coil, I suppose I'm the sole owner of his claim. Alas, the burdens of being the executor of his estate."

"A claim that sounds like it just paid off," Trammel said.

"I wouldn't count on it," Hagen said. "Verne Ayres was a better gambler than a prospector. He wouldn't know the difference between fool's gold and the genuine article if it leaped out of the ground and into his pocket." He offered another toast down to the corpse. "Sorry, old man, but I guess this is one claim that didn't pan out in your favor."

Trammel fought the urge to slap the drink out of Hagen's hand, pull him across the bar, and throw him in jail. He had murdered Verne Ayres just as sure as if he had followed him into a dark alley one night and knifed him to death.

But it was not Hagen's swindling that irked Trammel. Ayres knew the risk of going into debt with a man like Hagen. No one had forced him to walk into his gambling den that night. No one had forced him to sign over his claim to pay for one more turn of the cards. Trammel knew that was where Adam Hagen's true evil lay. He always found a way to use a man's weaknesses against him for his own benefit.

And it was all legal, even if it was not right. "All the money you've got, and you still feel the need to rip off an old grubber like Ayres."

Hagen's eyes slid over to Trammel before the glass touched his lips. "Careful, Buck. I don't respond well to criticism of my character."

But Trammel was not in a careful mood. He had just watched a man get gunned down over a claim that probably amounted to spare change in Hagen's deep pockets. "When is enough going to be enough for you, Adam? You ruined your father and burned his house to the ground. Your brother Caleb is over in City Hall, rotting in the next cell over from Lucien Clay. You're already well on your way to running most of Laramie. You'll be bigger than Clay ever was before long, if you're not already. What more do you want?"

Hagen appeared to think it over as he finally took his drink. He seemed to have made up his mind when he set the glass back on the bar. "More. I want more."

"More of what?"

"I don't honestly know," Hagen said. "I don't know what it is, or if there'll ever be enough, but whatever it is, I want more of it. Land. Gold. Property. Businesses. Women. Today it's this place. Tomorrow it might be something else. Works of art, perhaps. A bigger house or another empire to bring to its knees. All I know is that if it's worth having, I want it. As much of it as I can get. And I'm all too willing to do anything to get it."

Hagen seemed to remember himself and cast off the heavy words with another elegant shrug as he poured himself another drink. "Maybe one day I'll be satisfied, but today, old friend, is not that day."

No, Trammel imagined it was not. But he also knew the day would come sooner rather than later when Adam Hagen came up against something or someone he could not have. A man he could not beat. Something he could not buy at any price. And when he found it, he would pursue it until it finally destroyed him and cost him everything he had.

And once he was ruined, he would gladly start over, for

Trammel knew that, for men like Hagen, having something was never quite as sweet as chasing it.

And when that day finally came, Buck Trammel would be there to stop him, or make him pay for all the harm he had done in his life.

He watched Hagen swirl the whiskey in his glass. "I trust none of these details about my Ayres claim will be mentioned in whatever report you give to Judge Spicer?"

"The judge is a plain man," Trammel said. "He's only interested in having me testify to what I see, not what I think, or even what I know. Ayres was armed. He had assaulted the bartender and he *did* point his pistol in your general direction when you shot him. It was legal, but that doesn't mean it was right."

Hagen rested his hand against his chest. "That's a relief. I've had enough dealings with Lady Justice these past few months to last me a lifetime." He gestured toward the glass in front of Trammel. "You haven't touched your whiskey. I know it's not as good as the stuff I usually serve, but it's good enough, given the circumstances. I can even promise you won't go blind."

Trammel pushed himself away from the bar. "No, thanks. Unlike you, I've still got a job to do."

Hagen called after him as he left the saloon. "Don't forget to send the undertaker around when you get the chance. I'd like to reopen as soon as possible, and I can hardly do that with poor old Ayres here, stinking up the place. Though I suppose I could charge admission for people to look at him. Maybe he'll turn out to be worth something after all?"

Trammel decided it was best to ignore the comment. There was never much to be gained by sparring with Adam Hagen, either with words or with pistols. And it was tough to beat a man whose idea of victory changed each day.

CHAPTER 2

The long shadows of his cell's bars were cast along Lucien Clay as he lay on his bunk, lost in thought. It was never truly dark down there in the bowels of Laramie Prison. No matter the time of day or night, there always seemed to be lamplight somewhere, as if the dancing flame mocked his confinement. And without windows to the outside world, it was nearly impossible to measure time, except for the strict schedule the guards enforced each day.

The guards said the constant light in the dingy prison was for the inmates' safety as much as it was for their own. Clay imagined they also liked the idea that it prevented the prisoners from getting much rest. A weakened prisoner is an easier prisoner to handle.

Clay closed his eyes as he thought of the guards. They had been his tormentors all these months. His jailers. But soon, one of them would help him enjoy freedom once more. All he had to do was remain patient.

It was never truly quiet in prison, either. With so many men living in squalor beneath City Hall, there was always someone sniffling or snoring or sobbing or shuffling. His cell was so narrow that he could easily sit against the bars on one side of his cell and touch the other side with his feet. The cell was just long enough to fit his cot and nothing else. His world had been reduced to a cramped iron cell in the bowels of City Hall.

Clay had been locked up many times in many towns and cities for a variety of offenses. Being a vice peddler had its perils. But none of those places had been as wretched as Laramie Prison. He had not been allowed a visitor in more than a month, not that people were lined up around the block to see him. He had pled guilty to conspiracy to murder Rob Moran, a popular lawman in town. His plea had guaranteed he would not swing for the crime if he agreed to testify against Caleb Hagen, Adam's brother.

Sheriff Buck Trammel had also seen to it that Caleb Hagen was put in the next cell to Clay's, which only added to his torment.

Clay had decided against wasting money on attorneys and appeals and put whatever remained of his considerable fortune to better use. He had planted seeds that had already flowered and appeared ready for harvesting. He reminded himself to remain calm and soon all would be well.

But remaining calm was easier said than done, for in the next cell over, Caleb Hagen's feet continued to scrape against the floor as he constantly paced in his tiny cell. Clay was grateful he was not crying. He usually only did that when it was time to sleep.

"Curses on you for putting me in this mess, Lucien," Hagen said. "Curses on you for telling those infernal lies about me."

Clay had no pity for the man. This time the previous year, Caleb had been the leader of his late father's empire and had looked the part. He may have been raised at the family ranch in Blackstone, but he'd once had the soft look of a New York banker. His face had some of his dead father's sharp features, but any resemblance stopped there. Too many steak dinners and black cigars had made him thick around the middle and soft in the head.

Months in a cell had transformed Hagen from a captain of industry to a shell of who he once had been. His filthy prison garb hung loosely around his frame and his bearded cheeks had grown fallow from the slop the jailers passed off as food.

"Curse yourself instead," Clay told him for the countless time. "You and your brother-in-law wanted Moran dead as part of your petty family squabble. If you hadn't sent that boy to hire me to have Moran killed, neither of us would be stuck in here now."

"But we can still get out of this." Hagen grabbed hold of the bars, almost pleading. "All you have to do is recant your testimony against me. Tell them it was all a lie. Testify that I had nothing to do with planning Moran's death. Pin it all on my dead brother-in-law instead. He's the one who hired you, not me. And he's dead. No harm can come to him now."

"I'm sure the judge will ignore how convenient that is." Clay stretched on his bunk and clasped his hands behind his head. He could have set his pocket watch by Hagen's daily routines if he had been allowed to keep one. After breakfast and yard time, the pleas inevitably began, followed by whatever scheme he had spent the previous evening cooking up. When Clay remained unmoved by his desperation, Hagen would sputter in angry frustration for the rest of the day until it was time for Deputy Hal Haid to deliver their supper.

Clay had seen the delivery of the food not as an opportunity for nourishment but the chance to set his own plans for freedom in motion. It was the only bright spot in his day, which was quickly ruined by Hagen's whimpering once the guards ordered all candles extinguished for the night.

Clay reminded him, "Testifying against you is the only reason I haven't been hanged yet. Life sentence was the deal I made, and that's the deal I'm sticking with."

He smiled in the shadows. *At least for now.*

Hagen continued to pace in his cell, like a penned-in bull ready to charge. "Why won't you listen to reason? If you withdraw your testimony, they'll have no choice but to let me go while I'm working with my lawyers on my case. I might even be able to secure bail for you. Tell them Trammel forced you to confess just to frame me. You've got friends in town who can make sure the judge believes that. Everyone knows Trammel's a bully anyway."

Clay had already thought of that. "They'll never believe it. Not now."

But Hagen did not let facts get in the way of his dream. "I'll make them believe it. I'll buy off whoever I must. And once I'm free and clear of all charges, I'll hire the best lawyers money can buy to fight for you in court. Why, I'll have my own lawyer represent you. Free of charge, of course. I'm not talking about some backwoods hick lawyer like they have in these parts. I'm talking about the best legal minds in the country. From Chicago or Philadelphia or New York."

Lucien Clay did not have many joys left to him in life, so his only entertainment was listening to Caleb Hagen constantly claw at the prison walls, looking for a way out. This was at least the tenth time that week that he had made the same offer.

"Do you mean it, Caleb? Honestly and truly? Do you swear you'll get me out?"

Hagen tried to shake the bars in frustration. "I'll have my lawyer draw up papers to that effect if it'll make you feel any better. It'll be an iron-clad agreement."

"Papers he's sure to tear up as soon as I recant my story," Clay sneered. "You two would forget all about me before you made it to the station for the next train back to Chicago, or wherever it is you live. No thanks, Caleb. I've got plans of my own."

"Plans?" Hagen's mood brightened. "What plans?"

Clay shut his eyes and cursed himself for saying so much. Any glimmer of hope was bound to lift Hagen's sails. His big mouth would prove risky to his plans. He decided it was time to cut his losses and get some rest. He was expecting a visitor soon and he wanted to be at his best to receive his guest.

"Don't worry about me. Just worry about how your fancy attorney is going to get you out of here. Now, do us both a favor and worry in silence. I'd like to get some sleep before my meeting."

Hagen stifled a yell as he pulled away from the bars and left Lucien Clay alone.

Clay put the temporary quiet to good use and allowed sleep to take him.

When Barney, the elderly prison guard, brought him up to the receiving room later that day, Lucien Clay hated how his visitor looked at him. Pity, with a mix of disappointment. He had never been one to accept pity.

Like Caleb Hagen, prison had done Clay few favors in terms of his appearance. Buck Trammel had shattered his jaw with a single punch the previous year. He had been in ceaseless pain and had headaches and slurred speech for months. He had grown dependent on laudanum to dull his suffering. His mind, once sharp, had soon become lost in a blur of opiates and lost days. He could not help but wonder if he might have refused to play a role in Marshal Rob Moran's murder had he been thinking clearer.

He decided laudanum had not played a part in his decision. Killing the lawman was worth the risk and the great reward promised him.

But Doc Carson had not allowed Clay to have any laudanum during his imprisonment. After passing several bad weeks due to the ill effects of staying off the stuff, he had regained full control of his senses. His jaw was still crooked, which slurred his speech. But he had put his ongoing suffering to good use. It served to push him forward, even when all had seemed lost.

That same determination was the reason this stranger had come to see him today.

Barney looked at the prisoner and the guest with tired eyes as the large visitor stood to greet Clay.

"I'm Frank Bessler, your new attorney." His Texas accent was heavy but cultured. "Pleased to make your acquaintance, Mr. Clay."

Clay shook the big hand the Texan offered. He was a large man, almost the same size as Buck Trammel, though not quite. "Thank you for making the trip all the way from Texas, Mr. Bessler. I appreciate the effort."

Bessler had a healthy, dark beard that made his smile even brighter. His brown suit was clean and devoid of any wrinkles or hints of trail dust. A gold watch chain spanned his broad chest from one vest pocket to the other. Clay caught the faint whiff of shaving cream and hair tonic, which told him Bessler had just come from the barber. A good sign that Bessler might live up to his reputation.

As prisoner and attorney sat, Clay looked back at the prison guard. "Might as well leave us, Barney. My lawyer and I have things to discuss that aren't meant for your tender ears."

The toothless guard gummed his response. "You've got an hour, convict. Not a moment longer."

Clay waited until Barney shuffled into the hall and pulled the door shut behind him, leaving them alone in the cramped room across a crooked wooden table.

Bessler looked amused as he watched the old guard leave. "He looks like he's got one foot in the grave. No wonder you think busting out of this place will be easy."

Clay motioned for him to keep his voice down. "He's old, not deaf. Mind what you say in here. Words tend to carry in prison."

Bessler's look darkened. "And a man in your position ought to mind his tone when he speaks to me. I'm not one of your hired hands, Lucien. Not yet. And you're not the first client I've visited behind bars."

Clay had always bristled at familiarity from the men who worked for him, especially when they happened to be right. Clay was in no position to be haughty, and Bessler knew it.

"Just keep your voice down. I think they already expect I'm up to something."

Bessler's dark eyes narrowed. "What do you mean by that?"

"Meaning I usually don't have visitors these days," Clay explained. "Barney's bound to tell Trammel about it, and he'll get curious."

"Let him get curious. There's nothing wrong with a man in prison meeting with a lawyer. It happens every day."

Clay knew he did not have time to waste on arguing his point. Barney would be looking to take him back to his cell within the hour and they had much to discuss. "According to the notes Mayor Holm got to me, I hear you're good at what you do."

"I am, but we'll get to that." Bessler's smile flashed again. "But first, there's one thing about this whole setup that bothers me. I don't understand how you could've gotten yourself locked up, considering you've got the mayor in your pocket."

Clay felt his anger rise at the thought of it. Old shames rushed to the fore. "Because Buck Trammel isn't in my pocket and he's the one who put me here. Happy?"

"Not yet," Bessler said. "How did you get word to him from your cell? Walt Holm isn't the type who spends much time among prisoners."

Clay saw no reason to keep it from him. "The deputy who brings our dinner each night is a fella named Hal Haid. He used to be one of my best customers before I got locked up. He owed me quite a sum. I promised to forget about his debt if he agreed to take notes between me and Mayor

Holm. It was a harmless enough way for him to work off what he owes me. It certainly beats his wife finding out he wasn't always working late."

"You think this Haid character might've read your notes?"

"We always sealed them with wax. Don't worry. If he'd read them, I'd have known."

That seemed good enough to satisfy Bessler. "I'm surprised Walt played along," he said. "He's always been an old church mouse when it came to risking his neck, even back when we rode together."

Clay had always known Walter Holm was a corruptible man. It was why Clay had worked to install him as mayor of Laramie in the first place. He was as greedy as he was capable, which was why Clay had given Holm control of his fortune while he was in jail. Another man might have taken the money and run. But Holm had not wanted to risk Clay testifying in court about how they had worked to the detriment of Laramie for years. A bad reputation was hard for a man to outrun.

"I take it Holm has already given you your fee," Clay said.

"Half, which was more than fair. He said you already had a plan to get out of here without too much bloodshed. He didn't give me any details."

Clay was glad he knew that much. "That's because I didn't tell him everything. He's a politician, and that type isn't always known for their discretion."

"A wise choice," Bessler remarked. "Holm always had a habit of talking too much under the influence of good drink and female companionship. But there's no point in being as guarded with me. In fact, you'll have to be just the opposite if you want me to get you out of here. And you can rely on me to keep anything we discuss confidential. What Holm doesn't know can't hurt either of us. I'm putting my neck on the chopping block right next to yours."

Clay already liked the way Bessler thought. "Did Holm send you the details about my case?"

"He did, and I agree there's absolutely no way I can get you out of here legally. Your sentencing agreement all but makes that impossible. I'm sure you could agree to testify against Holm and all the others you've corrupted here in town, but I doubt it would make any difference to the judge. The best you could hope for is some extra yard time and marginally better food when the mood struck the guards."

Bessler sat forward and folded his large hands on the table. "We both know you didn't pay for me to come all the way here just for my reading of the law. Holm said you had a plan to break out of here. I'd like to hear it."

But Clay needed to know a few things before he could trust him. Even the slightest detail could be the difference between success and failure. "When did you arrive in Laramie?"

"Two days ago," Bessler told him. "I've put the time to good use by giving this town and this prison a good looking-over."

"And?"

"Laramie's not as backward as I'd heard," Bessler admitted. "I saw an old prospector shoot up a place called the Tinder Box just this morning. If a saloon was ever properly named, it's that dump. Doesn't seem to take much for a spark to turn into a blaze in these parts."

Clay frowned at the news. "That's because I'm not around to keep it under control. Adam Hagen took my place, and he isn't nearly as smart as he thinks he is. The Tinder Box always turned a tidy profit when I ran the place. He's going broke turning every saloon into a palace. Thinks he can turn Laramie into another Denver or Chicago."

"I hear Adam Hagen's quite a character. He's Caleb Hagen's brother, isn't he?"

Clay did not want to waste time explaining the complicated lineage of the Hagen family. "Tell me what you make of Trammel and his deputies."

Bessler drummed his thick fingers on the table. "They're good, and Trammel's got no shortage of deputies on his payroll. None of them look like they're easy targets, least of all Trammel."

Clay sneered. "You're not scared of him, are you?"

"Right down to my boots, mister," Bessler admitted. "I've heard talk of plenty of hard cases in my time, so I know the difference between bluster and the real thing. I hear Trammel's not much of a talker, so I'd wager he's the genuine article. Getting you out of here will be one thing. Keeping you out is something else entirely."

Clay could not blame him for being cautious. "What do you make of his deputies?"

"I've watched them work. They're smart. They know how to keep a lid on things without being bullies. They know just how far to push a man to keep him in line without causing a fight. And there's always one of them watching the street, even at night."

Clay did not like the sound of that. "They watch you?"

"I've received my fair share of attention these past few days. A man of my size doesn't exactly blend in, even in a bustling town like Laramie."

The more Bessler talked, the worse Clay felt about his prospects. "Do you think any of them recognized you?"

Bessler waved it off. "Not a chance. This is my first time in Wyoming and none of them looked familiar. The clerk over at the Continental Hotel told me one of the deputies stopped by to look at the guest register. The fool thought the notion of vigilant deputies would put my mind at ease, but I haven't received any unnecessary attention. And before you insult me by asking, they didn't notice me as I looked over the prison. I was very discreet."

"Your idea of discretion could be obvious as far as Trammel is concerned. How discreet were you?"

"I asked for a room at the back of the hotel," Bessler explained. "I told him I wanted something quiet to calm my nerves. The real reason was because the back of the hotel offers a perfect view of this prison. I did most of my work from up there."

Discretion was one of the reasons Mayor Holm had suggested he hire Bessler in the first place. He did not need another gunman like Major John Stanton. The assassin had lived up to his billing when he successfully killed Marshal Rob Moran.

But despite his skill with a gun, Stanton had not been good enough to go up against Buck Trammel in a straight-up fight. Few men were.

No, Clay needed a thinking man to get him out of this dungeon they called a prison.

"What do you think my chances are of breaking out of here?"

"It's possible." His thick Texas accent added a certain level of assurance to his words. "That's not to say it'll be easy. Or cheap."

Clay was not concerned about the price. "Holm will see to it you get your money after I'm free. He's prepared to wire it to any bank you say as soon as I give him the word. Today is Tuesday, and Mayor Holm works out of his law office on Tuesdays. Drop by his office when you leave here, and he'll be happy to give you your money. Tell him this phrase, 'The days are growing shorter.' That'll confirm that I've given him my permission to wire the balance of my remaining funds to the bank in Denver."

Clay thought it prudent to add, "And we'll have no trouble withdrawing it, as long as I'm there with you. In person."

Bessler smiled. "No one's looking to steal your money, Lucien. I've never stolen from a client yet and I don't plan on starting now. Just make sure you're ready to move every night after lights out. I'll be getting you out of here in a day or so at most."

Clay did not like the sound of that. "Don't you want to hear my plan?"

Bessler's chair creaked as he sat back in it. "No, and I never tell a client how I plan to spring them. Like you said, sound has a habit of traveling in jails, and I don't want you getting anxious and trying to help. Holm tells me you're one cold man, but if you start acting squirrelly, it might tip off one of the guards. What you don't know can't hurt either of us."

Clay tried to read Bessler's expression, but the lawyer's face was granite. He could remember playing in high stakes poker games that were not as challenging. "Don't make me insist."

Bessler drummed his thick fingers on the table as he thought it over. "I'd tell you, but it's going to cost you extra. Above and beyond what we've already agreed to."

Clay could hardly resent a man for having a mercenary nature. Bessler had not come all the way from Texas out of the goodness of his heart or because he believed in Clay's innocence.

Clay asked him the amount and Bessler told him. Clay agreed to it without hesitation.

And Bessler did not look happy about the easy victory. "That's it? No haggling?"

"My freedom's too valuable to haggle over," Clay said. "I've got the money, so I look at it as an investment. So quit stalling and talk. Barney isn't too good with telling time, so he's bound to be back here any moment."

Bessler seemed just as eager to get down to business and leaned closer to him across the table. "Going out the way I came in here is out. There's a great, big iron door between here and upstairs that's always guarded. If we tried to get out that way, it would mean shooting the guard. Even if I got down here and pulled you out of your cell, getting out would be impossible because everyone would hear the shot. That stairway would turn into a turkey shoot, with us as the turkeys. I don't think either of us want that."

Clay already knew what he was thinking. "That leaves the side door to the courtyard and stalls."

"Agreed, but we'll need to get the timing just right. I saw they have an old Negro man who works as a stable hand in the stalls back there. At first, I thought I might be able to use him as leverage to get inside, but I've been watching him closely. He never comes inside the prison and I don't think he has a key."

"That would be Old Bob," Clay remembered. "He's been working here since before I came to Laramie. They only pay him to stay with the horses. Even fixed up an old shack for himself to sleep in by the horses. I think he likes it. And you're right. He doesn't have a key to get inside. He's got one for those big iron doors that lead out to the street, though."

But Bessler was already past that. "I noticed an old man who goes through that way each night around midnight. Carries a black bag with him that makes me think he's a doctor. I've noticed that he likes to sit out in the courtyard by himself several times a day. Even wheels a chair out with him while he puffs away on his pipe for an hour or so at a time. I don't know why he doesn't just go out front and do it. It would certainly smell better than being next to the horses, but who am I to judge?"

Clay was glad it sounded like Bessler had been telling the truth about watching the place. "That would be Doc Carson. He's always been a solitary cuss. Spends so much time in here that he might as well have a cell of his own. He does most of his smoking and drinking in his office when he's not tending to prisoners. He has bad knees and hates taking stairs when he can avoid it. Says coming in the side entrance is better for his joints. Trammel even comes down to his office to make it easier on him."

"All the better for us. In fact, his predictability is essential to my plan. He always comes back here just before midnight. And each time, he wrestles something awful with those big iron doors into the courtyard."

"He likes to check in on us while we're sleeping." Clay's hopes in Bessler's plan began to dim. "I hope you don't think you can grab him on the street and use him to get in here. He'd sooner let you kill him than allow himself to be taken hostage. He'll cut loose with a holler and draw every gun on the street before you got five paces."

Bessler broke into another wide grin that unsettled Clay. "I know we just met each other, Lucien, but you ought to give me credit for a bit more creativity than that. I've already told you how I plan to do it. You just weren't listening." He pulled his watch from his vest pocket and checked the time. "We've still got a few minutes before the guard comes back. So, you'd best pay attention while I tell you exactly how I'm going to get you out of here. Tonight."